D0720974

TARA TAYLOR QUINN's

love affair with Harlequin Books began when she was fourteen years old and picked up a free promotional copy of a Harlequin Romance novel in her hometown grocery store. The relationship was cemented in 1993 when her first book, *Yesterday's Secrets,* was published by Harlequin Superromance. It received two Reviewer's Choice nominations and was a finalist for the RWA's RITA® Award for Best Long Contemporary in 1994. Tara has sold thirty-two books in less than nine years. Her first single title, *Sheltered in His Arms,* appeared in 2001. When she's not writing or fulfilling speaking engagements, Tara spends her time with her husband and commuting to Arizona State University with her daughter, a senior psychology major.

AMANDA STEVENS

knew at an early age that she wanted to be a writer, and began her first novel at the age of thirteen. While majoring in English at Houston Community College and the University of Houston, she was encouraged to write a romance novel by one of her instructors, who was himself writing a historical. Her first romance was sold to Silhouette Intimate Moments in 1985. She is now the author of over twenty-five romantic suspense novels, the recipient of a Career Achievement award for Romantic/Mystery from *Romantic Times* magazine, and was a 1999 RITA® Award finalist in the Gothic/Romantic Suspense category. Amanda lives in Houston, Texas, with her husband and their teenage twins.

TARA TAYLOR
QUINN

AMANDA
STEVENS

YESTERDAY'S
MEMORIES

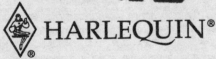

HARLEQUIN®

TORONTO • NEW YORK • LONDON
AMSTERDAM • PARIS • SYDNEY • HAMBURG
STOCKHOLM • ATHENS • TOKYO • MILAN • MADRID
PRAGUE • WARSAW • BUDAPEST • AUCKLAND

HARLEQUIN BOOKS

by Request—YESTERDAY'S MEMORIES

Copyright © 2003 by Harlequin Books S.A.

ISBN 0-373-23011-7

The publisher acknowledges the copyright holders of the individual works as follows:

FATHER: UNKNOWN
Copyright © 1998 by Tara Lee Reames

FADE TO BLACK
Copyright © 1994 by Marilyn Medlock Amann

This edition published by arrangement with Harlequin Books S.A.

Visit us at www.eHarlequin.com

Printed in U.S.A.

CONTENTS

FATHER: UNKNOWN
Tara Taylor Quinn

CHAPTER ONE

"YOUR NAME IS ANNA."

Anna. She wasn't sure she liked the name. Certainly didn't feel any affinity to it, any sense of ownership. Her heart started to pound.

"No one seems to know who you are," the doctor said almost conversationally. "You didn't have ID on you when they brought you in, just a locket around your neck engraved with that name. We were hoping you could tell us more."

Terror threatening to consume her, she shook her head. "Where am I?" Even her voice was unfamiliar, husky.

She tried not to flinch as he lifted her eyelids and shone his light into her eyes. "You're on the fifth floor of Madison General Hospital in New York City. I'm Dr. Gordon, a neurologist and your attending physician." The tall, thin white-coated man spoke as if reassuring a child.

New York.

"What day is it?"

"Tuesday. The first of July."

July. Summer.

"How long have I been here?"

"Since late yesterday afternoon."

She digested that piece of information slowly, but the cotton wool surrounding her mind remained alarmingly intact. Time meant nothing to her, either, it seemed. "What's wrong with me? Why don't I remember anything?" she cried.

"You took quite a bump on the head, and though the tests show no real damage, temporary memory loss isn't that unusual in this type of situation. If you'll just relax, things will probably start coming back to you almost immediately. In a few days you should be just fine," the doctor said with a smile, although he was watching her intently. "The baby doesn't seem to have suffered at all."

"Baby?" she whispered. *What baby? Where?* She looked around her at the sterile empty room. "I have a baby?"

"You're eight weeks pregnant, Anna," he said, feeling her pulse.

His watchful eyes continued to study her.

Anna. Pregnant. Pregnant Anna.

"None of this sounds familiar?" the doctor asked kindly.

She shook her head, and her fear increased when she saw the disappointment cross his face. Both he and the nurse who'd been in her room when she awoke had been kind to her. She clung to that kindness as Dr. Gordon's words failed to jar any memory from her at all.

"Well, just to be certain that there wasn't more damage than at first appeared, I'm going to write an order for more tests this afternoon. But don't worry, Anna, traumatic memory loss isn't uncommon. Chances are your memory will return shortly."

And what if it doesn't?

Dr. Gordon continued to explain her condition, speaking of a subway crash she had no recollection of, the trauma to her brain, the news bulletins being issued statewide in an attempt to reach anyone who knew her. But his words were like background noise, an irritation, nearly drowned out by the voice in her head aimlessly repeating the only words that meant anything to her—and yet meant, frighteningly, nothing at all. *Anna. Pregnant.*

She didn't feel like an Anna. She ran her hand along the flatness of her belly beneath the stark white hospital sheet. And she certainly didn't feel pregnant.

A baby. Surely the doctor was wrong. She'd remember something as important as a baby growing inside of her. She'd remember the man who'd helped put it there. Wouldn't she? Her chest constricted, making it difficult to breathe.

"Am I crazy, Doctor?"

"No! Of course not." He patted her foot beneath the covers. "The mind has its own ways of dealing with shock. Yours is merely doing its job, protecting you to get you through a hellish ordeal. You were one of the lucky ones, coming out of the crash virtually unscathed."

Anna nodded.

"Do you have any more questions?"

Of course she did. A million of them. But only one that mattered. And apparently one he couldn't answer. *Who* am *I?*

She shook her head again, harder. And then wished she hadn't as a wave of dizziness washed over her. She did have another question. *What's going to happen to me?* But she didn't ask it. She couldn't. Not yet. She was too afraid of the answer.

"We'll talk later," the doctor said, smiling down at

her. "Right now you just need to rest—and eat. You're far too thin."

Was she? Tears flooded Anna's eyes as she realized the doctor knew her body better than she did. Did she have freckles? Birthmarks he knew about and she didn't? Scars she wouldn't know the history of? What color were her eyes? Was there anyone she knew on the subway with her?

"Do you have a mirror?" she asked, hoping he couldn't hear the panic in her voice. How did you live in a stranger's body, in a stranger's mind?

"I'll have a nurse bring one in." Dr. Gordon turned away, almost as if he was finding this incredibly horrible situation as difficult as she was. "You probably have your own obstetrician, but I'm going to send Dr. Amy Litton in to see you later today to talk to you about vitamins and prenatal care. She was called in yesterday when your condition was first discovered. In the meantime try to rest, Anna. There'll be plenty of time for questions tomorrow."

Tomorrow. Anna lay completely still after the doctor left, her heart pounding as his last word brought on another attack of sheer terror. Tomorrow. How could she face tomorrow when she didn't even recognize today?

Dear God. What's to become of me? Slowly, concentrating, absorbing every sensation, she pulled her hands up the sides of her body and out from under the sheet she'd found tucked around her when she'd first awoken. Her skin was soft, her breasts firm, full. But she was bony, just like the doctor had said. Hadn't she had enough money to eat properly? And what about the baby? If there really was one, had she been taking care of it?

She reached for her hair with trembling fingers. A band at the back of her neck held it in place. So it was long. Long enough for a ponytail. Her fingers explored slowly. The strands weren't silky smooth as she somehow knew they usually were; she needed to wash it. Grabbing her ponytail, she pulled her hair around where she could see it. Blond.

She didn't know what she'd been expecting, but she didn't feel like a blonde any more than she felt like an Anna. Or an expectant mother.

Ceasing her exploration, Anna raised her fist to her mouth, stifling a sob, trying to remember something— anything. And drew a complete blank. What about her baby's father? Had he been on the subway with her? Was he lying in this very hospital, unidentified, as she was? Was he hurt? Or worse? Nausea assailed her.

What if her memory didn't come back as the doctor believed? How was she going to survive? How was she ever going to take care of herself when she didn't even know who she was? When she didn't know what she could do. If she was trained for anything. Where she came from. If she had anyone...or not.

She's pregnant. She has no memory. What's she going to do next? Anna suddenly stepped outside the situation, giving her problems to another woman, an imaginary unthreatening character over whom she had complete control. Something that felt strangely natural. All she had to do was decide what the woman was going to do next.

She's going to handle it. That's what. Somehow.

Deserting the imaginary woman, Anna slid her arms back beneath the sheet and closed her eyes. Her head hurt. A concussion, the doctor had said. A subway crash. She was lucky. Lucky. Trapped in a stranger's body, she didn't feel lucky at all.

WEEKDAY-EVENING newscaster Jason Whitaker choked on his coffee, barely setting the cup down before grabbing the remote control on the table beside him and jamming his thumb down on the rewind button. He'd been watching a clip that was scheduled for the six-o'clock news, reviewing the copy that went along with it. Thirty-seven people injured, two dead, one woman suffering from amnesia. And suddenly Anna's face had been there, transposing itself over the sketch of the woman he was going to be talking about.

Leaning forward in the chair in his dressing room, he watched the screen intently. It couldn't be... He'd just had one too many late nights. He should have gone straight home after the eleven-o'clock show last night, instead of stopping at the piano bar around the corner. He should have gone to bed at a decent hour for once, gotten some sleep—except that he'd known he wouldn't sleep. He'd have lain there in the bed he'd once shared with Anna, albeit in another city, and tear himself up wondering who she was lying with these days. Which was why he'd gone to the bar, instead.

The VCR clicked and Jason jabbed the start button. He was so tired he was seeing Anna everywhere. Even in the poor amnesiac from yesterday's subway crash. The woman shared her first name. Period. He'd better get a grip. Quickly. He hadn't seen Anna in months. It was time to be over her. To move on. To find a woman who wanted him. To find one *he* wanted.

He sat through the first part of the clip again, this time hardly registering the impossibly twisted subway train, the flattened steel of the maintenance vehicle it had collided with, the battered and broken wall that had ended the train's uncontrolled flight. Frightened people poured out of doors that had had to be forced open, some dragging bodies, others trampling over them. Emergency vehicles, police authorities, medical personnel scrambled on the screen. Tearful faces telling of panic, of despair, filled the background.

And then there she was again. Jason froze the frame. The vacant look in her eyes slammed into him, knocking the breath out of his lungs. He shook his head, trying to clear his vision, but she was still there. Not exactly as he remembered her, and yet there was no doubt that the Anna he was supposed to be reporting on was none other than the woman he'd left behind in California three months before—the woman who'd refused his offer of marriage. What was she doing in New York?

His blood pumped feverishly. Had she realized she couldn't live without him, after all? Had she come to her senses? Was she here to beg him to take her back?

The images from the clip suddenly crystallized. The tragic subway crash, the injured, the amnesia victim no one had claimed, the plea for anyone who knew the woman to contact Dr. Thomas Gordon at Madison General.

Oh, my God. The crash. Anna had been in the crash.

Blood running cold, he reached for the phone, dialing the number on the monitor in front of him.

"Dr. Thomas Gordon please." His words were clipped, and the pencil he'd picked up tapped furiously on the table.

"Who's calling, please?"

"Jason Whitaker, Channel Sixteen News." He used his position unabashedly. Anna had obviously suffered some kind of head injury. He had to know how bad it was. What else she'd suffered.

"One moment, sir."

The wait was endless. Jason was tempted to drop the phone and head immediately for Madison General. But with the Friday-afternoon New York City traffic, his chance of getting his answers any more quickly that way were nil.

"This is Tom Gordon."

"Jason Whitaker, Channel Sixteen News, Dr. Gordon. What can you tell me about your amnesia victim?"

"We sent a report to—"

"What's her current condition?" he said, cutting the doctor off. He knew about the report. He'd read and reread it. It didn't tell him what he needed to know.

"Relatively unchanged." The doctor sounded hesitant, and Jason couldn't really blame the man for taking him for an overzealous reporter looking for a scoop.

Throwing the pencil down on the table, taking a deep breath, he stared again at the monitor. "I think I may know her, Doc."

"You think you may? You aren't sure?"

"All right," Jason sighed, still not believing what his eyes insisted was true. "I do know her. Her name's Anna Hayden."

"You know her family? Where she comes from? Where she lives?" Suddenly the doctor was interviewing *him*.

"I know her family, where she comes from. I'm not sure where she's living," Jason said, still studying the vacant eyes of the pencil drawing on the television screen, the blurry photo beside it of the same woman, pale and sleeping. "I haven't seen or heard from her since I moved here three months ago."

"So she's not from New York?" the doctor asked, as if that explained something.

Jason shook his head, thinking of the little beach house Anna had shared with her sisters, those long-ago nights he and she had spent making love under the stars, the sound of the surf drowning out their cries....

"Mr. Whitaker?" The doctor's voice brought him firmly back to the present.

"She was born and raised in Oxnard, California, just north of LA. How bad is she, Doctor?"

"She's a very lucky lady, actually. A concussion, some minor contusions. Nothing that won't quickly heal. If she has someplace to go, I'll probably release her tomorrow."

Thank God. Jason expelled his breath, the knot in his stomach loosening a little.

"And her memory loss?"

"How well do you know Anna, Mr. Whitaker?"

Not nearly as well as I thought. "Very," he said. "And, please, call me Jason."

"Is there someone we can contact? Any family?"

"She has a sister. And parents, though I'm not even sure they're in the States," Jason said, suddenly afraid again. "Why? What's wrong with her, Doc?"

"I'm sorry, but I can only disclose the particulars of her case to a family member."

Frustrated, frightened and strangely hopeful as he considered Anna's presence in New York, Jason dropped the receiver back into the cradle after giving the doctor the information he needed. All he could do now was wait. And pray that Abby would call him.

He'd give her ten minutes, and then he was going to the hospital to get his information from Anna herself if he had to. He'd been in love with her for more than two years. He had a right to know whatever the doctor wasn't telling him.

And if she was alone in New York, she was going to need a friend.

ABIGALE HAYDEN gave a start, her gaze racing to the phone hanging on the wall in the kitchen of her beach cottage, daring to hope, even after two months of silence, that the caller would be Anna.

Hope dropped like lead in her stomach when the caller turned out to be male. How could Anna bear not to call? She had to be suffering the same agony at their separation that Abby was.

"Is this Abby Hayden?"

"Yes." Impatiently Abby waited for the telephone solicitor to recite his spiel so she could tell him she wasn't interested.

"I'm Dr. Thomas Gordon, a neurologist at Madison General Hospital in New York."

No, God. Please. No. She'd only assumed Anna had gone to New York. She could be wrong. She had to be wrong.

"Ms. Hayden? Are you there?"

"Yes."

"I have your sister, Anna, here, Ms. Hayden. She was on the subway that derailed…"

No! She couldn't lose Anna, too. She just couldn't. She still couldn't believe Audrey was gone, still had days when she just plain couldn't cope. If she lost Anna...

"...only minor bruises and contusions—"

"She's okay?" Abby interrupted frantically as the doctor's words started to register again. *God, please. Just let her be okay.*

"All things considered, she's a very lucky woman."

Abby's stomach clenched even more. "All things considered?" she asked, not liking the hesitancy she heard in the doctor's voice.

"Other than the memory loss I just told you about."

"Memory loss." Abby forced herself to pay attention. The doctor must think her an idiot.

"I'm afraid her amnesia is total at this point, Ms. Hayden. She didn't even know her own name."

"It's Anna." Abby blurted inanely, trying to absorb all the ramifications of the doctor's news through a fog of numbness. Anna couldn't remember her? Couldn't remember *them?* Frightened, Abby had never felt so adrift in her life.

The doctor told her more about Anna's condition; the slight concussion she'd suffered, her overall good health, her confusion. He told her about the engraved locket she'd been wearing that had been the only clue to her name.

"We all three have them," Abby said, ridiculously comforted by the fact that Anna was still wearing hers.

"Three?" Dr. Gordon asked.

"My two sisters and I," Abby said with barely a pause. "Is Anna going to be all right, Doctor? Will her memory return?" It had to return. Abby would sit with Anna every day, work with her around the clock, fill in every memory of every moment they'd ever lived if that was what it took to get her back.

"I expect it to return any time now, or at least portions of it, with the remainder following in bits and pieces. The blow she sustained wasn't particularly severe. I don't foresee any permanent damage."

"Thank God." Abby sank to the floor.

"I'd actually expected her to begin remembering already," the doctor continued, that hesitancy in his voice again. "The fact that she hasn't leads me to wonder if we're dealing with more than just shock here."

"Like what?" The fear was back stronger than ever.

"Ms. Hayden, has your sister suffered any emotional trauma lately? Anything from which she might want to escape?"

Abby almost laughed, except that she suspected the doctor would hear the hysteria in her voice. "Our sister, Audrey, died a little over a year ago."

"I'm sorry."

Abby blinked back tears when she heard the sincerity in Dr. Gordon's voice. "Me, too." She paused, took a deep breath, pushed away memories of that horrible day. "Anna handled it all pretty well, considering," she said. And then had to be honest. "Though Jason would probably know that better than I. He's probably the one you should be talking to."

"Jason Whitaker?"

"You know him?" Abby's heart rate sped up. Had she been right, then? Was Jason there with Anna now? Had the two of them managed to undo the damage Abby had done?

"I haven't actually met him. He called in answer to a story we'd put out asking for information."

"Did he say if he'd seen her recently?" Abby held her breath.

"To the contrary—he hadn't even known she was in New York. Said he hadn't heard from her in more than three months."

Oh, God.

"Do you have any idea what she's doing in New York?" the doctor asked gently. "Does she have a home here?"

Tears sprang to Abby's eyes once again, and again she forced them back. "I don't know." It was one of the hardest things she'd ever had to admit. "She called a meeting in my father's office about two months ago to tell us—my parents and me—that she was going away for a year. She said she had to prove to herself that she could get by without us to lean on. She wouldn't tell us where she was headed, and she said she wouldn't be phoning us. She made us promise we wouldn't follow or try to find her."

"And you haven't heard from her since?"

Not in fifty-nine hellish days. "No."

"Do you know if she went alone?"

"No. But I'd hoped she went to Jason."

"Apparently not."

"So what's she doing in New York?" Abby cried, more to herself than to Anna's doctor.

"That seems to be one of many things locked away in your sister's mind at the moment."

"There's more?" Abby asked.

"Anna's about eight weeks pregnant."

The fog swirled around Abby, cloaking her, making it nearly impossible for her to form coherent thoughts. Anna, pregnant? And Abby hadn't known? Hadn't felt…something? There had to be a mistake.

"How?" she asked, slowly getting to her feet.

The doctor coughed. "In the usual way, I suppose."

"Who's the father?"

"I was hoping you could shed some light on that."

Abby shook her head. She could think of no one. Only Jason. It had always been only Jason. And if he hadn't seen Anna...

"...so, I'd like to fax you some information on amnesia, various theories and treatments, if you have someplace you can receive a fax..."

Abby tuned in again in time to rattle off the fax number at the shop. And to inform the doctor, when he asked, that her parents were vacationing abroad, but that she'd leave word immediately for them to call her. Not that she expected much support from them once they learned Anna wasn't in any real danger.

"What happens next?" Abby asked, already looking through a drawer in the kitchen for the number of their travel agent.

"That, in part, depends on Anna. And on you, too." He paused, took a breath. "My recommendation is that you tell Anna nothing, let her remember on her own—particularly because we don't know what aspects of her life she might be trying to escape. But I want you to read the information I'm sending before you make any decisions."

Abby nodded, still looking for the number. "Is Jason with her?" she asked.

"Not yet," Dr. Gordon said. "I wasn't at liberty to apprise him of Anna's particulars without first checking with her family. Especially in a case like this when Anna can't possibly vouch for him herself."

"I'd trust Jason Whitaker with my life, Doctor," Abby answered immediately, almost defensively. "And Anna's, too." He'd been their strength after Audrey died—and so much more. He'd taught them to laugh again.

"Would you like me to call him?" the doctor asked.

"No." Abby stopped rummaging through the drawer. "I'll do it myself." The phone call wouldn't be easy, but she owed it to Jason. She owed him something else, as well, and knew, suddenly, that she'd just been handed a way to right the terrible wrong she'd done Anna and Jason. If she was strong enough.

"Dr. Gordon?" she said quickly, before she lost her courage.

"Yes?"

"As long as Jason's there and I'm not, and assuming he's willing, he's in charge." If Abby hadn't interfered, the right would have been his, anyway. He'd have been Anna's husband by now.

"You're sure?"

She'd never been less sure of anything in her life. "Any choices that have to be made come from him," she said firmly. And then, more for herself than for the doctor, she added, "I'll abide by whatever decisions he makes." With her eyes squeezed tight against escaping tears, she prayed to God that Jason would include her every step of the way.

Though, with her history of unanswered prayers, that didn't seem likely.

NINE AND A HALF MINUTES after he'd hung up from Dr. Gordon, Jason's telephone rang.

He grabbed the receiver. "Abby?"

"Jason?" Anna's sister was distraught, as he'd known she'd be. The amazing thing was she'd called him.

"I can't believe this is happening," she said, hardly

a trace of the old Abby in her subdued tone. "Dr. Gordon says you haven't seen her?"

"Only on a piece of footage. I was waiting to hear from you," Jason said, trying to gauge her mood—their relationship. "What else did Dr. Gordon say?"

"He said Anna's fine other than the amnesia," she told him. "He needs to know if there are any emotional traumas she might be trying to block." Abby paused. "I told him you would probably know that better than I."

He could hear the hurt in her tone, mingling with her worry. Not that he blamed her. He'd accused her of some pretty nasty things before leaving California. And she *did* have a tendency to control things, always thinking she knew best for everybody, but it hadn't really been her fault that Anna had chosen to stay with her only living triplet, instead of moving across the country with him.

"Did you tell him about Audrey?" Jason asked gently. He loved Abby like a sister. He was sorry he'd hurt her, sorry, too, that Anna's love for him had hurt her.

"Briefly." She paused, then said in a rush, "But then I discovered that I really don't know how Anna dealt with all that. I mean, she never talked to me about it very much." Another pause. "Which is why I told Dr. Gordon he was probably better off speaking with you." Her last words, an admission that had to have cost her plenty, were almost a whisper.

"She never talked to me much about it, either, Abby," he said, feeling compelled to ease her obvious suffering. "You know Anna, she's always been the type who keeps her pain to herself."

A heavy silence hung on the line. Jason would have

moved mountains to turn back time, to erase that last scene with Abby. He'd missed her. He'd missed them all.

"Will you talk to him, Jason? Please?" she finally asked.

"Sure. Of course. You know I will."

Another silence and then, tentatively, "So she hasn't been with you these past two months?" It sounded as if she was fighting the tears another person would have cried. Which was so like Abby. Always intent on remaining in control.

"I wish," he said. And then the significance of her question hit him. "You don't know where she's been? She's been away from home for two months?"

"I hoped she was with you." Abby lost her battle with the tears.

"I haven't heard from her since I left California. What's going on, Abby?"

"I don't know," she whispered, sniffing. He could picture her standing in the kitchen of the beach house, scrubbing at her nose with a tissue, her long blond hair falling around her shoulders. "She called a meeting with me and the folks just a few weeks after you left, said she was going away for a year—had to know whether or not she could make it on her own." Abby paused, taking a deep breath, and then continued, "She made us promise not to follow her or contact her until the year was up, at which time she promised to come home—at least for a visit."

His own disappointment was crushing. She'd been gone for two months. She hadn't just left home, just arrived in New York. She'd had two months to contact him. And she hadn't.

"What did I do, Jason? Why won't she talk to me anymore?" Abby cried.

"I don't think it's just you, Abby," he said, glancing again at the vacant stare on the sketch still frozen on his television monitor. "Audrey's death brought home to Anna that the three of you were three separate beings, not one whole as she'd always thought. Maybe she just needs to find out who her part of the threesome really is."

He hoped so. God he hoped so. Because until Anna truly believed she could survive apart from her identical sisters, she'd never be able to live her own life, to love.

"Maybe." Abby didn't sound convinced. And Jason had to admit that his reasoning was probably just wishful thinking.

"How soon are you flying out?" Jason asked, a little surprised she wasn't already on her way. Abby had pulled her sisters through every crisis in their lives.

"I'm going to reserve a flight for tomorrow, but I'll wait to hear from you before I buy the ticket. I won't come if Anna doesn't want me there."

Shocked, Jason said, "It sounds to me like she's not going to know what she wants." What the hell was going on?

"You'll call me as soon as you see her? As soon as you talk to Dr. Gordon?"

"Of course."

"Jason?" her voice was tentative again, but warmer. "You really haven't seen her since you left here?" she asked. "Not even once?"

"No."

"Oh."

"I'll call you later," he said, anxious to get to the hospital, to find out just what he was dealing with.

"Jason?" She hesitated. "I, uh, told Dr. Gordon that you're in charge." Another hesitation when Jason had no idea what to say. "For as long as you want to be," she finished.

Jason had waited too long for Abby to abdicate a single decision in Anna's life to quarrel over the fact that she was doing so three months too late. "Fine."

"You'll be there for her, won't you, Jason? No matter what you find?"

Her query was odd enough to send a fresh wave of apprehension through him. Was Anna's amnesia more serious than he thought? Was it permanent?

"As long as she needs me," he said, wondering if she ever really had. The Hayden sisters had grown up in their own little cocoon, buffered from the world by the unusual bond they shared, a bond made stronger by having been born to two people who were wonderful providers but terrible parents. He'd been a fool to think he could ever penetrate that cocoon, be a part of their world. But then, when it came to relationships, he'd always been something of a fool.

CHAPTER TWO

ANNA WANTED OUT. It was bad enough being mentally trapped, but to be stuck in a hospital room, too, was driving her insane. After another nap, a huge lunch and a visit from Dr. Litton, she was ready to get on with things. Whatever they were.

As she lay in bed, her restlessness grew. She needed to take a long walk, to smell the breeze. To do something.

But fear kept her paralyzed. What would she do? Where would she go? What clothes was she going to wear to get there? She could hardly wander around New York City dressed in a hospital gown. Her nurse had told her not to worry, that the city was assuming full liability; she'd have money for new clothes, might even end up a rich woman when all was said and done. Her nurse didn't seem to understand that money was the least of Anna's worries at the moment.

She'd had the second set of tests Dr. Gordon ordered, but she hadn't seen him again since she'd awoken that morning. Was it a bad sign that so many hours had passed and she still hadn't remembered a single thing? She was trying to relax like he'd said, but was beginning to suspect it was time to panic.

What happened to people like her? Were they institutionalized? Locked away until their only reality was the walls around them? If so, she'd rather have died in the subway crash.

Her gaze darted desperately about the small room—and alighted on the pamphlets Dr. Litton had left for her to read. The authorities couldn't put her away. At least not anytime soon. She was going to have a baby.

Picking up one of the pamphlets, Anna's panic eased just a bit. She liked Dr. Litton. Whether or not she ever remembered seeing another obstetrician, she wanted Dr. Litton to help her bring this baby into the world.

Baby. She was going to have a baby. Sometime around the middle of January.

As crazy as it seemed, Anna was glad.

DR. GORDON HAD a gentle bearing that bespoke calm, as well as confidence. Jason liked the middle-aged man immediately. Sitting in the doctor's office at Madison General, he listened intently while Dr. Gordon described Anna's condition.

"Her amnesia is a direct result of a blow to the lower left portion of her cranium. As the brain doesn't appear to be anything more than superficially bruised, I must wonder if perhaps her subconscious has used the impact as an opportunity to escape something that came before the crash," he said, joining Jason on the couch opposite his desk.

"You mean, something she saw just before the accident, something like that?" Jason asked.

"Possibly." The doctor's clasped hands lay across his stomach. "But I would expect the memory loss to cover just those few minutes if that were the case."

"Are you saying there's more to her condition than just the crash?"

"I believe she might be suffering from a post-traumatic stress form of amnesia, sometimes called hysterical amnesia."

Jason's blood ran cold. Was the doctor trying to tell him Anna's condition was permanent? That she was mentally ill?

"Which means what?" he asked. They'd handle it. Whatever it was, they'd handle it together. His right leg started to move up and down rapidly, the motion barely discernible, keeping time with his thoughts.

"Simply that she was suffering from an emotional crisis that was more than she believed she could bear. When she hit her head, lost consciousness, her subconscious grabbed the opportunity to escape."

"Permanently?"

"Most likely not," Dr. Gordon said. "When her subconscious believes she can handle whatever it is she's trying to escape from, her memory will return. Though probably not all at once."

Jason stared silently at the doctor, trying desperately to grasp the big picture. He had so many questions vying for attention, he couldn't settle on a single one of them.

"This reaction is really quite healthy in one sense," Dr. Gordon said, as if he knew Jason needed a little time to arrange his thoughts. "Rather than having a breakdown or falling prey to various other stress-induced mental and physical disorders, Anna is simply taking a vacation, gaining herself a little time to shore up the defenses necessary to handle whatever it is that's bothering her."

Jason's heart faltered as he realized the extent of the pain Anna must have been in to react like this. "How long do you think it's going to take?"

Shrugging, Dr. Gordon sat forward, steepling his fingers in front of him. "That's entirely up to Anna." He looked directly at Jason, his expression serious. "Her sister tells me you might be able to shed some light on whatever it is Anna's running from."

"Abby told you about Audrey?"

"Only that she died last year."

"Did she tell you the three of them were identical triplets?"

"No!" The doctor frowned. "But that explains a lot. The premature death of a sibling—only twenty-seven, Abby told me—is hard enough to cope with, but the loss of an identical sibling..."

Jason thought of that time, the horror. Hell, he'd been practically living at the beach house, ready to ask Anna to marry him, when their world had exploded around them.

"Audrey didn't just die, Doctor, she was murdered," he said, his throat dry. An entire year had passed—and the pain was still as fresh as if the murder had happened yesterday.

The doctor moved to the seat behind his desk, grabbing a pad of paper. "What happened?"

Jason shrugged. "No one knows for sure. After months of investigation the police determined that the whole thing was the result of an attempted assault that Audrey resisted."

"You say that as if you don't agree." Dr. Gordon looked up.

"I have no reason to doubt them, except that Audrey wasn't the type to resist...anything. She was the baby of the threesome and always seemed to take the easiest route."

"Did Anna accept the police explanation?"

Again Jason shrugged. "Let's just say she never expressed any disagreement with it. But then Anna has always kept her thoughts to herself. Comes from being the middle triplet I guess." His leg continued to vibrate, marking time.

"What about the girls' parents? Abby said this afternoon that they're in Italy. Do they travel a lot or were they around at the time of Audrey's murder?"

"They were around, as much as they ever are. The Haydens love their daughters, but they make much better entrepreneurs than they do—or ever did—parents." Jason thought of the handsome older couple, of how little he knew them, considering all the time he'd spent at their daughters' beach house the past couple of years. "The triplets weren't planned," he told the doctor. "I've pretty much figured out that practically from the stage they were in diapers, Abby stepped in to fill the void their parents' frequent absences left in the girls' lives. She's always watched out for them, made their business her business, bossed them around." He studied the diamond pattern in Dr. Gordon's tie. "But she's also, in all the years I've known them, put their needs before her own."

Dr. Gordon stopped writing and laid down his pen. "And yet Abby tells me that she hasn't seen or heard from her sister in over two months. From what you describe, this in itself is highly unusual."

"It is. I can hardly believe it." Standing, Jason paced slowly around the couch. "In all the time I've known Anna, she's never made a move without discussing it with Abby first." He shook his head. "I actually thought Anna's leaving was a good sign when Abby told me about it," he admitted. "I hoped it meant that Anna was finally beginning to believe she's a person in her own right, not just a third of a whole.''

''Seems logical.'' The doctor nodded. ''Or at least that Anna was ready to find out one way or the other. According to her sister, Anna said she was leaving to prove to herself that she could handle life on her own—apart from her family.''

Jason stopped pacing and placed his hands on the back of the couch. ''Do you think this could be what's behind her amnesia? Is she maybe allowing herself a respite from the compulsion to return to California, time to find out who she is apart from Abby?''

''I suppose it's possible,'' Dr. Gordon said, frowning again. ''She might even have been at war with herself—unable to make it on her own, unable to cope with *not* being able to make it alone.''

''You don't sound convinced.''

The doctor fixed Jason with an intent look and asked, ''Just what is your relationship with Anna?''

Jason resumed his pacing. With the past three months uppermost in his mind—that last terrible scene with Anna still haunting him—he wasn't sure how to answer.

''We're friends,'' he said finally, stopping once again behind the couch and clutching the frame.

''You said when you called earlier that you haven't seen her since you left California, that you didn't know she was in New York?'' Dr. Gordon continued to probe.

''That's correct,'' Jason admitted.

''Did her sister say anything to you about anyone else in Anna's life? Someone she may have been seeing? Either before she left home or just after?''

Jason shook his head. ''No one's heard from her in

two months. Why?'' he asked, although judging by the concern in the doctor's face, he was pretty sure he didn't want to know. Had Anna said someone's name in her sleep? Someone none of them knew?

''She's pregnant.''

Jason's knuckles turned white as he gripped the back of the couch. He'd heard wrong. He thought the doctor had said Anna was pregnant.

''Under the circumstances I can't help but wonder...'' Dr. Gordon's words were muted by the roaring in Jason's ears. ''...perhaps Anna's pregnancy is what she's hiding from. At no more than two months, she can't have known very long herself...''

Two months pregnant. God. No.

''...entirely possible she's not ready to handle the circumstances behind the child's conception.''

Conception. I haven't slept with her in over three months. Oh, God. No!

''You think she was raped?'' Jason's voice was a rasp. *Please, God, not my precious Anna. Anything but that.*

''It's possible.'' Dr. Gordon shrugged. ''But I don't think so. The amnesia appears to have affected only the personal portion of her memory, not the memory that controls basic needs. If she'd been raped, I would expect to see signs of fear for her physical self, even if she didn't understand why she felt those fears.''

The back of Jason's neck ached. ''So, what...'' his words trailed away. He couldn't believe it. Anna was pregnant. With another man's child. The world had tilted on its axis and he had a feeling it wasn't ever going to right itself again.

Dr. Gordon stood up, coming around to lean one hip on the corner of his desk. ''It's my belief that

Anna's amnesia is emotionally based,'' he said. ''That she's running from something. Perhaps she doesn't want the baby.'' He lifted a hand and let it drop back to his thigh. ''Maybe the father is married, or maybe it's someone her family wouldn't approve of, or even someone who didn't want her.''

None of which applied to Jason. He continued to grip the back of the couch, using it to hold himself upright. He thought he was going to puke. If, by some miracle, Anna's baby had been his, she'd have known she could come to him. She *would* have come to him simply because she would never have kept something like this from him.

The phone rang and Dr. Gordon excused himself, turning his back as he picked up the receiver and spoke quietly.

Jason continued to stand, still as a statue, his thoughts torturing him. Anna's family, her sister, would have been supportive if Anna was pregnant with his child. He'd been a part of them for so long he'd forgotten they weren't actually his family—until the day Anna had told him she wouldn't marry him, wouldn't move to New York with him. The day Anna had chosen Abby. Two days later Jason had hunted Abby down, hurling all his anguish, his pain at her.

But even that had been more like a brother furious with his sister than anything else.

Left to his thoughts as the doctor continued his low-voiced conversation, Jason faced the truth. Anna was no more than two months pregnant. He hadn't slept with her in more than three. Anna had been with someone else. Her baby wasn't his.

So what was wrong with the bastard? Why wasn't he here now, claiming her, claiming his child? Was he someone who, as Dr. Gordon suggested, would shock her family? Family was the one thing that mattered most to Anna—or at least Abby was. Anna truly didn't believe she could exist without Abby. He'd learned that the hard way. Had this other guy, too? Had Anna loved him and then sent him out of her life?

"Sorry about that," Dr. Gordon said, hanging up the phone. "My wife's pregnant with our first child at forty-one, and she's a nervous wreck." He shook his head. "We were all set to adopt, and my wife suddenly turns up pregnant. After more than ten years of trying."

Jason appreciated the doctor's attempt to lighten the moment, but he could barely manage a smile. He needed to throw something.

"You know, there's a remote possibility that Anna knew she was pregnant before she left home," Dr. Gordon said.

Jason remained silent, a raised eyebrow the only acknowledgment that he'd heard the other man.

"She could have left home to have the child in secret," the doctor continued. "She may have been planning to give the baby up for adoption without anyone ever knowing she'd had it. Hence her request for a year with no contact."

She'd left home only four weeks after he'd last seen her. Could the baby possibly be his, after all? Jason wondered. Had she taken their breakup to mean he wouldn't expect to know if he'd fathered a child? The thought wasn't pleasant.

"You said she's two months along. Could she be more? Say thirteen, fourteen weeks?"

Dr. Gordon shook his head. "I seriously doubt it. Judging by the baby's measurements from yesterday's ultrasound, eight weeks is just about max. Could be closer, in fact, to six or seven.''

"But you just said she may have known about the pregnancy before she left.''

The doctor shrugged. ''With early detection, women can sometimes know within days after conception,'' he said. ''Then again, she may have known only that she'd had unprotected intercourse at her fertile time.''

In that instant the vulnerable part of Jason that had somehow survived his childhood died. While he'd been making himself crazy with wanting Anna, she'd been making a baby with someone else. Hell, maybe there'd been someone else all along. Maybe that was why she wouldn't marry him. Maybe the unusual bond between Anna and Abby wasn't the problem at all—but rather, an excuse.

No. That didn't ring true. He knew that Anna would never have made love with another man while still sleeping with him. He knew, too, that her bond with Abby *had* been the biggest rift between them. Still, Jason couldn't escape one undeniable fact. Anna was pregnant and he wasn't the father.

She must have fallen head over heels in love with someone the second he left town. And if that was the case, he really had no one to blame but himself. He'd given her an ultimatum. And then he'd walked out on her.

Which was just what he wanted to do again.

Dr. Gordon's name suddenly came over the loudspeaker. ''I'm going to have to go,'' he said. ''If you don't mind, I'd like you to wait to visit Anna until I can go with you,'' he added, putting Anna's file back together.

Jason nodded, grateful for the reprieve.

"Can you meet me here this evening, say, around eight?"

Eight o'clock was right between shows. He could make it back. But he knew he'd have been there even if it wasn't convenient. "You think she might remember something when she sees me?" he asked, following the doctor out into the hall.

"It's possible," Tom Gordon said. "I think we need to be prepared for that eventuality. See you at eight," he called as he rounded the corner and was gone from sight.

Jason strode from the chilly hospital into the warm July sun, as if by leaving the building he could leave behind everything that waited for him there. Except that Anna was still in his heart, and he had to take that with him.

ABBY WAITED for his call. She had errands to run, some fabric to pick up for the shop, an order to deliver to the new kids' shop out by Beverly Center, but it all had to wait. When Jason heard what Dr. Gordon had to tell him, he was going to need to talk. Abby would have told him herself except she hadn't had that much courage. Hadn't been able to bring herself to hurt him again.

They hadn't parted well. And because of that last horrible scene, they'd both been awkward on the phone earlier. But he was family. By virtue of his love for her sister, his unending support to all of them when Audrey was killed the year before, he was family. Besides, as much as she hated the things he'd said to her that last day, the brutal accusations, she was grateful to him, too. If not for him, she probably never would have seen that she was ruining her sister's life with her controlling ways. When her sister had come to her telling her she was leaving, she'd have talked her into staying. Because she'd have been so sure that staying would have been best for Anna.

She wasn't sure about anything anymore. Except that Jason would call. Because of the baby. And she owed it to him to be there when he did. He was going to be devastated.

He'd been on her conscience for three long months. She'd never seen anyone as hurt, as bitter, as he'd been the day he'd stormed into the back of the shop. And he'd been right to accuse her of creating a rift between Anna and him.

She'd ruined his life. And probably Anna's, too. She'd never seen two people more in love, more suited to each other than Anna and Jason. And she'd been too selfish to free her only living triplet from *their* bond, to let Anna share an even closer bond with the man she loved. She'd been too blissfully blind to see that she had the power to hold Anna—or to let her go. She'd been so sure she and Anna were meant to live out their lives together, neither one making a decision without the other—almost as if she, Abby, had one part of their brain and Anna another. Audrey had had the third.

It had always been that way. The three of them together, through thick and thin, grades and boyfriends, lost friends and forgotten birthdays. No one had ever told them it would ever be any different. They were a package deal, their fate sealed in their mother's womb.

The phone rang, and Abby jumped, knocking over a stool as she grabbed for the telephone hanging on the wall.

It was Jason. And doing worse than she'd feared.

"You've heard," Abby said. She was having trouble comprehending that Anna was pregnant without her knowing, without her sharing in Anna's elation, her excitement, her fears. Jason had to be feeling ten times worse.

"Who is he?"

Tears sprang to her eyes at the raw emotion in his voice. "I don't know. I was praying it was you."

"No chance."

"Oh, God."

Silence fell heavily on the line. Abby felt as if she was coming unglued. She could hardly concentrate, couldn't make sense out of the past six hours at all. Her sister had been a victim in a serious accident, had amnesia and was pregnant, and she'd known nothing about any of it. Shouldn't she have sensed Anna's need? *Shouldn't Anna have reached out to her?*

"Have you seen her?" she asked, unable to stand the silence any longer.

"No." The single syllable was racked with pain.

Abby was almost afraid to ask. "Are you going to see her?" Anna would be all right if Jason was there. She didn't know why she was so sure of that, but she was.

"Of course," he said, and Abby heaved a sigh of relief. "Dr. Gordon was called away in the middle of our meeting," Jason continued, "but he asked me to wait to see her until he can go with me."

He didn't sound like he objected to the delay all that much. "Does he expect something to happen when she sees you?"

"I don't think he knows what to expect," Jason said on a sigh. "This is Anna's show all the way."

"She loved you, Jason, with all her heart," Abby felt compelled to tell him.

"Right." His sarcastic tone cracked across the wire.

"Those weeks after you left were awful." Abby insisted. "I've never seen Anna like that, not even after Audrey died."

"Yeah, well, apparently she recovered."

Abby had to find a way to make this all better. There was no one in the world she loved more than Anna—but Jason came in a close second. She'd always wanted a big brother, had often fantasized as a child about having someone older and stronger to look after them.

"Maybe he was just a one-night stand," Abby said in a rush. "You know, someone she turned to in a fit of loneliness, pretending he was you."

"Maybe."

He wasn't buying it and she couldn't blame him. But neither could she imagine, in any way, shape or form, that Anna had fallen in love with another man. Her sister was too besotted with Jason even to look at anyone else. Anna was the most steadfast person she'd ever known, and she'd given her heart completely to one man. She just wasn't the type to give it to another, not if she lived to be a hundred and never saw Jason again in her life. That was Anna. Though even Abby hadn't understood the depth of Anna's commitment—not until she'd seen what having to choose between conflicting commitments had done to her sister.

"What are you going to tell her?" Abby asked. She was almost afraid to hear the answer. Would Anna hate her when she heard about the part Abby had played in her life? If Anna had no memory of her love for her sister, Abby could well believe it.

"I don't know, yet," Jason said. "I suspect that's one of the things Dr. Gordon will go over before we see her."

He sounded tired and Abby's guilt grew.

"Call me, okay?"

"Yeah. You coming out?" he asked.

Abby shook her head, her tears finally brimming and falling down her face. "I don't know," she said. She wanted to—more than anything. But only if Anna and Jason both wanted her there. "I'll wait and see what happens tonight."

And she would. Wait right by the phone. She simply didn't know what else to do. Her entire life had consisted of taking care of her sisters, getting them out of scraps, Audrey mostly, guiding them, loving them when their parents weren't around to do it. But Audrey was dead. And Anna no longer remembered her. So what was left?

CHAPTER THREE

HE DID THE NEWS BROADCAST. He even gave the report on Anna. For all he knew, the father of her child was in the city somewhere, willing to claim her. Jason almost hoped another man *would* come forward—then he, Jason, would be free to walk away. But somehow, as he took a cab back to the hospital shortly before eight, he had a feeling that no matter what transpired, he wasn't going to be free from Anna Hayden for a very long time. Possibly never.

And in the meantime no one had reported her missing. She was all alone—and pregnant—in a strange city, thousands of miles from home. He couldn't walk away. He couldn't leave her lying there. But neither could he help wishing that the child she was carrying was his, that by some fluke her baby could really have been conceived fourteen weeks ago, instead of eight. That he actually had a right to be the one to care for her, to claim her.

The sick feeling increased as soon as he walked in the door of Dr. Gordon's office. There was nothing wrong with the room. Standard desk littered with charts, bland blue couch and matching armchairs, carpet, diplomas on the wall, and books. Lots of books. But Jason hated the room; he hated being there.

Hanging up the phone as Jason walked in, Dr. Gordon frowned. "That was the police," he said. "No one's come forward, yet."

Jason nodded, truly undecided whether this was good news or bad.

"Do you think she'll know me?" Jason asked the question that was uppermost in his mind. This wasn't how he'd pictured his reunion with Anna. In every single one of his fantasies, she not only knew who he was, but insisted she couldn't live without him.

The doctor leaned his hip on the corner of his desk. "It's possible she'll recognize you," he said. "But don't be surprised if she doesn't."

"Is she, you know, normal? Other than her memory, that is?" he asked quickly.

"Her intelligence hasn't been affected, if that's what you've been imagining," Dr. Gordon said, smiling. "Information is stored in many different areas of the brain. General learned information is separate from personal or emotional memories, for example. Apparently the only area in Anna's brain that's been affected is this last one," he said. "Which is, again, why I feel certain that she's suffering from hysterical amnesia."

At least somewhat relieved by the doctor's words, Jason asked, "So do we tell her who I am?"

The doctor gave Jason an assessing stare. "How recent is your personal history with her?"

"I'm that obvious?" Jason asked. It was impossible to feel embarrassed with this man.

"Not really," the doctor said. "But her pregnancy hit you hard."

Jason nodded. "I asked her to marry me a little over three months ago," he admitted. "She refused."

Dr. Gordon watched him for another moment and then got up to go sit behind his desk. "I'm sure there's more there, but I've heard enough to know that if she doesn't recognize you, we're going to have to proceed with caution.'' He pulled some printed material from a folder on top of his desk and handed it to Jason.

"I ran this off for you earlier," he said. "You're going to find that amnesia isn't treated like other mental illnesses. Some doctors are skeptical about its even being a valid diagnosis.''

"They'd think Anna's faking it?'' Jason asked.

The doctor shrugged.

"Do you think she is?''

"I'm certain she's not," Dr. Gordon said, leaning back in his chair. "But as you read, you'll find that even among the medical professionals who do recognize amnesia as a legitimate condition, there's a vast difference in beliefs when it comes to treatment.''

Jason looked down at the pages the doctor had given him, and then back at Dr. Gordon. The man had instilled trust from the moment Jason had met him.

"Go on," he said.

"All right, I will give you my recommendations, but with the understanding that after you've done some reading, you call in other opinions if you feel the need.''

"I'll fax the stuff to Abby tonight.''

The doctor shook his head. "No need," he said. "I've already done it. I spoke to her again a little over an hour ago.''

"And?''

"She agrees, though not enthusiastically, with my recommendation, but will abide by whatever you and Anna decide.''

She'd said the same to Jason earlier, but until that minute he hadn't really believed she'd follow through

on it. Abdicating decision making was so un-Abby-
like Jason felt his world tilt just a little bit more.
Maybe this was all just one hell of an alcohol-induced
nightmare.

But he knew it wasn't. Anna lay in a hospital bed
just floors away from him, their love not even a memory.

Jason set the papers down beside him. ''So what do
you recommend?''

''Assuming she doesn't recognize you, I'd say as
little as possible. Because as certain as I am that this
is temporary, I have to warn you that if you try to
force Anna to listen to what her mind's not ready to
deal with, you could very well send her into a permanent state of memory loss. If we knew for certain
what she's trying to escape, we could just avoid those
areas, but since we don't, the less said the better.''

Recognizing the sense in the doctor's words, Jason
nodded, but he didn't like what he was hearing. How
could he see Anna, possibly spend time with her and
act as though he hadn't spent the best two years of his
life with her? ''Can I tell her I know her at all?'' he
asked.

''Certainly,'' Dr. Gordon replied, steepling his fingers under his chin as he watched Jason. ''Tell her
you're an old friend of the family. Tell her she *has*
family. Even tell her that, according to her sister, she's
in New York on a sort of year's sabbatical from her
life. She should know that she demanded her family
leave her alone for a year. Anything to give her confidence in her own mental strength.

''What I wouldn't do,'' he continued, ''is tell her
anything emotionally threatening. I wouldn't tell her
that she's one of a set of triplets, for instance, which

means that it might very well be best to keep Anna and Abby apart for the time being. You said they're identical?''

"Completely," Jason said, nodding. Though *he'd* never had trouble telling them apart. By the time he'd met her sisters, he'd already been half in love with Anna. Their resemblance to each other had taken some getting used to, though; three gorgeous, blond-haired, brown-eyed beauties. But he'd never confused them. They were such different people, in spite of their physical sameness.

"Which means it would be impossible to keep Anna's multiple-birth status a secret if the two women met, and since being one of triplets is one of the things we suspect she's running from..."

Jason nodded, following the doctor's train of thought as the older man's words trailed off.

"I also wouldn't mention Audrey's murder or your own recent breakup," Dr. Gordon continued. "All these things combined are very likely a large part of what's paralyzing her."

"But there could be more," Jason said, thinking about what the doctor had already told him. "Something that happened in the past two months that we know nothing about. Something to do with the baby."

What hurt most of all was knowing Anna had been in New York, in trouble, and she hadn't called him. That, more than anything else, killed the hope he'd been harboring that she would one day come back to him.

"I suspect that Anna's suffering from not one huge trauma, but rather a combination of traumas—put together, they became too much for her. I'd say most definitely something in the past two months has contributed to her current condition.''

Jason nodded numbly as he accepted the need to ride this thing out. To let Anna remember her life in her own time. ''How soon can she leave here?'' he asked.

''Tomorrow if she has a place to go. Physically there's no reason for her to stay in the hospital.''

''She has a place.'' It didn't matter how stupid he knew it was, he couldn't have walked away from Anna if his life had depended on it.

Dr. Gordon stood up, accepting Jason's claim without further question, as if he'd been expecting the response. ''Are you ready to see her?''

As ready as he was going to get, Jason thought. But still… ''There's no chance she's three months pregnant?'' He felt compelled to try one more time.

Dr. Gordon shrugged, heading for the door. ''Anything is possible,'' he said—but he didn't sound like he believed it. ''Anna's underweight, which could make her baby small.''

The doctor stopped, looking at Jason, one male to another. ''You want my professional opinion?''

Jason looked away from the pity reflected in the other man's eyes. He was done fooling himself with false hopes, with dreams.

''Of course.''

''She's eight weeks along.''

Filled with apprehension, his stomach tied in knots, he followed the doctor from the room. After three months of being haunted by images of this moment, none of which were even remotely accurate, he was finally about to see the woman he loved again.

STROLLING DOWN the hallway for what seemed like the hundredth time, Anna studied everything around her. Surely something would spark a memory. A color, an emblem, a hairdo. Something must be familiar to her.

But nothing was. Except for the nurse who'd been caring for her most of the day. Anna smiled as the woman hurried past. Eileen. One of the three people Anna knew by name in the whole world. The other two were the doctors who'd visited her that day. Ready to climb the walls, instead of walking calmly beside them, she returned to her room and slipped back into bed, deciding it was more comfortable than the chair by the window. She knew, because she'd spent more time than she cared to think about in the chair that afternoon staring out into the summer sunshine, hoping to see someone or something she recognized, and then she'd remember.

There was no reason for her to remain in the hospital taking up a bed someone else might need. Physically she felt fine. Amazingly unaffected by the crash, considering the fact that she was two months pregnant.

But if she left the hospital, where would she go? How would she get there? What would she do once she arrived? Where would she get the money to survive? Especially if the city hadn't settled with the accident victims yet?

She started to shake when she came up with no answers. Because she had to do something. She could hardly raise her baby in a hospital room.

Nervously she reached for the chain around her neck, pulling the locket out from beneath her hospital gown. She'd kept the locket on all day because it had her name on the inside, but she didn't like wearing it.

Though it appeared to be good quality gold, it had a very odd shape. Reaching up, she unclasped the chain, pulling it from around her neck, and suddenly felt better than she had in hours. Freer. She could no more explain the odd sensation than she could say who'd fathered her child, but she decided to leave the chain off.

She lay back against the mound of pillows, the locket clutched in her fist. She was going to have to find someplace safe to keep it. As much as she didn't want to wear it, she couldn't bear the thought of losing it.

Men's voices could be heard just down the hall, and Anna sat up straighter in anticipation. *Dr. Gordon.* When you only knew three people in the world, it was an event to see one of them. And if anyone could make this feeling of panic go away, Dr. Gordon could.

They came into the room together, Dr. Gordon and an incredibly handsome man. He was tall, well over six feet, with thick blond hair and blue, blue eyes. She could tell because they were trained right on her. As Dr. Gordon came forward, the stranger's eyes never left Anna, never even glanced around the room. A part of her was aware that she should be uncomfortable, maybe even offended by that piercing stare, but instead, all she wanted to do was stare right back. Her heart sped up in excitement.

"Anna, I've brought someone to meet you," Dr. Gordon said, ushering the stranger forward. "This is Jason Whitaker, a longtime friend of your family."

Her heart continued its rapid beat, but now it was in fear. *She didn't recognize him at all.* Her gaze flew to Dr. Gordon as her mind tumbled over itself, searching frantically for something that just wasn't there.

Even faced with proof of her former existence, she couldn't recall any of it. Was this it, then? Was she trapped in this terrifying void forever?

"Hello, Anna." Her head jerked toward the stranger as he spoke. He had a wonderful voice. Just not one she'd ever heard before.

"Hello." She tried to act normally, but she could hear the panic in her voice.

"Anna—" Dr. Gordon started.

"It's okay, Anna," the man called Jason Whitaker interrupted. "Just try to relax."

And strangely, although he didn't sound the least bit relaxed himself, his words had some effect. The bands around her chest loosened enough for her to speak.

"But I don't know you," she said, staring at him, at his face, at his broad-shouldered physique. She'd never seen the man before in her life.

Her words hit him hard. Not only did he flinch, but she saw the quick flash of anguish in his eyes before he quickly recovered. "It's okay, honey," he said. "Dr. Gordon warned us this might happen."

He smiled at her and there was no doubt that that, at least, was genuine.

Suddenly the ramifications of the man's presence hit her and she sat straight up. "Us?" she asked. Dr. Gordon had introduced him as a friend of the family. Which meant she *had* a family. She clutched that one small piece of information for all she was worth.

"Who am I? Where are they?" she cried, looking around.

Jason glanced at the doctor and Anna's gaze followed. Filled with a sense of foreboding, she watched as the men came forward and flanked her bed. Jason reached for her hand, but pulled back before he made contact. She couldn't believe how much she'd wanted him to touch her.

"What is it? What's wrong?" she asked. Was her family dead? Had they been in the crash with her?

"You have a sister and parents living in Oxnard, California," Dr. Gordon finally said slowly.

A sister. Parents. The relief was so great it left her light-headed. She wasn't alone.

"Do they know…about me?" she asked. Were they on their way to see her? Take her home?

The doctor nodded. "Your sister does," he said. "Your parents are traveling in Europe and your sister's still trying to reach them."

A sister. Anna smiled. She was really glad to have a sister, someone she assumed would know her like no one else in the world could. Someone she could trust.

"What's her name?" she asked, looking from one man to the other.

"Abby." Jason's voice was odd, but Anna was too overwhelmed to do more than notice.

"Abby," she said, testing the name, liking it. The usual lack of familiarity didn't scare her as much now.

"Is she coming here to get me?" she asked, somehow knowing that if this Abby were there, everything else would be okay.

"That's up to you, Anna," Dr. Gordon told her, his face, as usual, a study in kindness.

Anna frowned. "Of course I want her here." Her sister would be able to fill in all the gaps in her life, wouldn't she? Abby could simply tell her everything she couldn't remember, until her mind was as full as if she'd never lost her memory.

Abby would know who'd fathered her child.

The two men looked at each other, and watching the silent exchange, Anna could see exactly when Jason Whitaker abdicated to Dr. Gordon, leaving the doctor to explain whatever they were hiding from her. What was going on here?

And then it hit her. Horrifyingly, embarrassingly. Was Jason Whitaker the father of her child? Was that why he was here?

"Did I sleep with you two months ago?" Anna blurted, in spite of the blush she could feel creeping up her throat and face. She was beyond manners. If Dr. Gordon and Jason knew something about her, she had to know, too.

Still suffering from acute embarrassment, still hardly comprehending what it might mean to have Jason Whitaker so intimately entangled in her life, crushing disappointment tore through her as he shook his head.

"I haven't seen you since I moved to New York three months ago," he said. He sounded sad, and she hated that he must pity her.

"I didn't even know you were in New York." He twisted the knife further.

Anna nodded. Her limited experience left her no clue what to say. How to handle such awkwardness was beyond her.

"You're in New York on a self-imposed sabbatical, Anna." Dr. Gordon freed her from the horrible moment.

"According to your sister," he continued, "you left home two months ago saying that you wanted to have a year apart from your family, that you needed to prove you could make it on your own. You demanded your family promise not to contact you for any reason during that year.''

''Two months ago?'' Anna asked. Right about the time she got pregnant—or right before.

Both men nodded. ''No one's heard from you since,'' Jason said.

''Did you tell my sister, uh, Abby, about my baby?'' Her eyes were pinned firmly on the doctor as she asked the question. She couldn't even look at Jason Whitaker.

The doctor nodded again. ''I did.''

''Does she know who the father is?'' Anna whispered. She had to know whose baby was growing inside her. She had to see the man, find out what part he was going to play in her life, in his child's life.

Tears flooded her eyes when the doctor shook his head. She was falling apart and she couldn't help it. A victim of the confusing and volatile emotions swarming around inside her, she had no memory of how to cope with them. She was losing it.

The touch of Jason Whitaker's hand distracted her. ''We wouldn't tell you, Anna, even if we knew,'' he said, his gaze full of something warm and powerful that she didn't understand, but that made her want to trust him.

''Do *you* know?'' she asked, tears running slowly down her face. The irony of her situation hadn't escaped her. She'd left home to find herself and, instead, had lost all recollection of herself completely.

''No.''

''I've told both Jason and Abby that I believe it would be harmful to fill you in on your past, Anna.'' Dr. Gordon broke the silence that had fallen. ''Your mind is hiding from something, and until your subconscious feels you're ready to cope with it, any attempt to force you to shoulder it could result in permanent memory loss."

"Oh." She wiped her tears with her free hand. Her head was hurting again.

"Amnesia is a gray area, Anna. Each case is different. And while some doctors would probably tell you that to be informed of your past might be for the best, I believe such a move is potentially dangerous."

"Dangerous," she repeated, and felt Jason squeeze her hand more tightly.

Dr. Gordon nodded and continued to gaze kindly down at her. "But I also believe, as do the associates I've conferred with, that when you're ready, you'll remember everything."

"But how long will that take?" she cried. Couldn't they understand she didn't have the time to just sit around and wait? She had to get on with her life—whatever it was.

The doctor shrugged. "That's entirely up to you, Anna."

"And what if I say I want to be told, anyway? In spite of the risk?"

"Then we'll tell you," Jason said immediately. "But according to Dr. Gordon, even if the information doesn't cause permanent memory loss, you won't know later if you're remembering things because you truly recall them, or only because you're remembering what we've told you."

"Keep in mind," Dr. Gordon added, "that neither your family nor Jason know anything about the occurrences of the past two months of your life."

Anna's gaze moved sharply between the two men, although she continued to cling to Jason's hand. "You think what my mind can't cope with is something that happened since I left home?''

"Possibly," the doctor answered. "It's more likely a combination of things."

Anna thought she'd experienced every kind of fear imaginable over the past hours, but nothing compared to the dread freezing her now as she contemplated doing anything that could impair her complete recovery. Nor was she honestly sure she wanted to know—at least not yet—what possible horrors had led her to this place, this time. And perhaps this pregnancy?

Pulling her hand from Jason's, she asked the doctor, "Do you think I was raped?"

She almost started to cry again, with relief this time, when he shook his head. "Apart from the bruises you suffered in the crash, there's no physical or psychological evidence of abuse," he said. "No old contusions, no neurotic fears when people get close to you, touch you."

"But if I don't remember anything, why would I act afraid?"

"You don't remember experiences, Anna, but fear for your physical safety is a conditioned response. In cases like yours, that's usually not something the patient loses."

"Okay." She needed to believe the doctor, to trust him, to trust someone. "Say we do it your way—no one tells me anything. What happens next?"

His brows raised, the doctor looked at Jason, who nodded. "Your sister has put Jason in charge of that," Dr. Gordon said. "And I'll be back to see you in the morning. If you're satisfied with what Jason has to offer, I'll release you then."

"Thank you," Anna murmured, watching as the

doctor turned and left the room. She continued to stare at the empty doorway until she'd worked up the courage to look at the man still looming over one side of the bed.

He wasn't watching the door. He was staring straight at her, and the longing she thought she glimpsed in his eyes before he quickly shadowed them made her feel incredibly sad, though she had no idea why.

"You're sure you're just a friend of the family?" she whispered, frustrated to the point of despair that she couldn't remember, that she had nothing to call upon to tell her the reason for his lost look—or her reaction to it.

"Positive," he said.

"And you really didn't sleep with me two months ago?"

He shook his head. "I wish I could tell you I had, Anna," he said with such finality she knew he spoke the truth.

Knew, too, inexplicably, that she wished his answer was different.

CHAPTER FOUR

"YOU WANT ME to come live with you?" Though Jason still stood beside her bed, Anna couldn't look at him, couldn't meet his eyes. Not because she was embarrassed by what he had in mind. She'd be an idiot to think that this gorgeous man could possibly have any sexual interest in a pregnant, currently demented family friend. He was taking pity on her, nothing more. No, what embarrassed her was her own reaction to his offer.

She *wanted* to go with him. She suddenly felt exposed, naked, vulnerable. She, who hated being a burden, who went out of her way not to bother anyone, wanted to saddle this man with an unexpected and very troubled houseguest.

"Oh!" she said suddenly, frantically retracing the pattern of her thoughts.

"What?" Jason leaned down. "What is it? Does your head hurt?" His worried gaze traveled over her. "Or…?"

"No! I…" How could she explain without sounding completely stupid? But looking into his eyes, how could she not? "I just had a thought, that's all. I knew something about myself. Really knew."

"You remembered something?"

She shrugged. Thinking back, she couldn't be sure how solid the feeling had been, was afraid to analyze it, afraid to dig too deeply, afraid she'd lose that little glimpse that was all she knew about herself. She was also afraid to test his reaction to her discovery. How well did he know her? Well enough to know she *hadn't* been overly concerned with being a bother in her other life? That these feelings were new, brought on by this horrendous situation? Not a part of her lost self at all?

"Whatever it was, it's gone," she said disappointedly, already convinced that her great self-discovery had been no discovery at all, but merely a reaction to her current circumstances. How could she possibly know whether or not she'd been a burden in someone's life when she didn't even know if she'd *been* in someone's life?

"It's okay, Anna." Jason sounded encouraging. "It's still a good sign. The doctor said things will probably come back only a little at a time."

She nodded, but it wasn't okay at all. He was suddenly too large, cramping her with his size, his broad determined shoulders blocking the door from her view, his optimism hanging over the room, pressing down on her, until her chest felt so tight it hurt to breathe. It took everything she had just to hold herself together. Optimism was beyond her.

Was this how it was to be? Was she to go through life looking for things that didn't exist, reading more into every situation because she so desperately wanted more to be there?

"My place is in Chelsea. It's fairly large for being in the city," Jason continued as though the last moments had never happened. "There's a loft bedroom, and a bedroom downstairs, as well."

Anna's gaze followed his back as he moved to the

window and gazed out into the night. There must be a woman someplace who wouldn't like a stranger moving into his home. No one as charming, as handsome as he was, would be living his life alone.

"You're welcome to stay as long as you like," he added.

He was being so nice. And without a dime to her name at the moment or anything else, for that matter, she had almost no immediate options. Still, she wasn't sure she could take him up on his offer, mostly because she wanted to so badly.

"You live alone?"

His shoulders stiffened, not markedly, but knowing nothing about him, about herself, her senses were acute to every nuance in her small world.

"Yes," he said, his voice as captivating as ever, no sign of the tension she'd witnessed—or thought she'd witnessed. "But you'll be perfectly safe. Your sister can vouch for me."

Funny, she'd never even considered her safety, although she supposed she should have. She was contemplating putting herself into this man's hands. Did she trust him so instinctively? Or had she just lost her common sense, along with her memories?

And what about her sister? Wouldn't *she* take her in? Would it really hurt to go back home to heal?

"Tell me something about Abby," Anna pleaded. "Anything." She'd agreed not to probe, but the blankness was more frightening than she could stand.

Jason spun around. "You've changed your mind, then? You want to go against the doctor's advice?" There was no condemnation in his voice, but there was urgency.

Anna shook her head. "I just need something a little

more tangible than a name. Something to hold on to.''
She felt ridiculous pouring her guts out to a perfect
stranger, and yet she couldn't stop herself. Because he
was easy to talk to, or because she was just so damn
needy, she didn't know.

Shoving his hands into his pockets, he watched her
silently. Anna could almost see the thoughts running
through his mind, see him discarding one after another. She waited for him to find something he could
share until she was ready to scream. Every thought he
was discarding was something she desperately wanted
to know.

"Is she close to me in age?" she finally blurted. Or
was this phantom sister a mere baby? Someone too far
removed from her in years to be truly close.

He deliberated for a couple of seconds. "Yes."

"Older or younger?"

Another hesitation. And then, "Older."

Anna laid her head back against the raised mattress
behind her. She was glad she had an older sister. The
thought was comforting.

"Do you really believe that whatever I'm running
from—" she flipped her hand up toward her recalci-
trant brain "—is back in California? That to go back,
to possibly force memories I'm apparently not ready
to face, could do permanent damage?"

"I do."

And he knew things she didn't know. Suddenly the
thought of California frightened her—and yet, at the
same time, called out to her.

"Would you like to speak to Abby?" Jason asked,
indicating the phone on the nightstand beside her bed.
"We can call her."

Turning, Anna glanced at the phone. Willing it to tell her what she should do.

"Is she home?" she whispered. Never had she been so tempted—at least, she didn't think she had. Just to hear her sister would be bliss. To have a voice on the other end of the line belong to her. Still, she couldn't forget the sabbatical she'd apparently taken from her family. Couldn't help but wonder why.

"She's home," Jason said, maintaining his position by the window. "Waiting to hear how you are."

Anna wondered what he thought she ought to do, but was reluctant to ask. He was leaving this completely up to her. Just as he should. So, had she and Abby had a fight? Was there a rift in their family? Had she, Anna, caused it? She didn't feel like the kind of person who would throw a tantrum or leave town in a huff, but then, she could hardly claim to know herself.

"She's waiting for me to call?" she asked.

"Or me."

Anna studied his face, looking for a sign, anything that would help her. His expression remained blank. Kind, but impassive.

"Do you think there was a valid reason for my going away?" How could she possibly know what to do when she had nothing to base a decision on?

"You weren't irresponsible, Anna," he said slowly, as though choosing his words carefully. "I fully believe that you thought things through and felt you had to leave."

"Do you know the reason?" She was being unfair, asking him for information that, were he to give it, could very well harm her permanently, but she couldn't help herself.

"Do you really want me to answer that?"

Yes. No! She wanted to get well.

"I'm not asking you to tell me the reason, Jason," she said, her voice stronger than it had been all day. "But give me a break here. I have no idea whether I'm apt to dream things up or to see clearly. Was my reasoning generally sound, or was it cockeyed?"

"Your reasoning was always sound."

His words were reassuring, but it was the steady look in his eyes, the way he spoke to her without words, that calmed the panic rising inside her.

She nodded, holding that gaze for another couple of seconds.

"Then I'm just going to have to trust myself, huh?" she finally said, trying for a grin and missing. "Until I know why I demanded no contact with my family, I'm going to abide by my wishes."

Jason nodded, saying nothing, but Anna could tell he was pleased. Satisfied she'd crossed one small hurdle successfully, she turned her thoughts to more immediate decisions. Like where did she go when the doctor released her tomorrow? With nothing to her name, not even a shirt on her back, her options were nil.

"I must have a place somewhere." She hadn't meant to voice the thought.

"If you do, we'll find it," Jason said. "I have most mornings free, and a bit of investigative skill left over from my reporter days. Finding your place'll be a piece of cake."

"And a job. Surely I was working."

"As soon as we find out where you were living, we'll be able to ask your landlord where you work.

Or your neighbors. You may even have a check stub lying around somewhere.''

There was that damned optimism again. But this time she welcomed it. She needed his encouragement. And he said he had investigative skills, too.

"What do you do?" she asked, suddenly realizing how little she knew about him.

He blinked, opened his mouth to speak and then closed it again. "I'm a newscaster," he finally said, still holding guard at the window.

"I knew that, didn't I?"

He nodded. And it hit her then how hard this had to be for him. How awkward and uncomfortable she must be making him feel. To be looking at a friend and yet speaking with a stranger. A stranger he was determined to help whether she agreed to his plan or not. And he was acting as though there was nothing to it, as if she hadn't already taken up more of his time than she had any right to, as if he, a busy news-caster, didn't have a million other things he could be doing. Would rather be doing. She made up her mind then and there to make this whole ordeal as easy on her benefactor as she could.

"This is really what you want—for me to come home with you?"

He crossed his arms over his chest. "Yes."

"And you honestly don't mind me camping out at your place until I find my own?"

"Nope." He stood still as a statue, waiting.

She wanted to ask once more if he was sure she wasn't going to be any trouble, but she didn't. Of course she was going to be trouble. She was going to be a complete nuisance for a day or two. She'd just have to make sure that it *was* only a day or two. Forty-eight hours to find her life. It would have to be enough.

"Then, thank you. I accept."

Jason glanced at his watch. "Okay, then, I've got to go," he said, moving toward the door almost as if, now that he had her acquiescence, he suddenly couldn't get away fast enough. "I'm on the air in half an hour. But I'll be back around ten in the morning."

Struck with sudden irrational fear as he departed, Anna lay perfectly still and closed her eyes. She might not remember anything, but at least she knew who she was now. And she wasn't all alone. She opened her eyes to stare at the telephone. She could always call the sister she'd left behind if she had to.

"Anna?" Jason's blond head appeared again around her open door.

With her stomach flip-flopping at the sound of his voice after she'd thought him gone, she met his gaze.

He pulled a card out of his jacket pocket and walked over to drop it on the nightstand. "That's my number," he said, backing slowly toward the door again. "If you need anything, call." A couple of more steps and he'd be history. "Anytime. I'm a light sleeper."

Her throat felt thick. "Thanks," she said, trying to smile without letting the tears fall.

Now he was at the door, standing there poised to leave, and yet, still there. She withstood his perusal, holding his gaze.

"It's good to see you again," he said finally. And then he was gone.

Her taut body relaxed back against the mattress, a tiny smile contrasting with the tears that dripped down her face as she reached for the television remote control. She just had to wait thirty minutes and he'd be there on her screen.

HE MADE IT to the station in time to change into his jacket. Barely. And he made it through the show, as well. Though not with his usual style. The natural repartee for which he'd become known wasn't flowing, his mind not on what he was saying but on the woman lying alone and frightened in a hospital bed across town.

"You feeling okay?" his co-anchor, Sunny Lawson, asked as soon as the On the Air light clicked off.

"Fine," he lied. He didn't need her attentions tonight.

She pouted her lovely lips at his curtness, her flirtatiousness as natural as her beauty. "What's wrong?"

"Nothing." Clearing his papers, Jason stood up, hoping to leave the set without hurting Sunny's feelings. She'd been a good friend during the months he'd been in town. He just wasn't fit company tonight.

Walking beside him, her heels clicking on the cement floor in front of their set, she suggested, "How 'bout a drink?" She linked her arm through his. "You can tell me all about it."

The offer was nothing new. He and Sunny often had a bite between shows or a drink afterward. "Not tonight," he said impatiently, realizing he should have suggested a rain check.

"Jason?" She stopped, hauling him to a standstill beside her. "You mad at me or the world in general?" she asked, frowning.

He opened his mouth to tell her about Anna. But the words didn't come. He didn't want to talk about Anna. Not yet. Not while he still felt so raw.

Leaning over, he planted a friendly kiss on Sunny's full lips. "I'm not angry. Just tired," he said, feeling a twinge of guilt as he kissed her again just to shut her up.

His guilt increased as the kiss worked. She smiled at him. "You should have left when I did last night, instead of staying for one more," she said.

"I know," he acknowledged. "Which is why I'm leaving tonight. Right now."

"Well, get some sleep, friend," she said, chuckling. "Your disposition could use some improvement."

"I'll be asleep the second I get home," he assured her, leaving her at her dressing-room door, feelings intact.

HE CALLED ABBY the second he got in. It was after midnight in New York, but only nine-thirty at the beach house in California.

"How is she?" Abby said in lieu of hello.

"Fine." He shrugged out of his sport coat and tossed it on the back of a kitchen chair. "Good. Really," he added as Abby's silence hung on the line. "Considering."

"You've seen her?"

Abby was crying and trying to hide it. He ached for her. For all of them.

"Yeah. She looked good, Ab, really."

"She looked the same?" Abby asked.

"Her hair was pulled back in a ponytail, but she was as beautiful as ever." Which was an understatement. To his starved eyes she'd been a vision, stealing the breath from his lungs.

"So what'd she say? Was—" Abby took a shaky

breath ''—was she crying?'' Then Abby lost her own
battle with tears completely.

Jason swallowed, hating the helplessness he felt, his
inability to make everything right for them. ''She
cried a little.'' He rubbed the back of his neck. ''She's
confused, Ab, frightened,'' he admitted. ''But she's
strong, too. In a way I've never really seen before.''
He took a breath and plunged ahead. ''She's coming
home with me tomorrow. She's going to stay at my
place until we can find out where she lives, where she
works.''

Abby digested that in silence, and Jason knew she
was drawing the right conclusions—just as he'd meant
her to. Anna had decided not to go home.

''I didn't think she'd stay in New York.''

''I know.'' Jason hadn't been sure, either, that Anna
would be strong enough to fight the temptation to run
to Abby. Whether she remembered home or not, some
habits were just too ingrained to break. He'd seen
Anna looking at the telephone, had felt her teetering
with indecision. But she'd refused to call. That was
when he'd known he was in for the long haul.

Silence once again stood between Abby and him.
Silent accusation, silent concession, silent relief.

''You told her about me?'' Abby finally asked.

''Of course.'' It bothered him she even had to ask,
that things had become so strained between them she'd
wonder such a thing. ''Although Dr. Gordon advised
against telling her you're triplets.''

''I know.'' She sighed. ''And as much as I hate it,
I think he's right.''

''I think so, too, Ab,'' he told her. ''And who
knows, it might only be for a few days. The doctor
said her memory could start coming back anytime.''

He didn't tell Abby about the brief flash Anna had had earlier that evening; he didn't want to get her hopes up, having her waiting for breakthroughs by the hour. Especially since this one had gone as quickly as it had come.

"I got hold of Mom and Dad." The words were too casual. "They're in France now."

"And?"

"They were horrified of course, but calmed right down when I told them you were with her."

"Are they coming home?"

"Not just yet." The words were almost defensive. "They're thinking about investing in some perfume company, already have meetings scheduled for next week," she explained in a rush. "I told them there wasn't any real danger. And it's not like we can see her."

No. But they could have come home for Abby's sake. Their eldest daughter was all alone, confused, hurting.

"Did you tell them about the pregnancy?"

"No."

Some things never changed. The elder Haydens sailed through life focused only on themselves and left Abby to bear the burdens.

"Anna was thrilled to know she had a sister," he said when Abby was silent for too long. "And though she'd already made the decision to abide by Dr. Gordon's advice, you should have heard her pumping me for information about you."

Abby chuckled through her tears. "She was always the smartest one of us."

From his tenth-floor window Jason looked out over the flickering lights of New York, wondering if one of the lights was Anna's, if she was sleeping. "Don't sell yourself short, Abby," he said. "You did a damn fine job holding the three of you together all these years." There. It was three months overdue, but it needed to be said.

"Yeah, right," she snorted. "Damn fine. That's why we're all living happily ever after."

The bitterness in her voice worried him. "You can't control fate, Ab," he told her sternly.

"That's not what you said three months ago," she reminded him. "I remember quite clearly you telling me I control everything."

He hadn't put it so nicely. "I'm sorry, Abby."

"I know," she said, her voice softer, more like the Abby he knew. "Me, too."

There was more Jason needed to say, but he'd be damned if he could come up with any words. Glib, smooth-tongued, always-know-what-to-say Whitaker was fresh out.

"The doctor said Anna came in with no ID on her except her locket," Abby said, rescuing him.

"Apparently her purse and whatever else she had with her was either destroyed in the crash or stolen during the mayhem that followed."

"That means she won't have her health-insurance card."

Right. Good. Something practical to think about. Jason grabbed a pencil, repeating the information Abby was reading to him from the health-insurance policy the triplets had through their shop.

"She's probably not going to need this," he said, the phone held to his ear with his shoulder as he wrote. "The city's liability insurance will cover all her medical expenses—and probably a lot more. The accident was so clearly the fault of a system's engineer—he was in the wrong place at the wrong time—that there's already talk of settlements.''

And then another thought struck him. ''What about her pregnancy?'' he asked. He was doing his damnedest not to think about that part of Anna's life at all. But she'd need to know. ''Will the shop's insurance cover that?''

''Yes.'' And that quickly, the tension was back. ''So…how are you doing?'' Abby's voice was soft.

''Fine,'' Jason lied. His insides felt ripped apart, but that was his own business.

''You'll keep in touch?''

''Of course.'' He should really turn on some lights. Except that he preferred the darkness.

''Jason?''

''Yeah?''

''Thanks.''

Grunting a reply, he rang off, stripped to his briefs and dropped to the hardwood floor, doing as many pushups as his tired body would allow. Forty-nine. Fifty. Getting involved with Anna again was sheer stupidity. One hundred. It was nothing short of lunacy. One hundred fifty. It was masochism. Two hundred. Suicide.

But he'd loved her once. Had actually, for the first time in his life, believed himself loved. And love meant you cared even when it hurt. It meant putting someone else's needs above your own. It meant loyalty and reliability. It meant all the things he'd always wanted but never known. It meant everything that was most important to him.

Rolling over, he lifted his legs an inch off the ground and crunched forward, pressing his lower back into the floor. One, two, three…fifty-one, fifty-two, fifty-three… Though he wouldn't have thought it possible, he'd underestimated how much he'd missed her. He'd also thought he'd suffered as hellishly as any one person could and still function, until she'd turned those big brown eyes on him—and hadn't known him from Adam.

One hundred twenty-one, one hundred twenty-two. She didn't know she'd sent him out of her life.

Jason spent the next hour moving his things to the downstairs bedroom. Whether she remembered growing up by the ocean or not, Anna would crave the openness of the loft just as he did, and he wanted her as comfortable as he could make her. Besides, he'd sleep better knowing she couldn't slip out without him knowing. His bedroom door was right at the bottom of the stairs.

Not that he thought for a second that Anna would run out on him. Or that she wouldn't be leaving just as soon as she was able. But old habits died hard. He couldn't stop people from leaving him. It was a fact of life—at least of *his* life. But he was damn well going to watch them go. He'd learned a long time ago that goodbye didn't hurt quite so badly when he knew it was coming.

It was when he cleared the last load of his clothes out of the closet that he saw the box he'd known was waiting there. Still taped up from the move from California, the small cardboard carton had one word scrawled across the top in black magic marker. *Anna.* Jason ripped it open.

He'd found a few of her things at his condo when he'd packed up so hurriedly to leave for New York. He hadn't been in any kind of mood to return them to her, to see her again. But he hadn't been able to toss them away, either. So like a fool, he'd thrown them in a box and carted them across the country with him.

A couple of pairs of silky bikini underwear. His body hardened immediately as he pictured her roaming around his condo back in California in them—and nothing else. Making them both breakfast or a midnight snack. Always fresh from lovemaking.

A long black spaghetti-strap nightgown he'd bought for her, but she'd never worn. Not because she hadn't liked it, but because once he got her to his place, he never gave her time to put it on.

And a couple of the loose-fitting, earth-toned dresses she wore almost every day of her life. Garments that would have looked drab on most women, but flowed lovingly around Anna's curves, giving her an air of womanly grace.

Jason smiled, remembering the first time he'd seen Anna standing on the street outside her shop in Oxnard, the wind whipping a dress just like one of these up around her hips while she'd laughingly tried to preserve some dignity. He hadn't had a hope in hell of escaping her allure. He'd been turned on then, as he pretended not to notice her gorgeous thighs, and ever since. Of course later, when he'd known she wore nothing under her dresses but silky bikini briefs, the damn garments had driven him crazy.

He was going to have to iron at least one of them. Three months in a box hadn't done them any favors. Both dresses had tints of mauve in them as did most of Anna's things. She'd told him once that she loved the shade because of its softness, its ability to meld with other colors without causing a stir. Only Jason had seen the fire hidden in her favorite hue.

After ironing and then showering, he finally lay down in his newly made bed sometime around three. And although he'd been up more than fifteen hours and was both mentally and physically exhausted, he still didn't sleep. In less than eight hours Anna was going to be here. In his home. With him. Just where he'd refused to allow himself to picture her for three torturous months.

And then she'd be leaving. Because while he'd been spending his nights trying not to remember her in his bed, she'd been in bed with someone else.

He'd deal with it. Anna wasn't his anymore. It was over. She'd told him so more than three months ago. He was a little slow, but he was getting it. Finally. She was just an old friend in need. He could handle this. No problem.

No problem to give her this chance to find out for herself who she really was. Anna Hayden. One person. Not Audrey, Anna and Abby.

All of this would be worth the effort if Anna discovered she could be Anna alone, not Anna, one-third of a whole—working a job she didn't love for a sister she did. Living a life that was content, but couldn't include the frightening, exhilarating experience of being completely, totally, in love. Couldn't include commitment to anyone but the other two-thirds. Anna, one-third of a whole, believing in her sister's opinion as much or more than she believed in her own. Believing that her strength and Abby's was to be found only in their togetherness.

Anna, one-third of a whole, and never really happy.

CHAPTER FIVE

SHE WAS GOING TO BE horribly embarrassed. She'd called the nurse, a new one since yesterday, and that harried woman had assured Anna that she'd see about getting her something to wear. But it was almost ten o'clock. Jason Whitaker was due to arrive momentarily, and Anna still had nothing on but a very short, very thin hospital gown with a slit all the way down the back. And her hair was still dirty. The hospital had been without hot water for most of the morning.

She considered calling the nurse one more time, but hated to be a bother. The woman was obviously busy taking care of people who really needed her. Sick people who were suffering. People who couldn't care for themselves. Anna felt like a fraud for even considering taking up the woman's time.

Of course the alternatives weren't much better. Either leave the hospital wrapped in a robe, assuming they'd let her borrow one, or ask Jason to go out and buy her some clothes with money she didn't have, and then come back and get her.

Or she could ask the doctor to delay her release for one more day, call her sister and have Abby wire her some money. Better yet, have Abby send her a plane ticket home.

Home. She closed her eyes, willing something, anything, to appear in the blankness—a picture, a feeling.

A memory. But try as she might, she couldn't raise a single image of the place where she'd grown up, or the people she'd known. Knew only that she didn't want to go there now. Not until she remembered why she'd left.

What she wanted to do was see Jason Whitaker. She wanted him to help her find her life. She wanted to get to know him again, this family friend who'd come to rescue her. Though she'd awoken this morning with the now familiar emptiness, the horror of living with a mind that had let her down, she'd also felt a flicker of anticipation. Simply because she was going to see Jason Whitaker again.

And therein lay her biggest fear of all.

Because she was scared to death he wasn't going to come get her. Surely, with time to consider the commitment he'd made, he'd change his mind. Any sensible person would. She could hardly blame him for not wanting to saddle himself with a crazy woman who also happened to be homeless, temporarily penniless, pregnant and who had absolutely no recollection of the father of her baby.

Jason had no way of knowing that his presence was the only thing that had made her feel safe since she'd opened her eyes the day before to a waking nightmare. That she was holding on to his offer to help her with every fiber of her being. That he made her believe she really could get her life back together, that somehow she'd find a way to be a mother to the child she knew she carried, but had yet to feel.

He owed her nothing. She hadn't even done him the courtesy of remembering him. Had no idea how close a family friend he was. He'd be a fool to come back. And if he didn't...

She'd been fighting her fears all morning, trying to concentrate on the mundane tasks necessary to prepare herself to go out in public, tracking down a toothbrush, washing her face, contemplating her nonexistent wardrobe. But as ten o'clock drew nearer, she could no longer keep her panic at bay.

He wasn't going to come. How could she possibly expect him to come? The walls started to close in on her. She was going to have to go back to California—without any idea what kind of a minefield she'd be walking into. Or maybe, worse yet, everyone would keep her reason for leaving a secret forever, treat her like some kind of invalid. What if they coddled her so much she'd never again have a life of her own, never be able to take care of herself, let alone be a good mother to her baby? She'd rather die first.

"Hey, sunshine, you ready to blow this joint?" Jason's cheerful voice put an end to her frantic soul searching.

Tongue-tied, Anna stared at him as he came through her door. He'd come back. And this morning, in form-fitting faded jeans and a polo shirt, he looked so classically gorgeously male he took her breath away.

When she didn't speak, he frowned, coming closer. "What's wrong?" he asked. He set a bag she hadn't even noticed he'd been carrying on the end of her bed.

"Nothing," she said, hot color spreading up her neck. How could she possibly ask this man to go buy her some underwear? She pulled the sheet up to her chin. "I, uh, have a small problem."

"Something we can fix, I hope?"

His warm blue eyes met her gaze directly, full of friendliness—and something more. Something she couldn't define or understand.

She couldn't do it. She just couldn't ask him for panties.

He picked up the paper bag he'd dropped on the end of the bed and tossed it onto her lap. ''Tell you what,'' he said, backing toward the door. ''I'll go get some coffee from the machine I saw down the hall while you get ready, and then we'll talk. Okay?''

He smiled, sending shivers all the way down to her toes, and she merely nodded. If there weren't clothes in this bag, she was going to crawl under the covers and never come out. And if there were, then he was the most amazing... He was a good friend. That was what he was. All he could ever be. Period. And she needed to get that straight right now. No matter how attractive she may find him, no matter how thoughtful and warm and kind, no matter how attached to him she was growing already, she was pregnant with another man's baby.

As soon as he was out the door, she ripped into the bag. Clothes. Thank God! Pulling them out of the bag as she climbed from the bed, she hurried into the bathroom. She was at least going to have the armor of decent covering the next time she came face-to-face with Jason Whitaker.

She liked his taste in clothes. The dress was loose and flowing, and the soft cotton felt good against her skin. As did the silky panties she found folded up inside the dress.

Blushing from head to toe, she slipped them on beneath the dress, chastising herself for thinking of the man who'd brought them as she slid them up her thighs. She might as well commit herself to the loony bin if she was going to start having romantic thoughts about her benefactor. Not only would it be sheer stu-

pidity to think that Jason could ever be attracted to
her, lunacy to read anything personal into his friendly
gestures, it was also impossible to involve herself with
anyone at this point in her life.

Somewhere in the world there lived a man with
whom she'd quite recently been intimate. A man she
hoped to God she loved, since she had his baby growing in her womb. A man who, if she saw him, may
just attract her more than Jason Whitaker did. It was
this crazy situation, that was all. Jason was the knight
saving the damsel in distress. And he was the only
attractive man she could ever remember seeing. Her
strong reaction to him was because of the situation. It
had to be.

And then it hit her. There'd been no tags on the
clothes she was wearing. The underwear, in fact, while
fresh and clean, was faded. She couldn't help wondering whom they belonged to or how well Jason
knew the woman. And couldn't seem to help the sick
jealousy that attacked her as she answered her own
question.

Swearing at herself, she yanked the band from her
hair, resecuring the ponytail with more force than necessary. One thing she knew for sure, she needed to
find her own place—damn quickly. Had to get out into
the world, meet so many people that rather than being
the sole individual in her life, Jason Whitaker was
merely one of a crowd. A huge crowd.

She was starting to obsess about him and was at
least rational enough to recognize the very real danger
in allowing herself to need him too much. He was
making it so easy for her to rely on him for everything.
But he was going to be gone from her life in just a
day or two, back to his own life, his own woman, and

she had to be able to stand by herself when he left. For her baby's sake and for her own. She couldn't afford another problem.

Her resolution to get away from him lasted right up until he came walking back into her room five minutes later. He smiled at her. And all she could do was smile back.

"You look good. Just like your old self."

His words gave her pause. It was so hard for her to accept that while she was getting to know a stranger, he was seeing an old friend. "I like the dress," she said. "Thanks."

He opened his mouth, closed it then opened it again to say simply, "You're welcome."

Anna had a burning urge to know what he'd almost said, but she didn't ask. She also didn't ask whose dress she was wearing. She wasn't ready to hear about another woman in his life.

"You ready to go?" he asked, looking the room over as if she might be forgetting something, as if she had something of her own to take with her. She followed his gaze around the stark room, struck again by the total emptiness that was her life.

"I don't know what I'm supposed to do about the bill," she admitted, something else that had been on her mind that morning. "I don't even know if I have health insurance."

"You do." Jason handed her a slip of paper. "That'll see you through until you can get a new card, but you won't need it today," he said. "The city is covering all your medical expenses. There'll probably be a settlement shortly, as well."

Anna stared at his forceful handwriting, wondering how many other things he knew about her that she didn't. She hated the way her condition made her so helplessly vulnerable, hated Jason seeing her like this. She swore to herself that she wouldn't rest until she'd taken back control of her life—and that once she had, she'd never let it go again. The insurance card was a good start. She no longer had to worry about financing her pregnancy. Now she just had to figure out how she supported herself.

"What kind of settlement?" she asked, sitting down in the wheelchair she had to be wheeled out of the hospital in.

Jason shrugged. "I don't know yet, but the city has already admitted liability. It's just up to their lawyers to determine amounts."

She turned to look at him as he pushed her from the room. "Do I need a lawyer?"

"I don't think so, honey. Only if you're not satisfied with whatever amount they offer."

"It was an accident, Jason," she said, crossing her arms over her chest. "They don't owe me anything."

"*They* seem to think they owe you something," he said, stopping at the nurses' station. "So I'd take what they offer—just to see you through until you're back on your feet."

Understanding that she would be less of a burden to him with money of her own, Anna just nodded and proceeded to sign the papers the nurse handed her. The sooner she was back in her own place the better. She had to believe that.

JASON THOUGHT it best to put off their investigating until the next day. "You're probably going to tire a little more easily than you're used to," he'd said.

And because she'd read his words to mean that he

had something else to do, she'd agreed with him. But after a brief shopping trip for some toiletries, another dress, purchased with money he'd lent her, and moving her few things into the beautiful loft bedroom in his apartment, she wished she hadn't agreed so readily. He wasn't going anywhere. And surely a possible bout of fatigue, heck, even passing out at his feet, was better than sitting intimately on his couch in the quiet of his apartment. She had nothing to say, no repertoire of small talk, of reminisces to draw upon. And the way he was looking at her, his eyes brimming with things she couldn't decipher, was making it hard for her to remember the reasons she couldn't allow him to mean anything to her.

"How well do I know you?" she asked suddenly. He had all the advantages and she had none. Had she been fond of him before? Was that why she was so instantly drawn to someone who, for all intents and purposes, was a complete stranger?

He shrugged, looking away. "I've known your family for several years."

"Well? Or just acquaintances?"

"Well."

"Did we see each other often?" she asked. She couldn't see how, if they were at all close, she hadn't been head over heels in love with him.

"We saw each other fairly often," he finally said.

"Why?" She couldn't have been in love with him. Loving Jason wasn't something she would ever forget. Not in a million years, or after a million bumps to her head. But even more, being her lover wasn't something he'd keep quiet about. Especially not now—not with her pregnant.

"You have a nice family, Anna. I enjoyed being with you all."

"Were you a friend of my parents?"

His right heel started to bounce, almost imperceptibly, his leg up and down. "Not until you introduced me to them."

"*I* introduced you?"

His leg was still. "You and Abby."

"Do you have a nice family, too?" Her bluntness made her uncomfortable, but the void where there should have been memories drove her on.

He shrugged. "They're nice people. I just don't see them much."

"They live faraway?"

His leg started to move again. "No."

She was treading on sensitive territory, and yet she wasn't getting any signals from him to stop. "Did you have a falling-out with them?"

He stretched his arm along the back of the couch, the tips of his fingers almost touching her shoulder. "My parents divorced when I was five," he said. "I grew up spending three days a week at one house and four at the other."

"Almost like a visitor," she said, frowning. "That must have been hard. Did you have a room in each house? Where'd you keep your toys?" She couldn't imagine anyone agreeing to raise a child that way.

He smiled sadly and she had a feeling she was seeing a part of Jason not many people saw, and wondered if he was telling her things he'd told her before. Or if, perhaps, the fact that he was to all intents and purposes a stranger to her made it easier for him to speak of things he usually kept to himself.

"For a while I had a room in both places," he said.

"Until my father moved closer to work and my mother remarried."

"What a tough way to grow up." She wondered if she'd ever met his parents. And if she had, if she'd been able to be civil to them. "I can't believe the courts allowed it."

"It was pretty unheard-of back then," he said. "It's not so unusual now. That way the child is still raised by both parents, has the benefit of a close relationship with both parents." His leg continued to bounce.

"Was that how it was with you?" she asked, filled with a need to understand everything she could about him.

"My father had his career." He shrugged. "Mom, her husband and new baby daughter. I always knew they cared—I just wasn't their first priority." He said the words easily, but Anna didn't believe for a second that his feelings were that uncomplicated.

And as he talked to her, as she caught a glimpse of the sensitive boy he'd been—sensitive to hurt, but sensitive to his parents' needs, as well—Anna wondered again why she hadn't been in love with him.

Had she already been in love with someone else? Someone who affected her even more deeply than he did?

"Were you ever in love?" she blurted. *Was I?*

He stiffened. "I thought I was."

It had to be difficult for him, hearing her ask things she should already know, but as long as he was willing to answer, she had to ask. And he'd just cleared up one mystery. There'd never been anything more than friendship between them because he'd been involved with someone else.

"What happened?" She curled her legs up beneath her.

"She chose someone else." And he was still hurting.

Anna couldn't imagine any woman turning Jason Whitaker away. Quite the opposite, in fact. She'd been picturing a string of broken hearts leading straight to his door. Maybe her own included. Maybe she'd loved him—and he'd loved someone else.

"I'm sorry."

He glanced over at her, a sardonic grin on his lips. "Don't be," he said. "It doesn't matter anymore." But somehow she knew it did.

"Did I know her?"

"Yes."

Anna wondered if she'd ever been as jealous of this unknown woman as she was of the woman whose dress she now wore. "Did I like her?"

He looked at her, his assessing gaze making her uncomfortable. "You never told me you didn't."

His fingers moved absently along the back of the couch, and Anna could feel every imaginary brush through the thin material of her dress, aware of him in a way that could only embarrass him, stir his pity. She was crazy. And pregnant. And the man was probably still in love with someone else.

"How long ago was this?" she asked.

"A few months." He looked away and then back again, his leg still. "Just before I came out to New York."

This woman was in California, then, Anna thought, worried by her sudden sense of relief. But worried even more by how deeply she felt the pain he was denying. In any way that mattered, she'd just met this man. "She was a fool," she said aloud.

He shrugged. "It's history."

She wasn't sure she believed him.

IT WAS A RELIEF to leave for work. Though he felt guilty about leaving Anna alone sooner than he had to, Jason gave himself enough time to walk part of the way to the station that balmy New York evening, catching a cab at Madison Square. People had been complaining about the summer humidity, but having grown up on the coast, Jason found New York's humidity no problem. And as much as he missed the ocean, he loved New York. He loved the rush, the life that surged around him every time he stepped outside his door. Everywhere were people with goals to achieve, important things to do, destinations to reach. He needed to get caught up again in the activity, the enthusiasm, remember who he was, the person he'd become since leaving California. He also needed to lose some of the tension that was building to an exploding point within him.

He needed a break from Anna.

She'd been in his home one afternoon and he was falling in love with her all over again. She was another man's woman now. A woman who was sitting in his apartment in the dress he'd stripped off her the last time she'd worn it, and she was carrying another man's child.

He'd had to leave before the anger building inside him spewed out and scalded them both. How could she have allowed another man to touch her, to know her, to leave his seed in her? And why wasn't she different because of it? Why was she still, even minus her memory, so much the Anna he'd known and loved more than anyone else, ever?

He'd have given his life for the woman. And she was giving life to another man's baby.

While he, like some kind of sick fool, still burned with desire for her. Her scent, her soft husky voice, the way she glided when she moved—all had driven him to the point of insanity that afternoon.

He understood how her separation from Abby had been more than Anna could bear. Understood that she badly needed this chance to emerge from the cocoon of her family to become a separate and complete individual. Accepted the fact that her mind was ensuring she got that chance.

But as the afternoon dragged on, even stronger than his need to take her to bed, stronger than his anger, was the hurt he'd thought he'd buried forever, rising closer and closer to the surface. He was having a hard time accepting, forgiving, that she'd forgotten *him*.

"Sleep improved your tongue, but it didn't seem to do much for your disposition," Sunny said as they left the set after the six-o'clock news.

She hadn't appreciated his curt acquiescence when she'd asked him out to dinner. But at least he'd been at his best on the air. His thoughts had flowed as freely as the cue cards, allowing him to add his own slant to the news he imparted the way his loyal viewers had come to expect. And if his grand performance had had anything to do with the fact that he knew Anna was watching him, he damn sure didn't want to know about it.

"Let me make a phone call and we can go to dinner," he said, tossing his station jacket on a chair just

inside the door of his dressing room. "But I'm buying."

For once she didn't argue with him.

Sunny drove a fire-engine red Mercedes convertible,
and Jason envied her only for having a garage close
enough to home to drive her car to work almost daily.
The Jaguar he'd brought with him from California was
every bit the vehicle her Mercedes was, but it was a
twenty-minute cab ride away, parked in a garage that
cost him nearly as much as his apartment did each
month.

Still, he appreciated a powerful car, and Sunny was
a good driver. Settling back in the passenger seat, he
enjoyed the view, the warm breeze in his hair, as she
maneuvered through midtown Manhattan toward the
seafood restaurant she currently favored on the Upper
East Side. Anna had already eaten, she'd assured him
when he'd called her from his dressing room. She'd
found the stash of TV dinners in his freezer and had
eaten one while watching his show. She was under-
standably exhausted and was planning to shower and
be in bed by nine o'clock. He was planning not to
think about her in that spaghetti-strap nightgown.

"So what's got you so uptight?" Sunny asked as
soon as they had their predinner drinks in front of
them.

"You remember that amnesia victim?" he asked
her, studying the ice in his glass. It was going to take
a lot more than a glass of scotch to put him to sleep
tonight.

"The one from the subway crash? Anna, didn't they
say?"

"Anna Hayden," he said. "I knew her in California."

"And?" she said when he paused. She'd stopped swishing her straw in her drink and was staring at him. Sunny wasn't going to like what he had to tell her.

"She's staying at my place for a few days."

"Why?" The softly spoken word hung between them.

He could tell her that Anna had no place else to go, that she knew no one else in the city. "Because I asked her to."

"Why?" she asked again. She'd made no secret of the fact that she'd been hoping for more between them than friendship. But he'd been honest, too. He wasn't ready for the kind of relationship Sunny wanted.

He took a sip of his drink, sending his co-anchor a warning look over his glass.

"I wanted to," he finally answered. It was the only part of the truth she'd care about.

She nudged her drink away. "How well did you know her in California?"

"Well."

Breaking eye contact with him for the first time since the conversation began, Sunny said, "Oh."

Jason sipped his drink, waiting. Knowing Sunny, she wasn't going to give up that easily. He'd known when he invited Anna home that Sunny wasn't going to like it. His relationship with her had started out as a publicity stunt. She was to be full of light sexual innuendoes and lots of personal approval as they worked together on the air, the idea being that if she approved of Channel Sixteen's new co-anchor, so would her loyal viewers. And if viewers tuned in to see a little chemistry between Sunny Lawson and her new co-anchor, so much the better.

In silence they ate their meal, lobster for Jason, crab

salad for Sunny. He'd have enjoyed the food a lot more if it wasn't sharing space with the rock in his gut. His relationship with Sunny was important to him, in more ways than one. Just not the way she wanted most.

When Jason had first come to town, not knowing a soul, he'd been only too willing to spend a lot of time with Sunny, to be seen about town with her, appear in all the right places with her on his arm—all in the name of business. She was a beautiful woman, and with her sharp mind, good company, too. But as they'd gradually grown more comfortable together, their relationship had become more than business. After three months of sharing dinners with her, working with her, drinking with her, Sunny had become a good friend.

She wanted to be his lover.

But as beautiful as Sunny was, as tempting as he found her, Jason did not intend to take her to bed. Sunny wasn't looking for a no-strings-attached affair, and he wasn't sure he'd ever want more than that with a woman again.

There was his job to consider as well. He cared about his job. A lot. And he had to work with Sunny. Though he'd given the show a much needed ratings boost, Channel Sixteen News had been hers long before he'd come along.

She waited until he'd pushed his plate away. "When's she leaving?" she asked.

"I don't know."

He couldn't give her any more than that.

"Are you sleeping with her?"

"No."

"Do you intend to?"

It was on the tip of his tongue to tell Sunny that

whether or not he slept with Anna was none of her business. But because she was a friend, because it was the truth, he answered her. "No."

Her shoulders relaxed. "Does she know that yet?" she asked in the voice that had made her famous.

"She's pregnant, Sunny." And then, when he saw the horror in her eyes, "The baby's not mine."

"Oh," she said. "Good."

Picking up her abandoned fork, she attacked her half-eaten salad with gusto and he waited while she ate, well aware of how beautiful she was, of the male eyes watching her appreciatively, of the envy surrounding him in the elite little restaurant. Well aware, too, that Sunny was his for the taking. He wondered if he'd eventually give in and take her to his bed without love. Good sex could go a long way toward covering up what wasn't there.

"You ready?" he asked as soon as she finally laid down her fork.

"Yes," she said, standing and waiting while he settled the check.

Any other time she'd have argued over whose turn it was to pay; tonight, she was claiming the right to have him buy her dinner. Jason didn't miss the message she was sending him. He was hers and she wasn't giving him up.

He could have told her she didn't have a damn thing to worry about where Anna was concerned. His housemate already had a man in her life. And she'd probably be running back to him just as soon as she remembered who he was.

CHAPTER SIX

ABBY AWOKE with a start. Cold sweat trickled down her back and she sat up, looking around her small bedroom in the back of the beach house. Something was wrong. Engulfed in fear, she slid soundlessly from the bed, eyes glued on the open door in front of her. Her own safety didn't matter, not until she assured herself that her sisters weren't hurt. She hadn't heard anything, but she never ignored her instincts. She'd awoken for a reason.

Slipping out her door and into the room immediately to her right, she saw the empty bed. Audrey's bed.

As reality crashed in, a cold calm settled around Abby's heart. Out of a lifetime of habit, she checked the rest of the cottage. But when she found it empty, as empty as her life, she lay slowly down on the kitchen floor, welcoming the coolness of the tile against her cheek, aware only then of the tears running down her face.

God, she hurt. Was going crazy with the pain. Not because she wasn't strong enough to shoulder it. She'd been feeling for three all her life. Whenever her sisters were in need, she knew. When one suffered, they all three suffered. They'd felt each other's thoughts— seemed to share a single soul. Just as they'd all shared a remarkable comfort in each other. The most agonizing heartache became less unbearable simply because it was shared.

But not anymore. Abby was alone now. And this solitary pain was much harder to bear than any she'd known before. Why was she still sensing things that no longer existed? Feeling bonds that had long been broken?

She ached so badly she wished she'd just die and be done with it. And no one knew she felt this way. Which was the worst part of all. For the first time in her life, no one knew.

ANNA FLEW out of bed before she was fully awake, running down the loft stairs with only one thought in mind. To get help. She had to get help.

Jason caught her by the shoulders just outside his bedroom door.

"Anna! What's wrong?"

"Let me go!" She fought his hold. She had to get help.

He held her captive. "What is it, honey? What's happened?"

She heard the concern in his voice, but she couldn't take time to explain. "I've got to get help!" she cried, still struggling to break away from him.

"Why? Are you in pain?" He pulled her closer, turning her face up to his.

His blue eyes bore into hers, full of worry—and something more. Something that reached down to soothe away the panic that had spread through her while she slept. She stared back at him, speechless, wondering how she could possibly explain her frantic urgency when she didn't understand it herself.

"Anna?" He continued to watch her.

She shook her head. Was she losing her mind?

"I..." She looked away, embarrassed, afraid. Confused.

"What frightened you, honey?" His voice was soft, understanding—and yet so very masculine.

"I... It was just..." What? How could she tell him without sounding crazy?

"Were you sleeping?" he asked, leading her over to the couch.

She nodded.

He sat down beside her, still holding on to one of her hands as he reached up to brush the hair from her face. It was a damp tangled mess.

"You just had a nightmare," he said gently. "Dr. Gordon warned us this might happen."

Still silent, she nodded again. Let him think that was all it was. Let her try and believe it.

"Were you dreaming about the crash?" he asked.

"Yes." She forced the word and barely got a whisper. That was how her dream had started, anyway. But there'd been more. Something that when she'd awoken hadn't vanished with the dream. Someone calling out to her, frantically, painfully, needing her so desperately she still felt the echo of it singeing her nerves.

Jason pulled her into his arms. "You're shivering," he said. "Are you cold?"

Shaking her head, she burrowed her face against him, realizing his chest was bare only when her cheek pressed against the warmth of his skin. *Please, God. Make me not be crazy,* she prayed, too weak to pull away from Jason even though she knew that snuggling against him wasn't right.

He settled back into the couch, cradling her. "Talk to me, Anna."

She wanted to. God knew she wanted to share everything with this man. These past few days, she'd been traveling the streets of New York with him on a so far fruitless search for her identity. Living with him, watching him on the news, hearing on the television show what he'd neglected to tell her himself—that his partner considered him the day's best catch—had so intensified her inappropriate attraction to Jason that being with him had, in some ways, become pure hell.

And in other ways, it seemed so natural. Jason knew her even if she didn't know herself. He knew what foods she liked best, what colors. He knew when she was bothered, when something amused her. Through him, she was gaining back bits of herself.

"Did I used to talk to you?" she asked now, allowing herself just a few seconds of touching him, of taking advantage of the strength he was so willing to share with her. Then she'd move, put the length of the couch between them, just as their lives pushed them apart in every other way.

"More than you talked to most people, I guess," he said. He'd considered her question carefully.

Anna was glad she didn't have to look at him. "Was I a pest?"

"Hell no!" His response was immediate, the first personal response he'd given her without first carefully choosing his words. "It used to drive me crazy the way you'd keep things to yourself," he continued. "If anything, I wished you'd open up more."

"I didn't talk much, huh?" Anna smiled. "Somehow that doesn't surprise me." In fact, this discovery felt gloriously right, familiar. Finally. Something felt familiar.

Jason tightened his hold on her. "You talked, Anna. Just not always about the things that mattered."

And what might those things have been? Maybe if she'd talked more, her mind wouldn't have needed to run and hide.

"Were we close, Jason?" She wanted to think that, though they hadn't been lovers, at least they'd been friends. Good friends. The kind of friend you could run to when the world was too much to bear.

Jason didn't answer. She'd whispered the words, so perhaps he hadn't heard.

As she lay there, her mind taunted her, playing absurd guessing games with his possible thoughts. How did you tactfully tell someone she wasn't your favorite person? Especially when that person was sitting half on top of you, helpless with need. How could he say that she'd been a difficult person to like? That while she was nice enough now, she'd been a pain in the ass in her other life? Or worse, how did he tell her that he'd tried his best to steer clear of her because of the embarrassing unrequited crush she'd made so obvious?

"Not as close as we are now," he answered after such a long time had passed she'd been certain her question had gone unnoticed.

Listening to his heart beat, she thought about his answer. *Not as close as we are now.* She wanted to ask him to explain, but was afraid to push him too far. She was afraid of his answer. Was something the matter with her that made it hard for people to get close to her? Had she been the type of person that someone good and decent like Jason wouldn't want to be close to?

The damn black hole that was her mind tormented

her with its silence, frustrating her, angering her. What the hell had happened to her? What had driven her to running away from herself?

"Is that why I didn't contact you when I came to New York?" The warmth of his arms gave her the courage to ask.

"There was no reason you should have," he said, his voice even, as though he was reporting the news. "You didn't even know where I lived."

She continued to lie pressed against him, the darkness loosening her tongue. "Did I know you'd moved to New York?"

"You knew I was going to."

"You didn't tell me goodbye when you left?"

"No."

So they must not have been all that close. "Did you tell my sister goodbye?"

"Yes," he said, still reporting impassively. "I saw her before I left. You'd gone down to San Diego. She said she'd say goodbye for me."

Which made perfect sense.

The warmth of Jason's hands radiated through the thin silk of her gown, and as she relaxed, Anna was suddenly too aware of them clasped just beneath her right breast. He was wearing nothing but a pair of thin cotton shorts, hastily donned, if the undone drawstring at the waistband was any indication.

And as she studied that waistband in the shadows, Anna noticed something else, something that sent her heart slamming against her ribs. He was aroused.

Her throat felt dry; her nipples tightened. She could move just a little bit lower and his hands would slide over her aching breast. Just a little bit lower...

"Do you have any idea who the father of my baby

is?'' Her words crashed into the intimate silence that had fallen around them. She had to keep her mind on what mattered, or she was going to make a terrible mistake. One she wouldn't be able to live with when she regained her memory—and her life.

''None.'' The word was clipped, his hold on her loosening.

''Are you just saying that, or do you really not know?''

He sat up on the edge of the couch, setting her away from him, leaning forward with his hands clasped between his knees. ''I had no idea you were seeing anyone.''

''But—''

''It's late, Anna,'' he interrupted. ''No more questions tonight, okay?''

''Just one more, Jason, please.'' She had to know. Especially after the way she'd just reacted to him, she had to know.

''What?'' He turned to look at her, frowning, his eyes shuttered in the shadows.

''Was I the type to sleep around?''

He jumped up from the couch. ''What kind of question is that?''

''Please, Jason,'' she begged, burying her pride to find the truth that was haunting her, the truth she feared almost as much as she feared never finding it. ''Was I the type to sleep around?''

He stared at her silently, a shadow in the dark. But his silence drove her on, her stomach knotting. Was it possible that *she* hadn't known who'd fathered her baby? Even before she'd lost her memory?

''I have to know.''

His shoulders relaxed, but the frown remained. "I wouldn't have thought so."

"You don't know for sure?"

"No. I don't know for sure."

IF THEY DIDN'T FIND her place soon, he was going to have to tell her who he was. Traipsing around Manhattan on foot in the hopes she'd notice something she'd missed from the cab had done nothing but tire her—and stretch his endurance so dangerously thin he was actually considering trying a little psychology of his own. He'd been tempted from the first moment he'd walked into her hospital room, when she looked at him with the eyes of a stranger. Tempted to lay her down in his bed, strip away her clothes and talk to her with his body as he'd done so often in the past. He just couldn't believe that once he'd made love to her she wouldn't remember him, wouldn't remember the love they'd shared.

"God, I hate that place," she said, her voice tired, worn. They were midtown, not far from the station, but several blocks from Central Park where he'd had the cab drop them off.

Feeling guilty for pushing her too far too fast in his own selfish need to get her out of his apartment before he did something he'd regret, it was a full moment before Jason saw what she was talking about.

Central Deli and Restaurant.

But she loved deli food. And Central was the best. On East Thirty-fourth Street it was a bit of a jog from the station, but the restaurant was good enough to be one of Sunny's current favorites. So why would Anna hate it?

How did she know she hated it? Jason stopped in

his tracks, the flow of Manhattan pedestrian traffic bumping into him, and Anna, too, as he pulled her to a halt beside him.

"You remembered something," he said.

Shock crossed her face, followed almost immediately by a smile that took his breath away. "Yeah," she said, grinning. "I guess I did."

The crowd moved around them, too intent on business to be slowed down by a couple of idiots grinning at each other on the sidewalk. "So why do you hate Central?" Jason asked.

"I haven't a clue." She laughed out loud at the absurdity of the situation.

Jason grinned, taking her hand as they finally had to give in and join the Friday after-work throng. He hadn't realized until that moment how worried he'd been that the doctor had been wrong, that Anna's memory loss was permanent, that maybe there *had* been some brain damage.

"Do you think I lived around here?" she asked him as they reached the end of the block.

"It's possible. We can check the phone book, call places nearby."

"I'll make a list tonight while you're at work."

Galvanized by Anna's small victory, Jason insisted on walking around the block three more times, making sure she didn't miss even a speck of gravel on the sidewalk. She'd been there before. Anything could spark a memory, lead them to her life, get her out of his.

And suddenly he wasn't sure he should push her. She'd remembered something. That was enough for one day. Telling her he had to get to work, he dropped her off at the apartment and took a cab to the station. And immediately called Abby.

HE AND ANNA spent the next morning sitting on his couch, the list of phone numbers she'd made the night before on the coffee table in front of them, taking turns with his mobile phone—but every call they made was another dead end. No landlord in the immediate vicinity of Central Deli had ever heard of Anna Hayden, no one had had a tenant missing for the past several days, not one they were aware of, anyway. No one recognized her description.

But Anna wouldn't be daunted. "I remembered that place, Jason," she said late that morning. "I *did* have a life here and I'm going to find it."

Jason couldn't help but admire her persistence, her surge of confidence springing from one small victory.

"Then get back on that phone, woman."

She picked the phone up and started to dial, but stopped. "You telling me what to do?" she asked, her eyes glinting with laughter.

"Not if you don't want me to." She never had liked to be ordered about; gently directed by Abby always, but never ordered.

"Good, 'cause I make my own decisions," she announced, dialing the next number on their list.

They were the sweetest words Jason had ever heard her utter.

THEY FINALLY HIT pay dirt midway through the afternoon. Jason had run through his introduction by rote, already hearing the negative response on the other end of the line before realizing he hadn't received one. The brisk woman wouldn't confirm that Anna was one of her tenants, said she managed so many buildings she couldn't keep track of who lived in them, but she agreed to look at her records.

She called back five minutes later, telling them to meet her at a brownstone in Gramercy, not too far from Central Deli.

A SATURDAY-AFTERNOON lull hung over the city, streets filled with more shopping bags than briefcases, but the traffic was steady, cabs honking, cars zipping in and out of spaces they should never have tried to inch through. And suddenly Anna wanted to stay right there, enjoying the sun on her skin, and watch the people, wonder where they were going and why. Anything but walk the two more blocks to the life that was waiting for her.

She wasn't going to be able to stand it if this was another dead end. If the apartment wasn't hers. And she was scared to death about what might happen if it *was*. Would she remember it? Remember everything? Was she ready to face whatever she'd run away from?

Did she want to go back?

Living with Jason was the only life she knew. And after just a few days, it was a life she was happy with.

So what if it wasn't real?

And what if she discovered her old life and still didn't remember it? If the apartment was hers and none of it was familiar? Could she carry on without any memories? Did she have any choice?

Butterflies swarmed her stomach as she and Jason approached the building. They'd covered the last few blocks silently, and Anna couldn't help wondering what he was thinking. Was he thanking his lucky stars that he was about to be rid of her?

She had to admit that as much as she liked living with him, as secure, as welcome, as he'd made her feel, she hated having to rely on him. Hated him knowing she had to rely on him. Hated being nothing more than a charity case.

She climbed the steps to the brownstone, praying the apartment they'd come to see was hers.

But what was she going to do when Jason left her there all alone?

CHAPTER SEVEN

ANNA HATED the apartment. Brown vinyl furniture, scarred tables, not even a view out the one tiny window. The only redeeming things about the place were its tidiness and gleaming wooden floor.

"I don't recognize any of it," she said, feeling like a trespasser in a stranger's home—a stranger's life. But Mrs. Walters had recognized Anna, had shown them Anna's name on the mailbox just before she'd given them the key to the apartment. She'd left before Anna could ask the woman any questions but not before making it clear that Anna could stay only as long as she wasn't a bother to anyone—they weren't in the health-care business—and as long as Anna paid her rent.

"Relax, Anna," Jason said. He was standing by the nook that served as a kitchen, watching her. "You rented it furnished and you've only lived here a couple of months."

Relax. She'd just been made to feel like some kind of freak by her landlady, she didn't recognize a single stick of furniture, didn't like it either. Somehow she didn't think this was a relaxing situation. Damn him and his optimism, anyway. What did he know about losing all knowledge of everything you'd been, everything you'd ever hoped or dreamed to be? What did he know about letting yourself down so badly?

Crossing to the far corner of the apartment, Anna flung open the closet door, revealing a sparse row of uncomfortable-looking cotton shorts and shirts. She hated the clothing more than she hated the furniture. "Did these come with the place, too?" she asked, doing her best to stave off an attack of panic with a show of anger.

It was bad enough that nothing was familiar, but she didn't even like the stuff she was seeing. What if she didn't like the woman she'd been any better?

Jason crossed the room, dismissing the clothes with barely a glance as he took her by the shoulders. "You must have wanted a change when you came to New York," he said, holding her gaze with his own. "You never wore shorts."

She wasn't ready to be mollified. Not even by him. "It's not a good change."

"So don't wear them," he said, rubbing her shoulders. "But stop being so hard on yourself."

More than his words, the look in his eyes spoke to her, telling her he believed in her, that he knew she'd make it through this awful time.

But how could she believe in herself when her loss of memory was proof of her inability to handle her life?

"It's been almost a week, Jason. Don't you think I should be getting somewhere by now?"

"Dr. Gordon said it could take a while. You remembered the deli. That's a start."

And with that she would have to be satisfied. Except she didn't feel satisfied at all. Looking around, she tried to see the room from another perspective, as if this were all happening to someone else. How should a woman in her situation react? What should she do? What was the answer?

She just didn't know.

A perfunctory search of the apartment turned up a checkbook with a balance that would see her through several months; there were lots of Saltine crackers stashed in a drawer of the end table by the pullout couch, in the bathroom cupboard, in the single kitchen cupboard with a couple of cans of soup to go with them. The only other personal items were a laptop computer Jason said she'd used to keep her personal finance records, and a beautiful music box shaped like a castle. Jason listened to the tune, rewound it and listened again. He seemed more than casually interested in the box, almost as if surprised to see it there; but when she asked him about it, he merely shrugged and said she'd received the box from a friend.

And—in a table drawer—a personal address book. Shaking, afraid to open it, she stared at the flowered cover.

Eyes closed, she held the book to her breast. Between its covers lay details of her life, people she'd known. And suddenly she couldn't open the book quickly enough. Scanning the pages so urgently she almost tore them, her gaze flitted from one entry to the next, until she reached the last page.

"Nothing," she said as the book fell from her fingers. "I don't recognize a single name, not a place, not a number. I don't even recognize the handwriting." Her eyes burned with tears, her heart with failure.

"I've never seen this before," Jason said. She heard him pick up the book, riffle through the pages, and just didn't care. She was a great big nothing. The father of her baby could be listed there, and she wouldn't even know it.

"They're all from back home," Jason said, having reached the last page of the book.

"You know them?"

"Every one of them."

"We were that close that you knew everyone I knew?"

Setting the book on the end table, Jason pivoted away from her. "We ran in the same circles, shared a lot of mutual friends," he said. "This book looks new, as if you copied those numbers all at the same time."

She'd noticed that, too. Every entry was in the same ink, the handwriting neat.

"And I never met a person, made a phone call, wrote down an address since coming to New York?" she asked. She couldn't help the bitterness she heard in her voice. It was as if she didn't even exist anymore.

"You had a planner you kept things in," Jason said as if just now remembering. "Everything from business cards to appointments. You carried it in your purse."

"Which was lost in the crash." She was not having a good day.

After knocking fruitlessly on the doors of her immediate neighbors—they were either not at home or said she'd kept so much to herself they knew nothing about her—Anna and Jason stood awkwardly in her apartment again, surrounded by furniture neither of them recognized. And then there was nothing else to do but say goodbye. Jason invited her to spend one last night at his place, but precisely because she was tempted, she declined his offer. It was Saturday night, and he was sure to have his pick of beautiful women with whom to spend it. His beautiful co-anchor, Sunny Lawson, for one. The woman had undoubtedly been more than patient.

Jason accepted her refusal easily, almost insultingly easily, but Anna couldn't blame him. Instead, she chastised herself for being hurt, made certain he saw none of her uncertainty as she waved to him at the door and kept herself well hidden as she watched him all the way down the block through her one small window.

Then, desultorily, she made another search of her apartment, acquainting herself with where she kept the silverware and napkins, what kind of makeup she used, her few pieces of jewelry. She added her locket, which she'd been keeping in the inside pocket of her new purse, to the box containing her other jewelry. And then pulled it right back out again, dropping it into an envelope before placing it back inside her purse.

Dr. Gordon had warned her about depression, so she continued to poke into drawers, touching her things, trying to get a sense of the woman she'd been, pretending that she cared. But she still felt as though she were trespassing in a stranger's life, one she couldn't identify with, one she wasn't sure she even wanted to know.

First thing tomorrow she was going shopping for some more dresses. Right after she packed up every last pair of shorts for the Salvation Army.

Finding the key to her mailbox in a corner of the kitchen drawer, Anna went down to check her mail, retrieving only a couple of bills and some solicitations. She returned the wave of a small dark-haired woman coming out of a door down the hall from her before locking herself back inside her apartment, making sure to secure all three locks as Jason had instructed.

The entire episode ate up fifteen minutes of an evening that stretched beyond eternity. With the walls of the small apartment closing in on her, increasing the agitation that already drove her day in and day out, she sank onto the couch, telling herself to relax, to hold on, to be patient and let her mind heal itself. Yet the future loomed ahead of her, a dark specter in the night, frightening her with its blankness. What was she going to do with the rest of her life? What was she going to do tonight, and tomorrow, and the day after that?

She had no idea where she'd worked, if she'd worked, but judging by the size of her checking account, work wasn't going to be of pressing concern anytime soon—she was going to be receiving a settlement from the city, as well. Besides, it wasn't as if she'd be much use to anyone at the moment, not having the slightest idea what she could do or memory of any training she'd had. And there was always the chance that her employer would view her exactly as her landlady had, a burden to be pitied. Nothing more.

For now, work was out.

Her stomach tightened, the horrible fear looming darkly over her again, consuming her. What was she going to do if she never remembered? And what was going to happen if she did? What horrible things would be there waiting? Would she still not be able to handle them? Would she flip out? Have a breakdown? Go mad?

She thought about calling Abby. About California. About going home. At least there she'd have someone to talk to. Someone to take care of her. Someone to commit her if she went over the edge.

And she thought about Jason. His tall athletic body. The way his eyes always made her feel warm, special. His laugh. His charm. His arousal the other night.... And she thought about Sunny Davis in his apartment, maybe that very moment.

She thought about the child she carried, the conception that had vanished from her memory as if it had never been. The man whose baby she carried. Then she started to cry. Was he out there somewhere thinking she'd deserted him? Or had he deserted her? Would he think her a weak fool for having a mind that checked out as it pleased?

Did *she* think herself a fool?

Anna stopped crying. Stood. Paced her small living room. And faced the truth. She did think herself a fool. And worse. She hated herself for refusing to deal with her life and escaping into this…emptiness. Hated the weakness, the cowardice surrounding her condition. But worst of all, she hated herself for wishing she could run back to Jason, bury herself in his arms and never remember at all.

HE BOUGHT HER groceries, called her four times a day, asked her to breakfast, to lunch, and beat the hell out of a racquetball while convincing himself that he was just being a friend, that he wasn't getting involved. That he'd be able to walk away.

He always had, hadn't he? Every time his mother called, he was there for her, no strings attached. No expectations. No recriminations when his birthday rolled around, Christmas, sometimes even a year or two with no word from her. Helping was what a man did. What a man *should* do.

"Jason?" He'd known it was Anna on the phone even before he answered it Tuesday morning. She was the only one who would dare call him before noon. In recent months, as his nights stretched till dawn, he hadn't been awake much before then.

"I found a file box in the back of the closet," she said. She was sounding stronger each day, taking control of her life. He admired the hell out of her. "There's this pay stub, just like you said there might be, from a place called Old World Alterations. It's in Little Italy."

Grabbing his keys off the coffee table, Jason said, "I'm on my way."

THE PLACE WAS a modern day sweatshop. Standing with Anna on the sidewalk outside the building that gray New York day, Jason stared with horror at all the women crammed into the small space, some sitting at sewing machines, others in hard-backed chairs, stitching by hand. No one spoke. No one smiled. But their fingers flew, racing to finish one job only to start another.

Sick to his stomach at the thought of Anna sitting in there like that, working as though she was a slave, Jason turned away. He'd seen enough. If Anna had worked there, she would no longer. He'd pay her damn rent if he had to. She wasn't going back in there.

Except she was. She reached for the door handle.

"Anna."

She dropped her hand and turned, surprised, almost as if she'd forgotten him.

"Do you remember being here?" he asked her.

She shook head distractedly.

"Do you know if I can sew?" she asked him.

The way she said it was so odd he had to ask, "Why?"

"I feel like I can sew," she said slowly.

She was remembering. "You can."

Someone bumped into her and she stepped back along the wall of the building. "Am I any good?"

"Very." She'd made money—a lot of it—sewing up Abby's designs for a line of children's wear that sold in exclusive shops all over Southern California.

Frowning, she looked at the women. "I don't think I like it," she said, sounding perplexed.

A sigh eased through Jason, releasing a spring of hope. He'd always suspected that sewing wasn't what Anna wanted to do, rather, what she did for Abby. But she'd never before admitted as much—even when he'd confronted her about it before leaving for New York. Perhaps, just perhaps, her memory loss was doing something for her he never could, getting her to know herself.

"Let's go in," Anna said. Her mind was obviously made up. She was going to follow up on this lead. Jason went with her inside.

"Anna!" The accented male voice came from someplace in the rear of the shop. "You've come back to us!"

Anna froze inside the door, immediately wary, though she had no idea why. The man sounded friendly enough. He'd been sitting at a desk and now he jumped up and came forward, weaving his thin body between the sewing machines.

Several women looked over at her behind his back, smiling tentatively, but then bowed their heads and resumed their work before she could return their smiles.

"I can't believe you've come back to us," the man said. Ignoring Jason, he reached for Anna's hand, kissing it before pulling her forward.

Anna wanted to slap him. In fact, the urge was so strong she had to move away.

She tried to concentrate on what he'd just said. He couldn't believe she'd come back. As though he hadn't been expecting to see her again. "I don't work here anymore?" she asked.

"Of course you work." He winked at her. "I give you lots of work!"

Jason stepped forward so that he stood between Anna and the man.

"You know about the subway crash," he said, his usual charm nonexistent. Anna had never seen him like this before.

"Oh!" The man hit his palm to his forehead. "It was you!" He looked at Anna. "The Anna they say was hurt. She was you?"

Anna nodded.

"And you still don't remember?"

Anna shook her head before realizing she was under no obligation to tell this man anything.

"My poor Anna," he said. "Come here and let your Roger make it all better." He tried to pull her into his arms, but Anna held back.

"My Roger?" she asked, managing little more than a whisper. Jason was frozen beside her.

"Of course you don't remember, but not to worry. I will remember for both of us." He grabbed Anna again, holding her close as he whispered, "What we had was good, no?"

Nausea overwhelmed her. It was all Anna could do not to be sick all over the man's dirty white shirt.

"You were so good, my little Anna." He kissed his fingertips.

Had she actually slept with this creep?

Oh, God. Was it his baby she carried?

With a quick look at Jason's horrified face, she dashed for the bathroom, getting there just in time to lose her breakfast. Hunched over the toilet, she heaved until she thought her ribs were going to break, but nothing could take away the sick feeling washing over her.

How could she go out there? Jason had heard the man. He'd obviously reached the same conclusion she had. And was disgusted. How could she ever face him again? How could she ever face herself?

Finally she rose, wetting a piece of paper towel under the sink and holding it against her burning face. If this was the life she'd left behind, she'd rather die than go back to it.

"Anna?" Jason's voice came through the door.

"Anna?" Roger's suggestive calling of her name nearly sent her back to the toilet.

"Ohhh, go away," she cried softly to herself, and opened the door.

"You're still sick from your crash?" Roger asked, not quite as enthusiastic once he got a look at her pale face.

All Anna could see was Jason, standing in front of the other man, his eyes searching her face intently. "You okay?"

She shook her head, silently begging him to get her out of there, to make the nightmare go away.

The phone rang and one of the women answered it, calling Roger to talk to someone named Baker.

"I'll be right back," he said to Anna as he walked off.

"Pssst."

Anna looked at Jason. Had he said something?

"Pssst."

A woman over by the door was trying to get her attention. Jason motioned Anna ahead, and they eased their way to the front of the shop.

"You no work here no more," the woman whispered in fractured English. She stared at the pair of men's slacks she was hemming by hand, her fingers never missing a stitch as they flew along the dark material.

Anna didn't respond, afraid to draw attention to the fact that the woman was speaking. But she nodded, hoping the woman would understand that she was listening.

"Quit, six, eight weeks ago. Very sudden. No one say why."

Exchanging a glance with Jason, Anna nodded again.

"Boss, he like you. Not like he like good worker." She lifted the pants to her mouth, cut the thread with her teeth and looked out the window.

The conversation was over.

Roger could still be heard in the back of the shop, speaking rapidly in a foreign language, glancing out every now and then, making certain Anna was still there. Jason grabbed Anna by the arm and pulled her out the door of the shop into the gloomy morning. She hurried silently beside him as he led her down the street, eager to put as much distance as she could between her and the disgusting slimy man whose touch had made her want to curl up and die. The man who could very well be the father of her baby.

JASON DIDN'T SLOW down. Not even after they'd traveled enough blocks and made enough turns to have lost the bastard should he *have* followed them. He continued to walk simply because he didn't know what else to do. He had to think, to make sense out of the past half hour, consider the woman he'd known and loved for more than two years and somehow find the truth.

"Am I carrying his child?" Anna's cry was so distraught passersby on the sidewalk stopped and stared.

"No!" Jason said, pulling her against him, sheltering her from a young man who was sending her furtive looks over his shoulder.

"How do you know?" she asked more softly. He could hear tears in her voice. Tears and something else—a distress so deep he knew she'd never recover if her fear turned into truth.

"I know you." But did he? "You'd never have gone for a man like that, Anna. Never."

The Anna he'd known wouldn't have. But the Anna he'd known would never have slept with another man only six weeks after leaving his bed. Or left Abby, either.

CHAPTER EIGHT

NEITHER OF THEM had an appetite for lunch and, at Anna's suggestion, headed back to her apartment. She had to search it again, tear it apart, look through everything she could find for something that would prove Roger was not the father of her child. Jason helped her look, but found nothing.

She had books—lots of those—blank computer disks, they even found the name of the obstetrician she'd made her first appointment with, one she missed the day after the subway crashed.

Getting out the phone directory, Jason started calling alteration shops in the area. None of them had employed or ever heard of Anna Hayden. Anna contacted the phone company, the electric company, asking for the job information recorded on her billing records. Old World Alterations.

"The first person someone calls after changing jobs usually isn't a utility company," Jason pointed out when she hung up the phone for the second time.

Anna felt like crying. She could feel the tears welling behind her lids and forced them away. On top of everything else, she wasn't going to cry on him. Jason hated tears.

Her head shot up, her heart beating against her ribs as she stared at him.

"What?" he asked.

She shook her head, flooded with confusing emotions, glee, fear, a sense of helpless foreboding left from the morning's ordeal—and hope. Grabbing her shoulders, Jason pulled her closer, holding her gaze. "What, Anna? You look like you've seen a ghost."

Her tears won the battle, trickling down her cheeks, but she smiled up at him, grateful beyond anything she'd ever known to have this one precious memory. This connection. To him.

"You hate tears," she said.

She laughed at the astonished look in his eyes. The delight. And was puzzled by the shadows that immediately followed. "You remember me?" he asked, letting her go.

She shook her head, still smiling in spite of his puzzling behavior. "Just that you hate tears." She really had known him before. Not that she'd ever doubted his word, but it was just so damn good to know something simply because she knew, not because she'd been told.

He nodded. "You're right. I do. Or I did. Until a friend pointed out how ridiculous I was to feel threatened by a simple expression of emotion." He continued to study her, his hands in the pockets of his chinos.

"Why would I know such a thing?"

"We went to see *While You Were Sleeping*. Your sister balled like a baby and I got on her case for it."

"*While You Were Sleeping?* Is that a movie?"

He nodded, still watching her.

"Why'd it make her cry?"

"Because all the woman in the movie wanted was to be part of a family and yet, in spite of her efforts, she was always on the outside looking in."

Sounded to Anna like something that might have

touched Jason, as well, knowing what she did about his lonely childhood.

"So who had the guts to tell you how ridiculous it was to feel threatened by tears?"

"You did." He turned away from her. "In Abby's defense."

For the first time in days he was measuring his words again. There was more to that story. He just wasn't telling her. But at the moment she was so giddy with her proof of his place in her life she couldn't worry about the secrets lurking just beyond her grasp.

She remembered knowing Jason.

HER NEWFOUND REMEMBRANCE, minute as it was, had a disturbing repercussion. Sitting on her couch, munching an early dinner, Anna watched Jason on the six-o'clock news that evening. She took pride in how he looked in his navy jacket with the station's emblem above the pocket; only Jason's broad shoulders could look that good. She loved the way his eyes crinkled when he smiled, approved of his witty repartee and generally felt privileged for knowing personally one of the city's most sought-after bachelors. And was shocked at the proprietary nature of her feelings.

When Sunny Lawson laid her perfectly manicured fingers on his forearm, Anna wanted to claw her eyes out. Afraid of the vehemence of the feeling, of what it meant, she forced herself to think about all the reasons Jason needed a woman like Sunny in his life, why, as a friend, she, Anna, had to hope they'd be very happy together. Why she had no business feeling jealous over a man she wasn't free to have. Even if she wasn't living in this half world of no memories, she had no right to Jason. She was bound to another man—and to the child she'd created with him.

Making herself watch Jason and Sunny together, Anna tried not to care. But no matter the logic of her reasoning, she couldn't stop her chest from tightening, her skin chilling, the butterflies invading her stomach.

And the more she panicked, the more panicked she grew. Was she so unstable that she was going to fall apart at everything? The woman she was now had only known Jason a matter of days. She couldn't possibly care for him so much that merely seeing another woman touch him was ripping her heart out.

But Jason was all she had. The only person she knew. It was natural for her to feel a bit possessive, she thought, trying to reassure herself. She just had to make certain she didn't get carried away with her possessiveness.

Jason had other friends. He played racquetball. One time when she'd been at his place, he'd received a phone call from a buddy of his in California. She wasn't the only person in his life by a long shot—wasn't even the most important person in his life.

Suddenly, out of nowhere, Anna was struck with the need to talk to Abby. Jason wasn't the only person in her life, either. He wasn't even the only one who cared. She knew Abby had been keeping in close contact with Jason. He'd told her so.

Picking up the phone with shaking fingers, Anna realized she didn't even know Abby's number. She refused to be daunted, dialing the operator, instead, requesting the area code for Oxnard, California, dialing long-distance information, only half-aware that she knew exactly how to do so. Yes, there was a listing for Abigale Hayden. Anna scribbled while an automated voice intoned the number.

She dialed the number quickly, giving herself no time to change her mind. She'd only talk for a couple of minutes. She just had to connect with someone who knew her, who hopefully loved her, unconditionally, as family was meant to. Someone who would still love her if Roger was the father of her baby. Someone who would love her even if she found herself hopelessly, dangerously attracted to another man. Someone who knew Jason.

But before the phone rang even once, Anna hung up, remembering Dr. Gordon's warning not to contact her family. And even more, his admonition to learn to trust herself. She'd had a real live memory that day. She couldn't give up now, couldn't let herself down. As the doctor had reminded her more than once, she'd requested a year away from her family for a reason. And that reason might very well be connected to the vacation her mind had taken.

She had to learn to trust herself. Regain some faith in herself. And that was going to take time. She had to take back control of her life or live forever like this—in a world without color, without depth, without memories.

Turning off the television set, Anna grabbed one of the many books stacked on her closet shelf, drew a hot bath and ordered herself to settle in and read. To focus her mind on something else for a while, to think about somebody else's problems. She made it through only a couple of pages before realizing that she'd read the story before. She couldn't remember how it ended, but she knew she'd read it.

And several hours later, as she lay in the middle of

the pullout bed, snuggled in her nightgown under the covers, and finished the book, she couldn't help re-plotting the ending. And that was something she'd done before, too.

HE SHOULD HAVE learned his lesson, but Jason couldn't seem to stop himself from spending most of his free time with Anna. She was like a drug, an ad-diction, had been since the first time he'd ever met her. He was also thinking about her too much, pre-occupied when he should have been focused—on the racquetball court, at the station, out with Sunny. But he couldn't just desert Anna. Not now. Not when she needed him. Not when her eyes lit up every time he walked into the room. Not when she said his name in that husky voice. Not when he...

It couldn't lead to anything. She had other priorities, people who came before he did in her life, in her heart. But where was the harm in helping her? He was a strong guy. He could handle it, he assured a couple of his buddies from California when they phoned. He was fine, he told his mother when, for once, she remem-bered to call to wish him happy birthday.

What he couldn't handle, couldn't accept, was walking away from a friend in need.

And Anna was a friend in need, he told himself the following Saturday. She needed a day out of the city. A day of freedom when she could be the same as everyone else around her, carefree, enjoying herself. A day at the beach. He wanted to take her somewhere that might spark a memory—of him, of the love they'd shared. They'd been on a beach the first time they'd made love. And the last time.

His Jaguar was waiting for him, sleek, its white

paint gleaming, the leather seats cool in the dark of the garage. Flipping the switch to put the top down, he waited for it to curl into the back of the car, securing the leather cover around the entire mechanism. Jason counted on very little in his life, invested his heart stingily, but he cared about his car. It was the one thing he'd really wanted that he'd had the power to get, to keep. He'd worked hard, demanding from his career what he couldn't demand from his personal life, fighting for the top spot in a competitive field, settling for nothing less. The Jag was his reward. And his reminder.

Anna had loved his car. She'd loved the wind blowing through her hair, unconcerned when the long strands became tangled because of her refusal to pull it back, laughing out loud when he pressed the accelerator to the floor, the thrill of speed turning her on.

"What a gorgeous machine!" When he collected her Saturday morning, her eyes lit up just as they'd used to. "Why haven't I seen it before now?"

She had. And she'd run her hands along its smooth contours just as she was doing now. "The closest garage I could find is fifteen miles away from my apartment," he said, opening her door for her.

She climbed in and he shut the door, asking, "You have your swimsuit?"

"I'm wearing it." Pulling down the top of her dress, she showed him.

Yep, she was wearing it. A tight-fitting one-piece black affair that showed him the cleavage he already knew intimately. Suddenly it was his turn to appreciate a sleek body. Except that he couldn't run his hands along this one the way she'd done moments before. Not anymore.

"You'll let me drive it sometime, won't you? After I get my new license?"

Jason froze, halfway around the car, staring at the back of her head. She finally turned, frowning at him.

"What?" she asked. "I'm a great driver." And then, "Aren't I?"

"Yeah, growing up near L.A. you have to be, but what makes you think I'd let you drive my car?"

She shrugged. "You're a nice guy."

Giving some inane reply, Jason continued on to his side of the car, sliding into the driver's seat with the ease of practice. For a second there he'd thought she'd remembered. In the old days, back when they loved each other, her driving his car had been a standing gag between them. She always wanted to. He always let her—and was nervous as a ninny sitting beside her the whole time. But she'd always made it up to him in the most glorious ways. More than once, before they'd ever made it out of the car....

"I met this girl in the hallway yesterday," Anna said, breaking into his thoughts as he headed out of the city. "Maggie Simmons."

"Someone you knew before?" He downshifted, trying to ignore the feel of his hand brushing against her leg. He moved over to the right lane.

"Not well." Anna frowned. "Like all the others she said I kept mostly to myself."

Jason nodded, content to listen to her. She'd been giving him hour-by-hour accounts of her day ever since she'd left the hospital, sharing more of her thoughts with him in the past two weeks than in the two years they'd been lovers. He would gladly have spent the rest of his life listening.

"Has it ever occurred to you that I'm not a very friendly person?" she asked.

Keeping his speed moderate so he could hear her, Jason considered her question. God, he hated the secrets between them. Not just the things she couldn't remember, but his lies by omission.

"You were always private, honey, but never unfriendly," he said, weighing his words. He wasn't a doctor. How the hell did he know how much he should tell her? And how, loving her as he had, did he stomach keeping the truth from her?

They drove silently for a while, Anna's expression smoothing as the Jag ate up the miles, putting more and more distance between them and the city.

Anna at last broke the silence. "Maggie told me something kind of odd."

"What's that?"

"Well, she's pretty sure I haven't worked in the past six weeks because I was always home."

"Nothing too odd about that if you were having troubles finding a job you wanted. It's not like you couldn't afford to take a little time off."

"My money isn't going to last forever."

Jason acknowledged the truth of that with a shrug. She was getting a settlement from the city, though not enough to live on for the rest of her life. But she had lots of time to worry about earning her keep and more pertinent things about which to worry.

"Anyway, Maggie said sometimes I'd come home carrying full garbage bags like some kind of bag lady." Anna said the words hesitantly, stealing a glance at him as if to assess his reaction.

Jason chuckled. "Surely you aren't thinking you were a bag lady."

"Of course not!" Anna said indignantly. "But you have to admit, it's odd."

"Only because you don't seem to have several garbage bags worth of stuff in your entire apartment."

"Oh, well, that's the other weird thing." Anna's hair flew about her face, brushing his shoulder as she turned her head toward him. "Apparently, after bringing in the bags, I'd be home all day, sometimes several days in a row, and then I'd leave again, carrying the same full bags."

"And what do you make of all this?"

"I did people's laundry?" She grinned at him.

Jason grinned back. "Where, in the tub?"

"I had a bird-sitting business and was smuggling in birdcages?"

He hooted with laughter. "You're afraid of birds."

She frowned at him. "Why on earth would anyone be afraid of a poor defenseless creature like a bird?"

"You saw Alfred Hitchcock's movie *The Birds* when you were little."

"And?" she prompted.

"Swarms of birds practically take over a town, and they attack people. It gets pretty ugly."

"I wonder why a little girl would be watching such a thing?"

He'd asked the same question when she'd first confessed her childhood fear. It was the first time she'd told him anything about growing up with only her sisters for guidance. The three had spent hours in front of the television watching programs they never should have seen, waiting patiently for the parents they adored to get home from work. There had been times when they'd fallen asleep, still waiting.

She wouldn't like the answer any better than he had.

"I wasn't there," was all he said. "Anyway, it wasn't birds. What else can you suggest?"

"I liked to shop, but suffered from buyer's remorse?"

Her stories got wilder the farther they drove. She was the bagman in a smuggling ring. A drunk—the bottles empty when she carried them back out, of course. A thief with a conscience, stealing and then returning what she stole. By the time they'd parked and gathered the cooler and blanket from the trunk, Jason had almost forgotten the troubles they'd left behind. For a moment out of time he had his Anna back.

Following Jason, Anna took a deep breath of the salty ocean air. "I love the beach, don't I?" she asked, but she didn't need the confirmation. Something else she just knew. Like she knew she was a good driver. Things were coming back. Too slowly, to be sure, but how glorious to begin to know herself. To really know the person in whose body she lived.

"You had a cottage on the beach," Jason told her, coming around the car.

Had she stayed there alone? she wanted to know, but didn't ask. She wasn't going to ruin this time with him by worrying about things she had no control over. Not today.

The sand felt like heaven between her toes. So familiar. So good. She could imagine herself lying in it, the grains closing around her body like a glove.

"Let's build a castle," she said suddenly, plopping down close to the water.

Dropping the blanket and cooler, Jason joined her. "Watch out," he warned, settling in as though he expected to be there awhile.

"Whatever for?" Anna asked. How difficult could

it be? Anyone could see that all you needed was the right mixture of water and sand to construct just about any shape you wanted. It didn't take a memory to pile up a bunch of sand.

Jason pulled off his shirt, threw it down and stretched out on it, his elbow in the sand, his hand supporting his head. "Just wait and see."

He looked resigned, expectant. And gorgeous.

"Did you play sports in school?" Anna forced her eyes back to the job at hand. The sun was hot enough without her thoughts making her even hotter.

"Quarterback of my high-school football team," he said, clearly pleased with himself.

She wasn't surprised. His body was a work of art.

"Did you go to college?"

He nodded. "On a swimming scholarship. Care to race me?"

Anna grabbed a cup out of the cooler, packing it with sand. "In a minute. Let me finish this," she said.

"That'll take more than a minute."

She didn't care if it took all day if it meant he'd still be lying there beside her. Her stomach was doing flip-flops just looking at him. But she couldn't make herself stop stealing covert glances.

"What school'd you go to?" she asked, making room for the small tower that had to go on one corner of the castle.

He'd gone to USC, had a masters degree in communication, could ski as well as he swam, spent summers playing beach volleyball and had lost his virginity when—

"What?" he snapped, sitting up when she asked that last question.

"Sorry," she said, using both hands to dig her moat. "It just slipped out."

When it came to Jason, she had sex on the brain. She was praying that was because she didn't have much else there at the moment. But she wasn't convinced.

"Sixteen."

"Hmm?" she said, trying her best to concentrate on the sand castle.

"I was sixteen. She was a present from my father. He was supposed to have taken me skiing for my birthday, but had to fly to New York on business at the last minute."

"Some present."

Had that woman been worth being ditched by his father? To some guys, probably so. Anna wasn't so sure about Jason. His priorities were different. People were important to him. Commitment, loyalty were important to him. This was perfectly clear to her, even after having only known him less than two weeks. Why else would he be continuing to help her if not for his loyalty to her family?

Remembering what he'd told her about his youth, Anna wondered if he'd ever come first in his parents' lives. Hadn't they seen what a special person they'd created? She couldn't imagine not wanting to spend every minute she could with her baby as it was growing up, whether he was a model child or not. Life passed so quickly.

"She was actually kind of nice," Jason added almost as an afterthought. "I dated her for a while, until I realized that just because she was seeing me didn't mean she wasn't also working as a prostitute."

Anna didn't want to hear any more about it. She was sorry she'd ever asked.

"I'm sorry, Jason," she said, knowing the words weren't going to do anything to dispel the memories she'd roused.

"Don't be." He filtered a fistful of sand through his fingers. "It was a long time ago. And hey, for a kid with adolescent hormones, great sex isn't anything to scoff at."

"That's some castle!" A young couple strolling down the beach stopped beside them, interrupting just as Anna was getting jealous of a seventeen-year-old memory.

"One of her more basic attempts," Jason said.

The girl leaned down, marveling at the nooks and crannies. "Basic! She's an artist!"

Anna dug her moat a little deeper, hating the attention she'd inadvertently drawn to herself.

"Gee, lady, you're good!" a little boy said.

One by one, people of all ages came over, little kids who wanted to make a castle, too, their parents, assorted couples, several teenagers, even an old codger down on the beach with his metal detector, looking for Lord only knew what kind of treasure. But they all had one thing in common—shared amazement at Anna's creation.

Jason being Jason struck up a conversation with just about every one of them as they wandered over. Anna, feeling tongue-tied and uncomfortable, marveled again at his charm, his talent for making people feel at ease.

Embarrassed by the continued attention, she finally suggested they break out the lunch he'd brought along. But before they opened the cooler, she insisted on moving as far down the beach as she could get from the castle she'd made.

"I had no idea I was going to cause such a stir," she said. Looking back at it, she couldn't help but be proud of her work. She really was good. She'd had no idea.

"I did."

"I've done this before, huh?" she asked. She should have known something was up by Jason's reaction when she'd first sat down in the sand.

"Your sand sculptures have won prizes," Jason said, helping her to spread their blanket.

Anna laughed. "Get out of here."

"Kids used to knock on your door just to ask you to come out and play in the sand."

She froze, her hand half in and half out of the cooler. She couldn't tell if he was pulling her leg or not, and it was suddenly important to her that he wasn't. For the first time since she'd awoken in this nightmare, she was discovering something about herself that she liked—a lot. She wanted to be the kind of person little kids knocked on the door to play with.

"Did I?" she asked.

"Of course."

Satisfied, feeling better than she had in days, she tucked her sandy damp dress beneath her and sat down to lunch.

She'd discovered a talent. She'd made a sand castle. She'd had fun.

CHAPTER NINE

BEDRAGGLED BUT SMILING, Anna climbed the steps to her apartment late that afternoon, meeting Maggie in the hallway.

"Looks like you had a day at the beach," Maggie said, pointing at Anna's damp and sandy dress. In spite of the bathing suit she had on, she'd never taken the dress off. She'd been too aware of Jason's half-naked body to be comfortable undressing with him so near, and too self-conscious of the fact that, though she wasn't yet showing, there was a baby growing inside her. She'd also seen that look in his eyes again.

"Jason took me," Anna said, smiling shyly at the other woman. She'd told Maggie about her amnesia when they'd met the day before, and also about Jason's rescue of her from nowhere land.

"You guys have dinner?" Maggie's short curls bobbed as she spoke, giving the impression that she was always on the move.

"No." Anna felt her stomach rumble even as she said the word. She may not feel pregnant yet, other than the occasional bouts of nausea, but she was hungry enough for two. "I imagine Jason had a date."

Maggie grinned. "It's so cool that you know him," she said.

Anna nodded, a little uncomfortable with Maggie's brash way, not sure how to respond. But she welcomed the woman's friendliness just the same. Especially when again faced with a lonely Saturday night of trying not to picture Jason with another woman. Anna and Jason spent days together. Never nights. She assumed he had less platonic ways to spend his evenings off than with a pregnant, confused family friend.

"So how about dinner? I made spaghetti and there's plenty," Maggie offered.

Anna shook her head instinctively and then stopped. "I'd like that," she said. "If it won't be too much of a bother."

"No bother at all. I'd love the company."

THE TWO HAD DINNER together twice more that next week. Once at Anna's. The other time at Maggie's. Maggie wanted to be an actress and waited tables four nights a week to make ends meet while she spent her days traipsing from one audition to the next. Anna didn't see what Maggie saw in her, a woman with no past, and feared sometimes that the only thing that kept Maggie coming back was pity. And yet Maggie's friendship felt genuine.

"Do you know if I was dating anyone?" Anna asked Maggie the following Thursday night. They were sitting in Maggie's apartment, and though she itched to tidy up some of the clutter, Anna liked being at her friend's place.

Maggie nodded, helping herself to another piece of the pepperoni pizza they'd ordered. "You mentioned having a date once or twice."

Suddenly not hungry, Anna asked, "Did you ever see the guy?"

"Yeah." Maggie frowned. "Once. I'm not even sure if it was the same guy each time. I just assumed it was. You weren't quite as easy to get to know back then.''

"From what I can tell, I was a really private person," Anna admitted. "I'm not really sure how to go about the friend thing."

Except that she knew she wanted Maggie's friendship. She looked forward to their evenings together, to having another woman around to talk to, laugh with.

"Relax." Maggie grinned. "You're doing fine."

"WHAT DO YOU DO during the day?" Maggie asked on Wednesday of the following week. They'd gone to a deli around the corner for dinner and were on their way back to the brownstone.

"I walk in Gramercy Park." She might have hated her apartment, but she adored the gated park, she'd discovered, which was for residents' use only. "And I read a lot." Hearing herself, Anna was embarrassed by how boring her life must seem to her actress friend.

"That's all? I'd go nuts." Ever dramatic, Maggie rolled her eyes and pressed a hand to her chest.

Anna supposed to someone like Maggie it sounded like a prison sentence, but to Anna, this time was a gift; she could feel herself growing stronger with every day that passed—although she suspected it wouldn't be long before she was going to have to find something to do. One could only sit around getting strong for so long. Then you had to do something with that strength. Trouble was, she had no idea what she wanted to do. What she *could* do. Other than sew— and build sand castles. She didn't want to sew, and building castles was a bit difficult in the city.

"I also see Jason," she said, hating that she was actually trying to win Maggie's approval with the admission. It was more important that she approve of herself.

"Now that I could handle." Maggie grinned. "You guys an item yet?"

Anna laughed, embarrassed. "Of course not."

"Why not? He's gorgeous. You're gorgeous. A match made in heaven."

"I'm pregnant." Anna couldn't believe it when she just blurted the words.

Maggie stopped in her tracks, staring openmouthed at Anna. "Pregnant?"

Anna nodded, watching her friend, wishing she'd kept quiet. But she was going to be starting to show soon, and if she planned to continue this friendship, Maggie was going to have to know.

"How?"

Anna shrugged. "The usual way, I suppose," she said, echoing words she'd heard from Dr. Gordon.

"You mean you don't remember?" Maggie's eyes widened, her New York accent more pronounced than usual. "It happened before…?"

Nodding again as Maggie's words trailed off, Anna started walking again. Maggie followed.

"Then you don't know who the father is?" Maggie asked, turning to watch Anna.

It sounded so horrible the way Maggie said it. Anna shook her head.

"Wow."

Exactly. But at least now Maggie knew.

"So how often you seeing Jason?" Maggie asked a few moments later.

"Almost every day."

Maggie stumbled. "You're kidding!"

"It's nothing, really," Anna said. But it was. She

cherished every moment of her time with Jason. "We're just doing the tourist bit. He's only been in this city three months and with the new job and all hasn't done any sight-seeing yet. And it's not like I remember any of it even if I have seen it."

"You're touring the city with him and you call that nothing?" Maggie screeched. "You know how much I'd give for one lunch with someone like him?" She clearly thought Anna needed some brain readjustment. If only she knew. Anna was glad to see their brown-stone just up ahead.

"It's completely platonic." If you didn't count the way her body had a mind of its own every time she was with Jason.

Maggie harrumphed. "Maybe you simply haven't figured out yet that he's nuts about you. A guy doesn't spend that much time with a girl unless he wants in her pants."

"Maggie!" After several days in Maggie's company Anna was still sometimes shocked by the other woman's New York bluntness. "And he's not nuts about me," she said. He couldn't be. Period. "He's just a friend. I think he feels sorry for me."

"Real sorry," Maggie said sarcastically. "Has he asked you up to his place yet?" Her question was accompanied by a sly lift of her eyebrows.

"I lived there for three days."

"I mean since then," Maggie said with exaspera-tion.

"No. And he doesn't come to my place, either," Anna said before Maggie could ask. "We go out in public, in broad daylight. That's the way one tours the city."

"Just wait," Maggie said. "He'll ask you up to see his etchings."

"Trust me, he saves his etchings for other women, Maggie. I never even see him after two or three in the afternoon."

Maggie gave a disappointed sigh. "Have it your way."

"It's the way it is." The way it had to stay.

"So what's he like?" Maggie asked, stepping sideways to avoid a little boy on a bicycle.

Anna smiled. "I don't know... Charming. Intelligent. Nice."

"You go out with a man like that and you call him *nice?*"

Anything else she might see in Jason she couldn't admit to herself, let alone Maggie. "He *is* nice." He was still taking pity on her, wasn't he? Although, if she was to be honest, there'd been more than one time since that night in his apartment when his interest in her had seemed like anything but pity. There was that peculiar look in his eyes...

"He's also to-die-for gorgeous, every inch male— even his eyes can knock you for a loop if you let them."

So Maggie had noticed. "He's just a friend, okay?" Anna couldn't think of him as anything else. To do so would be emotional suicide. If not now, then certainly when she regained her memory of the man whose child she carried.

"And he takes you out every day?"

"Not every day, but a lot." Anna was growing more and more uncomfortable with Maggie's questions. "We're seeing Manhattan one block at a time."

"You're in love with him, aren't you?" Maggie

said suddenly, stopping at the steps of their brown-stone.

"Of course not!" Hadn't Maggie been listening? "I'm not, Maggie," she added when her friend still looked unconvinced. "We're just friends."

"Well, if you're not in love with him, you should be." Maggie persisted. "Take a chance, girl. A relationship with that man would be...*incomparable*."

Somehow Anna knew that, her lack of anything to compare it to notwithstanding. But that changed nothing. "Maggie, I'm pregnant."

"So?"

"So, the baby's not Jason's."

"Does he know?"

"Of course."

"Then what's the problem?"

"The problem is that there's a man out there I don't remember right now, but who I loved enough to make a baby with."

"Maybe. Maybe not."

Anna prayed every day that she'd loved her baby's father. She didn't want to be the type of woman who'd get pregnant for any other reason. If she hadn't loved the man... The very thought terrified her. Because if she hadn't loved the man, she could be carrying the child of a creep like Roger. Or a man who'd forced her...

"Besides, what would Jason want with someone like me?" she asked, wishing she'd just stayed home that night. She'd really been having a good day.

"Have you looked in the mirror lately, girl?" Maggie asked. "You're nuts if you don't try to make it with this guy."

And suddenly, as much as Anna loved having her

new friend around, she felt the strongest urge to turn and run. To get as far away from Maggie as she could go. Her chest felt tight, every breath a struggle as, standing outside in the balmy New York evening, walls started closing in on her.

She couldn't let herself be talked into something she felt was wrong. She had to make her own decisions. Even if it meant that Maggie didn't want to be her friend anymore.

And as for what Maggie'd suggested, what kind of man would Jason be if he was willing to settle for someone like her? Someone who came to him, not only memoryless, but pregnant with another man's child?

A man who didn't love her, that was what he'd be. Because with the way he'd grown up, never coming first in his parents' lives, there was no possibility he was going to allow himself to settle for second place again. And second place was all she had to offer.

WAITING TO DRIVE across the Verrazano Narrows Bridge onto Staten Island Saturday morning, Jason smiled to himself. Life had a way of slipping in surprising little twists and turns that made the impossible almost seem possible. He would never have believed a month ago that he'd be joining a queue of summer tourists with Anna at his side. He wouldn't have believed she'd ever be at his side again, period.

As usual she was wearing one of her lightweight, sexy-as-hell dresses, though one Jason had never seen before—something she must have picked up on one of the shopping expeditions she'd told him about. He approved of her choice. The colors were bolder than she usually wore. So many little changes.

"I saw Dr. Gordon yesterday," she said, her long hair wind-tousled. "His wife had her baby last week—a little boy. Both are home and doing fine."

"Good for them!" Jason tried to inject the same enthusiastic note he'd heard in Anna's voice into his own, in spite of the surprising flash of jealousy that flared in him. So the doctor and his wife shared something he and Anna didn't share—a child. The best of both of them in one package. He could almost picture the little towhead he and Anna would have had. But it wasn't to be. Still, he had more today than he'd had a month ago. It should be enough.

"So what did he have to say about you?" He stole a sideways glance.

"He says my confidence is growing."

"It is." Three weeks ago Anna had relied on him for everything.

The sun highlighted the gold in her hair. "I asked him about calling Abby."

Jason froze. So the bond the triplets shared *was* reaching her even now?

"What'd he say?" Not yet. He wasn't ready yet.

"That to rock the boat at this point could very well cause a setback," she reported. "He still says it's best if I remember on my own."

"And he's confident you will?"

Anna stared straight ahead as Jason inched his Jag closer to the bridge. "Absolutely. According to him all these little things coming back are just the beginning."

"Like the sand castle."

"Yeah." She paused, frowning. "You know, I had the oddest sensation last night, almost like a memory, but it wasn't that tangible."

"A feeling?"

He wanted so badly for her to remember their love. And dreaded the day when she did. He didn't really hold out any hope that he and Anna would ever be together again. So much more than her sister stood between them now.

"Yes, a feeling—that describes it as well as anything," she finally said.

"What happened?"

"Maggie was nagging me and suddenly I got really claustrophobic." Anna was still frowning, still watching the traffic inching ahead of them. "I mean, I really resented her for a minute there. I enjoy Maggie's company a lot, but I've got to make my own decisions."

If only the old you could hear yourself now, my love.

"There's nothing wrong with that." Jason pulled the Jag closer to the suspension bridge.

She shrugged. "I don't know, maybe I overreacted, but I've got precious little control over anything right now. At least let me control my decisions."

"You're not overreacting, Anna. It's just like Dr. Gordon said. Trusting yourself means trusting your own decisions."

"You're right, of course." She twisted in the seat to face him. "And a good friend. Thanks."

Hold that thought, he urged silently. He wasn't so sure how happy she was going to be with him when she remembered everything.

"You know, it's odd," she said a few minutes later. "But lately I've been more at peace with my amnesia."

"Yeah?" So she was okay with this, too, the two of them living in the here and now, in their own little world?

"It's just that when I get these feelings, they're so strong, you know? I didn't simply not appreciate Maggie's nagging. I had to physically restrain myself from running away from her. For a second there I thought I might pass out or something."

Looking her over carefully, Jason asked, "Do you feel okay now?"

"Of course. Fine." She brushed her hair back from her face. "But it makes me think that maybe I do need this time to heal from whatever happened. The intensity of some of my reactions scares me."

"You're afraid of remembering?" *Oh, Anna, if only I really knew the extent of our problem here. If only I had all the answers.*

She looked away, out her side of the car. "Sometimes."

Thankful for the traffic that kept them at a standstill, Jason turned her to face him, holding her chin in his hand, forcing her to look at him. "That's nothing to be ashamed of, Anna."

He could see the tears welling in her eyes as she searched his gaze. Relaxing his hold, he moved his thumb along her jaw, needing to kiss her more right then than at any other time he could remember.

"Thank you," she whispered.

"For what?" *Wanting to kiss her senseless?*

"Knowing me so well."

Oh. That. In her other life she'd been able to read him just as clearly. "It's the truth, Anna. Fear is natural."

"Are you ever afraid?"

Her eyes implored him for the truth, looking for reassurance. Dumbstruck, Jason sat there staring at her. He used to be afraid sometimes, back when he still counted on his parents to be parents. He could remember being at a football game, afraid as the quarters went by that his father wasn't going to make it to see him play again. Afraid that he'd go to his mother's house, after four days at his father's, only to find he'd lost his bedroom. But sleeping on couches hadn't been so bad, and that was all so long ago, back when he'd depended on other people for his happiness.

And fear?

He continued to stare at her—until a horn sounded behind him. Jerking away from Anna, he put the car in gear and shot forward. He was concerned. Concerned she'd remember everything. Concerned she wouldn't. Concerned about the baby she carried, about the man who'd fathered it. Concerned she was going to see his own misrepresentation of their relationship as a betrayal, in spite of the doctor's advice. Because parts of him saw it that way, himself. Concerned he'd never again be able to hold her in his arms, lose himself within her honeyed depths. Concerned he'd never be home again. That he'd carry the ache of her loss with him to his grave. Yeah, he was concerned.

He was not afraid.

CHAPTER TEN

STATEN ISLAND deserved better. Its beautiful shore-lines, magnificent rolling hills sprinkled with grand homes, and miles of trails waiting to be explored didn't receive even a tenth of Jason's attention. He was too distracted by Anna's nearness. They visited Conference House, a stone manor that had served as the only site of a Revolutionary War conference. But while noteworthy, if one cared to take notes, the Revolutionary War was far in the distant past—and Anna was the present.

He took her through historic Richmond Town, visited the Staten Island Institute of Arts and Sciences and debated with her about the exhibits, comparing them to pieces they'd seen at the Museum of Modern Art earlier in the week. He was challenged by her thinking, pleased with her new openness—telling him what she thought rather than leaving him to guess—and entranced by her laughter. At her request, he walked with her through innumerable gift shops. She pointed out trinkets, commented on likenesses to things they'd seen, bought a deck of cards. All he saw was Anna. All he heard was Anna. All he wanted was Anna.

And she wanted him, too. He'd been her lover for almost two years, her friend before that. He knew when Anna was turned on.

They toured the Alice Austen House Museum that afternoon and then it was time to go home, to get away from Anna before darkness spread over the city, cloaking them in its intimacy. To avoid temptation.

"Let's stay for dinner," he heard himself say, instead, as they climbed back into the car.

After a full day of being with Anna, Jason wasn't ready to reenter the real world, temptation be damned. "I saw a pamphlet back there." He indicated the cottage that housed the pioneer photography collection they'd just viewed. "It advertised waterfront dining just a few miles from here."

Anna stopped, her seat belt pulled out but not yet fastened. "Don't you have a date?"

The question sounded so wrong coming from her. "No."

"Why not? It's Saturday night."

Because, after a two-year commitment to her, one he'd expected to last forever, he had no desire for other women. "Never got around to asking."

She studied him closely. "But you *are* dating someone, right?"

For a woman who wanted him, she was doing a damn good job of convincing him she didn't. "No, Anna, I'm not currently dating anyone."

"But you have to be!"

He wasn't sure it was panic he heard in her voice until he turned and read it in her eyes loud and clear. Just then a family walked by the convertible, staring at them; Anna looked down at her lap. Starting the Jaguar, Jason roared out of the parking lot and sped along Hylan Boulevard past the Gateway National Recreation Area, turning off at the first semiprivate cove he found along the shore. He stopped the car and stared out at the ocean.

"Now, you want to tell me why I have to be dating?" he asked.

Anna hadn't said a word since he'd left Austen House. She still didn't.

His gut turned hard as a rock when he saw the hunted expression on her face. Reaching over, he took her hand. "Anna?"

"You get this look in your eyes sometimes." Her words were a mere whisper on the ocean breeze.

He waited for her to continue, fully aware she hadn't pulled her hand out of his grasp.

"I recognize the look, Jason." Her own eyes burned with heat.

Shit.

"And?"

She gazed at him, shook her head and got out of the car. A breeze from the ocean whipped her dress up, swirling the thin material about her thighs, reminding Jason of the first time he'd seen her. As then, he had no choice but to follow her. Down the small copse to the beach beyond.

But the laughter that had been in her eyes when he caught up with her that first time was nowhere to be found now. Sandals in hand, she just kept walking, her face a mask.

"I feel like such a fool," she said.

"Why?" He was the one making a royal mess of things. He had the facts. He knew better.

"Because if I'm wrong..." She stopped walking, turning to look at him. "Except I'm not, am I?"

He shook his head. "I want you, Anna, if that's what you mean."

Looking away, she started to walk again, silently. Jason could only keep pace with her, waiting, watching. She had to make the decisions.

"Why now?" she asked suddenly. "Why not when I knew you before?"

Okay, Dr. Gordon. What now? "I can't answer that, Anna," he said, carefully weighing his words. She was going to remember their past someday—along with today. "Except to say that I see things in you now that weren't there before."

"What things?"

"You're more independent," he said, strolling slowly beside her on the deserted stretch of beach, the late afternoon bringing a chill to the air.

"Really?" She seemed pleased.

"Really." He smiled at her. "And stronger, too."

"I don't feel very strong."

Grabbing hold of her hand, Jason stopped her, reaching up to brush her hair back from her face, his hand lingering on the softness of her cheek.

"Is it so very wrong to admit that we're attracted to each other?" he asked.

Winning her heart a second time hadn't been what he'd had in mind at all, but what kind of fool would turn his back on this chance?

Jason withstood her gaze as she stared up at him. He wanted her. She wanted him. And for now, he and she were all that existed.

"Yes," she finally said, breaking eye contact with him. She took his hand and held it against her cheek. "It's very wrong, Jason."

"Why?"

She dropped his hand and continued her trek up the beach. "You know why."

She wasn't talking about her amnesia. "Because you're pregnant."

"That's a start."

"I'm sure you're not the first pregnant woman to have a romance."

Dropping her sandals, Anna plopped down in the sand, scooping up a handful and letting it run through her fingers. "And when my memory comes back?" she asked, her voice stronger, bitter. "What if I discover I love someone else?"

"And what if you don't?"

He sat down beside her, and took her hand. "Anna, would it help if I tell you that I won't hold you to anything? That you call all the shots? That if, once you remember, you choose someone else, I won't stand in your way?"

The longing in her eyes as she stared silently up at him was all it took. All reasoning, all conscience vanished. With the familiarity of having loved her before, he lowered his mouth to hers.

ANNA WAS LOST at the touch of his lips. He felt so right in a world that had been nothing but wrong. Her mouth opened to his automatically, as if possessing a mind of its own. And because her body seemed to know exactly what to do when she hadn't a clue, she listened to it.

Easing her back onto the sand, Jason moved over her, sliding one leg between hers, molding their bodies to a perfect fit, his lips caressing hers all the while.

Like a starved woman, Anna returned kiss for kiss, finding in Jason's arms everything she'd been looking for—a sense of home, and a strength beyond anything she'd ever be able to muster on her own. Fire, too.

Fire that ignited a matching flame in her veins. One that threatened to consume her if she didn't have more of him.

His hands, never still, caressed her body, pleasuring her in ways she'd never imagined until finally, blissfully, they found her breasts. Not just cupping them, as she'd longed for so many times over the past weeks, but moving back and forth, back and forth across her hardened nipples, sending shock waves of sensation through her.

"So perfect," he whispered against her lips, continuing to torture first one breast and then the other with his light caresses, only ceasing when Anna arced her body, pressing his hand more firmly against her aching breast.

"So full," he said.

Anna fell back to the sand, turning her head, breaking the kiss, pushing him away with both hands. Yes, they were full. Fuller than normal, or so she'd been told. Because she was pregnant.

"Anna?" Jason's voice sounded drugged, or as if it came from far off. "What's wrong, honey?"

"I'm sorry," she said when she could speak. Rolling away, she sat up a few feet from him, hugging her knees to her throbbing breasts.

It took him a minute. She saw his struggle, saw the cords in his neck tense as he tried to compose himself. Eventually he, too, sat up, his hands on his knees as he stared silently out at the ocean.

"Did you remember something?" he finally asked, his voice level, resigned.

Not in the way he probably meant. "Yes."

He flinched, but gave no other indication that he'd heard her, strengthening Anna's resolve to let things go no further between them. Because Jason wasn't going to protect his heart. With his eternal optimism he would enter into the relationship with high hopes. But if the worst happened, if she suddenly remembered another man, one who already had her undying love, Jason would simply allow her to walk away from him.

Even though he knew that doing so would kill him.

"I remembered the baby," she said. She owed him complete honesty. If they were going to salvage their friendship, one that had become as essential to her as the air she breathed, they had to talk openly about this.

"And his father?" Jason asked, still deadpan, still gazing at the ocean. If he hoped to convince her he didn't care, he'd failed miserably. Or maybe it was himself he was trying to convince. One thing was clear, he wasn't going to try to urge her to forget whatever it was she'd remembered.

"No, Jason." She shook her head. "Just the fact that I'm pregnant."

He looked at her then, relief in his eyes. "That's all?"

Nodding, Anna gave him a sad smile. "I don't know what I did in the past, Jason, but the person I am today, the person I'm learning to live with, the person I have to like, can't make love without commitment."

"I don't have a problem with making a commitment," he said.

"I know."

He shifted over until his thigh pressed against hers in the sand. "So what's the problem?"

"*I* can't make any commitments, Jason," she said, not bothering to hide her pain from him. At least it told him she cared. "Until I know what promises I've already made, I'm not free to make any more."

He didn't move away. Didn't move at all. Just sat staring out at the ocean.

"I'll understand if you'd like to take me back to Manhattan and forget you ever knew me."

He was silent so long she wasn't sure he was even still listening to her. Not that she blamed him. All she'd done was take, take, take since he'd first walked into her hospital room. Strength, money, peace of mind, time. He'd given them all freely. And she had nothing to give in return.

"No chance of getting naked, huh?" His outrageous words dropped into the silence and suddenly Anna felt giddy with relief. He was going to get them through this.

"None," she lied.

"Then my next choice is dinner on the waterfront."

"But what about—"

"Anna," Jason interrupted, taking her hand, "look at me."

She did. When he gazed at her like that, she couldn't look anywhere else.

"I understand, and it's okay," he said, enunciating every word. "When your memory returns, we'll have this discussion again. Until then, I'll wait."

Her eyes wet with tears, she touched his sweet handsome face. "What did I ever do to deserve you?"

"Someday, when I have you in my arms, I'll tell you."

She prayed that someday she'd be able to take him up on his offer.

HE CALLED ABBY much later that night. He'd finally dropped Anna off sometime past midnight, walking her to her door but not asking to come inside. It wouldn't have taken much to get her to acquiesce and, once inside, to bed her. But then he'd have been as bad as Abby, overriding Anna's decision with his own. He had no choice but to respect her judgment.

But damn, doing the right thing felt like hell.

All things considered, they'd had a great evening, almost like the old days—laughing, simply enjoying being together. Being able to feast his eyes openly on her had helped. There was more honesty in their relationship now. And for the time being, he could live with that. Was determined to have this chance—and to be prepared to walk away.

Abby's phone rang so long he was ready to hang up, a bit relieved to see that Abby had found something to do with her Saturday evening besides sit at home.

"Hello?"

The voice that answered, just as he was putting the receiver down, barely resembled his old friend.

"Abby?" he asked, frowning.

"Yes?"

"Am I interrupting something?" Did Abby have a man there? Wonder of wonders. He'd never known the oldest Hayden girl to bring a man home.

"No. I'm just sitting here."

"Alone?"

"Yeah."

Oh. "Something good on the tube?" He remembered some cozy evenings back when Audrey was alive. Abby would make popcorn and coerce everyone to sit down and watch some show or other she was sure they'd all enjoy. And they usually had.

"Nah."

"You working up something spectacular to introduce in the fall?" He wasn't sure how Abby kept coming up with ideas for her children's-wear designs fast enough to keep her growing clientele happy.

"No. Just sitting."

"Anna saw the doctor yesterday."

"And?" She sounded almost afraid to ask. Suddenly Jason wondered if he and Anna weren't the only ones frightened of her memory.

"He's happy with her progress, her growing confidence."

There was another long pause and then, "How is she, Jason?"

"She misses you."

"Oh, God, I miss her, too..." And that was when Jason heard the tears Abby had been trying to hide. She'd been sitting in that cottage on the beach all alone on a Saturday night, crying.

FIFTEEN MINUTES after hanging up the phone Jason was still sitting on his couch in the dark—his thoughts far from pleasant. While he'd been convinced that Anna would only be free to live a full life if she could separate her identity from Abby's, he'd also honestly believed that in the long run Abby, too, was going to be happier. He was no longer so sure.

Hell, what did he know? He'd never been a part of a relationship of the sort Abby, Anna and Audrey had shared from birth. Had never really been part of a family.

Maybe being together was the way the sisters were meant to be, the only way they could be happy. Maybe there was a greater reason for their multiple birth than simple genetics, a connection stronger than physical resemblance and blood ties. A connection beyond understanding.

A connection that threatened him more than anything else in his life.

He'd been so sure that he'd had all the answers, that he knew exactly what the problems were between Anna and him. But looking back now, he was seeing something else. Something that sickened him. Could he possibly have been jealous of the closeness Anna shared with her sisters? Had his New York job offer merely been an excuse to make her choose, once and for all, between her sisters and him? Had he been so shallow, so immature?

God, he hoped not.

And if he had? And Anna had seen through his righteous indignation to the selfish man beneath? And Anna remembered?

Breaking out in a cold sweat, Jason dropped to the floor. One. Two. Three...

CHAPTER ELEVEN

JASON WAS ON THE PHONE first thing the next morning, Sunday or no. He couldn't wait anymore. He had to know what he was up against. He had to find the father of Anna's child.

She may have to remember on her own, but nothing said he couldn't find out in the meantime. Not only would he be better prepared to help her deal with the memory, especially if it was distressing, but he, too, would be better protected. Knowledge was power. And Jason needed all the power he could get.

Calling his contacts in California, as well as the fact-finding sources he'd encountered since coming to New York, felt good. Right. At least he was doing something. He couldn't fight what he didn't know. And he planned to fight.

Unless it turned out that Anna truly loved the man who'd fathered her child just weeks after Jason moved out of her life. In that case he'd walk. A thing much easier done sooner than later.

Again, he had to know.

He also put down a retainer on one of New York's best private investigators. If anyone could find out who Anna Hayden had been sleeping with, Smith Whitehall could. A Harvard graduate, the man not only knew how to turn up dirt in a bottle of glass cleaner, he was smart.

And then Jason set out himself, visiting all the places he would expect Anna to visit upon arriving in New York, showing her picture around, asking questions. He'd have sent out an all-points bulletin on the evening news if he could have found a way to do so without humiliating Anna.

"Yeah, I've seen her," a clerk in a bookstore close to Gramercy Park told Jason late Sunday afternoon. "Not lately, though."

"Was she ever with anyone?" Jason asked casually, his heart pounding. *Say no. Say yes. Say she didn't love him.*

"Nope." The clerk shook her head. "Always came in alone. Always bought a lot of books, though. Fiction, but nonfiction, too. Art-history stuff. I suppose she could've been buying for two."

Nodding, Jason thanked the clerk and walked out. He was getting nowhere. New Yorkers were a tough bunch to crack, too concerned about their own backs to notice other people. He'd spent an entire day traipsing the town for nothing. An entire day he could have spent with Anna.

Shit. He was losing it, big time. And all for a woman who'd already sent him out of her life once. Once home, Jason changed into cotton shorts and a T-shirt, grabbed his racquetball gear and headed for the club. He'd stay until midnight if that was how long it took to beat some sense into himself.

He knew better than to look to anyone else for his personal happiness, to need to be the most important person in another's life. Knew all the inherent dangers of doing so firsthand. Had, as a boy, lived with the fear of rejection as his constant companion. He wasn't going to be afraid again. Not ever.

ANNA INVITED MAGGIE to go secondhand-clothes shopping Tuesday evening. She'd seen Jason that day and was too restless to be content with her own company. Being with him was better than ever—and worse. It was ten times harder to keep her desire under control when she knew he wanted her, too.

"What do you want with used stuff?" Maggie asked. She was sitting on the only counter in Anna's kitchen eating Anna's last apple.

"It's got character," Anna told her. Besides which, it was cheap and she needed some more dresses. With the baby on the way, Anna was growing more and more aware of the limits of her bank account.

"You've already got plenty of character," Maggie said, surprising Anna with her praise.

"You think so?"

"You might've lost your memory, but even you have to know that much," Maggie said. "And you've got looks, too, dammit. If I didn't like you so much, I might have to hate you."

"So you'll come?" Anna asked.

Begrudgingly Maggie followed Anna into three different shops, grumbling when Anna bought exactly what Maggie told her not to buy, more of her "flower child" dresses as Maggie called them.

"You need some shorts, girl," Maggie said. "Show off your legs."

"I need dresses," Anna countered. "To hide my belly."

"No kidding?" Maggie looked at the part of Anna's anatomy in question. "You're starting to show?"

"I don't know. I'm three months along and I'm starting to look bloated. It's embarrassing."

Maggie laughed. "What're you gonna do when you're big as an elephant?"

"Don't," Anna groaned. "Let me get used to bloated, first." And let her not think about four or five months down the road. Who knew where she'd be then, who she'd be, or with whom. It scared her witless every time she thought about it. So she tried not to.

"I sure wish I knew what I used to do," she complained to Maggie on the walk home. "I'm getting restless."

"Which means you're getting better," Maggie said. "You've got that computer on your dresser—can you type?" she asked. "You could get a part-time job as a secretary or receptionist or something. Lord knows you have the looks for it."

"I'm not even sure how to turn the thing on," Anna admitted. And she hadn't wanted to admit to Jason yet another failure, another thing she no longer knew. Plain and simple, she'd been too proud to ask for help.

"Even I know that much," Maggie said over her shoulder as they climbed the steps of the brownstone. "Come on, together we can figure it out."

ONCE MAGGIE HAD the laptop open and on, Anna suddenly took it from there. There were no conscious memories, but she knew how to move about in the first couple of programs fairly well. She spent the rest of that evening fooling around with the computer, surprised to find how many things she just automatically knew to do.

She'd just discovered her personal financial file the next morning when the telephone rang. Assuming it was Jason, she grabbed it up on the first ring.

"Hi!" she said. She couldn't wait to tell him that she had an account in a bank in California with enough money to see her through a couple of years, baby expenses included. Then she'd have to go to work. But, God willing, by then she'd have regained her memory.

"Hello, yourself, sexy lady."

Anna froze, wanting to drop the phone back in its cradle and pretend she'd never picked it up. But as horrified as she was to hear Roger on the other end of the line, she had to know why he was calling her. Was he going to claim his child? Expect visitation rights?

"What do you want?"

"You know my voice," he said a little less enthusiastically. "Does this mean you've recovered from your unfortunate affliction?"

He made her sound like some kind of half-witted freak. "My memory hasn't returned yet."

"It's been three weeks and one day since you were so naughty and ran out on me, Anna. Are you ready to kiss and make up?" His voice was oiled with sickening innuendo. "I promise to take good care of you."

"Never."

"I see you've still got a lot to learn, Anna. Lovers' tiffs aren't meant to last forever. Come back to work, let me take care of you, and you won't have to worry your pretty little head anymore."

"Never," she repeated. Still fighting the urge to slam the phone down, Anna hung on. Did he know about the baby? Surely, if he was the father, she'd have told him about the baby. The woman she was now certainly would have.

"But, Anna, it's summer! We can go to the beach," he said, as if coaxing a child. "I'll take you down the coast, just you and me. No one will know about you."

His voice lowered. "You won't have to use your mind at all."

Yeah, but she could guess what she would have to use. She'd rather die.

"I'll make you happier than you've ever been," he said confidently, as if he actually thought there was a chance she'd go away with him.

"I'm pregnant, Roger."

"Son of a bitch! You threatened me with a lawsuit for stealing a little kiss and here all along you were screwing some other man?"

"I didn't sleep with you?" Anna asked, almost dizzy with relief.

"You aren't going to pin your bastard on me, you little bitch. Other than that one kiss, I never touched you—"

Anna clicked the off button on her mobile phone and laid it calmly beside her computer.

Two seconds later she picked it back up, dialed automatically and held her breath, praying he was home.

"Jason? He's not the father!" she cried the minute he picked up his phone.

"Who isn't?"

"Roger. He called just now. I never slept with him."

"Why'd he call?" Jason didn't seem to be sharing her joy.

"He wanted me to go to the beach with him."

"If he calls again, you let me know," Jason said. "We'll get him for harassment."

As thrilled as she was at the protectiveness in his voice, Anna stomped her foot.

"Didn't you hear me?" she practically hollered. "He's not the baby's father."

"I didn't think he was, Anna. You'd never sleep with a jerk like that."

Anna was grinning when she hung up the phone after promising to be ready to accompany Jason to lunch in half an hour. He'd had a lot more faith in her than she'd had herself. She was damn lucky he'd been in New York when that subway crashed.

A WEEK PASSED and there continued to be no word on a man in Anna's life. Jason hung up from his daily call from Whitehall, frustrated as hell. No news was supposed to be good news. But in this case, it was still just no news. Because it was beyond doubt that somewhere out there was a man who'd impregnated Anna. She was starting to show. Not obviously, probably not at all to someone who wasn't as intimately acquainted with her body as he was. But when he'd slid his arm around her on their walk through Gramercy Park the day before, he'd felt the difference.

It had bothered him so much, this evidence of another man's having touched her, he'd dropped his arm, then contented himself with simply holding her hand. And for the first time since Staten Island, he'd broken his promise to himself and to her. He'd kissed her goodbye. He hadn't lingered, just a quick peck. Because he'd had to leave his mark on her like some macho jerk. An insecure one at that. The fact that she'd clung to him made him that much more of a heel. That kiss hadn't been about loving. It had been about jealousy, plain and simple.

So for the fourth time in three days it was back to the gym for him. To things he could control, things he was good at, things he could count on. But for the first time in months he lost a match.

JASON WAS LATE. Which wasn't all that unusual. Anna, on the other hand, had been pacing her small apartment since fifteen minutes before he was due to arrive. It was this way a lot recently, her nerves stretched tight with impatience. It had been two weeks since the night she'd finally admitted to the restlessness that was slowly consuming her. She was sick and tired of sitting around storing her strength and waiting for her mind to heal. She needed something to do.

When Jason called, saying that he'd gotten caught on the phone, that it would be another forty-five minutes before he'd be by to take her to Chinatown, she almost snapped at him.

She sat down at her computer, instead. Jason was a saint, and there was no way she was going to take her growing tension out on him. But she'd already played the few games installed on her computer a hundred times apiece. She was bored as hell.

Desultorily flipping through the directory of her hard drive, she found several files she didn't recognize, having really explored only program files to this point. She clicked on the first unfamiliar file. It contained only a series of unreadable formating codes. As did the second, third and fourth.

She clicked on the fifth file, surprised when her word-processing program opened up. What she saw was entirely readable. And there was a lot of it, paragraph upon paragraph. Her heart started pumping furiously, butterflies swarming in her stomach as she scrolled through the pages.

She closed her eyes, frightened suddenly, wishing she could turn off the machine, return to the tedium of sitting and waiting. Something safe. Something she was sure she could do.

But the words continued to flow in her mind, words she recognized. Exciting her, balancing her panic. She couldn't exit the file, couldn't turn off the machine, couldn't get up and walk away. She had to read.

Starting with the first page, she read every word, knowing some of them *before* she read them. It was a story. A compelling one. Of a young man...

And Anna knew this man better than she knew herself. Knew his desires and goals. Knew his fears. Even his hobbies. She knew because she'd admired him most of her life.

The pages were the beginning of a book, a biography. The story of John Henry Walker, a nineteenth-century New York artist whose tragic life was filled with triumph. A man who, orphaned at a young age, grew up in squalor, an unwanted ward of the state. A man whose first wife was killed by outlaws, whose baby girl died of tuberculosis. A gifted impressionist. A loving husband, a revered father. She'd come to New York to research his story.

She was so engrossed in her reading, she didn't hear Jason's knock on the apartment door. Until his knock became a pounding accompanied by his voice calling her name.

"You won't believe it!" she cried when she threw open her door.

"Are you okay?" He looked her over swiftly.

"Better than okay. Magnificent! Terrific! Oh, Jason, I know why I came to New York!"

His face drained of color and he shut the door behind him. "You remembered everything?"

"Yes. No!" she grabbed his arm, dragging him over to the computer. "I haven't regained my memory, just a small part of it. Look!'' she cried exultantly, pointing at the screen.

Jason looked from her to the computer screen and back again, as though wondering if she'd finally flipped her lid completely. "It's a paper of some sort," he said.

"It's a book, Jason!'' She could hardly contain her excitement. This book was a huge part of her, of who she'd been before the accident. "I remember writing it!'' She tapped the computer screen. "This is why I came to New York!''

"You wrote it?'' he asked, clearly shocked.

"Yep!'' She *did* have a worthy endeavor. "It's about an American artist—an obscure American artist—named John Henry Walker. Some of his work is still on display here in New York.''

"John Henry Walker?'' Jason asked, frowning. "You had a print of his hanging in your cottage in California.''

Anna was so relieved to hear that she almost cried. She wasn't losing her mind. She was remembering. "I think I like art.''

"You minored in it in college,'' Jason said.

"I have a college degree?''

Jason's glance was shuttered suddenly, as though he was remembering he was supposed to be watching what he told her. "You earned a B.A. in English,'' he finally said.

Leaning over, he looked more closely at the words covering the computer screen. "Is this finished?''

"No.'' She shook her head. "I don't remember how far I was into it, but judging from the number of pages, it's only about half-done.''

Scrolling through the pages, he asked, "You haven't read it all?"

She grinned, shaking her head again. "I just found it half an hour ago."

After reading a couple of paragraphs, Jason went back and read the first two pages.

"This is really good," he said, turning to look at her.

"You think so?" She'd thought so, too, but she still put more stock in his opinion than her own.

Jason straightened, pulling her against him and kissing her full on the mouth. "I know so," he said.

As if suddenly realizing what he was doing, where he was, the temptation that was even now blazing into flames between them, he set her gently away. "If you'd like, I can take a copy of this with me and print it out for you at the station."

Though she missed his warmth, Anna was too grateful for what she'd discovered to mourn for things she couldn't have.

"Great! Sure. If it's not too much trouble," she said, still practically dancing with excitement. She couldn't wait to immerse herself in the life of the man she'd admired most of her life. To read the whole book, or the finished portion of it, anyway.

Finally she had a little piece of the real Anna Hayden.

THERE WAS A MESSAGE from Smith Whitehall waiting for Jason when he stopped home to change before work that afternoon. The man had a lead, was chasing it down and would call back. Jason flipped off the machine, the day suddenly bleak. This was not good news. And yet it was the news he'd been waiting to hear. The question was, was he ready to hear it? Was he ready to give Anna up?

But then, how could he give up what he didn't have to begin with?

HAVING GONE into the station early enough to print out Anna's manuscript, Jason was sitting on the couch in his dressing-room-cum-office reviewing the day's stories.

"You're here!" Sunny came into his office without knocking. She was wearing one of the short tight skirts she always wore on the air, her white silk blouse displaying a fair amount of cleavage.

Jason nodded, continuing to read, hoping she'd get the hint and leave him alone.

"What's the occasion? Lately you've barely gotten here in time to go on," she said, her tone a little resentful.

"I've been busy, Sunny. You know that." He wasn't in the mood for a showdown with his partner.

"I know." Her voice softened as she sat down close to him on the couch—too close. Running one perfectly manicured finger along his arm, she laid her head against his shoulder.

It wasn't the first time she'd cuddled up to him. In fact, he'd probably encouraged the closeness a time or two. But it wasn't enough. He had to resist the urge to shrug her away from him, to jump up off the couch and put as much room between him and Sunny as he could. He didn't want her touch. He wanted Anna's.

Still, a small part of him wanted to wrap his arms around Sunny, place his mouth on hers and ease the ache that had been burning inside him for weeks. Maybe even find a moment or two of forgetfulness.

But although she might be able to ease his physical ache, it would only be momentary. And the self-loathing that was sure to follow would be far worse than the original problem. If all he had was himself, he was damn sure going to be someone he could be proud of.

"Why don't you come back to my place after the last show tonight?" she invited softly.

"Sunny—"

"I'll even make breakfast in the morning," she interrupted. For Sunny that was major. She hated to cook.

"I need to get home tonight." He had a manuscript to read.

"Why?" Her finger strayed higher, moving toward his chest. "Don't you think it's time our relationship progressed a little?"

He braced himself against her practiced seduction. His body had been too ready for too long not to be tempted by the beautiful woman beside him.

"We're friends, Sunny. Good friends. I never intimated that we'd be more," he reminded her.

"It's because of that woman you're helping, isn't it?" she asked, sounding jealous.

He didn't want to think about Anna. Thinking about her only made the ache worse. The ache Sunny was offering to ease. One she wanted to ease.

"I'm not seeing her tonight, if that's what you mean," he said.

"Then why not come home with me? It's not like you two have anything going, right?"

He shifted slightly away from her before he threw good judgment to the wind and drew her onto his lap.

"We're friends." Unfortunately the new position had her breast pressing against his arm.

"But you don't owe her anything."

She was right of course. The person he owed something more to was himself. He had to look at himself in the morning. He wanted to like what he saw. And using Sunny for his own selfish release wasn't something he'd be able to look upon too fondly, no matter how he tried to rationalize.

"She has nightmares sometimes," he heard himself explaining. "I told her she can call—"

"She calls you in the middle of the night?" Sunny sat up, her eyes reflecting her hurt as she pushed away from him.

Jason wondered how a face could be so beautiful and make him feel so uncomfortable at the same time. "Once or twice."

"So how much longer are you going to be at the beck and call of this poor family friend?" she demanded.

All trace of desire fled. "You make her sound like some dim-witted hanger-on," he said, biting down on his anger.

"Your words, not mine."

Jason stood, walking to the door. "Let's get one thing straight," he said. "Every woman should hope to be as smart and courageous as Anna." He held the door open for Sunny to leave. "If you can't accept that, then we have nothing more to say."

Sunny rose—graceful, classy and way too disappointed as she walked slowly toward him. "You *are* involved with her, aren't you."

"No," he said. "I've just known her a long time,

and I admire the heck out of the way she's handling this whole thing.''

But while Sunny seemed to accept his denial for now, Jason wasn't so easily convinced. He might not have fallen in love with Anna all over again, but if his instant defense of her was any indication, he was starting to care more than he wanted to. With that in mind and considering the call from Whitehall that afternoon, he needed to take a serious look at what he was letting himself in for.

LATE THAT NIGHT, after two hours of engrossed page turning, Jason set Anna's manuscript carefully down on the coffee table in front of him. She was good. Better than good. Anna possessed a talent for pulling the reader so completely into the story, that Jason actually thought the man's thoughts, hoped his hopes.

As he put down the manuscript, Anna's earlier words rang in his ears. She'd come to New York to sell this book—not to see him.

CHAPTER TWELVE

EXCITED, NERVOUS, a bit frightened, Anna stood outside Jason's apartment building at nine o'clock the next morning. She'd never just popped in on him, hadn't really planned to do so now. But she was on her way to an ultrasound appointment, and she didn't want to go alone.

Her fear wasn't logical. Seeing the child growing within her wasn't going to tell them anything about the conception. Still she was frightened. She really wanted Jason to go with her. But could she ask him to do this? Considering their encounter on the beach on Staten Island, was it fair of her to ask?

And yet, considering his willingness to accept her, pregnant and all, was she really out of line to want him there?

Time continued to tick away, people stared at her as they passed her on the street, and still she couldn't make up her mind. Looking around her, she noticed a phone booth a couple of buildings down. She'd call him. Should have called him before she'd ever left home.

He answered on the fourth ring, and the first thing Anna could tell was that he'd been asleep. The second was that he wasn't in the best of moods, though he did try to cover that up.

"No, Anna, don't apologize," he said quickly. "I told you to call me anytime. Is something wrong?"

He sounded concerned. Anna felt a little better.

"Not really," she said. She still had an hour before her appointment. There was time for him to get dressed and accompany her. But should she bother him?

"Did you remember something?"

"No." Should she ask? Would he want her to? "I just..."

"What?" He still sounded sleepy.

"I have an ultrasound appointment this morning. I just wondered if you wanted to come along," she said quickly.

"Are you having problems?" he asked.

"No, not at all. It's strictly procedure." This was a bad idea.

"It doesn't hurt, does it?"

Not unless you considered her uncomfortably full bladder. "No."

"What time's the appointment?"

She heard the hesitancy in his voice. As if he wanted to come. And at the same time didn't. She should never have called.

"Ten-thirty."

"I'm sorry, honey, but you'll have to go without me," he said. He didn't sound sorry—more like relieved. "I have a meeting at the station at eleven."

"That's all right, Jason. It was no big deal," she said, embarrassed, trying not to feel hurt. Jason had already gone above and beyond the call of duty. She'd been wrong to expect him to step into the shoes of a man he'd never met, a man who might very well appear at any time and claim them. And her.

THE LIGHT on her answering machine was blinking. Dropping the bag of groceries she'd carried in, Anna hurried to the machine. She'd been so busy writing the past several days she'd hardly seen Jason at all. She missed him. A lot.

Jabbing impatiently at the button, she waited through three beeps to hear his message, hoping he wanted to take her to lunch. Monday was broccoli soup day at the deli. Not only was she lonely, she was starving, too.

"Hello, Anna dear." The unfamiliar deep baritone startled her. "I'm sorry to have missed you. Business is going to keep me here much longer than I expected. I'm in Italy this month and part of next, and then back to London for more meetings." More than his words, the regret and genuine affection in the man's voice spoke to Anna. With both hands she rubbed the swell of her belly. "I'll be in touch the second I'm back in New York, my dear," the voice continued, "with great hopes you'll still be free to take up where we left off. Until then, happy writing."

The machine re-wound, clicking off, and Anna stood there staring at it. She had no idea who the man was or where they'd left off. Remembered nothing, felt nothing at hearing his voice. But she was suddenly, sickeningly afraid he'd fathered a child he knew nothing about. By the sounds of things he'd been in Europe awhile. Possibly before she'd found out that she carried his child?

Oh, God. Her unattended groceries scattered, the frozen foods melting on the hardwood floor, Anna sank to her knees and wept.

"You look like a rag."

Anna chuckled wanly, taking the chain off her door to admit her friend. "Thanks, Mag," she said dryly. "I can always count on you to cheer me up."

"Hey." Maggie held up her hands, sauntering over to sprawl on Anna's couch, her feet resting on the arm. "You're the one who invited me to dinner." But Anna saw the concerned glance her friend gave her on her way past. She sat down in the chair at her computer desk, needing the support for her back.

"You cry when you're preggie and the kid comes out a grouch." Maggie grabbed an apple from the bowl on the coffee table that Anna kept specifically for her.

"There was a message on my machine today from some guy in Europe," Anna blurted. "He's there on business and says he hopes we can take up where we left off." She had to tell someone, and she couldn't bring herself to talk to Jason about it. "I think he might be the father."

Maggie sat up. "Yeah? Wow, that's great!"

Anna nodded, wishing she felt half as excited as Maggie about the news. What she felt was a bone-deep dread.

"So you remembered? Recognized his voice? Something?"

"No." As hard as she fought them, tears filled her eyes again. "Nothing happened, Maggie."

"It's okay, kid." Maggie's voice was uncharacteristically gentle. "You know the doc said it'll take time. When you're ready, you'll remember this guy."

Anna shook her head. "I don't want him to be the father of my baby," she whispered, ashamed, frightened, as lost as she'd felt in the hospital after the crash.

She needed Jason.

Maggie set her half-eaten apple back in the bowl. "So what makes you so sure this guy's it?"

"He almost has to be, doesn't he?" She rested her chin on her hands. "There's nobody else beating down my door."

"Still doesn't make him the daddy."

No, it didn't. But this man, whoever he was, was the only logical choice. She'd apparently been seeing him. And she was sure she wasn't the type to date two men at once.

"He must have money if he's got business all over Europe," Maggie surmised.

"Yeah." But though Maggie clearly saw this as a plus, Anna didn't care.

"He's probably that guy I saw you with," Maggie said, frowning. "He was always wearing natty suits. Seemed real important."

"What'd he look like?" If the man had fathered her child, she should at least learn the color of his hair.

Maggie shrugged, picking up her apple. "Tall, thin, dark hair. Fortyish."

Twelve years older than I am. Seven years older than Jason. Old enough to have a nearly grown family of his own. Maybe past the time in his life when he wanted to start a new family. She started to cry again.

"Buck up, kid!" Maggie said. "You don't owe the guy anything."

"If he's my baby's father, I do!"

"That's a big 'if,' and no, you don't. He took off for Europe without you, right?"

Anna nodded.

"And he only *hopes* you'll be free when he makes it back, right?" Maggie took another bite of apple, chomping contentedly.

Anna nodded again. It all seemed so hopeless. The baby didn't even seem real yet, and here she was, having to accept a complete stranger as its father.

"There you have it, then." Maggie tossed the apple core in the trash. "You guys obviously don't have a commitment at all."

"We have one big commitment," Anna said, rubbing her stomach. "He just may not know about it yet."

"A baby's a responsibility, Anna, not a commitment," Maggie said, her voice more serious than Anna had ever heard. "Say you get your memory back, you remember the guy, the baby's the result of one night with a little too much champagne, a little too much loneliness—no love. You gonna marry the guy?"

"No." Surprised at how quickly the answer came to her, Anna suddenly felt better than she had since she'd listened to that wretched message. No one could force her to do anything she didn't want to do.

"He may not want to marry you, have you thought of that?" Maggie tossed out the question.

She hadn't. Feeling incredibly stupid, Anna realized she'd never even considered the possibility that the man wouldn't expect her to marry him.

Jason's image as he'd kissed her on the beach on Staten Island filled her mind. He'd wanted her then, baby and all. Was it possible that things could work out for them? Someday?

"Of course, when you get your memory back, if it turns out this guy is the father and you do love him, it's good that he called," Maggie said cheerily.

Maggie's words plummeted Anna straight back into the depths. She had nothing to give to Jason. Not while there was still a possibility she was in love with a man she couldn't seem to remember.

OTHER THAN BRINGING HER a new printer, reams of paper and extra diskettes, Jason stayed away from Anna for six days. Long enough to win a racquetball tournament at the club and to drink himself into a celebratory stupor with the guys afterward. Long enough to convince Sunny he hadn't fallen in love with his old family friend. To gather his defenses about him. To drive himself completely crazy with wanting Anna, with worry.

She was pregnant and virtually alone in one of the most dangerous cities in the world. And she had no memory of her life prior to the past seven weeks.

He'd planned to wait until he heard something concrete from Whitehall before spending any more time with Anna, but the lead the man had mentioned was on simmer because a contact was on vacation. Finally Jason couldn't stay away any longer. He still hadn't come to terms with her pregnancy, with the other man in her life. Still wasn't certain he could stop himself from falling for her all over again. But he was sure of one thing. The past week had been hell. So while he still could, he wanted to spend as much time with Anna as possible.

Feeling guilty, he rapped on her door Tuesday morning. He'd been wrong to leave her on her own so long.

No answer.

Jason rapped again. Harder. She didn't usually leave the apartment in the morning. Though she'd never outright admitted it, he knew she was still suffering from occasional bouts of morning sickness.

The vacant look on her face when at last she opened the door changed to instant welcome when she saw who was standing there.

"Jason!" Throwing her arms around him, she hugged him tightly. His arms came around her automatically as he gloried in her softness, ignoring for the moment the evidence of her pregnancy.

"I'm sorry, Anna," he felt compelled to say. "I didn't mean to desert you." But he *had* meant to. And he'd been wrong.

"No, Jason, don't be sorry." Her sweet smile tore at him. "I understand. You have things to do." Smoothing the frown from his brow, she said, "It's okay, really."

"How are you?" he asked, still holding her. He couldn't seem to let her go.

"Fine. Especially now that you're here. I've missed you."

"I missed you, too."

Looking into her big brown eyes, seeing the desire there, he either had to kiss her or get away from her.

He couldn't kiss her. He had to keep enough distance to retain his sanity when they eventually found the man who'd slept with her.

Seeing her computer blinking over her shoulder, he let her go and crossed to it. "You've been working?"

She chuckled. "All the time."

"It's going okay?" His gaze met and settled on hers. Damn, she looked good. Her hair was tousled, her face was devoid of makeup—exactly as she'd looked waking up in his bed.

"Ideas are flowing so fast I'm afraid of losing them," she said, grinning.

She was doing fine. Just fine. Jason was glad, relieved. Whatever happened, Anna was going to be okay.

"You want to go out for breakfast?" He had to get out of her apartment. She was too close, too tempting. He couldn't stop thinking about Staten Island.

"Sure." She grabbed her purse. "So, what've you been doing besides working?"

What could he tell her? That racquetball had been more important than seeing her? That he'd taken Sunny out several times?

As easy as Anna was making it, Jason couldn't just pretend that there hadn't been a problem, that there wasn't still a problem. She might not remember their relationship, but he did. And the one thing that had made it so different, so remarkable, was the complete honesty between them.

"Staying away from you." The words were out of his mouth before he could stop them.

"What?"

"I've been avoiding you."

Anna's purse hit the floor. Her face white, she sank onto the couch, her eyes stricken. She didn't say a word. Just looked at him.

"I was wrong." The confession didn't make him feel any better. Her either, apparently.

"To the contrary, your reasons were probably quite valid." Her calm impersonal tone cut him to the quick.

This was Anna when she was hurting the most. She'd perfected the art of covering up. *Don't let it show*. He could almost hear the ingrained words repeating themselves in her head.

"Valid or not, avoiding you wasn't the answer." He sat down beside her, taking her hands in both of his, holding tight when she tried to pull away. "But we have to talk about this, Anna."

"Why are you doing this?" she asked. "Why do you hang around, keep coming back?"

That was easy. "Because I care."

Her gaze searched his relentlessly. "As an old family friend?"

"No."

"Oh." She looked down at her lap. He looked, too, and was surprised to see how much larger she'd become in just six days.

"I tried to stay away. It didn't work."

Anna nodded, feeling stupid. She'd had no idea. All the while she'd been working, content with the knowledge that Jason was just a phone call away, he'd been contemplating changing his number.

Jason's hand suddenly moved, and Anna flinched as it covered the swell of her stomach.

"Don't." She pushed his hand away, embarrassed. She would have given anything for Jason to have been the man who'd put the child there.

"Do you want me to go?"

Her gaze flew to his. "No!" she said. And then, more softly, "I care, too, Jason. A lot." Frightening as the admission was, it was also a huge relief.

Bringing his hand back to gently caress the baby again, Jason said, "We have to talk about it, Anna," He tapped her stomach with one finger. "This little guy's a part of you."

"She's a girl." He was right. They couldn't keep pretending the baby didn't exist.

His hand stilled. "You know for sure?"

She nodded. "I found out last week during the ultrasound."

Not only wasn't it fair to either of them to keep pretending the child didn't exist, it wasn't fair to her daughter. Something shifted in Anna's heart as she finally allowed herself to acknowledge the tiny being inside her. She was bearing a child. And a part of her was very very glad.

"Was everything all right?"

"Fine." The baby was growing right on schedule— which made Anna about fifteen weeks pregnant.

"I'm sorry I let you down." He was troubled. And that troubled Anna.

"Oh, Jason, don't," Anna said, laying her hand on top of his. "You've done so much for me. There's no way you've let me down."

Jason's gaze held hers, seeking what she didn't know. But she knew when he found it. He smiled at her, squeezing her hand.

"Have you thought of names?"

Hell, no. She'd barely thought of the child as real until two seconds ago. She shook her head.

"What happens next?" he asked, rubbing her stomach again, staring at it as if he could actually see the little girl growing inside.

"Not much for a while," she said, her eyes misting with tears as she watched him. Oh, God, why couldn't it have been him?

"I continue my monthly checkups clear up until the last month," she continued. "Take my vitamins, get fatter."

"This isn't fat," Jason said, almost sounding like a proud papa for a moment as he continued to rub her stomach. One thing she'd learned about Jason over the past weeks, something she greatly admired, was how completely he jumped into everything he did. He'd decided to acknowledge her baby, and now she couldn't get him away from it.

Unfortunately his fingers weren't just communicating with the child in her womb; they were sending erotic messages to her.

She forced herself to concentrate on his original question—the months ahead. "If I can find a partner, I'd like to take childbirth classes."

If she'd been looking for a way to stop Jason's attentions, she'd found it. He pulled his hand away, sitting stiffly beside her, not touching her at all.

The ensuing silence screamed with the offer he wasn't making.

"What about after she's born?" His quiet words fell into the awkwardness she'd created. "Have you thought about what you're going to do?"

Anna shrugged. "I guess that all depends on where I'm living."

"Where?" He turned to look at her, shocked. "You're thinking about leaving New York?"

If his stiffness a moment before had hurt her, his dismay now made up for it.

"I meant whether I'm still living in this vacuum or in the real world."

And there was the crux of their problem. The past weeks, the time they'd spent together, the relationship they were building—none of these were real.

Taking her hand, Jason pulled her up and into his arms. "I want to be a part of that world, Anna."

No more than she wanted him there. Still... "Nothing's changed," she whispered. She wasn't free to make promises, no matter how badly she wanted to make them.

"Just tell me you won't disappear without a word.

No matter what happens, what you remember or when, you'll come to me first? Talk to me about it?''

His request was fair. It was even one she could grant. "Of course."

He smiled at her, kissing her lightly. "Then there *is* a commitment we can make."

"Yes?" She was desperate enough to listen, even knowing he was wrong.

"We can promise each other the present."

It wasn't at all orthodox. It solved nothing, as the present became past with each new minute. "I promise you my present," she whispered, her eyes welling with tears as she looked up at him.

"And I give you mine."

Jason offered to attend the childbirth classes with her.

WHITEHALL'S LEAD turned out to be nothing—wrong person, wrong place. They knew from questioning Anna's landlord that Anna had been accompanied by a man on at least one occasion, but hadn't managed to find out anything about him. Jason had already questioned all of Anna's neighbors himself, knew what a dead end that was. On a hunch Jason had Whitehall check every literary agent in New York, but a month later, nothing was still all they had.

Sitting in Anna's apartment one Tuesday in mid-September, waiting for her to finish getting ready for their lunch date, Jason wasn't even sure he wanted Whitehall's answers. Anna was nineteen weeks pregnant. In all that time, no one had shown up on her doorstep. Maybe their luck would hold out for another fifty years.

"Jason! Come here, she's awake!" Anna called from the bathroom.

He was up in a flash, striding across the apartment as fast as the cramped quarters allowed. He'd missed the last two times. He wasn't about to miss a third.

"Where?" he asked, reaching for her belly the second he was in the door.

"Here." Stretching her dress across her stomach, she took his hand, placing it just under her left ribs.

Jason waited, feeling Anna's heart beat, but nothing else. Damn. Did the little girl somehow know it was him? Had she recognized his voice when he'd walked in the room?

Waiting impatiently, refusing to budge until Anna's daughter gave in, Jason continued to cup Anna's stomach. *Come on, darling, move for me,* he encouraged silently.

The flutter against his hand startled him so much he pulled back instantly. Shocked, he looked up into Anna's laughing eyes.

"Put it back, silly." She grinned, guiding his hand to the right spot.

"It's amazing!" Jason said seconds later. Until that moment the life forming in Anna had been a source of pain to him. Suddenly the child was nothing but incredible joy.

His gaze met Anna's, the wonder, the awe of life's creation passing between them there in her cramped little bathroom.

"I wish she were yours," Anna whispered softly.

Not as much as I do, sweet Anna. Not nearly as much as I do.

Unable to say a word, Jason broke his own rule and leaned down to kiss her.

THEY WERE FINALLY READY to leave the apartment when her phone rang. Still tingling from the shock of Jason's kiss, Anna fumbled with the receiver, nearly dropping it before getting it to her ear.

A woman's voice greeted her in German. It sounded harried, apologetic and wonderfully familiar.

"Rosa!" Anna said. *"Guten Tag."*

The older woman spoke rapidly, apologizing profusely in her native tongue for disturbing Anna, aware that Anna was writing, that Anna would call if and when she had some extra time for sewing. But Rosa was in a terrible bind. Just had two seamstresses come down with the flu and had a whole series of jobs due out that week. Please, could Anna help her just this once? She didn't have anyone else to call.

Anna assured Rosa that of course she'd be glad to help and was halfway through her commiseration with Rosa's predicament before she noticed the odd way Jason was looking at her. That's when she realized she herself was speaking fluent German.

And just as suddenly she knew that she'd studied German because she didn't want to study Spanish. Though what relevance that piece of information had was completely lost on her.

Quickly explaining her condition to Rosa, she asked for directions to Rosa's shop, saying she'd be by later that afternoon to pick up a batch of jobs. Rosa started to cry when she heard what Anna had been through, trying to retract her request for help fearing that she was putting too much on Anna's shoulders, but finally giving in when Anna assured Rosa that she'd welcome something extra to do.

Rosa did, however, insist on bringing the sewing to

Anna. She couldn't get away that day, but she'd come by first thing the next morning.

"Rosa?" Anna asked, just before she hung up. She just had to know one thing, she explained. Did she pick up her sewing in garbage bags and return them the same way?

"Ja." Rosa went off on another spurt of German, worrying about Anna, assuring her she'd do anything she could to help.

Maybe Rosa would know who Anna used to consort with. Maybe she'd be able to help Anna find out who'd fathered her child.

CHAPTER THIRTEEN

ABBY NEVER CALLED anymore. Jason dialed the beach cottage for the third time that week, frowning when he realized he was the only one keeping in contact these days. The past months were taking one hell of a toll on Abby.

She answered on the fifth ring. "Yes?"

"What, you can't say hello anymore?"

"Jason!" There was a little more life in her reply as she recognized his voice. "Nothing's wrong, is there? You just called two days ago."

"Everything's fine," he quickly told her. He knew it was hell for Abby being so far away when Anna—the sister she'd spent her entire life caring for—was going through such a difficult time. Jason understood, which was why he called so often.

"I felt the baby move today," he told her.

"No kidding!" It sounded like Abby might even be grinning. "Is Anna getting huge, then?"

"Not yet, but she's definitely showing."

"Will you send me a picture?" The wistful tone was back.

Jason agreed readily, then said, "She had a call today from some German woman who owns an alterations shop. Anna had been doing piece work for her."

"That's one mystery solved."

"Anna spoke to the woman in fluent German."

"She remembered her German?"

"Not only that, she told me over lunch that she remembered studying it because she didn't want to study Spanish."

Silence thrummed over the line. Jason had expected Abby to find the news encouraging. Slowly but surely Anna was remembering.

"I never knew she didn't want to learn Spanish. I just thought she liked German," Abby finally said. It sounded as if she was crying again.

"What's wrong with her not liking Spanish?" Jason asked, lying back on his couch, exhausted. Tired of trying to find answers that didn't seem to exist.

"I made all three of us sign up for it," Abby finally said. "Living so close to Mexico, with so many Spanish-speaking people, I thought it would be good for us to be fluent." She stopped, took a deep breath.

Jason waited.

"Both my sisters agreed, but the first day of class, Anna didn't show up. She'd gotten Mom to change her schedule at the last minute. They just told me she really liked German."

"Maybe she did."

"Or maybe she was trying to get away from me even then."

"She wanted to think for herself, Abby," he said softly, the back of his hand over his eyes. "Not to get away from you."

"I'm not so sure."

"I am."

"Because she wouldn't leave me to move to New York?"

It hurt to hear her say it even after all this time. "That's one sure sign."

"Did you ever think that maybe we're the real reason for Anna's amnesia?" Abby sounded as worn-out as he felt.

"That she needed to find her own identity, you mean?" he asked. Of course he'd thought of it, they'd all discussed it—he, Abby and Dr. Gordon. But while the doctor had seen that as a contributing factor, he'd been sure there was more going on with Anna than an identity crisis. Something far more disturbing.

"No. I mean, maybe by forcing her to choose, we forced her to escape, instead."

Sitting up, Jason frowned. It was past midnight. He was beyond playing mental gymnastics with Anna's sister. "I don't follow you."

"Think about it, Jason. If Anna loved us both equally—shared an equal though different bond, an equal loyalty—we both betrayed her by forcing her to choose one bond over the other. To make one of us happy, she had to desert the other. For someone as intensely loyal, as deeply committed as Anna, it was an impossible situation."

Abby had had a lot of time to think. And what she said made sense.

"So how do we get her back?"

"Wait. Just like the doctor told us," Abby said, sounding more like the bossy woman Jason had grown to love. "It's when we have her back that it's our turn to go to work. We can't make her choose anymore, Jason."

"You're prepared to give her up?" Jason asked.

"Are you?"

"Of course not."

"Then how can you ask it of me?" Her voice was

barely above a whisper. But Jason had no trouble hearing her message. *Or of Anna?*

"I'm an ass," he said, finally seeing what he'd done all those months ago. He'd let the insecurities he thought he'd left behind years before overrule his good sense. Anna was an identical triplet whose bond with her sister had grown as necessary to her as breathing over the years. Moving her to New York wouldn't have changed that. It would only have made Anna miserable. Just as miserable as Abby was now.

And because he was a jealous fool, feeling shut out by a bond that was stronger than anything he'd ever known, anything he could ever share, he'd laid down an ultimatum.

"I'll quit my job, move back to California," he said, surprised to find that he wasn't as upset as he should have been at the thought. He'd been so proud when the offer had come in.

Or had his excitement been charged with the knowledge that he now had a legitimate excuse to force Anna's hand, to make her prove she'd forsake all others for him? To get her away from her sister?

He didn't know. But one thing was for sure—the job alone had not made him happy. He needed Anna. And although he'd sworn he'd never again allow himself to come second to a woman he'd committed his all to, wasn't second still better than nothing? If he knew going in not to expect any more than that?

"Jason?" Abby's voice was oddly hesitant.

"Yeah?"

"Don't quit your job yet."

"I'm not going to lose her again, Abby."

"You may not have a choice."

He'd thought Abby was on his side. All these weeks

she'd been encouraging his involvement with Anna. "We were meant to be together, Abby. She may not remember our past, but she's fallen in love all over again."

"And how's she going to feel when she remembers the choice we forced on her? Do you think she's going to be fond of either one of us?"

He didn't know. Dammit, he didn't know. "The move back to California should settle that."

"Maybe. But where's her guarantee it won't happen again?"

"She'll have my word. Besides, life never carries guarantees. Anna's smart enough to know that."

"There's another possibility. What if, when she remembers, there's another man she loves more?"

Her words sliced into him and he couldn't answer her. *God, did she hate him this much?*

"I'm worried about you, Jason," Abby finally whispered. She was crying again. "You're the best there is and you're getting in too deep."

"You'd rather I just walked away?"

"No." She sniffed. "I'd rather you just marry her before she comes to her senses."

The thought had crossed his mind.

"But I know you. You won't do anything even remotely so dishonest."

"Thanks for that, I think." God, he'd never felt so weary of spirit. Why did he go on? But with Anna still within reach, how could he not?

"I wish you weren't so damn honest. Because when Anna remembers who the father of her baby is, she may very well choose him even if she loves you more. And knowing you, you're going to let her go—and that just might kill you."

"You think letting her go now is going to hurt any less?"

"Just be careful, okay?"

"Yeah." He'd be careful.

If only he could figure out how.

"OH MY! HOW DID THAT happen?" Rosa exclaimed in German, standing in Anna's doorway the next morning. The plump gray-haired woman was staring at Anna's stomach.

Anna looked down, too, as if she might find a spot on her dress, something she'd spilled. But her head remained bowed. "I don't remember."

Rosa didn't seem nearly as bothered as Anna was by the humiliating admission. "I'll bet it was that nice man you brought with you sometimes," Rosa said pleasantly, her old-fashioned brown dress crinkling as she walked by Anna to set her bag of sewing down beside the couch.

"I brought someone with me?" Anna asked. Her embarrassment fled in light of possible answers to questions she'd almost given up asking.

"A man, yes," Rosa nodded. "He was tall, nice-looking, if you like them skinny. Older than you."

Sounds just like the man Maggie described. Anna looked blankly at Rosa; she didn't remember this man at all.

"Clark, you called him," Rosa told her.

Clark. Anna felt sick to her stomach. She didn't want him to have a name. She'd wanted Maggie to be wrong, to have imagined the man. *And the voice on the answering machine?* She'd erased that.

"He had dark hair?" Anna heard herself ask. But she didn't want to know. Didn't want this man to exist.

"Yes, he did." Rosa's heavy, flat-soled shoes against the hard wood floors sounded like cannon shots as the woman approached Anna again. "You remember him?" she asked.

Anna shook her head, shame washing over her. Not only did she not remember this man, she didn't *want* to remember him, didn't even want him to exist.

Rosa clucked when she saw the stricken look on Anna's face. "Oh, he'll understand, dear. He was always so nice to you, carried your bags, took you nice places."

Anna tried to smile at the older woman, all the while feeling more and more trapped. Tied up in so many knots she'd never get out, never be free.

"Sounds like I spent a lot of time with him," she said, and knew she hadn't hidden her distress very well when Rosa took her hand and led her to the couch.

"A bit, I think," Rosa said. "But don't you worry about it now, dear. You just rest here." She pulled the blanket off the back of the couch, laying it over Anna's legs. "You've got that little one to think about now."

Yes, she'd think about the baby. And Jason. The past was past. She was living in the present. A present she'd promised to Jason.

BECAUSE DRIVING in the country was one of Anna's favorite things to do, Jason took her out most weekends. He loved to see the smile on her face as they sped down quiet country roads.

"I feel so free out here," Anna confessed one Saturday in early October.

He glanced over at her, seeing her hair falling about

her shoulders in a golden halo. "You don't feel free in the city?"

Shrugging, she said, "My problems are there."

"You shouldn't worry so much, Anna." Jason frowned. "Dr. Gordon gave you a great report just last week."

"I know." She nodded. "And it's not even worry so much as it is feeling trapped by my own mind."

He was happy with their present. A small part of him wished she, too, could be satisfied with just today, although he knew he was asking the impossible.

And were he to be completely honest with himself, he'd have to admit he was only happy with the present because he refused to consider the future. But ignoring it was getting harder and harder.

"Do you want to start asking questions? Call Abby?" he asked.

Anna took a long time answering him, telling him without words of the battle taking place within her. He needed to do something to help her. But he sat beside her, instead, completely helpless.

Finally, shaking her head, she said simply, "No."

"Then we'll wait."

"Are you disappointed in me?"

The car swerved as Jason stared at her. "Good Lord, no!" How could she even imagine such a thing?

"You don't think I'm a coward for wanting to wait?"

Jason pulled to the side of the road and stopped. Then he took both her hands in his and leaned over to kiss her gently. "You're the farthest thing from a coward, Anna Hayden," he said, kissing her again. "You're brave—" another kiss "—and strong." He brought his lips to hers one more time.

"Strong enough to hear the truth?" she asked when he finally pulled away from her.

"Strong enough to make your own decisions." He sat back in his seat, still holding her hand. "And for the record I think you've made the right one."

Her eyes clouded. "Because you don't think I'm ready?"

"Because I trust Dr. Gordon, and he thinks you're going to remember on your own."

Jason's heart jumped when she pulled on his hand and planted a big kiss on his mouth. "Thank you," she said, smiling as she let him go.

"You're very welcome." Jason ran his finger along her cheek. She was so beautiful, his Anna. Except that she wasn't his Anna. At least not yet.

"TELL ME MORE about Jason Whitaker," she said later that afternoon when the Jag was headed back toward the city.

"What do you want to know?" This was one of the hardest parts for him, looking at the woman he'd shared his heart and soul with and having her act as if she'd only known him for a few months.

"Why are you still single?"

The flippant answer that came automatically to his lips froze when he glanced at her earnest expression. She cared about his answer.

"You know about my last relationship," he reminded her.

"The woman who turned you down?" She was frowning.

Guiding the Jag around a curve, he studied the landscape. "Mm-hmm." Such a beautiful day—and so filled with land mines.

"What about before her?" Anna asked. "You're thirty-three—you had to have had some other relationships." Her husky voice drew him.

"I lived with a girl my last couple of years of college." Which was something he'd never told her before.

"What happened?" Her eyes shimmered with ready understanding.

"She could never get over her first love, a guy who left her at the altar to marry a woman almost twice her age."

"I'm sorry."

Jason shrugged. "I was young," he admitted. "Just made a bad choice." He grinned at Anna. "I didn't really love her, anyway—at least, it only took me about a week to get over her."

Anna smiled back at him, connecting with him the way she used to when they'd had entire conversations without ever saying a word.

"So what about after her?" Anna asked.

"There was only one other serious relationship...." One the old Anna had known all about. In fact, he'd met her the day it had fallen apart. He'd only spoken three words to Anna that day, but her smile had carried him through a very difficult afternoon.

"She wasn't in love with someone else, too, was she?" Anna asked.

Jason shook his head, welcoming the lights of the city ahead. "Nope. The law was her first love."

"She was a lawyer?"

"A defense attorney."

"Oh." Anna sounded almost intimidated. "So what happened?"

"My grandmother died. Sheila chose to bail a new

client out of jail rather than accompany me to the funeral. The guy didn't want to wait a few hours. I decided then that I didn't want to wait around anymore, either.''

''I can't believe she did that!'' Anna's eyes were wide, just as they'd been the last time he'd told her this story. ''Did she know your grandmother?''

''My grandmother introduced us.''

THE INSTRUCTOR Anna wanted for her childbirth classes, a woman who came highly recommended by Dr. Litton, already had a full roster during Anna's last trimester, leaving Anna the choice to take the classes during her second trimester or take them from someone else. Anna chose to take the classes early, starting in mid-October.

His leather jacket over his arm and nervous as an expectant father, Jason showed up at Anna's apartment half an hour early the first night of classes, extra pillows in hand.

''These okay?'' he asked, thrusting the pillows, still in their packaging, at her when she opened the door.

''Fine.'' Anna grinned. ''Any pillows would have done—I only have one.''

She looked great, her long-sleeved brown flowered dress matching her eyes. She was going to be able to get through her whole pregnancy without having to buy maternity clothes. Her loosely cut dresses came in handy for more than the freedom of movement she'd always claimed from them.

''Where's Maggie?'' he asked, looking around when Anna disappeared through the open bathroom door. Maggie had laughingly promised to send them off with a glass of champagne. Jason had hoped to have more than one.

"She got a job!" Anna called, coming out of the bathroom with a tube of mascara in her hand. "She's playing a female cop in an NBC pilot. She flew to California this afternoon."

As happy as he was for Maggie, Jason was sorry to see her go. She'd been a good friend to Anna. And he'd really been counting on that champagne.

HIS FANTASY WORLD shattered the minute they walked into the classroom. It wasn't until he saw the size of the stomachs of the women who were in their third trimester, saw how far Anna had yet to go, that he was forced to acknowledge the dangerous pretense he'd embarked on. And the small hope, that chance in a million that Anna was carrying his child, that the doctor had been six weeks off on Anna's due date, died a very painful death.

But because everyone, Anna included, was watching him, waiting for him to take his place beside her, Jason didn't give in to the impulse to bolt. Like the mature grown man he was, he sat down beside her on the mat and proceeded to learn how to help her bring another man's child into the world.

Unfortunately mature grown men experienced agony right along with the rest of them.

THAT FIRST CLASS introduced a new intimacy into a relationship already on the verge of becoming far too personal. Feeling like a wanton woman, Anna started to flood with desire at the merest glance from Jason, at the unexpected sound of his voice on the telephone. And every time he helped her practice for the birth of her daughter, every time she lay back and lifted her pelvis for him to shove a pillow beneath her, she ached with the need to pull him down on top of her. More than one time she had to bite her lip to stop herself from begging him to make love to her.

Instead, she directed her emotion into the biography she was writing, pouring her longings onto the page, her frustrations, her desires, knowing that if nothing else came from this nightmare time of her life, she was writing a good book.

In the evenings she sat, drained, watching Jason on the news and sewing for Rosa.

Then one afternoon toward the end of October, a letter came in the mail from a literary agent in Manhattan. It seemed she'd sent three chapters of her manuscript to the agency back in June. They liked them. Enough to want to see the entire manuscript as soon as she could send it.

It wasn't a sale. But it was more than she'd even dared hope and her spirits soared.

Coming down long enough to dial Jason's number, Anna hung up in disappointment when he didn't answer. He'd been invited to take part in a celebrity touch-football game that afternoon to benefit homeless shelters in the city, and she'd hoped he would already have arrived home.

She tried again between newscasts that evening and finally reached him when she was half-asleep late that night. He was as delighted as she'd known he'd be, and more, he sounded proud. Even invited her out to dinner on the Upper East Side the next night to celebrate. But only after she promised that when she was a famous celebrity, she'd still remember him.

As if she'd ever forget him.

Anna hung up with a huge grin on her face. Amnesia or no, she felt good about herself. She'd built a new life. A happy life.

Lying on her side in bed, cradling her unborn child, Anna finally had the courage to admit what she'd been hiding from for months. She didn't want to remember anymore, didn't want to find the father of her child. She didn't care if she'd loved him before the accident—she didn't love him now. And the reason she didn't love him was that she was passionately in love with Jason Whitaker.

But the admission didn't bring her relief. Instead, she started to cry, stopping herself only when she remembered Maggie's words about crying women having grouchy babies. Not that there was any truth to that. Still, her sobs couldn't be good for her daughter, this tiny being who was a hundred percent dependent on her, Anna, to give her a good life.

Could she do that? Her chest tightened. Until she found out who she was, what did she have to offer this child? Not even a father. And what if, when she remembered her past, she found herself irrevocably bound to another man?

What if the past she was running from turned out to have been immoral, or so painful she couldn't face it?

Until she knew what she'd done, what she'd been, she wasn't free to love Jason. Nor fully equipped to be a mother to the child who'd be arriving in less than three months.

Tossing and turning, Anna finally drifted off, but only after forcing herself to practice the breathing techniques she and Jason had been working on. But sleep, when it came, brought, instead of relief, only more nightmares.

HER HEAD POUNDING, she called Dr. Gordon first thing in the morning. Wasn't there something more he could do? Because until she got her life back, she couldn't go forward.

No, the doctor told her. The most she could do for herself was just relax. Allow her mind whatever time it needed to heal itself. Getting upset was only going to slow the process. She should take heart from the memories she'd had, resting assured that the remainder would follow. In the meantime concentrate on her book, on shopping for baby things—on relaxing.

Unfortunately the doctor saying so didn't make it happen.

LIKE SOME DIRTY TRICK, more than three months after he'd hired Smith Whitehall, Jason finally got some answers on Halloween. Jason was sitting in his office an hour before he was due on the air, going over the day's stories, when his phone rang.

Whitehall had a name for him—Clark Summerfield. The eldest son of a family with old money, a New York businessman with fingers in numerous financial pies, he'd been dating Anna for several weeks before being called out of the country on business. There was no evidence that Summerfield and Anna had ever slept together, no indication of nights spent at each other's homes or records of any hotel stays. However, Whitehall was certain Summerfield was the only man Anna had seen on a personal basis since arriving in New York—and there was no one in California at all, not since Jason.

Cold with dread, Jason spent the next half hour calling several of his New York contacts, needing factual and frank character assessments of Clark Summerfield.

The accolades came in almost immediately. Clark Summerfield was a prince. A widower for many years, he had no children, worked hard, although he didn't have to, and attended every family get together. He donated heavily to charities. Before Anna, he'd often been seen escorting his mother or unmarried sister to business functions. He'd celebrated his fortieth birthday the previous spring. His only fault, if you could call it one, seemed to be his workaholic tendencies.

And the fact that he wasn't the least bit athletic. Anna loved sports. Or at least, she'd always been eager to watch Jason's various athletic ventures.

So, his rival had a name. A damn good name. A damn good life. One that in other circumstances, he could see Anna being happy with. Summerfield was a man Anna could love.

Jason went on the air, he exchanged quips with Sunny, even had dinner with her in between shows. And he did it all with a frozen heart.

For the first time in a long time that night Jason went home and did some serious drinking. He hoped the alcohol would warm him up a bit, make him feel again. And maybe it did, because by the end of the evening he felt as if he had died and gone to hell.

But if he had, his rival was there with him, taunting him. Clark Summerfield. New York's number-one catch. Hell, maybe America's number-one catch. And, it seemed, Anna's sweetheart.

Sometime around three o'clock in the morning, six or seven whiskeys under, he started to think. If Summerfield was the father of Anna's baby, wouldn't she have told the man? And wouldn't he, respectable responsible man that he was, have stood by her? Married her?

Or was this guy's image a sham? Had he simply used Anna and then deserted her in her hour of need? Conveniently finding it necessary to wheel and deal in Europe for the next several months.

Had this been the blow that had done her in?

No, if Summerfield was that much of a jerk, someone would know. Anna wouldn't have been the first scorned woman. Men like that left a trail of them.

So maybe he'd left before Anna had known she was pregnant. Maybe she hadn't had a chance to contact him before the crash had wiped away all evidence of his existence.

And maybe Summerfield wasn't the father, after all. As good as Whitehall was, wouldn't he have found some evidence if Summerfield and Anna were lovers? Even if they'd only had sex once? Of course, they could have done that in the car or on the beach....

It was also possible, based on the lack of any other evidence, that Anna's mysterious lover had died. Perhaps that was the tragedy she was running from. No. Whitehall would definitely have been able to determine that.

Perhaps the guy was running from something himself, purposely covering his tracks. Maybe he'd been a swindler, a professional crook who changed identities and ate nice girls like Anna for bedtime snacks.

So what if the man never turned up? What then? Jason couldn't base his future on what ifs. Was it wrong for him to want to come first in someone's life? No matter how hard he'd tried, he'd always played second fiddle—to his father's career, his mother's second marriage, her new daughter, his college love's other man, the law, even to a prostitute's career. He'd been eating leftovers his entire life.

But weren't leftovers better than starving? And the bottom line was, did he have any choice? He'd been in love with Anna Hayden since the first moment he'd seen her. He had a pretty good idea the feeling wasn't going to disappear now, just because his head told him he'd be safer not to care.

Dizzy with the circles his thoughts were running, Jason finally fell across his bed, still half-dressed, just as dawn was breaking over the city. One fact remained. The father of Anna's child wasn't here. Jason was. And possession was nine-tenths of the law.

HE WAS GOING to lose her. In the cold light of day, his head pounding in protest, Jason had to face the truth. Clark Summerfield was the only logical choice for the father of Anna's baby. He simply wasn't aware of the child he'd created. When he was, a man like Clark would ask her to marry him immediately. And Anna, loyal as she was, would marry him out of duty. Wouldn't she?

Or would she?

Anna had changed, was sticking up for what she wanted. Would that new determination extend to rejecting what she didn't want?

Summerfield was in Europe during Anna's greatest hour of need. Which meant he must not know anything about the crash or her amnesia. Had he known, he'd have flown home to see her through this difficult time. But if there was commitment between them, wouldn't there also be communication?

And if there were no commitment...

Jason had won her love once. While the field was clear, he at least had to try again. But he'd do it with his eyes wide open, knowing the risks. No more pretending.

CHAPTER FOURTEEN

JASON SENT HER FLOWERS. They arrived Saturday afternoon just before his phone call asking her out on a date. An official date. Dress comfortably, he told her. They were going on a cruise around the harbor.

At six and a half months pregnant, Anna didn't have any idea how she could feel sexy and romantic, but when she opened the door an hour later, when Jason looked at her as though he'd like to make love to her right there on the floor, she'd never felt sexier. Dressed in a long-sleeved ankle-length flannel tent with a thick cardigan sweater on top, she felt like every man's dream centerfold. Maybe pregnancy made your hormones rage.

The cruise was idyllic, quixotic—and deserted. No one else was crazy enough to cruise around the harbor at night on the first of November. But snuggled against Jason in the wool blanket he'd brought, Anna couldn't think of anything more romantic.

They ate assorted cheeses accompanied by a homemade French loaf and grapes, popping them into each other's mouths, licking the juice from each other's fingers—and lips. Jason drank wine, Anna, mineral water. And they talked. About the world. About people. About life. Jason believed in so many of the things she found most important. Family. Loyalty. Commitment.

After they'd eaten he pulled her back against him on the secluded bench. The blanket enveloping them in their own private world, he linked his hands beneath the swell of her belly, holding her and the baby both.

Happy, drugged with the night, the romance, she snuggled into him, content to remain as she was forever.

The baby moved, her little foot dragging across the bottom of Anna's stomach.

"She's awake, Mama," Jason whispered in her ear.

"It's 'cause she knows you're here." Anna was convinced that the baby recognized Jason's voice, his touch. These days she seemed to become active whenever he was around.

Jason laughed, following the baby's progress with one hand, poking her gently, playing with her. Anna didn't see how any moment could be more perfect.

"There's a daddy position open if you're interested." The words slipped out before she could stop them.

And she wished she had when she felt Jason stiffen behind her. "I'm not her father."

She was spoiling the most perfect evening of her life, but she couldn't stop herself. When she'd awoken in that hospital all those months ago, she'd had to start fresh, fill the horrible void that was all she knew. She'd created a new life for herself, a good life, and that hadn't come easy or without a fight. If convincing Jason they were meant to be together took another fight, so be it.

"Not biologically," she said, placing her arms over his, keeping his hands on her belly. "But in every other way—in my heart and, I believe, in hers—you're already her father."

"And what happens to me when you find out who her father is, when he returns to your lives claiming what's rightfully his?" Jason's words weren't an accusation; that wouldn't have hurt so much. They were resigned.

It was time to speak up or lose him forever. "He doesn't matter anymore." The confession was difficult to make, not because she wasn't completely certain of its truth, but because it left her so vulnerable. "He can't matter," she continued, her voice breaking. "Because I'm completely in love with you."

Jason's heart soared. Which made the plunge to despair that followed all the more painful. He didn't doubt that she believed what she was saying. But how could she possibly be sure of her feelings without a yardstick to measure them by?

Then, too, she'd claimed tearfully to love him when he'd asked—okay, demanded—that she come to New York with him. Yet less than two months later she'd become pregnant by another man.

"You don't know how desperately I want to believe you," he finally said, her honesty deserving the same from him.

She turned to face him, clearly shocked. "You don't believe me?"

Jason kissed her slowly, tenderly. He'd always been able to show her so much more than he could say.

"I believe you feel that way now," he said when he raised his head.

"You don't think I know my own heart." Her head fell against his chest, and her gaze turned to the bay.

"You know what's there now, Anna, but what about when it fills back up with all the emotions you've forgotten?" He couldn't believe her words, couldn't count on them. He'd only get hurt. And he couldn't go through that again.

Her silence wasn't a good sign. He had to help her see that they had to know for sure. "I'm here," he said quietly into the darkness. "I'm the only one here." He chose his words carefully, needing her to understand. "But we have to face the fact that somewhere there's another man about whom you could have felt the very same way."

"How do I convince you he just doesn't matter anymore?"

"Until you remember him, you can't, Anna," he said, his voice strong. He wasn't going to let her sway him on this. He couldn't. It would kill him to believe her now, only to have her regret her decision when her memory finally returned. "Until you remember what it is you're giving up, you can't know if you want to."

"And what if I don't ever remember?" Her question fell between them, a question they'd both asked themselves a hundred times. A question neither one could answer.

JASON CALLED Dr. Gordon first thing Monday morning. He rushed through pleasantries, assuring the doctor that Anna was fine, the baby was fine, he was fine, and then got straight to the point.

"What are the chances that Anna will never remember?" When was it time to tell her the truth? At least about them. To tell her that she'd opted not to marry him when he'd asked her last spring. To give her at least those facts and then let her decide if she still wanted him to be the father of the child she carried. If she still wanted him.

The doctor was silent so long Jason was almost afraid to hear his answer. "You know something I don't know?" Jason finally asked him.

"No," Dr. Gordon said, the word drawn out. "I'm just not sure I can give you any percentages, Jason." He paused. "Of course there's always been a possibility that Anna won't ever regain the memories she's lost."

"Does it grow stronger as time passes?"

"No."

"So five years from now she could be sitting in a restaurant or driving down the road and suddenly have it all come flooding back?" Five years' worth of living, of loving, only to lose it all?

"Or it could come in little snatches, just as it's been doing."

"I want to marry her, Doctor."

"I'm not surprised." Dr. Gordon sighed. "But I can't tell you I think it's a good idea right now. Too much still rests in the balance."

"It's not fair to Anna, is what you're saying," Jason stated flatly. He'd already reached that conclusion himself. It was just convincing her he was having troubles with. "How can she make such a lasting commitment when she doesn't know what she's leaving behind?"

"Exactly."

The doctor was only confirming what he already knew. And it sounded just as hopeless coming from someone else.

"It also wouldn't be fair to you, Jason," Dr. Gordon continued.

"I'm not worried about that." He brushed the doctor's words aside. He'd given up on fair a long time ago. Now he simply kept himself safe. If he didn't count on anything, didn't look for things that weren't there, he'd be fine. "I'm just not sure I can convince Anna to wait another five years to start living her life."

"You'd have a hard time convincing me if I were in her position."

"She says she isn't going to wait until she's eighty and then, when she's too old to do anything but die, decide that her memory isn't coming back." They'd been her last words to him the night before when, in her apartment, they'd had a replay of the conversation from Saturday night. Jason had a feeling that they'd continue to replay it until he gave in.

"She has a point."

"So you think I should tell her about her past? At least about my part in it?" he asked, hopeful for the go-ahead. It was his only chance.

The doctor took a moment to think, but his answer was disappointing. "I really believe it's too soon, Jason. She's a strong woman, stronger now probably than she ever was before, but we have to remember that none of us knows what she's running from, what prompted her amnesia."

"And you don't think she's strong enough to handle whatever it is even now?" Because Jason did.

"Probably she is strong enough. But if she no longer wants to remember, if she no longer has any reason to try, you might be committing her to permanent darkness." He took a deep breath. "She's growing increasingly more frustrated. Her determination to know her own mind is becoming all-important, her need to make her own decisions stronger than ever.

These are all signs of imminent recovery. I can't urge strongly enough that you give her more time.''

Jason could find nothing in the doctor's words he could fault. ''I'll give her until the baby's due,'' he said. ''If she never remembers who fathered her child, if she never remembers the circumstances that led to her amnesia, I can live with that. But I'll never be able to live with myself if we bring this child into a relationship based on a lie.''

There would be no argument on that point.

THE NIGHT SUNNY argued with him on the air, Jason knew he had some other decisions to make. His co-anchor, knowing he'd been seeing a lot of Anna, was trying to get his attention.

''Lighten up, Sunny,'' he said softly during a commercial break. Cameramen were milling around, someone from makeup came over to blot the perspiration on Jason's brow. Now wasn't the time for a showdown, but he hated to see Sunny humiliate herself on the air. She was a damn good newscaster. And she'd been a good friend.

''I don't know what you're talking about,'' she said, her voice sweet enough. But she wasn't as relaxed as she sounded. He watched her tap the end of her pencil on the desk in front of them.

''Will you at least agree to wait until we're in private?'' he asked.

Sunny's assistant came forward to adjust the collar on Sunny's blouse. ''Wait for what?'' Sunny asked when the girl stepped away.

''I promise we'll talk, Sunny. Tonight. Right after the show.'' He smiled at the technician who adjusted his mike.

"The show. Sometimes I wonder if that's all you've ever cared about," she said. "Well, don't forget, I helped make you, Jason. And if all it took was my opinion, my acceptance, to gain your entrance into this town, then my opinion can just as easily guarantee your exit."

"Five seconds!" The voice boomed from the darkness in front of them.

Feeling sorry for Sunny, Jason braced himself for a difficult second half. His ability was one thing he was sure of. If she thought she had any power over his career, she had an eye-opener ahead of her.

ANNA WATCHED the news that night, Friday, almost a week after her cruise with Jason, feeling restless and bothered. She'd become used to Sunny Lawson's proprietary air with Jason, or told herself she had, anyway, but that night, either Anna was even more insecure than she thought, or Ms. Lawson had turned up the heat.

Busy with the little overalls she was stitching—a pattern she'd drawn herself and cut from an old newspaper—Anna hadn't noticed anything all that unusual about the first half of the newscast, other than an occasional uncharacteristic barb from Sunny. But during the second half of the show, Sunny not only touched Jason, she actually rubbed his arm a time or two. She was acting like a woman confident of her man's affection, confident her overtures would be accepted.

Licking her lips, Sunny smiled sexily at Jason as she told him they'd have to discuss their differing opinions on a recent parochial-school levy in a more private venue. Everyone watching was meant to know that the last thing Sunny and Jason would be discussing was school levies. That they'd be too involved in more...physical pursuits to discuss anything at all. Anna stabbed herself in the thumb.

Jason had explained about Sunny months before, assuring Anna that any personal relationship he and Sunny pretended to share was just that—pretend. He'd told her about the publicity campaign the station had devised to introduce him to his New York viewers. He'd told her how Sunny had become a friend, someone who's company he enjoyed. Not someone he wanted to have as a lover.

Anna knew all this. She even believed it. So why did Sunny's hand on Jason's arm make her feel so small, so insignificant?

SUNNY FOLLOWED HIM to his dressing room. Shutting the door behind her, she helped herself to a drink from the sideboard, fixing him one, too. Liquid courage.

"Lillie's having a mystery party next weekend on the yacht," she said, settling back against the smooth leather of his couch. Lillie was Sunny's best friend and a bit too shallow, too materialistic for Jason's taste.

He stood at the desk, the drink she'd brought him untouched. He didn't loosen his tie and didn't remove his jacket. He simply stood, not saying a word.

"It's from four on Saturday till whenever on Sunday."

He remained there, unmoving, unbending, by the desk. In his professional life, at least, he was in control. Always. He'd accept nothing less. And he had the feeling Sunny was actually trying to issue him an ultimatum.

"We're invited." She was no longer looking at him, drinking her martini more quickly than she should.

He still said nothing. Did nothing.

"If you pick me up at four-thirty, we should get there late enough to make an entrance."

He wondered where Sunny had gotten the idea that he'd ever change his mind about them. He'd been clear from the start that a friend was all she could expect him to be.

"I'm sorry, Sunny, but I can't go."

Her gaze shot up, locking with his. "Of course you're going," she said with an attempt at a laugh.

"No, I'm not." Jason enunciated the words carefully.

"Don't be stupid Jason." She set her glass down, stood, came over to the desk. "Didn't you hear me earlier?" She placed her hands on his shoulders, leaning her body into his. "The show's mine. You want it, you take me."

"Don't do this to yourself, Sunny," he said, pleading with her to come to her senses before she did irreparable damage to their relationship.

As she pulled away, the look she gave him was a mixture of desperation and hurt. "I'll have you moved to weekends," she blustered.

"I don't think so."

Picking up the phone, Jason dialed the station manager's office.

And less than two minutes later hung up.

"You play nice or take weekends," he said. "The choice is yours." He didn't wait around for Sunny's reaction—or her decision.

DURING THE LAST childbirth class they watched a movie of a woman giving birth. Anna decided one thing instantly. Jason definitely wasn't going to be there for the birth. There was no way his first sight of her naked was going to be like that. She couldn't get out of the class fast enough, away from the chattering couples, the cheery instructor.

Wonder if she'd be feeling that cheery if it were her going through the ordeal, Anna thought sourly, her head bent as she walked out to hail a cab.

"Wasn't that the most amazing thing you've ever seen?" Jason asked, catching up with her at the curb. "Here, honey, put this on before you catch a chill." He handed Anna the coat she'd left behind in the classroom.

Amazing? She snuggled into her coat. "Thanks."

Lifting her chin and looking into her eyes, he asked, "You okay?"

Anna's glance fell. Hell, no, she wasn't okay.

"Anna?"

His gorgeous blue eyes were warm with understanding. He knew.

"I'm scared," she admitted, her breath misting in the cold air between them.

Silently cupping her face with his hands, he lowered his head to kiss her, the touch of his lips a distraction, a reassurance, a reaffirmation of how far she'd come, how strong she really was.

"I'll be there with you, honey, every step of the way."

"You promise?" She held his gaze. "No matter what happens between now and January?" She was asking a lot, but dammit, this was one thing she couldn't do alone, no matter how badly she wanted to.

"I do."

His words were promising far more than his attendance at her daughter's birth. They both knew that.

CHAPTER FIFTEEN

JASON WAS IN HIS KITCHEN when the phone rang Thanksgiving afternoon. Anna, having lain her increasingly cumbersome body back against the couch for a minute, reached lazily for the receiver. "Hello?"

"Is this..." A young woman rattled off Jason's phone number.

Instantly on edge, Anna sat up. "Yes."

"Is Jason there?"

"Who's calling please?" She had no business asking, no right to monitor his calls. Suddenly she felt ill.

"Is he there?"

Anna didn't answer. She was too busy trying to see through the haze that was enveloping her. Sunny wouldn't be calling; Jason had told her his co-anchor had taken a cruise for the holiday weekend—with the new man in her life.

"May I speak with him please?" The woman was determined. Anna just wanted to hang up.

"Just a moment," she said, setting the phone down. She felt awful, light-headed. Must have overexerted herself in the kitchen, but she'd been so determined to prepare a perfect holiday dinner complete with all the trimmings for Jason.

"Anna? What is it?" Jason asked, coming out of the kitchen where he'd been lifting the Thanksgiving turkey out of the oven for her.

"Huh?" she asked, looking up at him. "Oh, nothing... I mean, the phone's for you." She couldn't think, didn't want to think.

"I didn't hear it ring," he said, looking first at her and then the phone.

She lay back, suddenly afraid she was going to be sick. "It did," she finally said.

Forcing herself to concentrate, she listened when he picked up the phone.

"Hello?" A pause during which Anna's stomach clenched again. And then, "Oh! Hi!"

Did he have to sound so cheerful? "Uh, yeah." This with a furtive glance her way.

Intending to lay right there and figure out what this mysterious woman could possibly want with Jason, why he was suddenly uncomfortable with her listening in, Anna was forced, instead, to bolt for the bathroom—giving him plenty of time to have whatever private conversation he wanted.

JASON DIDN'T TELL HER who'd been on the phone. And she refused to ask. He didn't owe her any explanations. Except that she needed one. She fought with herself the rest of the afternoon, barely touching her dinner, right up to the moment he dropped her off at her door that night. She didn't want to know, didn't want to be hurt. And didn't see how she could go another minute not knowing—loving him as she did.

He'd said he was bringing her home early because she was tired, because she'd been so violently ill earlier in the day. And he seemed genuinely concerned. But Anna couldn't help wondering if he had somewhere else to be. Someone else to see.

Not that she'd blame him. She just had to know.

"Who was she?" she finally blurted as he slid her
key into the lock, her proximity to her own apartment
giving her the courage to face whatever might be coming. If the news was devastating, she only had to make
it a few feet to her bed, then slip under the covers and
escape.

Jason didn't look at her or even ask who she meant.
He obviously hadn't forgotten the call, either. "Nobody," he said, flipping on a light before standing
back to let her enter.

Anna's nausea returned. For "nobody" the woman
really bothered her, though Anna figured that was un-
derstandable. No matter how much she wanted to, she
couldn't promise Jason anything, not yet. Maybe
never. The phone call had brought home to her just
how untenable that made her position.

He had every right to find promises elsewhere.

"There's no reason to lie to me, Jason," she said,
standing in front of him, feeling like a beached whale
as she imagined how beautiful the other woman surely
was.

Helping her off with her coat, he stopped, looking
down at her, his eyes serious. "Yes, Anna, there is."

He couldn't have surprised her more if he'd slapped
her. "Why?"

THE DESPAIR IN HER EYES finally decided Jason. This
had gone on as long as he could let it. If the past
needed to be buried, that was just too bad. He wasn't
going to let it interfere with the future.

"Come," he said, drawing her over to the couch,
aware of how reluctantly she followed. She'd been
through so much, his poor darling. And he had a feeling things were going to get worse.

"Anna, how did you feel when you answered that phone today?" he asked. He'd been worried about Anna's violent reaction to the call. And he wasn't the only one who'd worried.

"Well, if she hadn't evaded me so obviously, it probably would have been okay," Anna said defensively.

Oh, honey, if only you knew. He'd never felt so helpless, watching her, not knowing what to say, what *not* to say.

"It's okay, Jason, I understand," she said, obviously misreading the look of pain in his eyes. He hurt for her, not for himself.

He shook his head slowly, brushing her hair back from her face. "No, honey, you don't," he said, ready to take the plunge, and yet not ready.

"Yes, I do, Jason, and it's really all right." She was trying so hard to mean what she said it broke his heart. "I won't hold you to your promise to hang around until the baby's born," she rushed on. "You've been wonderful to stand by me this long, but you don't owe me anything."

"It was Abby."

Anna's eyes went wide, blank, and she started to shake.

"Oh, God." The words were anguished.

Pulling her against him, rocking her as he held her, Jason told her about the call and the two others he'd made later in the day, both times when she'd been in the bathroom, reassuring Abby that no harm had been done. Abby had miscalculated the time when she knew Anna was due at Jason's. And then realized what had happened and been terrified, knowing that hearing her voice could very well have risked Anna's future health.

What he didn't tell Anna was how devastated that call had left Abby. To have actually spoken to Anna, to have had her on the phone, hearing her voice—and still not be recognized had shaken Abby to the core. Nor did he tell her how worried they still were. Both from Anna's first nauseous reaction to having spoken with her sister, and the fact that Abby's voice hadn't sparked any memory at all.

"I could have talked to her—" Anna's words, thick with tears, broke off.

"You can always talk to her, honey."

She swiped at the tears on her face. "Dr. Gordon says I should wait."

But the doctor's way wasn't working. "And is that what you want to do?" This was Anna's show now.

"I don't know what I want." Her voice broke again. "Hold me, Jason," she begged. "Please, just hold me."

He did. But his arms couldn't take away the fear. For either of them.

AUDREY. ANNA SAT straight up in bed, looking around at the predawn gray of her apartment as if she'd find someone there. Audrey. She wanted to name the baby Audrey.

Although not knowing how she knew that or why, Anna had never been more sure of anything in her life. *If the baby was a girl, she was to be called Audrey.* Anna was having a real live honest-to-goodness memory. A resurgence of a thought she'd had before she knew the sex of her child, a thought she'd had before the accident.

She'd been walking in Gramercy Park, and she'd just found out she was pregnant. She'd decided to name the baby Audrey if it was a girl. And she'd hoped it was a girl. Surrounding the memory was a feeling that someone would be very pleased about her decision—once she was free to speak of it.

Still frustratingly locked away was why she couldn't speak of it or who would be pleased.

Tempted to call Jason, in spite of the hour, a new worry held Anna back. Something—or someone had been calling out to her more and more often lately. Before it had only been in dreams, like the nightmare she'd had at Jason's just after she'd left the hospital. But in the three days since Thanksgiving, she'd been experiencing the oddest sensations while wide awake, almost as though someone else were there in her mind, calling her name, needing her.

Terrified, she had no idea what to do—and half suspected she was losing her mind, after all. Which was one reason she didn't tell Jason. She couldn't bear to have him see her go crazy. To place such a horrible burden on him.

But there was a second reason she didn't call. She was horribly frightfully suspicious that she was remembering someone—and that the someone was the man who'd fathered her child. Who else would have such an intense emotional hold on her? A bond that was reaching out to her even through her darkness?

Queasy, shivering, Anna burrowed beneath her covers, her arms cradling her child, holding on by the barest thread to logic, to reason.

She only had one thing to focus on right now. One thing that mattered. In only seven weeks she was going to give birth to her daughter. To Audrey.

To say Jason was shocked when Anna told him what she planned to name her baby was an understatement. Fortunately she did so over the telephone and he was able to hide his reaction. She was remembering. She had to be remembering. And for that reason alone he didn't tell her the significance behind the name.

He was achingly aware of what the return of her memory would mean. Every day as her baby grew, so did the tension between them. They were living on borrowed time. They both knew that.

Jason was sitting with Anna in her apartment the first Saturday in December, his leg bobbing swiftly and almost imperceptibly as they watched another movie. They'd been spending most afternoons that way since Thanksgiving, and he had to get out, to do something besides wait quietly for his world to come crashing down around him. He was spending far too much time watching Anna's expression, waiting for the light of memory to come into her eyes. Dreading what would happen when it did.

And today was worse, knowing as he did that, since it was a weekend, he didn't have to leave for work in a matter of hours. That he could stay right there with her as darkness fell over the city. And stay. And stay. Now, before her memory came between them.

"Isn't it about time to buy her some stuff?" He asked, his hand resting on Anna's stomach, waiting for Audrey to wake up.

"I've been looking through catalogs," Anna said, grabbing one from under a pile of books on the coffee table. "I found the furniture I want, but as small as this place is, I figured I'd wait until I was a little closer to my due date before I started getting any of it. I was thinking about looking for a larger place.'' She'd received her settlement check from the city the week before.

Flipping through the well-worn pages of the catalog, she found the nursery ensemble she'd chosen.

''All that color's great,'' Jason told her approvingly. The crib and changing table were white with colorful balloon motifs. The baby would only have to open her eyes to be entertained.

''See, there're sheets, receiving blankets, hooded towels, sleepers—everything to match.'' She pointed to the next page.

Standing up, Jason said, ''So let's go get 'em.''

''Now?'' She looked up at him. They'd just finished lunch. She usually rested after lunch.

''Sure now.'' He suddenly wanted to do it all, to take part in everything that was yet to be done to prepare for Audrey's imminent birth, and to do so as soon as possible. Because he didn't know from one day to the next if there'd continue to be a role for him to play.

''But where will I put it all?''

Looking around the cramped apartment, Jason could see her problem. And suddenly he had the perfect solution. Or at least as close to perfect as he could get, considering his limited options.

''We'll set it up in the downstairs bedroom in my place. I'll move back up to the loft.''

''Your place?'' she asked. But she didn't sound at all displeased with the suggestion.

''Sure,'' he said, grabbing her coat. ''I've got the room.''

And if he had the baby's things, didn't he stand at

least some chance of eventually having the baby? And her mother, too?

"But won't it be a lot of trouble to move it all again?"

Jason shrugged. The possible trouble would be worth the chance to have her stay. "Your chances of finding a place you want before she's born are pretty slim," he said, which was one thing they both knew to be the truth. Waiting lists for New York apartments, at least ones she'd want to raise Audrey in, were a mile long. "You guys can room with me until something comes up."

Neither examined the plan, knowing that to do so would only borrow trouble. Instead, avoiding each other's eyes, they locked hands and went on a shopping spree.

"WE DID GOOD, don't you think?" Anna looked around Jason's spare bedroom on Sunday night, tired but happy.

"We did great!" he said, the pride in his voice sending little thrills clear through her. This was how expecting a child was meant to be. A man and woman, their love electrifying the air between them, filled with anticipation as they surveyed the crib that would soon bear a tiny body, the changing table filled with tiny T-shirts and sleepers, bottles waiting to be filled, diapers to be worn.

"You don't think we went a little overboard?" she asked, looking around them. They'd bought out half of New York in less than twenty-four hours.

"This little one's worked damn hard to get here," Jason said, wrapping his arms around her from behind, his hands spreading over her stomach. "She deserves to have her necessities waiting for her."

Anna grinned at him over her shoulder. "I'm just not convinced that a life-size bear that plays nursery rhymes can be considered a necessity." She covered his hands with hers, leaning back into him, loving the solid strength of his body. A body she'd not yet discovered, and yet felt as if she knew so well.

"Sure it was," Jason said. "He matched the crib."

"And the curtains?" She looked at them, hung at the window to pull out the creases. They were playing a dangerous game. But curtains could be rehung.

"You want someone peeping in at her while she sleeps?" Jason asked.

"On the tenth floor?"

Her gaze locked with his over her shoulder. He'd never actually asked her to move in with him, but they were both talking as if such a move was a foregone conclusion.

"Anna?" Jason's voice was hesitant, unlike him. "If, after the baby's born, we're still where we are now, would you consider making this her home?"

If we're still where we are now. If she was still without half her senses, he meant. If she still didn't know who Audrey's rightful father was.

She should tell him no. She had to tell him no. None of this was fair to Jason, but moving in with him, being a family, was downright cruel.

"For how long?" she whispered when she'd meant to decline his offer. "Not just until I can get into someplace bigger than what I have now?"

She felt him shrug as his arms fell away. Cold, suddenly bereft, she took his hand gladly when he offered it, following him out to the living room.

He sat down on the couch and pulled her down beside him, still holding her hand. His gaze locked with hers.

"I want her here," he said. "I want you both here forever."

Her heart flip-flopped. She'd been living to hear those words since she'd first come home from the hospital with Jason, maybe even before. And then reality set in. "But..."

"Shh. Hear me out." He placed one finger against her lips. "I want to marry you, Anna."

Tears sprang to her eyes. She didn't think it was possible to hurt so much. "Oh, Jason, I want that, too, so much."

He nodded. Swallowed. And then started again. "I can't ask you to do that, Anna. It wouldn't be fair."

"To you," she said, her tears still welling as she held his gaze. "I know."

Shaking his head, he said gently, "To you." He reached up and dried her eyes. "I'd be taking advantage of you if I married you now when you're at your most vulnerable. When you have no idea what you'd be giving up."

"You mean Audrey's biological." It was how she'd come to think of the man.

"Her what?"

"Her biological, as in the biological source of half of her existence."

"He's a man, Anna," Jason said, although she could see what the words cost him. "He's her father."

She couldn't allow him to go that far. "No, Jason." She shook her head. "He's not a father."

As if he knew she was prepared to argue semantics with him all day if that was what it took, he nodded slowly. "He exists. Someplace in your memory he exists." A pause. "And there's more."

Frowning up at him, she asked, "What?"

"You have no idea how you felt about me before, but if your memory returns, that will come back to you, too. And whether you believe it or not right now, that memory could very well change how you feel about me."

Anna's stomach clenched. She hated the sudden turn the conversation had taken. "Didn't I like you?" It was something she'd never even considered.

"Yes."

But his eyes told her there was more.

"Was I angry with you?"

"Yes."

Frightened, she grasped his hand more tightly. No. She didn't want there to be any problems between them.

"Did I have reason to be angry?" she whispered, her heart thudding.

She'd pretty much decided that she was ready to deal with whatever it was she'd been avoiding remembering now that she was stronger, now that she had Jason by her side. She'd never once considered the fact that he might be part of the problem.

"Yes."

She pulled away from him and then, seeing the pain in his eyes, grabbed his hand back again. "You wouldn't ever have hurt me deliberately, Jason, I know that," she said, the conviction in her words coming straight from her heart. There were just some things a body knew, no matter what.

Jason acknowledged her trust with a nod, a slow smile spreading across his face. "Never," he said.

"Do you want to tell me this horrible thing you did?" she asked, trying to make light of it.

Jason studied her for a long moment. "Do you want me to?"

No. She didn't. She didn't want to know any of it, to have had a past at all. She was happy with the present. A present they'd promised each other. Why couldn't they just leave it at that?

"What do you think Dr. Gordon would say?" She knew she was copping out even as she said it. But while she'd been convinced she was strong enough to handle the return of her memory, she'd also planned on having Jason to turn to, to help her pick up the pieces.

"He said you're probably strong enough to hear what I have to say."

Her fear increased. "You've already talked to him about it?"

Jason nodded. "I'd planned to tell you, anyway, before the baby's born."

"And he agreed?"

For the first time Jason looked away, and Anna breathed a small sigh of relief. He wasn't sure.

"He advised me to wait. Going by what you've already remembered, your chances of complete recovery are excellent, and so anything we might tell you could hamper that recovery." He said the words in one breath.

"Then I'd like to wait."

"Okay, we'll wait." He didn't even try to convince her otherwise.

"Will you tell me one thing?" she asked, missing the emotional closeness they'd been sharing these past weeks.

"I'm ready to tell you whatever you want to know," Jason said, sounding resigned.

"This thing that made me angry, was it something horrible enough to make me run from myself?"

"Not by itself, no," he said, choosing his words as carefully as he had those first few days she'd been with him. He was going to honor her decision not to be told about her past. "We had a nasty quarrel. The stance I was taking was unfair. But that was all."

Anna started breathing easier.

She grinned up at him. "I can live with that."

"Here? After the baby's born?" Jason asked, his eyes serious.

Anna nodded. She'd learned to trust herself these past months, and Jason's home, in his life, was where she wanted to be. "But if six months after the baby's born I still haven't recovered my memory, I'm going to be expecting a marriage proposal, anyway."

Shocked by her own boldness, Anna nevertheless held his gaze.

"I'll do better than that," Jason said, pulling her into his arms. "You have it now, due and payable six months after Audrey's born."

She wanted the proposal more than anything else. And yet, as part of her rejoiced, another part shivered. So much could happen in the next seven and a half months.

CHAPTER SIXTEEN

JASON HELD ANNA for a long time, reluctant to let her go, knowing that every minute of his time with her was to be cherished as though it was his last. Knowing that every moment might very well *be* his last.

She felt so good in his arms, so right, even pregnant by another man. This time was his. His and hers. And if, with the regaining of her memory, he lost it all, he at least would have had something he'd never had before. Unconditional love. Total commitment. An acceptance of his proposal of marriage. Even if just for today.

Pulling Anna closer, Jason inhaled her natural scent. Anna. His woman. He couldn't get enough of her.

"I love you," she whispered against his neck.

And because this was his moment, he answered her. "I love you, too, Anna." He raised her face, kissed her deeply. "Please remember that."

Her eyes clouded, almost as if she'd heard the desperation he'd thought he'd concealed. Before she could delve into things better left buried for now, he kissed her again, lifting her, settling her on his lap, on the aching hardness he'd grown almost accustomed to these past months.

Or thought he had until she moved against him, creating a friction she'd created so many times before.

Her dress slipped up her body, bearing thighs firm

and long and so painfully familiar. He knew every freckle, every shadow there—and other places, too. He ran his hands along one smooth thigh, back and forth, up and down, caressing her, remembering. Until her long legs wrapped around him, straddling him, cradling him.

And he was lost.

With the ease of exploring familiar territory, Jason seduced Anna, knowing where to touch, how to caress, how hard and how soft, how much to tease. He knew because she'd taught him; he'd insisted she teach him. And he'd taught her, too.

Breaking off a long satisfying kiss, Anna drew her tongue down his neck, unbuttoning his flannel shirt as she went. Artfully flicking his sensitive flesh with the tip of her tongue, she ignited him as she'd done so many times in the past, the only difference being that, instead of laughing up at him as she'd done in the days when confidence had made her bold, her eyes were shyly downcast.

And even this turned him on. To seduce Anna all over again, to relive those shockingly erotic days of teaching her how to give him love, how to take it for herself. A gift few men were honored with twice.

Then, as she settled herself more completely against him, things were suddenly different. She didn't fit as she used to. Her stomach protruded between them.

Oh, God. He let go of her thigh. What in hell was he thinking?

"We can't," he said, unable to hide the agony in his voice as he pulled away from her.

She stared up at him, her eyes clouded with passion. "What?"

"The baby." He could barely get the words out. He

was struggling to breathe, to hold her calmly, to not lose his control in an agony of want.

Pulling herself farther up his body, she traced his ear with her tongue. Hadn't she heard him? He had to stop. Now.

"It's okay." He barely heard the whispered words through the roaring of his blood.

When he didn't respond, didn't do more than sit there holding her, holding on, she whispered something else, her words sending the blood straight back to his groin.

"I asked Dr. Litton when I saw her last week."

Her announcement stunned him. She'd been that sure? Or, his body throbbing harder with the thought, just that needy? Jason held her firmly away from him, watching her as he demanded, "And?" His hands were shaking with the effort it was taking not to carry her upstairs to his bed.

"I'm still seven weeks away," she said. "As long as it's not uncomfortable and we're careful..." Her voice trailed off as she lowered her eyes.

His own sweet Anna. Bold yet shy. Needy and yet not wanting to ask anything for herself. Even in love. He was going to enjoy teaching her how to ask all over again.

"Then let's be careful, my love." He was already carrying her up the stairs to the loft as he said the words.

ANNA HAD NEVER BEEN so thoroughly loved. Even without a single memory of anything to compare it to, she knew making love had never been so good. Not only did she catch fire everywhere Jason touched, she sensed his love, as well, and a reverence she wasn't sure she deserved but knew she returned with every fiber of her being. She was his totally, completely.

When she sat astride him, lowered herself down on him, she found not only a physical joy beyond anything she'd imagined, but an emotional release she felt she'd been craving for as long as she'd lived.

At first, when it became obvious to her that she knew what she was doing, that a man's intimate touch was achingly familiar, she worried that she might be remembering another place, another time. Another man's touch.

But soon, as Jason stroked and kissed and encouraged her to do the same, she had no thoughts other than Jason. Loving him.

"You're so beautiful," he whispered, every muscle in his body straining with the obvious effort it was taking him to be gentle.

The truth of his words were reflected in his eyes. And in that moment Anna felt beautiful.

"I could get real used to this," she said, watching him, the concentration on his face, the love in his eyes.

"Good."

He held her motionless on top of him and Anna frowned, eager to reach the destination she'd been climbing toward for months.

"Just giving us a minute to slow down," he said, his words coming with an effort. "To prolong the pleasure." Then he gasped, thrusting so deeply she felt the sensation to her fingertips and toes.

There was nothing slow about their loving then.

JASON HAD TOUCHED heaven, confirmed not only its existence, but that it was everything he'd hoped it would be. He held Anna, rolling with her until she was lying on her side facing him, his body still connected to hers. He was home.

"That was incredible," he said, needing her to know that what they'd just experienced hadn't been ordinary at all—not even for them.

"Mm-hmm," Anna said, moving her body against his, getting him aroused all over again.

"You're sure?" he asked, his body already fully hard within her.

She moved with him, giving herself to him completely. For now, this one night, this one time, he knew there was no part of her already reserved, already spoken for. For this one night he was first.

As Jason moved slowly within her, holding her gaze with his own, speaking on so many levels and connecting on every one of them, he couldn't help thinking that their lives would always be like this if she never regained her memory. And for just a second he hoped for exactly that.

But only for a second. Her beautiful brown eyes were filled with love but only a present love. His love had its roots in their past, had a depth hers would always be lacking. It would never be enough. For either of them.

He loved all of Anna—before and after. For both their sakes she needed to know herself, to love herself, too.

SHE'D STEPPED OUTSIDE her self again, was watching as she walked in Gramercy Park, stumbling because she hadn't seen the uneven sidewalk through her tears. She even knew why she was crying. What she couldn't figure out was why she was there all alone.

She'd never been alone before in her life.

And then there were two of her. Only she was in a different park, the ground covered with soft white sand, instead of grass. There was a sand castle nearby and she was laughing. Both of her were laughing at something beyond the castle. Something she couldn't see.

No. Wait. She'd miscounted. There weren't two. There were three of her. And all three were crying. They must know about Jason, she thought. They're all crying because I can't remember anything so I can't marry Jason.

Except that Jason hadn't asked her to marry him yet. This was before the crash. But the tears didn't stop. Had Anna caused all this pain? She wanted to tell them she was sorry, but all three ignored her. They'd reached the end of their endurance, found a hurdle they couldn't vault.

She was losing her mind—but not the pain. It wasn't ever going to go away. No matter how hard she cried, how hard all three of them cried, they couldn't change the—

With a start Anna sat bolt upright in bed. Remembering wasn't the shock it should have been; it wasn't even surprising or new. It was a solid wall of agony. An agony so familiar she knew she'd never forgotten it, not for an instant. Had been carrying it with her every day since the accident. And before.

Dr. Gordon had told her an incident, something deeply important, could very well trigger her memory when she was ready. Making love with Jason must have been that important. But she didn't think she was ever going to be ready.

She was Anna Hayden. Of Abby, Anna and Audrey Hayden.

Oh, God. Memories assailed her. Audrey. And Abby. "Abby!"

Her voice startled her, scaring her, bringing the nightmare to life. She felt arms steal around her, allowed them to hold her only because she hurt too much to fight them off.

They weren't three anymore. "No!" she shouted, shaking her head, refusing to accept the picture in her mind. She couldn't bear the memory. Couldn't go back to living with the pain day in and day out. But the memories continued, pouring in so quickly she thought she might collapse from the onslaught.

Audrey. Beautiful vibrant laughing Audrey. Still. Terrifyingly unnaturally still. Covered in blood. Her face. *Oh, God.* She saw her identical sister's face. No one else. Only her. She'd been the one to find Audrey out on the beach. Had gone there to build a sand castle.

She'd screamed, could still hear her screams even now. They deafened her, sickened her. Covering her ears, Anna rocked from side to side. No! Stop!

But the pictures, the sounds, the smells just kept coming. She hadn't been strong enough, even then, to handle things on her own, to call the police, to spare her sister Abby at least that much. Instead, she'd stood there shaking and screamed for her. She'd thought that was all she'd done. All those months after the accident, she'd thought all she'd done was stand there and scream, the smell of Audrey's death enveloping her. But that hadn't been all. First she'd rolled her dead sister over. She'd rolled her over so Abby hadn't had to see her face.

"Ohhh nooo, please!" she cried. "Please stop!"

She shook her head again and again, trying to dislodge the pictures. Anything to make them go away.

The funeral had been closed-casket. At the time she'd been too thankful to question the decision her parents had made without even seeing their daughter first. Now suddenly she knew why. They'd probably been told...

Rocking, crying, holding herself, Anna was no longer aware of the arms that held her, couldn't feel anything but the agony. A pain so deep there was no way to recover, to ever be again the innocent woman who'd walked out of the beach house that day.

And Abby. *Oh, God, Abby!* It was Abby who'd been calling out to her these past weeks. Abby who was hurting, who was needing her. Abby, who'd also had a part of her soul destroyed. "Abby!" she cried. She needed her sister. Needed that part of herself.

JASON JUST HELD ON, sweat running off his body as he listened to Anna's anguished cries. He'd never witnessed such suffering, had no idea what to do for her, how to help, how to reach her. He just knew he couldn't let her go, couldn't let her be alone when she came back out of this hell of hers. If she came back. His throat dry, his body starting to shake, it hit him that he might be losing her forever.

She'd remembered. Though she'd still said nothing but Abby's name, nothing else could have rent this much pain from her. But as he sat there holding her, the memories no longer mattered. Anna mattered. And her torment was breaking his heart.

His helplessness rendering him powerless, he just held on.

"Shh," he whispered over and over, rocking her,

brushing the tangled hair back from her face. "I'm here, honey. I'm right here," he kept saying.

Whether or not she could hear him, he kept repeating the litany, hoping that even a trace of the comfort he had to offer would reach her, help her fight her way back.

"Oh, God."

The anguish in her voice tore at him. It was so hard to believe it was only hours ago he'd heard her crying in ecstasy. Their lovemaking must have triggered her memory. Subconsciously she'd remembered loving him before.

Anna continued to cry out against whatever visions she was seeing, locked all alone in a world he couldn't share.

Why? he asked over and over. *Why her?*

Fighting him again, she kicked the covers away.

"Anna! What is it, honey? Talk to me." He spoke firmly, urgently.

She continued to wrestle with no direction. Then one arm wrapped around his, holding him in a death grip.

"Talk to me, honey," he said again. "Let me help."

Pushing frantically at the hair tangled about her face, she continued to sob.

"I saw her!" she cried suddenly. "I saw her face." And then, as if the admission drained the last of her strength, she went limp in his arms.

"Whose face, honey?" Jason hoped to God he was doing the right thing in making her talk.

"Audrey's. I saw her face." The words were mumbled, as if she'd finally given up.

Unsure whether she was speaking of the baby she

carried or the sister she'd lost, Jason asked, "When? Where?" Had Audrey visited her in a dream? He'd never been a big believer in the supernatural, but Anna couldn't be imagining whatever horrors were playing themselves out in her mind.

"That day—" She broke off, started to sob again. "On the beach..." More gasps. "I saw her face."

"What day?" he asked softly. When Audrey was killed, she'd been found facedown in the sand. Anna was remembering something else. If only he knew what.

"The blood!" she cried, and then moaned, burying her face against his chest. "Her beautiful face."

Jason held Anna more tightly, as though by sheer force of will he could erase her mind once again. Anna had found Audrey, but the police had made her leave—made Abby leave—before anyone had touched the body. Neither had seen the extent of the damage caused by the murderer's knife. Unless...

Jason swallowed, took a deep breath. "Tell me about it, Anna," he said, his voice gentle but commanding. He had to get it out of her before she escaped back to a place where nobody could reach her. "Tell me what you saw."

"Her face—" She broke off, sobbing. "I c-couldn't even r-r-recognize her." A spasm of hiccups choked her words. "But I saw her neck...her neck...her necklace..."

Cold to the bone, sickened, Jason knew. Audrey hadn't been found facedown. Anna had seen her and then wiped the sight away. But the vision had remained in her subconscious, preying on her without her even being aware of it, waiting.

"Her n-n-nose was g-gone."

Sick to his stomach, Jason had heard enough. "Shh," he whispered. "I'm here, honey," he crooned.

"Her ch-cheeks and m-mouth..." She tried to breathe, couldn't, tried again, her voice shaking with sobs. "So much b-blood."

Oh, Anna. Beautiful strong silent Anna. You didn't have to do this all alone. We would have helped you.

Suddenly she stopped. Stopped crying, stopped speaking. Stopped breathing. Panic shot through him and he sat up, intending to force his own breath into her lungs until she was ready to take over on her own, a part of him trying to devise a plan that would allow him to be in two places at once—breathing for Anna and on the phone getting help.

He lay her down, her closed eyes scaring the hell out of him. But before he could do more than prop her neck with pillows, a shudder tore through her. She was breathing again. Tears running down her face, she lay completely still and cried.

Unable to bear her pain, Jason reached for her again, and her eyes opened. She looked at him as though only just realizing he was there. "Oh, Jason!" she cried. "Her eyes, they were open and glassy and they weren't laughing at all." Her husky voice was thick with tears, but sounding more like her own.

"Anna. Lovely Anna." He swallowed, exerting every ounce of control he had to hold back his own emotion, cradling her against him.

And then, leaning back to look up at him, she asked, "You knew Audrey, didn't you Jason? Were you our friend back then, too?"

He nodded, unable to speak. Hadn't she remembered him?

"I'm glad," she said, smiling through a fresh spate

of tears. "Oh, God, Jason, how could I have forgotten something like this?"

He didn't have any answers for her. Only platitudes she'd heard before. Leaning back against the pillows, he held her close, surrounding her with strength, with love. It was all he could do.

She cried quietly now, speaking little. "Thank you," she said at one point.

Brushing his hand gently across her cheek, he said, "You don't have to thank me, love."

She nodded, as if accepting the truth of his words.

A long time later, still crying but much calmer, she pulled away just enough to look up at him. "I rolled her over," she said, as though confessing a crime.

"You did the right thing, Anna."

She shook her head. "I couldn't bear to look at her."

"There was no reason to."

She started to cry harder, still so full of raw anguish she overflowed with it. "Death smells awful."

Jason had smelled death once, during his early days as a reporter. He'd never forget the sickly sweet stench that had permeated the air, choking him. He'd been so violently sick to his stomach he'd had to leave the scene.

"I love you, Anna." The words were torn from his throat. He'd take her pain, her memories, upon himself if he knew of a way.

"I love you, too," she said, sitting up and gazing at him, the love in her eyes still fresh, still new. There was no recognition of the former love they'd shared.

NUMB, ANNA LAY in the bed with Jason, her head on his chest. He'd made her get up, put on one of his shirts, afraid she was going to catch a chill. But he'd taken only a brief moment to yank on a pair of cotton shorts himself before pulling her right back down into the comfort of his arms, the covers close around them.

But still she shook. Her whole body trembled as her mind wandered, stumbled, shied away and wandered some more. So many things, so many memories to revisit. Her childhood, growing up with her sisters. The time she'd broken her arm and Abby had been the one to sit up half the night with her, trying to take her mind off the pain of her broken bone setting in the cast. She remembered the jokes they'd played on their teachers, on their long slew of baby-sitters and nannies. But never on their parents.

Desperate for time with them, the girls had always been perfect angels whenever their parents were around. Except of course when they'd done some stupid kid thing, like the time their parents took them out to dinner at the Beverly Hills Hotel and Anna had spilled her drink on the table and into their father's lap. Or when Audrey had gotten lost at an amusement park, and the nanny of the week had panicked and called her father out of an important meeting.

Anna remembered the time Abby had bloodied Jimmy Roberts's nose for calling Anna a bookworm. The year her mother had surprised them with three birthday cakes—for her three little angels, she'd said. And Anna remembered Audrey, always hugging everyone....

All of these memories and more she shared with Jason, talking long into the night, one memory resurfacing after another. But every memory was tainted with bone-deep sadness. It was over.

"Poor Abby," she said, her eyes welling with tears

as she thought of her older sister. Older by twenty minutes chronologically, older by years in every other way. "She grew up so fast." And had lost so much.

"Too fast and yet not unhappily," Jason said. "Abby's a born caregiver."

Anna had to remember that he'd known them before, that some of what she was telling him might not be new to him. But then, why was he still new to her?

She sat up, frowning. "There're still some blank spots."

He nodded. "Dr. Gordon said there might be, that your memory probably wouldn't come back all at once."

Anna started to shake again. "I can't take any more, Jason." She'd rather die than go through another night like last night.

"You're a strong woman, Anna, stronger now than ever before," he said, his hand rubbing her arm, warming her.

And in some ways she knew he was right. She was stronger now. If nothing else, these past months had given her that.

"It's funny," she said. "I remember leaving California. It was just like Abby said—I had to prove to myself I was a complete entity on my own." She chuckled without humor. "I guess I've done that, huh?"

"Absolutely," Jason agreed, his breath brushing the top of her head.

"The shop," she said, suddenly remembering the business she'd built with her sisters, the reason she was such a good seamstress. Knowing, too, that the overalls she'd been sewing for her baby were Abby's design. "I left her all alone with the shop."

"And it's doing just fine," Jason said. "Abby hired a couple of women who love her designs almost as much as she does."

Anna was glad. She'd hated spending her days sewing when her own creativity had been clamoring for release. But she'd owed Abby and hadn't begrudged her sister her chance. Or herself the opportunity to do something for Abby for a change. Even Audrey had done her share at the shop without grumbling.

Frowning, Anna said, "I even remember making my family promise to leave me alone for an entire year." She could picture the scene as if it had happened yesterday. Her parents had been stunned, Abby devastated.

But in the end they'd given her the promise she'd demanded.

"I just can't remember why it was so important," she said weakly. How could she remember hurting her sister so horribly and not remember why she'd done so?

"It'll come back to you, Anna," Jason said. "You just need to be patient."

"And you?" Anna sat up again, staring at him. "Why can't I remember you at all?"

Jason shrugged, breaking eye contact. She couldn't blame him for being uncomfortable. How must it make him feel for her to claim to love him but to have forgotten him so completely?

And then there was the other person she'd forgotten....

"I still can't remember the biological," she said softly. She was frustrated and frightened and so damn tired. What horrors remained to jump out at her? And would she be able to cope when they did?

CHAPTER SEVENTEEN

DAWN WAS BREAKING over the city when Anna finally fell silent. Believing she'd fallen asleep, Jason lay completely still, cushioning her head on his chest. And although he had a lot to think about, to consider, to accept, at the moment only one thought occupied his mind. Anna hadn't run for the telephone—for Abby. She'd remembered and had come through her emotional crisis without her sister.

And then, as if his mind had conjured the action, she sat up, slipping silently from the bed.

"You calling Abby?" he asked, resigned and maybe even a little relieved. She'd made it through her crisis. That was all that mattered. For the rest he'd been wrong. Wrong to expect her to leave a bond that was as necessary to her happiness as food and air. One that had been forged long before she'd even known him. One that had seen her through her entire life, made her who she was. The woman he loved.

Surprised when Anna shook her head and walked past the phone, Jason climbed out of bed and followed her. She'd turned her purse upside down and was shaking out the contents, sifting through them. Pulling an envelope from the pile, she opened it, dumping a chain and locket into her hand. He recognized it immediately.

"I thought it was such an odd shape," she said,

holding the locket lovingly in her slender hands. "It's odd because it's only a third of a whole. Put together, the three parts form a heart."

Jason nodded silently, although he knew she wasn't looking at him. His throat thick, he watched Anna, seeing her—all of her—for the first time. He'd thought he'd wanted her to be whole, and all the while he'd been the one tearing her apart. Refusing to see an important part of who she was simply because it was a part he couldn't share.

"Our parents bought the original locket when we were born," she murmured. "They had it cut into three and then made into three separate lockets."

Even with her head bent, Jason could see that she smiled.

"They made us wear them always so they could tell us apart." Her finger brushed over her name.

"As we grew up, the lockets were a sign of our loyalty. We agreed never to take them off." She shrugged. "Other girls had best-friend necklaces. We had our lockets."

He ached to hold her, but didn't.

"It was also a symbol of our own separate identities," she said, telling Jason something she'd never told him before. "We were always part of a whole and yet different, too. I can remember Abby telling us that once when we were little. Audrey had been crying because Abby's locket was bigger than hers. Abby explained that hers was biggest because she was the oldest. Mine was next, and Audrey's was the smallest. That we were the same and yet special in our own ways."

"I didn't know that." Jason spoke for the first time since following her out of the bedroom.

She glanced from the locket to him, as though surprised to see him there. Frowning, she said, "You know, it's funny, but I don't think I've thought of that in years."

She handed the locket to Jason. "Would you help me fasten it?" she asked, holding her hair up off her shoulders.

She wanted him to fasten around her neck the symbol of what had driven them apart, asking him to give her back to the relationship he'd tried to take her from. She was asking him to share her, to know he was never going to be the single most important person in her life.

He fastened the locket.

MONDAY MORNING, just as soon as she was alone in her own apartment, Anna called Maggie.

"Hey, preggie, what's up?"

You were right about Jason and me all along, Maggie. We're lovers now. And it was even better than I imagined. Better than you'd probably imagined. And...I remembered some things. "Your apartment was rented."

"Yeah, well, I don't think I'm coming back."

"You got the job?" Anna asked, happy for her friend.

"Don't know yet, but the pilot's finished and it looks great."

"Oh, Maggie, that's wonderful!"

"I got me an agent, Anna," Maggie said, her usual sardonic attitude slipping. "He says I'm good."

"You *are* good, Maggie." Damn good.

They talked about a couple of other auditions Maggie had been on, and Maggie actually made Anna laugh when she told her about the job she'd lost for a cookie commercial. Maggie as a life-size macaroon Anna couldn't see.

"Where are you staying?" Anna asked when she could finally get a word in. She'd had a crazy idea during the cab ride home this morning.

"A dump on Sunset Boulevard."

Anna paced her apartment, her phone pressed to her ear. "You got a car yet?"

"Yeah, you could call it that. It used to be a compact sometime before the last wreck or two."

"Does it run?"

"Of course. You think I'm throwing my money away on something that isn't reliable?" Maggie demanded. "It's not pretty, but it works."

Crossing her fingers, Anna plopped down on the couch. "I've got a favor to ask, Mags."

"So ask."

"It's my sister, Abby."

"You talked to her?" Maggie asked, suddenly alert.

"No." Anna paused. She was afraid to call. Not until she remembered why it was so important that she left. "But I remembered her."

Maggie's silence spoke volumes. "Not everything," Anna answered the unspoken question quickly. She wasn't up for an interrogation, not yet. Maybe not ever. But this was something she had to do.

"Abby's all alone, Maggie. I want you to live with her."

"Whoa!" Maggie was probably backing away as far as her telephone would allow. Her New York friend was not used to California's laid-back ways.

"She has a three-bedroom cottage on the beach,

Mags,'' Anna said before Maggie made up her mind once and for all. Once she'd done that, there was no changing it. ''And she's only about forty-five minutes from the city, depending on traffic.''

''I'm not worried about traffic, Anna. It's your sister. You ask her about this?''

''She won't mind, Maggie,'' Anna said. ''I know she won't.'' Abby would never turn away a person in need, whether she wanted to or not. And Abby needed Maggie much more than Maggie needed a decent place to stay. ''You can have my room.''

''Your room?''

''Yeah. The cottage is half-mine.''

''You and your sister lived together?''

''Yes, until I came here.'' Anna took a deep breath. ''She's all alone, Maggie, and not, you know, doing all that great. She could use having you around.''

''Right.''

''You kept me sane, didn't you?''

''You're easy Anna.''

''Abby's a lot like me.'' Well, okay, maybe not in some ways. But she had a feeling Maggie and Abby would hit it off. And couldn't bear the idea of Abby being alone one more day.

''I don't know, Anna.''

She was losing her—she could hear it in Maggie's voice. ''It's right on the beach, Mags. Think of all the beachboys.''

''I'm getting enough pretty boys in the city.''

''You can have my room at no charge.''

She'd hit a chord there. She could tell by Maggie's silence.

''Please, Maggie, for me?'' she asked.

"I'll go meet her," Maggie said grudgingly. "How do I find her?"

Anna rattled off the number at the shop. If Abby wasn't in, someone there would know where to find her.

"And Maggie?"

"Yeah?"

"I don't want you shocked or anything, but when you see her…?"

"What, she looks like Godzilla or something?"

"No." Anna smiled mistily. "She looks exactly like me."

ANNA SPENT the next couple of days making herself crazy. Every waking moment was eaten up with remembering—and searching for the lost pieces of the puzzle that had become her life. More and more frightened by the number of things still unknown to her, she became desperate to discover them, to get the ordeal over with once and for all. To own her life before her baby was born.

And for every memory she had, she conjured up an imaginary one that could explain the gaping holes still left in the picture. The largest hole, the one that mattered most to her, was Jason. Why couldn't she remember him? What was so threatening about an old family friend? She didn't know why it took her so long to come up with the answer—not when it was so obvious. Her only explanation was that she'd simply been too self-absorbed to see.

Sitting with Jason at lunch on Wednesday, she worked up the courage to confront him.

"Tell me about you and Abby."

She watched him put down his sandwich, her stomach a mass of knots. She'd been feeling poorly all morning—ever since she'd figured it all out.

"What do you want to know?"

"Whatever you need to tell me."

"We're friends."

"And?"

He splayed his hands, then dropped them to the table on each side of his plate. "That's all."

She believed differently. And her subconscious agreed—which was why it wouldn't allow her to remember Jason, especially since they'd spent the last three nights together in his bed.

"She was the one you went to see before you left town," Anna said.

"I had something to say to her." His sandwich still lay untouched on the plate in front of him.

"What?"

"That Audrey was gone, you were an adult, and it was time she concentrated on her own life."

Anna frowned. That sounded more like a friend than... "What about that phone call on Thanksgiving?"

"You know about that, Anna." Jason was frowning. "She was alone, it was a holiday, and she wanted to connect with you in the only way she could."

"You're sure that's all it was?" Because there had to have been some reason he'd grown so close to her family, something that kept him coming back. And she already knew it wasn't her. She'd have remembered loving Jason. She was sure of that—especially now that she knew what loving him was like. And besides, if they'd been lovers, he'd have told her. The pain he felt because he wasn't Audrey's father was too real to ignore.

"Of course I'm sure," he said impatiently. "What else could there be?"

"You two could have been in love."

The shock on Jason's face alone drove that suspicion from her mind. "We could have been, but we weren't," he said calmly, staring her down.

Bowing her head, Anna felt herself blush. Okay. She'd missed the boat again. Apparently that was something she was good at.

Light-headed with relief, she actually giggled. At least her beloved and her beloved sister weren't lovers.

ANNA HAD EXPECTED to feel better after her conversation with Jason, but as the evening wore on, she only felt worse. She wanted—needed—to call her sister. She hadn't heard from Maggie, didn't know how Abby was doing, if she was all right. And yet, Abby knew Anna's memory had returned. Anna could only surmise that Abby was respecting Anna's original request, her stipulation for silence between them. She just didn't know why. Her head hurt from trying to make sense of it all.

What was still out there for her to know? What had happened between she and Abby? Why had she extracted the promise in the first place? Why couldn't she remember Jason? And where in hell was the biological? He had to be that Clark guy. But why couldn't she remember him?

Audrey kicked her so hard she doubled over on her couch. She was waiting for Jason's second newscast to come on so she could admire his thick blond hair, the way his mouth curved when he smiled, his eyes. All the while knowing she'd be admiring the rest of him the minute he got home.

The baby kicked again, stealing the breath from Anna's lungs. She lay still.

The third kick scared her a little bit, coming as it did so low in her belly and in her back at the same time. Either the baby had turned miraculously fast, or she had six legs.

Halfway through the news, her water broke. Jason spoke to her from the television set, his blue eyes warm as they gazed straight at her. She could do this. That was what he was telling her. She was sure of it. She could do this. Never taking her eyes from his face, she reached for the phone.

Twenty minutes later Jason was at the door, a cab holding downstairs. The wait had almost killed her. Especially the last ten minutes when those steady blue eyes had been missing from her television screen.

CHAPTER EIGHTEEN

THERE WAS NO TIME to tell her the truth, in spite of his vow to do so before they had the baby. Jason threw Anna's coat around her shoulders, lifted her off the couch and carried her down the stairs. Six weeks early, Audrey was one determined little girl. *God, please get us there in time. Let them both be okay.*

"We've got plenty of time, Anna. Just relax, honey," he said, helping her into the cab. His heart thundered in his chest.

Please let them have found Dr. Litton. Have her waiting at the door.

"That's it Anna, one, two, three." He breathed with her, holding her in the backseat as the driver swerved in and out of the Wednesday-night traffic.

There was nothing else he could do. Nothing else but worry.

"We have to move my stuff to your place," Anna said after what seemed to Jason a particularly long contraction.

Stuff? Who the hell cared about stuff? How could she think about that at a time like this? They were having a baby here.

"Sure, honey," he said. "We'll do that."

"Right away, Jason." Her voice was stronger. "We'll probably be ready to come home tomorrow or the next day."

Okay. Fine. Whatever. "I'll move everything in the morning." *Now would you just concentrate on what you're doing, please?*

"I can't believe I'm finally going to get to see her," she said, resting her head against Jason's shoulder. She sounded as if she might be going to sleep.

They were having a baby. He was scared to death and she was going to sleep. Nobody had said anything about sleeping during the childbirth classes they'd taken. Sleeping wasn't in the job description. But sure enough she was actually going to sleep.

Right up until the next contraction. That was when Jason went back to work. At least he knew what to do. "One, two, three," he breathed. "Easy now, honey."

"I want to paint her bedroom red," Anna panted through the pain.

Red. Right. "Breathe, Anna."

"And the ceiling blue with a bright yellow sun."

"Uh-huh." And they thought she was actually going to have this baby? Why in hell had they gone to the classes if she wasn't willing to do anything right?

She chattered on about the room as the spasm passed, her voice getting drowsy again. Jason was almost glad this time. If she could just sleep until they got to the hospital, he'd have Dr. Litton to assist him in getting this job done. He didn't think they were going to get much help from Anna.

"I'd love a burger, Jason," she said suddenly. "You think we have time to stop for a burger?"

A burger! She just didn't get it. Giving birth was serious stuff. So much could go wrong...

"With pickles on it, please?" she asked sleepily. "Lots of pickles. Tell the driver to stop."

Jason wasn't sure how much more of this he could take.

But once they got to the hospital, Anna seemed to get more with the program. Dr. Litton was waiting for them in emergency, quickly checked Anna and determined they had time to get her up to a birthing room. Jason was doubtful. However, bowing to Dr. Litton's greater experience, he kept his opinion to himself and pushed Anna's wheelchair silently. And prayed for all he was worth.

THINGS MOVED so quickly Anna didn't have time to be afraid. She smiled at Jason when he appeared, garbed in a green surgical suit, in the door of her birthing room.

"This where the party is?" he asked.

She nodded. "Mm-hmm." They could get on with it now. He was here.

"Anna?" He looked as if he had something important to say.

"Yes?"

He paused. Glanced at the IV in her arm, at the monitor hooked to her stomach. "I love you."

That was all she needed to hear. "I love you, too."

She couldn't believe how excited she was. Soon, very soon, she was going to meet her daughter, see her, hold her.

"I'd expected to be scared," she confessed to Jason. "But with you here I just know everything's going to be fine."

He smiled at her. "Of course it's going to be fine."

It must have been a lot warmer in the room than she thought. Sweat was darkening the cotton surgical garb Jason wore.

GET 2

HOW TO GET YOUR 2 FREE BOOKS AND FREE GIFT!

1. Peel off the MIRA® sticker on the front cover. Place it in the space provided at right. This automatically entitles you to receive two free books and an exciting surprise gift.

2. Send back this card and you'll get 2 "The Best of the Best™" books. These books have a combined cover price of $11.98 or more in the U.S. and $13.98 or more in Canada, but they are yours to keep absolutely FREE!

3. There's no catch. You're under no obligation to buy anything. We charge nothing – ZERO – for your first shipment. And you don't have to make any minimum number of purchases – not even one!

4. We call this line "The Best of the Best" because each month you'll receive the best books by some of today's most popular authors. These authors show up time and time again on all the major bestseller lists and their books sell out as soon as they hit the stores. You'll like the convenience of getting them delivered to your home at our special discount prices . . . and you'll love your *Heart to Heart* subscriber newsletter featuring author news, horoscopes, recipes, book reviews and much more!

5. We hope that after receiving your free books you'll want to remain a subscriber. But the choice is yours – to continue or cancel, anytime at all! So why not take us up on our invitation, with no risk of any kind. You'll be glad you did!

6. And remember...we'll send you a surprise gift ABSOLUTELY FREE just for giving THE BEST OF THE BEST a try.

SPECIAL FREE GIFT

We'll send you a fabulous surprise gift absolutely FREE, simply for accepting our no-risk offer!

Visit us online at
www.mirabooks.com

® and TM are registered trademark of Harlequin Enterprises Limited.

BOOKS FREE!

Hurry!

Return this card promptly to GET 2 FREE BOOKS & A FREE GIFT!

The Best of the Best ™

YES! Please send me the 2 FREE "The Best of the Best" books and FREE gift for which I qualify. I understand that I am under no obligation to purchase anything further, as explained on the back and on the opposite page.

Affix peel-off MIRA sticker here

385 MDL DRTA   185 MDL DR59

FIRST NAME	LAST NAME

ADDRESS

APT.#	CITY

STATE/PROV.	ZIP/POSTAL CODE

▼ DETACH AND MAIL CARD TODAY! ▼

(P-BB3-03) ©1998 MIRA BOOKS

THE BEST OF THE BEST™ — Here's How it Works:

Accepting your 2 free books and gift places you under no obligation to buy anything. You may keep the books and gift and return the shipping statement marked "cancel." If you do not cancel, about a month later we will send you 4 additional books and bill you just $4.74 each in the U.S., or $5.24 each in Canada, plus 25¢ shipping & handling per book and applicable taxes if any.* That's the complete price and — compared to cover prices starting from $5.99 each in the U.S. and $6.99 each in Canada — it's quite a bargain! You may cancel at any time, but if you choose to continue, every month we'll send you 4 more books, which you may either purchase at the discount price or return to us and cancel your subscription.

*Terms and prices subject to change without notice. Sales tax applicable in N.Y. Canadian residents will be charged applicable provincial taxes and GST. Credit or Debit balances in a customer's account(s) may be offset by any other outstanding balance owed by or to the customer.

If offer card is missing write to: The Best of the Best, 3010 Walden Ave., P.O. Box 1867, Buffalo, NY 14240-1867

BUSINESS REPLY MAIL

FIRST-CLASS MAIL   PERMIT NO. 717-003   BUFFALO, NY

POSTAGE WILL BE PAID BY ADDRESSEE

THE BEST OF THE BEST
3010 WALDEN AVE
PO BOX 1867
BUFFALO NY 14240-9952

NO POSTAGE
NECESSARY
IF MAILED
IN THE
UNITED STATES

Watching the monitor for her, Jason handled labor like a pro. He could tell from the lines on the screen just when her next pain was due and had her already breathing properly by the time it hit. He counted. He cajoled. He offered his arm for her to squeeze and ignored her when she yelled at him to shut up.

A nurse wheeled in what looked like a portable incubator just as Dr. Litton stopped by for one of her periodic visits. Anna looked from the machine to Jason, and then up at the doctor.

"What…?"

"She's close to six weeks early, Anna," Dr. Litton said calmly. "We have to be prepared."

"Jason?" Anna cried, fear choking her as she reached for his hand.

He held her, but looked at the doctor. "Have you any reason to expect trouble?" he asked.

"None at all. We wouldn't be in this room if we did."

"What's the immediate danger?"

"Probably none," the doctor said, smiling at Anna. "The baby's been perfectly active, her heart's strong, everything looks good. But with an early baby I like to be extra careful."

"You worried?" Anna asked Jason as soon as the doctor left the room.

He shook his head, smiling as he smoothed her hair out against her pillow. "Not at all. She knows what she's doing."

That was enough for Anna. If Jason wasn't worried, she had no reason to worry, either.

Jason's scrubs were drenched by the time she'd fully dilated, and by then she was pretty hot herself. And exhausted beyond belief. As the worst pain yet subsided, she wanted nothing more than to go to sleep. They were all going to have to take a break.

"Come on, Anna, it's time to get to work," Dr. Litton said from the end of the makeshift bed.

After she had a little sleep. Then she'd do all the work they needed.

"Now, honey. Push!" Jason instructed, watching the monitor.

She pushed. And wished to God she'd gone to sleep.

"Again!" Jason said.

She pushed again. Jason wasn't watching the monitor anymore. He was keeping company with Dr. Litton, both of them at a party she couldn't get down to attend.

"I see her hair!" Jason said, his eyes glowing with a light she'd never seen before. It made her want to push again, harder.

Jason's face her cue, Anna did her job, pushing when she was told, holding back as she had to. She watched the birth, not from the mirror they'd mounted for her, but through her lover's eyes.

Then, just as the baby surfaced, as her body found a relief so powerful she cried, she saw an expression on Jason's face she'd seen before. Once. In another life. The intensity of his yearning, the look of pain that resulted from unrequited longing, was completely familiar to her. It was an image she'd been carrying in her heart every day since she'd sent him from her life. She remembered him.

She remembered everything.

"Seven pounds!" a nurse declared, holding the newborn on a scale to one side of Anna's bed.

"Seven?" Dr. Litton was still working on Anna, but

glanced over her shoulder at the nurse. "That much? Are you sure? Better check it again."

A pause fell over the suddenly still room.

"Still seven," the nurse said.

Clearly surprised, the doctor checked the scale herself.

Ignoring Jason completely, Anna was vaguely aware of the doctor and nurse, but her gaze was glued firmly on her baby girl. Audrey. A new life for one lost.

A baby born right on time.

Jason stepped back, his ears buzzing, his heart thumping heavily. He had answers to all his questions. As long as Anna and Audrey wanted him in their lives—in any capacity—he would be there. Period. Being someone's first priority was nothing compared to being needed, to being part of a family, to loving. He'd been playing second fiddle all his life. Was good at it. Memories, other loves, be damned. The past, the future. Nothing mattered except being whatever, whoever, his two girls needed him to be for however long they needed him.

So MANY FEELINGS exploding inside her, so many thoughts clamoring for attention, she wondered if she'd ever see clearly again. Anna lay in her hospital bed the rest of that day, assimilating all that had happened before her accident, all that had happened since and what was yet to happen. And holding Audrey. Almost constantly holding the baby girl who was everything she'd ever hoped her to be and more. So much more.

She'd already made the decision to breast-feed her daughter, and so she'd had Audrey moved right into bed with her, feeding her when necessary, holding her while she slept. Keeping her close. At times throughout that long day, she felt as if Audrey was the only person she'd ever be close to again.

Anger, pain, guilt, all cascaded down on her until she had to send Jason home, telling him to go ahead and go in to work, that she needed to sleep. Unaware she'd remembered, he wanted to talk. She didn't have any idea what to say. Playing for time, she insisted, that she had to rest as much as possible before they released her the next morning.

Except that, of course, she didn't rest after he kissed her softly goodbye and left. She watched Audrey. Cried over her. Nursed her even though her milk wasn't in yet. Loved her. And thought. She'd bought herself one day. It didn't seem nearly long enough.

BEFORE SHE KNEW IT, before she was ready, she was back in Jason's apartment firmly ensconced on his couch, a blanket tucked snugly around her and the baby she held.

"You're sure you're comfortable?" Jason asked, hovering at the other end of the couch, almost as though he was afraid to touch her—or the baby he'd yet to hold.

Nervous as she was, she couldn't smile at him, but she tried. "Fine."

He nodded, then hovered some more, moving pillows out of her way, the coffee table closer. He was aware that something was wrong. He'd been avoiding her eyes all morning. And now that she'd combined the Jason she'd known before the crash with the Jason she knew now, she could read him like a book. Just as he'd been reading her all these months.

"You should have told me." So many emotions roiling inside her, and anger won out. "I can't believe you didn't tell me."

He stopped dead, just stood frozen beside her.

"All these months and you never said a word."

Pale-faced, he sat down, no longer avoiding her eyes. "When did you remember?" he asked simply.

"Yesterday, the second she was born."

He nodded. "The birth brought it all back."

"No." She shook her head. "You did. I was watching your face." Anna sighed, her anger draining away. He'd done what he'd thought right. Jason always did what he thought right. If only his thinking wasn't skewered by his upbringing. He'd done what he thought right, yet he'd been so wrong, too.

"Dr. Gordon knew," he told her, but not in way of defense. "He said it was possible I was somehow mixed up in whatever you were running from, and so telling you who I was could force you to deal with a relationship you weren't ready to handle."

"After all we'd shared, Jason, you didn't know me better than that?" Her anger was back, but maybe just to camouflage the pain.

His jaw tightened. "We hadn't shared anything in quite a while," he reminded her. "And you were pregnant."

The words hung between them, his unasked question underlined by her silence.

"When are you going to stop being a martyr, Jason?" She couldn't look at him, couldn't bear to hurt him. Yet the words had to be said. Should have been said seven months ago.

"You mind explaining that?" He was angry.

She looked down at her sleeping daughter. *For you,*

my darling. For all of us. Then she took a deep breath and spoke.

"You settle, Jason. Always." She glanced at him, saw the stoicism settle on his face as he prepared, once again, to take whatever was handed him. "You make it damn near impossible for people *not* to put everything else first, to think of you last. You're so undemanding one could almost believe you have no needs at all." Almost. But not quite. She'd seen the longing on his face.

He remained silent. She wasn't even sure he was listening.

"Think about it, Jason. Did you ever ask your father to be at a game?" She'd had so much time to think those two months she'd been alone in New York. Time to figure it all out, to see where she'd been wrong—and where he'd been wrong. She just hadn't had the faith in herself to know that she could do anything about it.

"He knew when they were."

"But did you *ask* him to be there?"

His silence gave her the answer. "And what about that girl in college? Did you ever try to win her love away from the guy who'd dumped her?"

"You don't win love."

"Yes, you do, Jason." She forced back tears. "Sometimes without doing anything more than being yourself." Which is how he'd won *hers.* He'd certainly never asked for it. "Love isn't easy—it doesn't just fall in your lap and stay there happily ever after. You have to work at it, grasp it with both hands and be determined to keep it, or it's going to just slip away." Her last words were barely more than a whisper, her throat thick with unshed tears. This was a concept he had to understand.

The room fell silent again. Finally Anna couldn't stand it any longer. "And what about your lawyer friend?"

"What about her?" Jason asked, sounding suddenly confident. "I asked her to go to that funeral."

"Yes, but in all the years you'd been with her, had you ever before asked her to put her job second? Or had you given her the impression that you *expected* her job to come first?"

Again his silence spoke volumes. "Don't you see, Jason, not only are you living proof of self-fulfilled prophecies, you actually make people feel that they're pleasing you by doing as they please. That to be lavished with attention would turn you off."

Another glance in his direction. If he couldn't understand this, couldn't see it, their life together was over.

But even if their relationship was going to end, she owed him. Because she'd been wrong, too. The woman she'd been before had never even tried to communicate this to Jason, had never dared voice her doubts, her fears. She'd been too much of a coward to speak up, too afraid of being a problem. Swallowing back her tears, she held Audrey close to her heart and faced Jason head-on.

"I'm just as guilty as you are, Jason," she said. "I did you—us—a terrible wrong, and I don't know if I'll ever be able to forgive myself for that." Once again she pictured that look on his face. She'd seen it twice. The first time, when she'd walked out of his life in California, refusing to leave her sister and go with him. And the second she'd brought a baby into the world, a baby he'd so very much wanted to be his own.

"There's nothing to forgive," he said softly, gruffly. "I never should have asked. It was unfair, cruel, to expect you to leave Abby so far behind."

"Leaving Abby wasn't the problem, Jason. Or at least, not all of it."

His shocked gaze collided with her sad one. "Moving away wouldn't have made any difference to the bond I share with Abby. What we share isn't dependent on physical closeness.

"And that was the problem, wasn't it?" she asked, still holding his gaze. "Neither of you was willing to share the part of me you each had."

He nodded. "If it means anything to you, we've actually both realized that. We know how wrong we were to expect you to sacrifice one for the other."

"You and Abby have talked about this?"

"In depth."

"And you're friends again?" She could hardly dare hope.

"Closer than ever, I think." He paused, looked down, and then met and held her gaze unwaveringly. "We were wrong, Anna, insisting that we wanted all or nothing. Abby swears—" he stopped, swallowed and continued "—no *I* swear never to do that to you again. To love you is to love all of you, including the part that belongs exclusively to your sister."

That was one hell of an admission coming from Jason. And a prayer come true for Anna. She was free to love both of them. If only...

"Do you know why I chose not to come to New York, Jason?"

He looked away. "You're going to tell me it was

because I led you to believe I expected you to say no.''

So he had been listening. Had heard. "You did, but that's not why I said no.''

His gaze flew back to her. "Then why?''

"Because I honestly didn't believe you loved me. Not completely. Not as wholeheartedly as I knew I was going to need to be loved if I was going to sever my relationship with my sister.''

"After the two years we spent together?'' he asked, scowling. "How could you not know I loved you? I told you so all the time.''

"Because you didn't need me, Jason. Not really. You always held a part of yourself back, relied only on yourself, protecting yourself for that moment when I'd let you down.'' She paused, looked down at the child in her arms. "I needed you to need me as much as I needed you.''

"And if I'd let you know that I needed you, you'd have come with me?'' he asked, even now expecting a negative answer.

"I did come, Jason.''

His eyes were pinpoints of steel, boring into her. "You came to sell your book.''

"I came to be with you.''

JASON WANTED to believe her. More than anything in his life, he wanted to believe her. But his heart couldn't accept what she was telling him. He'd been a selfish jerk. Why would she have come here to be with him?

"You were here for more than two months,'' he reminded her.

Her eyes filled with tears, and a full minute passed

before she managed to get any words out. "After you left California, I hated myself. I hated you and Abby, too, but mostly just myself for not being strong enough to stand up to either of you."

Jason was hating himself pretty thoroughly at the moment, too.

"And I was terrified," she continued, her words making him hate himself more. He'd done this to her. "I was afraid that I couldn't get along on my own. When I reached deep down inside, looking for some imaginary well of strength to draw on, I found that there wasn't one. Not in me alone. Not without Abby. And I knew you were right. As painful, as terrifying as it was, I had to get away from my sister. I had to know I could rely on myself alone."

She stared down at the baby, and Jason looked away. He couldn't look at the child. Sooner or later she was going to tell him about the father. And that she was returning to the man.

"When I broke your heart, I broke mine, too," she said now, crying softly.

Reaching over, Jason brushed the tears from her face, then handed her a tissue. The baby didn't so much as stir.

"I came to New York to be close to you." She wasn't giving up on that one. He still didn't believe her.

"But I didn't contact you, couldn't contact you, until I'd proved to myself that I wasn't just transferring my dependence on Abby to you. I had to come to you whole or not at all."

After a lifetime of disappointment Jason had no idea how to handle anything else. Stunned, he just sat there, listening as two months of anguish poured out of Anna.

Those first days were harder than she ever would have imagined, but Jason could imagine it. She'd done this for him? She told him about being forced to quit her job when her boss tried to put the moves on her, how she was desperate to work—not because she needed immediate cash, but because she needed to be permanently independent for her own peace of mind. Independent of Abby. Of the shop. She told him how she'd always wanted to write, that working on John Henry Walker's biography was the only thing that had kept her going at times. She told him about finding Rosa and how much she'd liked the older lady.

And Anna saw him on the news. Saw him enjoying Sunny's attentions, saw how easy they were together. She knew she was losing him and that it was her own fault. And his, too, for not fighting for her, for their love. For letting something so wonderful slip away.

She was out walking one night less than a week after she'd left California, afraid, lonely. She walked for hours and still had to hail a cab to take her where she'd been wanting to go for weeks. The television station. That was the first time she'd seen him with Sunny off the air. Seen how close they were. She'd followed them to the Central Deli and Restaurant. And though she told herself to forget it, she started almost a daily ritual, taking a cab ride down to the deli between newscasts. And each time she saw him with Sunny, she died another death.

"If only you'd come to me." The words were torn from Jason.

She looked at him, her lips trembling. "I couldn't."

Of course she couldn't. He'd moved on—or so she'd thought.

"I met a man, Clark Summerfield, coming out of the deli one night shortly after I first saw you and Sunny there." *Here it comes, the part I've been waiting for.* And suddenly, with the truth at hand, he knew he never wanted to hear it.

"You want something to drink?" he asked.

Startled, Anna looked at him, shook her head and continued. "I was crying, and Clark saw me, came over, insisted on having his driver take me home in his limousine."

"You cold?" Jason asked, standing. "I can turn up the heat."

"I'm fine, Jason."

"What about her? Maybe she's cold." He still didn't look at the baby. Clark's baby. Twenty-four hours ago he'd been willing to settle for that.

"I spent a lot of time with Clark," she said. "He was nice. Mostly he was a much needed balm to a broken heart."

Okay, okay. He got the picture.

"I tried to convince myself I'd be happy without you," she said, her voice thick with tears.

Jason's own throat was uncomfortably tight. They'd made such a mess of things. Both of them. And ruined something beautiful in the process.

"And then came the day I couldn't avoid putting off doing the home pregnancy test I'd bought," Anna said. Her words were like a knife in Jason's heart. "I was getting sick every morning."

Was this the penance he was to pay for not fighting for her in the first place, this cruel blow-by-blow?

"When it was positive, my first instinct was to run home to Abby."

Why not straight to nice, balm-for-the-heart Summerfield?

"But as much as I was hurting, as terrified as I was, I couldn't run anymore. For myself, but also for her." She smiled down at the baby in her arms. "Then, more than ever, I had to know that I was a whole person. How else was I ever going to face raising a baby by myself?"

By herself? Jason stood frozen, every nerve ending tuned to her, listening intently.

"What about Summerfield?"

She frowned. "He'd left for an extended business trip to Europe." She sounded as if she couldn't have cared less.

So he didn't know yet?

There was hope. Not a lot. But enough to speak up.

"Anna?" He sat down, gently taking her free hand in his, his thumb running along her palm. He brushed the hair back from her face with his other hand, his eyes trained on hers.

"You were right," he said. "I do settle." The admission cost him. Far more than he'd expected. Because once made, he couldn't take it back. Couldn't allow himself to settle ever again.

"Growing up as I did, it was just easier."

She nodded, her eyes brimming with tears. "I know."

"I guess it just became habit. I didn't even realize I was doing it."

Anna nodded, waiting.

"Habits are hard to break."

"I know."

Her eyes shadowed with fear, she waited for him to continue.

"But I can't settle for a life without you."

She smiled, her lashes wet with tears.

"I love you, Anna, so very much."

"I love you, too, Jason." Her whispered words drove him on.

"But there are some things I have to have."

She nodded again, still smiling through her tears.

"I have to know that I'm the only man in your life." He couldn't live with the fear that Summerfield may one day return, discover he had a daughter, insist on a place in her mother's life.

"Absolutely." Her reply came swiftly. "You always have been."

"And always will be." This wasn't negotiable.

"As long as we both shall live."

He needed to kiss her, to hold her close to the heart he'd just bared for her. But there was a seven-pound baby lying between them. He knew she was there. Just couldn't bring himself to look at her.

"I'll gladly raise your daughter, Anna," he said, still holding her gaze, holding it almost desperately. "But only if I have your word that you'll allow me to be a *real* father to her." He stopped. Looked away, then back. "If I'm to love her, I have to do so as though she was my own."

He wouldn't settle for any less.

Tears pouring down her cheeks, Anna said, "I never slept with Clark, Jason."

He stared at her, sure he'd heard wrong.

"I'm not saying he wasn't interested, but he travels so much he knew he couldn't make a commitment— and I couldn't settle for anything less."

She really hadn't slept with him?

"Besides, he knew I was in love with you. He told me before he left for Europe that if, when he got back, I was still single, he was going to set out to steal me away from you."

"You never slept with him?" Jason couldn't quite grasp the gift she was giving him.

Anna snuggled the baby briefly, then held Audrey out to him.

"Take her," she whispered. "*You're* her biological." And then she grinned.

Jason stared at Anna for another full minute, then down at Audrey. His baby. His daughter. His and Anna's.

"She's *mine?*" he asked.

Anna nodded. "Even ultrasounds can be wrong. She's small, but she's all yours." Jason's heart full to overflowing, he took the sleeping baby from her mother's arms.

"Hello, Daddy's darling," he said, tears in his eyes as he gathered his daughter to his chest.

Audrey stirred, opened her eyes, then fell back to sleep with a little sigh. In that instant Jason knew he was never going to have to settle again.

His gaze left his sleeping daughter only long enough to run lovingly over her mother.

"Will you marry me, Anna?" he asked.

"I'd be honored to marry you, Jason," she answered softly.

After a lifetime of loneliness Jason had a family.

FADE TO BLACK
Amanda Stevens

Prologue

"And if it's a boy, I think we should name him Max."

"You know I hate that name," Jessica Kincaid complained as she pressed down a loose corner of the circus-motif wallpaper in the newly redecorated nursery. "Besides, what makes you so sure it's a boy?"

"Well, Maxine then," Pierce teased her, stretching to paste the last of the glittering stars to the ceiling. Suddenly the ladder he stood on teetered, and Pierce grabbed for a handhold. His arms flailed wide as the ladder toppled and crashed to the floor. Jessica cried out in alarm, but as usual Pierce landed on his feet.

Jessica's hand went to her heart. "Are you all right?"

"Right as rain, sweetheart." Pierce bent to drop a light kiss on the top of her head. "Don't you know by now I have nine lives?"

"By my count, you're getting dangerously close to

the last one," Jessica remarked dryly, referring to her husband's penchant for adventure and excitement. Whether it was snow skiing or parasailing, driving a car or riding a motorcycle, nothing ever seemed quite fast enough for Pierce Kincaid. He seemed to relish living on the edge, and he often left Jessica breathless in more ways than one.

Why he had ever been attracted to someone as shy and hopelessly introverted as she, Jessica still couldn't understand, but their marriage had already survived two wonderful years. Not only survived, but flourished. And now with the baby on the way, everything in her life seemed like a dream come true. A dream she prayed would never end.

She reached up and caressed Pierce's cheek with her fingertips. "I wouldn't be able to bear it if anything ever happened to you. You're my whole life, Pierce. I love you so much."

He touched the teardrop on her cheek in wonder. "What's this?" he asked gently. "Why the tears?"

"Hormones," she whispered, but it was more than that. Sometimes when Jessica looked at Pierce, she still couldn't believe how happy they were. Sometimes in the dead of night, with Pierce sleeping peacefully beside her, she would wake up, certain that something would happen to take it all away from her. Just like it had when she was a little girl.

Sensing her need, Pierce took her in his arms. "I'll always be here, Jesse. For you and the baby. We're a real family now. Nothing can change that."

He kissed her again, then turned and, in typical fashion, quickly changed the mood and the subject. But he kept one arm protectively around her shoulders. "I think a celebration is definitely in order here. We've finally remodeled one room in this monstrosity we optimistically call a house, business is picking up at the shop, and Max here will be making his debut in another couple of months. So what do you say, my love? Dinner and dancing tonight? A movie? Or shall we turn in early and celebrate in bed? And I might add that I'm particularly fond of the third choice.'' His dark eyes teased her as his head lowered to kiss her again, but the phone in the hallway rang, interrupting them. He nuzzled her neck. ''Hold that thought,'' he murmured, then turned and left the room.

Moments later when he came back, his smile was missing. The glint in his eyes had disappeared. It wasn't the first time Jessica had noticed his troubled look, but he would never let on to her that anything was wrong. In spite of what he'd said earlier, she couldn't help wondering if he might be having problems with the business.

''Pierce, is something wrong?'' she asked anxiously, touching his arm.

His expression instantly altered as he smiled down at her. ''Everything's fine. Now, where were we?'' He reached for her, pulling her into his arms and holding her close, as if he could somehow protect her from the outside world. Or, from whatever might be troubling him. ''Have you decided what you're in the mood for tonight?''

''Actually…'' Jessica trailed off, trying to shake the dark premonition stealing over her. Her own expression turned coy as she skimmed one finger down the front of his shirt. ''I have this irresistible urge for…''

Pierce's voice deepened. ''For what? For once, tell me exactly what you want, Jesse.''

"I want...some ice cream," she admitted. "I'm dying for butter pecan ice cream."

He groaned. "That's all?"

"Well...for starters."

"In that case, I'd better get to the store." He paused at the door and looked back, lifting his brows suggestively. "Need anything else? Whipped cream? Jell-O?"

"I'm seven months pregnant, Pierce," Jessica reminded him, but the look he gave her had her heart racing just the same.

"And sexier than ever," he added with a wink. "I'll be back in a flash."

By Jessica's calculations, it should have taken Pierce no more than ten minutes to walk to the store, no more than ten minutes inside, no more than ten minutes to get back home.

When he'd been gone an hour, she started to worry.

When he'd been gone two hours, she drove to the store and looked for him, but no one remembered seeing him.

When he'd been gone three hours, she called her brother, Jay Greene, who was a naval officer at the Pentagon in nearby Washington, D.C.

When Pierce had been gone four hours, she called the area hospitals while Jay searched the streets.

At midnight, when he'd been gone ten hours, Jessica sat in the darkened nursery, hugging a teddy bear to her chest as she rocked back and forth, her dry eyes burning with grief. A star had fallen from the ceiling and lay shimmering on the floor near her feet.

It seemed like an omen to Jessica, that fallen star.

Like a symbol of all her lost dreams, her hopeless prayers, her unshed tears.

Because Pierce Kincaid, her beloved husband, had vanished in broad daylight without a trace.

Chapter 1

Five years later...

Where in the world was he?

Jessica glanced at her watch for the umpteenth time as she gave the chocolate batter the requisite fifty stirs. Sundays were the only full days she had to spend with her son, and she'd promised him this morning they'd make brownies together. She'd been out of eggs, though, so she'd sent Max next door to borrow one from her best friend, Sharon McReynolds.

"That was your first mistake," she muttered. Sharon's daughter, Allie, had just acquired a new kitten, a white fluff ball named Snowflake, that attracted five-year-old Max like metal to a magnet.

Jessica grimaced, envisioning the conversation that would ensue with her son as soon as he returned. "Allie's not even as old as I am, Mom, and she has a pet. Why can't I have one?"

Jessica knew the routine by heart because they'd been through it every afternoon for the past four days, ever since Sharon had taken Allie to the animal shelter to pick out a kitten. Explaining to Max that Allie's mom didn't work outside the home and, therefore, had more time than Jessica did to help take care of a pet did no good.

She knew Max already felt cheated because he had to go to the baby-sitter's after morning kindergarten while Allie got to go home and spend the afternoon with her mom. Jessica knew Max thought it also unfair that Allie had a daddy to take her to the zoo on Saturday mornings and work on special projects with her on Sunday afternoons.

Allie had a real family, with a mother *and* a father. Max didn't.

Jessica suspected her son's penchant for superheroes was his own way of trying to make up for the lack of a male role model in his life. Superman and all the other comic-book characters that Max loved and tried to emulate were substitutes for the father he'd never had.

Sometimes Max pretended that his own father was a superhero, off fighting bad guys. That's why he couldn't be here with them now. In spite of the fact that Jessica had told Max his father was dead, she knew that deep down, her son had never really believed it.

Sighing deeply, Jessica wiped a stray lock of hair from her forehead with the back of her hand as she stared out the window, trying to catch a glimpse of Max's red cape as he came through the hedge. Wiping her hands on a dish towel, she reached for the phone just as she heard the screen door on the back porch slam shut. Without turning, Jessica picked up the spoon and began stirring the brownie mix again.

"What took you so long, sweetie?" she asked over her shoulder, trying to hide her impatience. She knew full well what Max's explanation would be.

"You'll never believe what happened."

The deep, masculine voice that responded shocked Jessica to the core. A chill shot up her spine. She whirled to see a tall, dark stranger emptying a bag of groceries into her freezer.

Scream! she commanded. But to Jessica's horror, not a sound escaped her throat.

Run! she ordered, but her feet remained rooted to the floor.

The man stood with his back to her, but even in her terror, Jessica saw that he was tall and lean with dark, unkempt hair. The blue jeans he wore looked old and threadbare, and the cotton shirt was shredded at the hem, as if it had been caught on something sharp.

"It was the weirdest thing, Jesse." He closed the freezer door and opened the refrigerator. "Have you ever arrived somewhere without knowing how you got there? I mean, I left the house, and the next thing I know I'm in front of the ice-cream freezer at Crandall's, and I have no idea how I got there." He chuckled softly as he shook his head. "Anyway, once I finally found the ice cream, I remembered we were out of milk, and then I saw the grapes, and one thing led to another. I forgot the whipped cream, though."

He folded the sack and turned, smiling.

Jessica's knees threatened to buckle. "Dear God." Her hand flew to her mouth. It couldn't be! It couldn't be possible! She clutched the counter for support as she stared at the man, at the darkly handsome face that seemed so familiar and yet so strange.

The brown eyes stared back at her in confusion. "What the devil's the matter with you? You look like you've just seen a ghost."

"You *are* a ghost," Jessica whispered in horror. "You must be."

He started toward her, but she shrank away, her hands still frantically gripping the edge of the counter. "Don't touch me," she pleaded. Then he seemed to look at her, really look at her, for the first time, and he stopped dead in his tracks, as if he'd just been struck by lightning.

For one breathless moment, they eyed each other in utter disbelief.

"Jesse?" His voice was a hushed question. The confusion in his eyes deepened to horror as he continued to stare at her. His gaze roamed over her long black hair, scrutinized her face, studied her slender figure. Then lingered on her flat stomach. "What... what's going on here? Your hair...your face...dear God, the baby...." His voice trailed off as he scrubbed his eyes with his hands. "I must be dreaming," he muttered.

Jessica cowered away from the apparition before her, denied the vision that stood not four feet away. It couldn't be him. It wasn't possible. Not after five years. *Five years!*

She'd long ago resigned herself to the possibility that her husband had met some tragic death because the other alternative—that Pierce had simply tired of their life together and walked away—would have been, in many ways, harder for her to accept. She'd had so many losses in her life. So many abandonments.

But if Pierce had died all those years ago, there was absolutely no explanation for the specter that stood before her now. No *earthly* explanation.

Jessica had the slightly hysterical notion that if she reached out and touched him, her hand would pass right through him. A shiver crawled up her spine as the hair on the back of her neck stood on end. Almost reluctantly she let her gaze move over him.

Whether ghost or man, something about him was different, she realized. He looked older and leaner and…hurt. There were lines on his face she didn't remember, but the scars were the worst. Pierce's face had been so handsome, so perfect. This man was a dark, frightening stranger.

That's it! she thought suddenly. This man *was* a stranger. A stranger who was a dead ringer for Pierce. A new wave of fear washed over her as she stared at him. She began edging toward the door.

"Who are you?" she demanded, but her voice trembled with terror.

He looked at her incredulously. "For God's sake, stop it. You're scaring the hell out of me, Jesse. Is this some kind of sick joke? How can you look so different?" He paused, letting his gaze roam over her again as his eyes clouded in confusion. "My God, I hardly recognize you, but how can that be? How the hell can that be? I've only been gone half an hour."

Jessica could feel the color draining from her face. "Half an hour? My husband has been missing for five years," she whispered.

"Five years?" He gaped at her in horror. "What are you talking about?"

Jessica put trembling hands to her face. "Who *are* you?"

"You know who I am."

"Please tell me your name," she begged. "I have to hear you say it."

Slowly he crossed the tile floor toward her. The knees of his jeans were ripped and his ragged tennis shoes were muddy. A long, jagged scar creased his right forearm, drawing Jessica's gaze for a second longer before she lifted her eyes to his.

The brown eyes were shuttered now, completely unreadable. She didn't know him. He was a complete stranger to her.

He said slowly, "My name is Pierce Kincaid. Now kindly tell me who the hell you are. And where is my wife?"

A stunned hush fell over the room.

It was the kind of silence that always follows some mind-boggling revelation. But why that should be, Pierce couldn't imagine. Why his appearance in his own home should shock anyone was beyond him, but he had the oddest feeling that he'd walked into the last few minutes of a movie, and though the climax was exciting, he had no idea what the hell was going on.

The woman standing before him—face ashen, eyes wide with shock—looked like Jesse, except...different. Her hair was the color of Jesse's, but instead of the short bob of curls with which he was so familiar, it cascaded down the woman's back in gleaming, luscious waves. The wide silver eyes, fringed with thick black lashes, were colder and harder than his wife's. And where Jesse's figure was thin, almost frail-looking, this woman's body was gently rounded with womanly curves.

Pierce felt something stir within him, and he frowned in disgust. He hadn't so much as looked at another woman since he and Jesse were married, and yet this stranger elicited a response from him that seemed disturbingly familiar.

Who was she? A relative? That would explain the overwhelming resemblance. He'd never met any of Jesse's family except for her brother. She rarely talked about her, but Pierce knew Jesse had a sister somewhere. Maybe the woman had simply shown up at their doorstep while he'd been out.

He tried to temper his own shock with a tentative smile. "Are you Jesse's sister?" he asked as he took another step toward her. The woman flinched away, but the coldness in her eyes warmed for a moment with a flash of anger. Doggedly he held out his hand to her. "I'm Jessica's husband."

He watched the last shred of fear fade away from her eyes as a sort of horrified realization dawned in those magnetic gray depths. With an almost visible struggle for control, she pulled herself up straight. She faced him squarely, her eyes dropping to his outstretched hand, then returning to meet his gaze. "Why, you arrogant son of a bitch. What kind of fool do you think I am?"

Her hand swept upward so quickly it seemed to surprise them both. It connected with his cheek, and the stinging sensation triggered an automatic reaction from Pierce. He grabbed her, shoved her up against the edge of the counter and pinned her arms behind her back with one hand while his other hand fastened around her throat.

For one heart-pounding moment, brown eyes stared into gray.

Her face swam before his eyes, a hazy image from a dark dream. Pierce was no stranger to fear. He knew what it looked like, what it smelled like, what it felt like. He could see fear in her eyes again. Could feel her flesh tremble beneath his fingers. For one brief moment, it gave him an almost perverse sense of gratification to be the one to inflict it.

Then the mists cleared, and the face before him was once again a sweet, lovely, familiar face—a face far removed from the blackness, from the explosion of pain behind his eyes. As abruptly as he'd seized her, Pierce released her. He backed away, shocked and sickened by his own reaction.

"My God—" His hands moved to his eyes, as if he could rub away the searing pain in his head. *Black it out,* he mentally instructed himself. *Fade to black.*

The pain subsided, but his stomach still roiled in sickening waves. What the hell was the matter with him? He could easily have hurt her, and he didn't even understand why. He was beginning to think he didn't understand anything. The whole scene seemed so disjointed, like a nightmare fragmented into bits and pieces he couldn't seem to fit together in any way that made sense.

"I don't know why I did that," he mumbled.

She didn't say a word, just stood there looking at him like an animal trapped in a corner. He wished she'd say something, do something to help him understand, to help him put the puzzle together. "Can you…just tell me your name?" he asked with a desperate edge to his voice.

Her fingers were at her throat, massaging the vicious

red mark left by his hand. She moistened her lips with the tip of her tongue, "I think you already know," she said, as the quiver in her voice shook Pierce anew. He felt his muscles tighten with awareness, with anticipation, as if preparing for a situation fraught with danger.

Their gazes clung for one electric moment, and then she whispered into the silence, "I'm Jesse."

Jessica thought for a moment he would collapse. He staggered backward, supporting himself against the counter much as she'd done earlier. Her own knees were shaking so badly she could hardly stand. The sound of her heartbeat seemed to echo through the silence.

Pierce had come back. Somehow, some way, her husband had found his way back to her. But why had he left? Where had he been? And, dear God, why was he here now after all this time? The questions exploded in her head, mirroring the confusion and shock in Pierce's brown eyes.

She closed her eyes, trying to shut him out, but the man standing before her drew her gaze against her will. He looked at once so dear and familiar, and yet so strange and frightening. His once handsome face was haggard and deeply lined. His body, once powerful and athletic, had thinned to gauntness. A narrow white scar sliced the left side of his face, marring what had once been a perfect jawline.

She reached a trembling hand up to touch it. "What happened to you?" she whispered. "Where in God's name have you been?"

He recoiled from her touch, and Jessica instantly drew her hand back, nursing it against her heart as if to hide the bitterness of his rejection. His brown eyes were bleak, distant now. The eyes of a stranger.

"I don't know," he said numbly.

"You don't know what happened to you?" She knew her voice sounded disbelieving, but Jessica couldn't help it. The whole situation was unbelievable. Incredible, but terrifyingly real. "You don't know where you've been for five years? Were you in an accident? Is that how you got those scars?"

Pierce put an unsteady hand to his temple. "I have no idea what you're talking about," he said.

"Are you saying…you don't remember *anything?*"

He shook his head. "I don't know. I remember leaving here to go get ice cream. The next thing I know, I'm standing in front of the freezer in the store. I get the ice cream, I walk back here, and in the space of half an hour, everything has changed. It's like…a nightmare. Am I going crazy, Jesse?"

At that moment, Jessica wasn't completely sure of her own sanity. Her heart was beating against her chest so quickly and so hard that for a second she thought she might actually pass out. She took a deep breath, trying to calm herself. "You walked out that door five years ago," she said shakily, "and until you walked back in a few minutes ago, I hadn't seen or heard from you in all that time. I thought you were dead."

If he noticed the faint note of betrayal in her voice, he chose to ignore it, concentrating instead on her words. "*Five years?* That's impossible!"

"Look at me," she said desperately. "You said yourself I look different. I *am* different. I'm five years older."

His proprietary gaze raked over her, stirring something in Jessica she thought had long since died. She struggled to keep her expression calm, composed, but her mind reeled in confusion. The dark gaze probed her face, making her only too aware of the changes five years had wrought in her appearance.

"If what you say is true, then that must mean—" he trailed off as his gaze dropped to her flat stomach once again "—that must mean...you've had the baby."

In the last few minutes, Jessica's emotions had run the gamut—terror, shock, disbelief, anger and maybe even a glimmer of joy. But the emotion she felt now overwhelmed all the others. The fierce protectiveness for her child settled around her like an impenetrable shield.

Max was *hers*. She'd given birth to him all alone. She'd raised him single-handedly. She'd made the sacrifices, she'd worked the endless hours to provide for a child she loved more than life itself. No one would take that away from her. Max was the one thing in her life she had ever been able to count on.

She opened her mouth—to say what, she was never quite sure—but suddenly the back door slammed, and both of them jumped. In unison, Jessica and Pierce whirled toward the kitchen doorway where five-year-old Max, clad in jeans, a T-shirt and a shiny red Superman cape, stood staring up at them.

The dark hair, the huge brown eyes, the stubborn set of his jaw and chin—all were identical to the stranger who stared back at him.

The very air quivered with emotion. Max's solemn little eyes took the stranger's measure and seemed to find him lacking. His gaze shifted to Jessica then back to Pierce. He squinted his eyes. "Who are you, mister?" he demanded suspiciously.

Jessica's own gaze was locked on Pierce's white face. She could see a muscle throb in his cheek, saw emotion after emotion sweep across his features. There was no mistaking Max's identity. He looked exactly like his father. Pierce took a tentative step toward him.

The slight movement roused Jessica. She made an involuntary sound of protest which drew both pairs of male eyes. She knelt and opened her arms, and Max flew across the room to her. She hugged him tightly against her as both of them stared up at Pierce.

"My God," he said woodenly as he gazed at mother and son across the room, "I don't even know if I'm dead or alive."

He didn't wait for a response but turned and walked through the swinging door of the kitchen. Jessica wanted to go after him but found that her heart was suddenly pulling her in two different directions as Max's little arms caught around her neck and held on for dear life.

"That man's scary, Mom," he whispered, clinging to her. "Is he going to hurt us?"

"No, darling, he won't hurt us," Jessica soothed, hugging him. But even as she gave voice to her denial, she could feel the tender flesh of her neck where Pierce's hand—a real, flesh-and-blood hand—had pressed.

A warning pounded in her brain. *He's a stranger,* she thought. The man somewhere in her house was not the Pierce she had known and loved. Wherever he had been, whatever he'd gone through in the past five years had changed him. She only had to look into those haunted eyes to know that.

Maybe she'd never known him, she thought with a

jolt. She'd shared her life with him, shared his bed, but had she ever really known him?

She thought now, as she'd done for those five years, of all the times he'd been away during their marriage. So many of the trips had been unexpected it seemed now in retrospect. Sometimes when he'd been gone, she hadn't heard from him for days at a time, but the answer to that had seemed very plausible. Many of the remote areas he traveled to in Europe and Asia, looking for treasures for The Lost Attic, his antique shop, didn't have easily accessible telephones. In fact, Jessica had been to some of those off-the-beaten-track places with him.

Back then, it had never occurred to her to question Pierce's absences, the lack of phone calls. She'd simply accepted it. But maybe she should have questioned Pierce. Maybe she wouldn't have gone through the hell she'd gone through the past five years if she'd taken the time to know Pierce Kincaid a little better.

She'd believed what she'd wanted to believe, she realized now, because she'd wanted a home and family so badly. Someone to love her.

Jessica untangled Max's arms from her neck and stood. "Come on, honey. Let's go back over to Sharon's house. You'd like to play with Allie and Snowflake for a little while longer, wouldn't you?"

Max stared up at her with rounded brown eyes. "Are you coming back here?"

"Yes."

"To talk to him?"

"Yes."

Max clung to her hand. "I want to stay with you, Mom. I don't think I like him. I don't want him to hurt you."

She bent and smoothed the dark hair from his forehead. "You don't have to worry about me, Max. I'll be fine. Now, come on. I'll walk you over."

As she and Max stepped outside, Jessica thought how normal everything looked, how perfectly ordinary a spring morning it was. The blue morning glory blossoms that climbed the trellis walls of the summerhouse were opened wide to the early sun. A mild breeze rippled through the trees, stirring the scent of roses and mimosa, and somewhere down the street a lawn mower droned.

Everything was the same, and yet nothing was. Five years ago, when Pierce disappeared, Jessica had thought her life was over. For the first few months, all she'd hoped and prayed for was that he would one day come back to her. As long as no trace of him was found, she couldn't let go of the hope that he was still alive.

But the first time she'd held her tiny son in her arms, the realization had finally hit her. Pierce wasn't coming back. She'd counted on him for everything, depended on him to take care of her, but he was gone. Suddenly she had no one to rely on but herself.

Max had given her life new purpose. Not only had she been both mother and father to her son, but she'd taken over Pierce's antique business, learned everything about it there was to learn, and it had continued to grow into a thriving concern.

She'd accomplished a lot in the past five years, but those accomplishments had demanded restitution. She'd changed, so much so that sometimes when she stared at her reflection in the mirror, she hardly recognized herself. There wasn't a trace of the old, dependent Jesse. She didn't need anyone anymore. Certainly not a man who had walked out on her five years ago. For whatever reason.

Her hand tightened on Max's. She felt his fingers squeeze hers back in response, and Jessica's heart melted with love. She would do anything, anything to protect her little boy.

Together they slipped through the opening in the thick hedge that divided the two properties. Sharon sat on the back porch steps, watching Allie and Snowflake romp in the shady grass beneath an elm tree.

"I knew you couldn't keep Max away," Sharon called gaily. "Might as well come have a cup of coffee while the two of them torment poor Snowflake up a tree."

"Max, come watch!" Allie squealed as she enticed the kitten with a ball of twine. Her squeaky laughter peeled across the yard, an irresistible invitation, but still Max hung back, hugging his mother's leg.

"Go play, Max," Jessica urged.

He looked up at her. "I want to stay with you," he insisted.

Sharon reached over and ruffled his hair. "What's the matter, Superman? How come so shy all of a sudden?"

"There's a strange man at our house," Max announced solemnly, as if that explained everything.

Sharon's cornflower eyes widened as she lifted her gaze to Jessica's. One brow lifted. "How interesting."

Jessica could see the curiosity in her friend's eyes, but didn't bother to explain. How could she, when she didn't understand it herself? "Can Max stay over here for a little while, Sharon? It's really important."

"Well, of course. You know he's always welcome." She turned to Max and grinned. "Allie's been trying to teach Snowflake a new trick. I think she could use a few pointers from Superman.''

That did it. Sharon knew exactly how to appeal to Max's male pride. He took off toward Allie and the kitten, his red cape billowing in the wind.

Sharon returned her curious gaze to Jessica. ''You want to tell me what's going on?''

Jessica sighed. ''I'm not even sure *I* know. I just need some time to deal with…a problem.''

Sharon shrugged. ''You know where to find me if you need me,'' she said, and Jessica knew her friend wouldn't pry any further. Sharon had learned a long time ago that Jessica wouldn't talk about anything until she was ready.

Jessica turned back toward her house, stopping for a moment to take one last look at her son. Sharon had joined the kids, and all three of them were shrieking with laughter as the kitten rolled and tumbled and became hopelessly entangled with string.

As Jessica stood watching them, she had to fight the overwhelming urge to join them, to try to return her world to the nice, sane place it had been that morning when she'd gotten out of bed. But there in her friend's backyard, with the sound of children's laughter filling the air and the scent of spring flowers drifting on the breeze, the realization hit her full force.

Her world would never be the same again.

''Pierce?'' Jessica called tentatively, feeling the strangeness of the name on her tongue. She felt a ripple of anxiety in the pit of her stomach, as if saying his name provided irrefutable proof that the stranger in her house was indeed her dead husband.

Jessica shoved open the swinging door to the dining

room and stepped through, then went on into the living room. The room had been completely renovated nearly three years ago. The dark paneling Jessica had always hated had been replaced by Sheetrock painted a cool robin's-egg blue and decorated with Allenburg watercolors she'd acquired through the shop.

Light from the French doors gleamed on the hardwood floors and highlighted the thick Aubusson rug she'd splurged on just last month. A grouping of chintz-covered sofas and oversize chairs flanked the brick fireplace, and the carved oak mantel held dozens of photos of Max, all lovingly displayed in antique pewter frames.

The pictures looked rearranged, Jessica thought, as if someone had picked them up one by one and hadn't bothered returning them to their original positions. Her eyes moved to the curved staircase, upward to the sunny landing and beyond. Her bedroom was at the top of the stairs, a huge suite which took up most of the second floor except for Max's bedroom. The third floor contained only a converted attic, which Jessica was in the process of turning into a game room.

The hair at the back of her neck prickled with unease. Somewhere in this house a stranger roamed, looking at her things, touching them, laying claim to them.

When Pierce had left, the only room that had been remodeled in the fifty-plus-year-old Georgian-style house had been the nursery. That same room had long since been transformed to accommodate a growing boy's tastes and interests. Was Pierce in there now?

The thought unsettled Jessica more than she cared to admit. Her eyes lit on the phone, and suddenly she wondered if she should call the police, her brother, *someone* to help her deal with this situation.

She closed her eyes and rested her head against the wall. No one could help her. No one could even comprehend what she was feeling at this moment. Even she didn't understand. Because in spite of her fear, in spite of her questions and her doubts, one small part of her heart still rejoiced.

Pierce was alive!

The miracle she'd prayed for for so long had finally happened. She should be down on her knees giving thanks, except for one small detail. Jessica had given up believing in miracles a long time ago. Resolutely she opened her eyes and started toward the stairs, halting when she noticed the powder-room door off the foyer stood open.

"Pierce?" There was no answer, but still she crossed the hardwood floor and entered the small washroom, assuring herself that everything was intact. And then her eyes fastened on the mirror, saw her reflection, and she knew. Pierce wasn't in there, but he had been. He'd gazed into that same mirror, saw his reflection, and he'd learned the awful truth about himself.

Jessica backed out of the bathroom, frantic now to find him.

"Pierce!" She called his name as she stood in the hallway. Colored light filtered through the leaded diamond panes in the front door and spilled onto the polished planks of the floor. The wavering, jewellike shadows drew Jessica's gaze downward, then toward the source. The front door was closed, but the dead bolt had been drawn back, and now it was Jessica who had to face the truth.

Pierce Kincaid had walked out on her one more time.

Chapter 2

A little while later, Jessica sat on the window seat in the dining room and watched the street for her brother's car. How long had it been since she'd cried? she wondered. Not since Max had been born. Not since she'd decided that never again would she depend on anyone but herself. Not since she'd vowed that she would never love again because everyone she'd ever loved had left her.

Except Max.

She drew up her knees and wrapped her arms around them, hugging them close. It was an instinctive response to her pain and confusion. For the first few days in every foster home she'd ever been assigned to, Jessica had similarly retreated into herself, had hugged herself tightly as though recalling the feel of her mother's arms around her. Finally, though, after so many homes she'd lost count, she could no longer remember her mother's face, much less the warmth of her arms.

The orphanage had been better because at least there she'd had Jay. The two of them had clung to each other those first few months after their older sister, Janet, had left them there. Their mother had died, their father had disappeared, and eighteen-year-old Janet hadn't wanted to be saddled with two kids, so one cold December morning, she'd dropped Jessica and Jay at the state-run orphanage in Richmond.

After a year, twelve-year-old Jay had gotten lucky. He'd been adopted by an aging couple in Washington, D.C., who had always wanted a son and realized they were too old to begin raising an infant.

Jessica hadn't been so fortunate. She'd been plain and skinny with unruly hair and eyes far too big and too sad for her ten-year-old face. She'd been shy and sickly and had never developed much of a personality. No one had wanted such an unattractive child.

After Jay left, Jessica had been sent to one foster home after another. She'd bonded fairly well with the first couple, but when the man's job had forced them to move out of state, Jessica had been emotionally ripped apart again. After that, she kept herself aloof, sustaining herself on sparse letters from her brother and on the even sparser memories of her mother.

And then, years later, she'd met Pierce. It was the summer she'd graduated business school and moved to Edgewood, a suburb of D.C., to be close to Jay. Jessica had always sworn it was fate that caused her to answer the ad Jay showed her in a neighborhood newspaper about a bookkeeping position at an antique store not far from her new address. Fate, and perhaps a touch of desperation. She didn't expect the job to pay much, but she'd been making the rounds at employment agencies for weeks with no luck.

Pierce Kincaid, the proprietor of The Lost Attic, had taken one look at her frail body, her faded blue dress, her scuffed shoes, and hired her on the spot.

Pity, she'd accused him later.

Love at first sight, he'd countered.

Jessica still remembered the exact moment when she first laid eyes on him. His assistant was about to turn her away when Pierce walked out of his office and changed her life with one heart-stealing smile.

"I'm Pierce Kincaid," he said, dismissing the assistant with a curt nod of his head. "Welcome to The Lost Attic. What can I do for you?"

Jessica's first thought was that he was the most handsome man she'd ever seen. He had longish dark hair that curled at the nape, and dark, penetrating eyes fringed with thick lashes. He was casually dressed in jeans, a white T-shirt and a gray sport coat, and as he leaned against the counter, he gave her another smile, one that managed to look both mysterious and openly inviting.

"I—I've come about the job," Jessica stammered, her poise completely shattered by his attention.

"Wonderful. How soon would you be able to start?"

His enthusiasm caught her off guard. "Now. Immediately."

"As in today?"

"*Today?* But I—"

"You said immediately," he reminded her, a subtle gleam in his eyes. "I'm rarely here, you see, and I need someone I can depend on to handle things while I'm away. My previous bookkeeper up and quit without notice. Financial statements are due, tax payments are late, the bank is screaming about overdrafts, and I'm due in Copenhagen tomorrow morning. Frankly, I'm desperate. So can you start today, Ms....?''

"Greene. Jessica Greene. And yes I can," she added quickly, before he could change his mind.

He grinned. "Great. Let me show you your office then."

"But don't you even want to see my résumé?" She'd worked so hard on it, had even splurged on a rental typewriter.

He shook his head. "I know a good thing when I see it."

Nonplussed, Jessica gazed around the shop, admiring the treasures. "You have a wonderful store," she murmured.

"Do you know anything about antiques?"

"No. But I know a lot about bookkeeping."

He smiled, and Jessica felt a tingle all the way to her toes. "That's fine. I tell you what, Jessica. You teach me enough bookkeeping so that I know my way around a ledger, and I'll teach you everything I know about antiques. And then some. How does that sound?"

It sounded wonderful. Too good to be true, in fact. Within days, Jessica had settled into the routine of her new job. When she'd been working for Pierce for three months, true to his word, he began teaching her about antiques.

"This is a Lowell," he'd say as he showed her an exquisite glass sculpture. "See the marking on the bottom? Lowells aren't as famous as Steubens, of course, but the designs are original and highly detailed. Andrew Lowell died so young, there aren't many of his pieces around and most of the ones that are documented are in private collections. But I found this in a little shop on the outskirts of Paris. The owner didn't realize what he had.''

Jessica was like a sponge. She drank in every word Pierce uttered, exclaimed over the beauty of each and every piece he brought back from his treasure hunts. She loved being surrounded by beautiful things with fascinating histories, possibly because her own past was so dismal. She adored having Pierce spend hours talking to her, devoting his time solely to her. She'd never had so much attention before.

When she'd been working for him for six months, he gave her a raise and added responsibilities. He began leaving her in charge when he went on his regular jaunts overseas. When he returned, he'd tell her intriguing stories about the places he'd been to and the people he'd met as they pored over his findings.

''Pop quiz today, Jessica. Tell me how we can be certain this is an authentic Allenburg watercolor?'' he would ask, a teasing glint in his dark eyes as he and Jessica unwrapped the paintings.

With a magnifying glass, Jessica would locate the tiny hidden water lily which identified the artist's work, and Pierce would smile his approval. ''Excellent. Perhaps you deserve a reward,'' he would say, with that mysterious, sexy smile that always sent her heart racing. And then he'd take her out to lunch at some little out-of-the-way place, which would have both excellent service and scrumptious food. And for the rest of the day, Jessica would feel special and pampered.

When she'd been with Pierce a year, he began taking her on buying trips with him occasionally. Slowly but surely, under Pierce's expert tutelage, Jessica began to blossom, to come out of her self-imposed exile. And slowly but surely she was falling madly, passionately, desperately in love with her boss.

When she'd been with Pierce fifteen months, he asked her to marry him. They were in Paris, and at first Jessica convinced herself that the romantic ambiance of the city of light, the effusive flow of champagne at the Cochon d'or had made Pierce impulsive.

"If I were impulsive," he explained, staring at her over the flickering candle on their discreetly located table, "I would have proposed to you the first time I laid eyes on you. Because I knew even then that you and I were meant to be, Jesse. You knew it, too, didn't you?"

"Yes," she whispered. "I knew it."

"Then say you'll marry me," he demanded, his eyes glowing with triumph.

"I'll marry you," she said, and then he lifted her hand and slipped a beautiful antique diamond and garnet ring onto her finger.

"You won't regret it. I'll make you so happy you'll forget all about the past."

"I already have," she vowed.

Weeks later, they were married and settled into their home in a lovely neighborhood only a few miles from the shop. Edgewood, located a few miles from Langley, Virginia, and across the river from Washington, D.C., was home to a lot of government and military employees. Though not as pricey as Georgetown or Alexandria, it still boasted many of the same attractions: tree-shaded sidewalks, cobblestone streets, elegant old Federal and Georgian homes, as well as a close proximity to the nation's capital.

Jessica loved her job at the shop, but she gladly gave it up to concentrate on remodeling and redecorating their home. She had no higher aspiration than to be the perfect wife and mother. She loved Pierce dearly, needed him desperately.

How could she have known back then that the one person she held most dear, loved more than life itself, would eventually leave her just like all the others had?

Jessica rested her forehead against her knees as she closed her eyes, trying to push away the memories. Why? she asked herself over and over.

Why had Pierce left her?

And why had he come back?

How could he not remember five years of his life? And yet that was exactly what he'd told her. What had been five years of grief and loneliness, struggle and frustration for Jessica had only been a mere thirty minutes in time to him. What could have happened to him?

He'd been hurt. She could tell that by the scars on his face and arm. It made her shudder to think what he might have gone through. There was only a shadow remaining of the man she'd known, loved, adored. But was that shadow merely a mirage? Was there anything left of the man from her past?

At that moment, Jessica wasn't sure she could handle the truth—whatever it turned out to be.

Pierce walked the streets. By force of sheer will, his tired legs carried him farther and farther away from that house. From his home. From his wife. From his son.

The image of those huge dark eyes in that solemn little face brought stinging tears to his own eyes. He rubbed the back of his hand across them, trying to erase the vision as he wiped away the moisture. He had a son. Dear god, a five-year-old boy he didn't even know.

And Jesse. Sweet, lovely, fragile Jesse. She seemed so cold, so hard, so suspicious. But five years had elapsed, she'd said. Five years! How could that be? How the hell could that be? Pierce asked himself desperately.

Just a moment in time for him had been five years of limbo for her. One glance in the mirror had told him she wasn't lying—not that Jesse ever would. Not his Jesse, he thought as his fingers moved to touch the scar on his face.

But the woman back there, the cold-eyed, beautiful stranger was not his wife. He felt something of the loss and betrayal now that she must have felt so long ago when he hadn't come back, and he despaired for them both.

A car horn blasted in his ear, and Pierce jumped back from the curb, startled to alertness. The driver shook his fist at him as the car zoomed through the intersection.

Pierce paid him scant attention. Automatically he waited for the traffic light to change, then walked aimlessly across the street. A bright red Coca-Cola sign flashed in the morning sun over a corner café, reminding him rather urgently that he was hungry. He couldn't remember the last time he'd eaten. He couldn't remember anything, in fact, beyond two hours ago.

That wasn't exactly true, he realized. Ever since he'd seen Jesse's shocked face, he'd been experiencing certain…impressions. Impressions of darkness and pain, of wandering around hopelessly lost but knowing all the while there was some place he should be, had to be. That certainty had driven him relentlessly through the mists until, almost as if he'd awakened from a long, deep sleep, he'd found himself at the grocery store and everything had clicked back into place.

For Pierce, the world had stopped for five years, then started back up again in exactly the same place. But why? And how?

He gazed at the scar on his left arm. What the hell had happened to him?

Checking his pockets, he pulled out the bills and change he'd gotten back from the twenty he'd used at the grocery store earlier. He had no idea where the money had come from. Someone must have given it to him....

Suddenly the street noises faded. His surroundings disappeared. For just a flash of time, Pierce was back on an island, standing on the beach, staring at the sky. A bird soared high overhead, silhouetted in the brilliant sunlight. It was an image that instantly brought back feelings of anger and betrayal. A nagging premonition of danger. And then a man's voice at his shoulder. "You'll need money. Here's all I can spare. Go home now. Find your family and protect them."

The vision vanished, leaving Pierce with a pounding headache in the warm morning sunshine.

Find your family and protect them.

Against what? Against whom?

For a moment, Pierce fought an almost overpowering urge to turn around, to go back home and make sure Jesse and his son were okay. But they'd managed just fine for five years without him. How could he help them now? How could he protect them from something he couldn't even remember?

Wearily he put his hands to his temples, massaging away the pain as the memories and the feelings began to evaporate in the sunshine.

His stomach rumbled again—a demand for fuel—and Pierce knew that whatever had to be faced would best be done by getting back his strength. Besides, Jesse needed some space, and he needed time to figure out what to do.

He opened the glass door of the café and stepped inside. As disreputable as the place seemed to be, his appearance still garnered a few curious looks. He chose a table in the back and carefully studied the one-page menu. The meager selections tempted his appetite beyond reason, making him wonder again just how long it had been since he'd eaten. He chose a club sandwich, then checked his money again after the waitress had taken his order.

The bells over the door chimed, and Pierce's head swung around, his gaze immediately scrutinizing the man who had just walked in. He was tall and thin with light brown hair and a thick mustache. He took a seat at the counter, and Pierce studied the man's back for a full thirty seconds, not understanding his own wariness.

Did he know that man?

Caution. It was a deeply ingrained command, an almost instinctive behavior. Pierce's gaze scoured the room, then came back to his own hands resting on the chipped Formica tabletop. They were trembling—from fatigue and hunger as well as emotion—but what caught his attention now was the raw, broken skin across his knuckles. He studied his hands as though they belonged to a stranger. They were scarred and dirty, the nails broken. Disgusted, he rose from his seat and located the men's room nearby.

Trying to avoid his reflection in the mirror, Pierce scrubbed his hands with hot water and soap. The raw places on his knuckles stung, but he ignored the pain, automatically blacking it out. When his hands were as clean as he could get them, he filled the basin with cold water and plunged his face into it, hoping the icy shock would restore his memory.

Why was it he could remember Jesse and their life together so clearly, so vividly, and not anything about the immediate past? He could remember his childhood, his parents and the sterile, loveless home he'd grown up in. He remembered college at Georgetown and even friends he hadn't seen or heard from in years. He could remember traveling in Europe and Asia before he'd met Jesse, and the secret he'd deliberately kept from her, the side of himself he'd never told her about.

Guilt welled inside him as he thought about the evasions and half truths he'd told her for years. She'd innocently accepted each and every one without question.

Except for the past five years, the memories were all coming back to him now, pouring through his mind so fast he felt a little dizzy.

For years, before he'd met Jesse, Pierce had been a specialized agent for a very elite agency that operated within the CIA. Very few operatives even had knowledge of the group whose specialty was deep cover. Pierce had been recruited out of college because he had a certain reputation for living on the edge and because of the antique business he'd inherited from his parents. It gave him the perfect excuse to travel around the world without arousing questions. His real identity had become a deep cover for him, the very best kind because no one ever suspected.

Not even Jesse.

He gazed at his reflection in the mirror. He'd never told her even after they'd married—not just because of the oath he'd sworn to uphold—but because he'd always thought the less she knew the safer she'd be. It had been his duty to protect her.

It still was.

The washroom door swung open, and Pierce whipped his head around, his hand reaching for a weapon he knew instinctively he hadn't had in years. The man who'd been sitting at the bar now stepped inside the room. He gave Pierce barely a glance as he headed for a basin and began washing his hands. Quickly Pierce drained the sink, then combed his fingers through his damp hair, trying without much success to look a little more presentable.

The man was studying him in the mirror. Pierce turned and their gazes met. He searched the man's face for some sign of recognition. Something other than the niggle of suspicion was worrying him.

"Nice day, isn't it?" the man asked pleasantly as he dried his hands on a paper towel.

"It'll probably rain this afternoon," Pierce replied automatically, not exactly sure where the response had come from.

Somehow the answer seemed expected. Something flashed in the man's blue eyes, and then he smiled slightly, his mustache tilting at one corner. "One thing's for sure. You can never predict the weather this time of year. Be a fool to try." Then he turned, tossed the paper towel in the trash bin and exited the washroom.

Shaken by the encounter and having no idea why, Pierce waited a few seconds, then followed the man out. The stranger was seated at the counter again and didn't look around. But Pierce's appetite was gone. He tossed some bills onto the table and hurried through the café door.

Outside, the sun blinded him. Pierce leaned against the building's redbrick facade as the full realization of his plight hit him square in the face. He'd just spent the last of his money, he was still hungry, and he had absolutely nowhere to go.

Wiping a streak of sweat from his temple, he pushed himself away from the building and started walking down the street.

"Now, let me get this straight," Jay Greene said as he sat across the kitchen table from Jessica. "You're telling me that Pierce Kincaid—a man who disappeared five years ago—strolled through your back door this morning as if he'd only been gone half an hour?"

Jessica nodded weakly. "He even brought me the ice cream I'd sent him out to get that day, right down to the correct flavor."

"And you have no idea where he is now?"

"I took Max next door, and when I came back, he was gone. That was this morning, Jay. He looked so tired, so...ill. I can't help but think of him out there wandering the streets. It'll be dark soon—" The look on Jay's face stopped her.

"I wouldn't get carried away with the pity just yet,

Jesse. This whole memory thing seems a little too convenient for me.''

''You think he's lying?'' Her voice sounded anxious, shaky.

''Wouldn't be the first time a husband just up and
took off. Think about it.''

She had thought about it. Endlessly. ''But…we
were so happy,'' Jessica protested. ''We were both
excited about the baby. The shop was doing great,
we'd just bought this house—''

''And maybe he woke up one morning and decided
he couldn't handle the responsibilities anymore. It
happens, and Pierce Kincaid was always a bit foot-
loose, if you ask me. You said yourself he ran the
business in a haphazard fashion, and frankly he never
struck me as the family-man type.

''Now, out of the blue, he appears on your doorstep,
just when you've gotten your own life in order. Look
at this place, Jesse. It's worth a small fortune, and so
is the shop. When he tired of whatever the hell he was
doing, why wouldn't he want to come back here?''

Jessica stared absently out the window. Jay wasn't
telling her anything she hadn't thought of herself, but
it still wasn't easy to hear. It wasn't easy to think that
Pierce might have walked out on her. That he had lied
about his feelings for her.

She had been so sure. So sure their love had been
real.

A breeze lifted the hem of the pale blue curtains as
it carried in the evening scents—honeysuckle, clover
and roses. Years ago, after long days at the shop, she
and Pierce would sit on the back porch and sip wine
while they watched the first stars twinkle out. Twilight
had always been a special time of day for them, a time

when the cares of the day melted away into the coming darkness.

Had none of that meant as much to him as it had to her?

As if echoing her thoughts, Jay covered her hand with his and asked softly, "How do you feel about him now, Jesse? What was it like seeing him again?"

She sighed. "I'm not sure. I know you're right. I do have to be careful, but you didn't see him. I think he must have been in some sort of accident. He has all these scars. Do you think—could he have been kidnapped five years ago? Held all this time?"

"With no ransom note?" Her brother looked skeptical. "It's possible. Hell, anything's possible. But victims who're kidnapped either in a robbery or for sport usually turn up dead. Five years is a long time to hold someone captive."

"I know," Jessica agreed, her tone bleak. "I just keep asking myself where he could have been all this time. What could have happened to him?"

"Did he have any identification on him?"

Jessica shrugged. "I don't know. I didn't ask to see it. I didn't need to."

"You're that sure it was him?" Jay's icy gray eyes scrutinized her face.

"It *was* him. It was Pierce."

Jay swept his hand through his brown hair, setting it on end. He shook his head. "Damn, what a mess. You know I'll do what I can, but I couldn't find out anything about him five years ago. It was as if he disappeared off the face of the earth. We may not have any better luck now."

"I just want you to find him," she whispered desperately. "Whatever he's done, wherever he's been—he needs help."

"*Your* help?"

Jessica hesitated for a moment, biting her lip. "He's still my husband."

"Technically," her brother agreed grimly. "All right, I'll see what I can do." He took out a pen and pad and began jotting down notes. "Give me a general physical description of how he looked, what he was wearing and all that. And how about a cup of coffee? This looks to be a long night," he said with a sigh.

Jessica rose from the table and reached for a cup, but the barking of a neighbor's dog stilled her movements. A shadow swept across the open window, so swiftly she thought at first she'd imagined it. Then came a scraping noise on the back porch, as if someone had bumped into a chair.

Jessica's gaze flew to Jay's, her heart hammering in her chest. He lifted a finger to his lips, silencing her. Slowly he reached for the light switch just as the sound of the back-door buzzer ripped through the quiet. Jessica gasped and Jay cursed softly as both their gazes fastened on the dark silhouette outside her kitchen door.

Chapter 3

At Jay's nod, Jessica rose and went to answer the back door. Heart still pounding, she turned the knob and drew back the door. Pierce stood on the porch, his pale, gaunt features highlighted by the light from the open doorway. If possible, he looked even more weary than he had that morning.

For the longest moment, he and Jessica stared at one another. Neither of them spoke, but the tension crackled between them like a live wire in an electrical storm.

Then his hands slipped into the front pockets of his jeans and he shrugged, a gesture that was at once familiar and dear. The ghost of a smile touched his lips. "I seemed to have lost my key," he said wryly.

They both seemed to waver with indecision. Then with a little gasping sob, Jessica took a step toward him as Pierce moved toward her. His arms went around her and held her tightly as she clung to him, her eyes squeezed shut against the intense emotions spiraling through her.

Pierce was alive!

For a moment, everything else vanished from Jessica's mind. She just wanted to hold him, assure herself that this was no dream. He buried his face in her hair, and she could feel his arms trembling as they held her, could feel his heart beating against hers. One hand came up and brushed through her tangled curls.

"I'm sorry," he whispered raggedly. "Maybe I shouldn't have come back here, but...I had to. I had to see you again, to make sure you were all right...."

"It's okay," she said, her voice cracking with deep emotion. She could feel the leanness of his body against her, the sharply defined ridges of his ribs through the ragged shirt. Pierce had once been so virile and muscular. To see him now made Jessica's heart ache with sorrow.

But even now, when he'd been through God knows what, she could still sense remnants of strength in his arms, a hint of the same confidence she had always admired so much. Pierce was not a man who would be taken down without a fight.

That thought struck her with cold reality. Was that why he had all the scars? Had he been fighting for his life all this time? *Dear God...*

As if sensing her thoughts, she felt his posture stiffen. She lifted her head and saw that he was staring over her shoulder, his dark eyes wary once more.

"Hello, Jay," he said with a thin smile. "Aren't you out of uniform?"

Jessica had forgotten all about her brother. Awkwardness now settled over the room like a funeral pall. She tried to pull away from Pierce, but his arms held her for a fraction longer, as if staking his claim before letting her go.

"I didn't think this was an official visit," Jay said. But even without his uniform, he stood military straight, his cool gaze taking Pierce's measure without blinking.

Jessica backed away, her gaze darting from Pierce to Jay. Her brother's expression must have been identical to the one she'd worn that morning. The mixture of suspicion, disbelief, anger and even touches of fear echoed in Jay's gray eyes.

It seemed a million years before either of them spoke again. Jessica's heart raced with tension as she stared up at Pierce, once again taking in the haggard features, the scar.

Pierce smiled. "You haven't changed a bit."

"Not where my responsibilities are concerned," Jay agreed. "Shall we all sit down? Jesse, can you get us some coffee?"

The command finally motivated her. Jessica headed toward the coffeepot, relieved to have something to do. She could feel Pierce's dark eyes on her, following her every movement. Reluctantly her own gaze lifted to meet his. Something flashed between them—a memory? A feeling? Jessica wasn't sure. But all of a sudden, she felt a tiny shiver of warning scurry up her spine.

Pierce's proprietary gaze moved over her, greedily, familiarly, making her body tingle with memories she'd long ago suppressed. He was looking at her the way she remembered him looking at her. The brown eyes were narrowed slightly, the long, thick lashes hooding his expression, but Jessica knew what he was thinking. She'd always known.

She said the first thing that came to her mind. "You look hungry."

"Starving." His eyes never left her mouth.

Her face flamed at the inadvertent—or not so inadvertent—innuendo. Nervously she wiped her moist palms on a paper towel as she moved past him toward the refrigerator.

"Actually, what I'd really like to do is get cleaned up," Pierce said. He started toward the kitchen door, then checked himself as he looked back at her. "Is that all right?"

"Of course."

He hesitated, his gaze unreadable. "Where?"

That jolted her. Where, indeed? She'd long since removed his belongings from her bedroom, except for a few mementos she couldn't bring herself to part with. The idea of him once again occupying that room was distinctly uncomfortable.

The question of where he should shower brought up a whole new set of problems for Jessica. Where would he stay? Where would he sleep? What did he expect from her? They were still legally married, but five years was a long time. Even if he had no memory of their separation, the reality of those long, lonely years still breathed a life of their own inside Jessica's heart. Surely he didn't expect just to waltz back in and pick up where they'd left off five years ago.

But if he was really suffering from amnesia, then that's exactly what he would expect. His feelings hadn't changed—even if hers had.

Her gaze lifted again, and Pierce's eyes trapped her with a look she thought seemed slightly reproachful, as if he'd read her exact thoughts. She blushed again and said almost defiantly, "Sometime ago, I moved all your things into the guest room downstairs. You'll find fresh towels in the bathroom. Everything you need...."

Her voice trailed off at his look. Not everything, he seemed to be communicating. Then he turned and disappeared through the swinging door to the dining room.

Silence quivered in the air for a long moment, then Jay said, "Well, I'll be damned. I wouldn't have believed it if I hadn't seen it with my own eyes."

With shaking fingers, Jessica pulled the makings of a sandwich from the refrigerator and placed each item carefully on the counter. "So...what do you think?" she asked, not daring to meet her brother's eyes. He'd already seen more than she would have wanted him to. Her reaction when she'd first seen Pierce at the door had been purely spontaneous, an overreaction to the tumultuous emotions racing through her. She hadn't stopped to think about what she was doing, about the wrong signals she might be sending to Pierce.

Now she did stop to think, and she regretted the embrace because it had instantly created a bond between them, an intimacy that was far more than she could deal with right now. She was glad Pierce was alive. More than glad. Joyful. Thankful. They'd conceived a son together. But the years apart had been longer than the years they'd had together. There was no way they could ever go back to what they'd once had.

She hoped to God Pierce understood that.

Jay got up and carried his cup across the room to the coffeepot. He poured himself a fresh cup, took a tentative sip, and grimaced. "Damn, Jesse, I wish you'd learn to make a decent cup of coffee."

"My mind was elsewhere, okay?" she snapped.

"Hey, don't bite *my* head off. I'm an innocent bystander in all this."

"Sorry." She dropped down at the kitchen table and propped her chin in her hand. "What am I supposed to do?" she asked in desperation. "I don't even know him anymore, and he doesn't know me. I don't know where he's been, what he's done, why he's back. I'm not even the same person he left five years ago. I've grown up. I've taken charge of my life. I don't—"

"Need him anymore?" Jay nodded. "I'm sure he'll find that out soon enough, if he sticks around."

"What do you mean *if?*" Jessica raked impatient fingers through her hair as she stared at her brother. "You think he's going to leave me…leave again?"

Jay shrugged as he brought his coffee to the table and sat down again. "Let's just say I'm trying to keep an open mind. Wherever he's been, he's had trouble. You only have to look at him to know that much. What I can't help wondering is what kind. And if he's bringing it back here with him."

Jessica's silver gaze rested on Jay's stern countenance. "Meaning he could be on the run?"

Her brother merely shrugged as he lifted the cup to his lips. But his gray eyes were darkened with worry. "Max is next door with Sharon, right?"

His tone was a little too casual. Jessica found herself shivering with an eerie premonition as she nodded. "She called earlier and asked if he could stay the night. Under the circumstances, I thought it was a good idea."

"So do I."

Their gazes met again, and Jessica saw her own uneasiness mirrored in Jay's eyes. But before either of them could speak, the kitchen door swung inward and Pierce stepped into the room.

Jessica's gaze instantly collided with his. He looked better, she had to admit. Much better. His dark hair, still glistening with dampness, had been carefully combed and the days-old growth of beard had been scraped away, accentuating even more dramatically the white scar down his cheek, the deep creases around his eyes and mouth.

The jeans he'd put on were old and worn, a pair he used to favor for puttering around the house. But even though they were frayed at the hem and shiny at the knees, they were far better than the disreputable pair he'd discarded. They hung loosely on his gaunt frame, reminding Jessica of how snugly they had once fitted him, how sexy he'd always looked in them.

He wore a blue cotton shirt—sleeves rolled up, tail out—that triggered yet another memory for Jessica. He'd worn a blue shirt the day he'd disappeared. Had he remembered that, too, or was his selection an ironic coincidence?

He returned her appraisal, the deep brown eyes warm and seeking as they moved slowly over her face and then downward. Her own jeans fitted a little *too* snugly. She'd always been pencil thin, but after Max was born, she'd filled out and had never been able to drop the extra ten pounds. Actually, she'd always been happy with the added weight, but now she found herself wondering what Pierce thought.

The sudden warmth spiraling through her veins shocked her. And scared her. It had been a long time since she'd felt sexual desire. Not since Pierce had left.

Sex with him had been wonderful because it was with *him*. But before she'd met him and after he'd left, abstinence had never been a problem for her.

Pierce had always teased her that she was like a car engine on a frosty morning. She had to be warmed up properly to get the best mileage. Jessica's cheeks heated at the memory.

Finally breaking eye contact, she jumped up from the table and busily began assembling his sandwich. Pierce sat down at the table across from Jay, and the two men eyed each other stonily, reminding Jessica that, to her despair, they'd never been the best of friends. She placed the plate in front of Pierce, and their hands touched briefly before Jessica drew hers back.

"What would you like to drink?" she asked in a brisk tone.

"It's been a long time since I've had a beer," he suggested with a smile that sent a new wave of awareness washing over her.

"How would you know that?" Jay asked quietly. "I thought you lost your memory."

Pierce's head swiveled so that his eyes met Jessica's. "It's just an impression, not a memory. I think I've done without a lot of things."

The bottle almost slipped from Jessica's fingers. Hands shaking, she poured the beer into a mug and set it beside Pierce's plate, careful this time to avoid his touch. She sat down at the table and watched him attack the sandwich.

His appetite seemed ravenous, though she could tell he tried to curb his urgency. The sandwich disappeared in seconds.

"Would you like another one?" she asked softly, her heart feeling as if it would break in two.

The idea of seconds seemed to shock him for a moment. Then he said, "If you're sure it wouldn't be too much trouble."

It took Jessica a long time to make the second sandwich. She stood at the counter, her back to the men as she tried to gather her shattered poise. But as soon as she wiped away the silent tears from her face, a new batch would take their place. Instinctively she knew she wouldn't let him see her pity. That was the worst thing she could do to a man like Pierce.

At last, sniffing as unobtrusively as she could, Jessica placed the sandwich on the table and said hurriedly, "If you'll excuse me for a moment, I, uh, have something to do in the other room."

She all but fled the kitchen, leaving dead silence in her wake.

After a few seconds, Pierce picked up the other sandwich and began eating. Jay reached into the inside pocket of his jacket and withdrew a pack of cigarettes and lit up, leisurely blowing a thin stream of smoke skyward.

"I thought you'd quit," Pierce said as he eyed his brother-in-law curiously.

"I've quit several times since you left. If I hadn't already started again this last time, I'm sure I would have after tonight."

Pierce's brows arched. "I'm glad I don't have to take the responsibility then."

Jay blew a trail of smoke from the corner of his mouth as he spoke. "What about your other responsibilities? You as anxious to dismiss those?"

"Meaning?"

"Jessica and Max. You left them high and dry five years ago. If it wasn't for Jesse's grit and determination, I'm not sure what they would have done."

"You don't have to remind me of my responsibilities to my wife and son. I'll take care of them from now on."

Jay crushed his cigarette in his saucer as he stared at Pierce. "You still don't get it, do you? They don't need you to take care of them. Jesse's managed just fine without you. More than fine. The business you left behind is booming, thanks to her. This house is worth a small fortune, and Max, well, Max won't even know you, will he?"

It was a reality Pierce had been trying to come to terms with since he'd stared into those wide, accusing eyes this morning. Max. How strange that Jessica had named him that after she'd fought him so hard about it. It gave Pierce a small thrill of happiness to know that even after he'd left, Jessica had still wanted to please him.

"Look." Jay folded his arms on the table and leaned toward Pierce. "Let's cut through the crap, shall we? This memory business may work with Jesse, but it won't wash with me. I can recognize a man in trouble when I see one, and I'd say you, my friend, are definitely in trouble. You don't have to tell me what, you don't have to tell me how or when or who. All you have to tell me, Kincaid, is *why?* Why did you come back here?"

"This is my home."

"*Was* your home."

Brown eyes challenged gray. It gratified Pierce to see Jay glance away first. He'd always thought his brother-in-law a little too cocky, a little too self-possessed. Pierce could spot a phony when he saw one, but he'd never had the heart to tell Jesse just how one-sided her sibling devotion was.

"This is my home," he said, feeling the warmth of anger stealing over him. "I don't have to justify myself to you. I may owe Jesse an explanation, one I don't have at the moment, but let's get one thing straight. I don't owe you a damned thing."

The air buzzed with tension. Jay's gray eyes glinted with steely anger as he half rose from his seat. The unspoken challenge lay in the air between them like a gauntlet thrown to the ground. Slowly Pierce stood up.

"What's going on in here?"

Both male heads whipped around to find Jessica standing in the doorway, watching them with an expression that wavered between curiosity and disgust. Her assessing gaze went from one to the other as she did her own summation of the situation.

Jay spoke first. "I need to be shoving off, Jessica. But I don't want to leave until I know everything's all right here."

Her expression softened as she smiled at her brother. "I'm okay. Thanks for coming over."

Jay's gaze returned to Pierce. "Can I drop you somewhere?" he asked bluntly.

The question struck Pierce like a physical blow. He was being asked to leave his own home. For one black moment, it was all he could do to curb the sudden rage hurtling through him. He turned to face Jessica who still hovered in the doorway. He tilted a brow in question.

Her gaze burned into Pierce's until his heart started to pound. What was she thinking? he wondered. Did she still feel anything at all for him? It was impossible to think that for him only a moment ago they had been in love, happy, and now she might feel nothing at all for him except pity.

God help him, he could stand anything but that.

Jessica took a deep breath and released it as if she was gathering her courage for what she needed to say. Pierce's own breath seemed suspended somewhere in his throat.

"This is your home, too, Pierce," she said finally. "I can't ask you to leave. Not when...." Her voice trailed off as she gazed at him, the gray of her eyes turning to mist. Pierce knew how he must look to her, and it made him cringe.

"Go on," he said evenly.

Her gaze dropped. "Not when you obviously need a place to stay."

"Jessica, for God's sake, what do you think you're doing?" Jay objected. "He can't stay here. What about Max?"

"What about Max?" Pierce said in a deadly quiet voice that seemed to hold both brother and sister in thrall.

"My God, man, you have to know what this will do to him. He's only five years old."

"I'll take care of Max," Jessica said, and the firm note of resolve in her voice surprised Pierce. Once she would have turned to him to make such an important decision.

Five years, he thought again. Five years of his life gone in the blink of an eye. How much more was lost to him than just that time?

"I hope to hell you know what you're doing," Jay muttered angrily as he pushed past them both and strode out of the kitchen.

Jessica chewed her bottom lip, a nervous habit Pierce remembered so well. It heartened him to know that at least some things hadn't changed.

"I'll be right back," she said, then turned and hurried after her brother. Pierce hesitated a moment, then pushed through the door, too, distracted once again by all the changes Jesse had carried out on the house. Changes they had once planned to work on together.

Had she done all this by herself? he wondered as he walked through the formal dining room. The decor was elegant, but somehow the room left him cold. It was almost too perfect, he thought, remembering the house he'd grown up in. There was no life in it. No warmth. No love. It was a room that matched the hard chill in Jessica's eyes.

He walked through to the living room and looked around. He liked this room better. The pictures of Max in here added a homey touch that somehow soothed him.

Jessica had walked her brother to the door, and now they both stood in the foyer, their furtive whispers attesting to the nature of their conversation.

Pierce crossed the hardwood floor to the fireplace and picked up one of the pictures of Max he'd studied so intently that morning. A baseball cap angled over the boy's forehead as his brown eyes squinted into the sun. There was a rip in his shorts and a scab on one scrawny knee.

Pierce's heart melted. He'd loved the baby Jesse had been carrying, and now he loved this little boy with an intensity that astounded him.

Jessica stood at the end of the sofa and watched Pierce. He didn't look up, and she realized he hadn't heard her come in. She watched him trace a finger

gently along the photo, and the look of fierce possessiveness that came over his face shocked her. Her
heart skidded with warning as her own defenses rose
in reaction.

Pierce glanced up, and the expression in his eyes
confirmed her deepest fears. When he spoke, his voice
gave rise to new ones. Jessica trembled with dread as
his gaze continued to hold hers.

''Where is he, Jessica? Where's my son?''

Chapter 4

Jessica tried to keep her voice controlled. She didn't want to give away her fear, didn't want to appear weak or vulnerable even to Pierce. Especially to Pierce. "Max isn't here," she said, glancing away.

"Where is he?"

"He's somewhere...safe."

"Safe? That's a strange term to use."

Her eyes challenged him. "Is it?"

He lifted his brow, and the scar twisted it, giving him an almost sinister appearance. "Are you implying that I'm a threat to our son? Or to you?"

Jessica hesitated, then said, "You barely resemble the man I knew back then. You've obviously been hurt. Maybe you're even in some sort of trouble. God knows what might have happened to you since you left. You've been gone for five years, Pierce. *Five years.* I don't even know who you are anymore," she finished in a whisper.

His voice lowered. "I'm your husband."

"Technically," she said, borrowing Jay's term. Jessica took a deep breath and let it out, trying to calm her pounding heart. She walked over to the window and stared out into the darkness. "Can you even begin to imagine what this is like for me? All those years you were gone and not one word, not one clue, and now suddenly here you are, acting like nothing's happened. Acting like you think…everything should be the same between us. It's not. It's not the same." She turned and faced him. "It'll never be the same again."

His eyes close briefly. "Don't say that."

"Why not? It's the truth. I don't want to hurt you, but the sooner we face it, the better off we'll both be."

"My God, Jesse." He spread his hands in appeal. "You're acting like you think I left because I wanted to. And given your background, I guess I can understand that. My…disappearance—whatever you want to call it—must have seemed like the ultimate betrayal to you. You must have felt as though I had deserted you, too."

"You can't know how I felt," she said, crossing her arms.

"No, I guess I can't," he agreed. "But one thing I do know. I didn't leave you because I wanted to."

Her chin lifted a fraction. "Then why did you leave me?"

"I've already told you," he said helplessly. "I don't know what happened."

"You have no idea?"

Pierce hesitated, as if searching for the right words. "I have no memory of the past five years," he finally said.

"It's incredible," she whispered. "So hard to believe."

"Yes, it is," he agreed. "It's even hard for me to believe. So I guess I have to ask you, Jesse, given the circumstances, where does this leave us? Where do we go from here?"

Jessica made a futile gesture with her hand. "I don't know. I think the first thing you should do is see a doctor, but beyond that...I just don't know...." Her words trailed off as she glanced away. She couldn't bear to look at him any longer. Couldn't bear to see what the past five years had done to him. To her. "You need a place to stay for the time being. I won't ask you to leave, Pierce. I...can't."

"Is it just pity you feel for me, then? I know how I look to you," he said, with a derisive smile. "As you said, I'm hardly the man I once was."

"That's not what I said," she flared out. "It has nothing to do with the way you look. At least not in the way you mean. It has everything to do with where you've been these past five years. What you've been doing. Why you left me in the first place."

Her anger deepened as she forced herself to meet his dark gaze. Her voice grew shaky with emotion as she spread her hands in supplication. "Can't you understand? Maybe you didn't leave because you wanted to, but that doesn't change the fact that you *did* leave me. I thought you were *dead*. All these years, I've mourned you, and now I find out it was all for nothing. It was all a lie."

"You sound disappointed, Jesse."

His observation startled her. Made her feel just a trifle uneasy about herself. *Was* she disappointed? Or was she just feeling hurt and confused? Angry and betrayed and…wronged. "I feel a lot of things," she admitted. "Not the least of which is fear."

"I would never hurt you."

"You already have," she said. "You have no idea."

"But not intentionally. Never intentionally." Pierce took a step toward her, but stopped when she flinched away. "You have to believe that, Jesse. I don't know what happened five years ago. I don't know where I've been, what I've done, why I couldn't come back to you. I wish to God I did."

He raised his hand to massage his right temple. His eyes closed for a moment as though he were experiencing excruciating pain. "It's something I have to figure out. I have all these bits and pieces of memories floating around inside my head, and somehow I have to fit them all together again. I know none of this makes any sense to you right now. To me, either. But the one thing I do know is that I never stopped loving you."

"How can you possibly know that?" she demanded. "If you have no memory of the past five years, how can you be so sure there wasn't someone else?"

He lifted his gaze to hers. "Because there could never be anyone else. At least…not for me."

It took Jessica a few seconds to register the note of accusation in his tone. The brown of his eyes deepened almost to black. His gaze was intense, probing, his voice a little too calm. Jessica felt a chill of apprehension as he said slowly, "Perhaps that should have been my first question. I'm almost afraid to ask it, though."

Jessica glanced away guiltily.

"With good reason, it would seem. Is there some-one else?" he persisted.

She hesitated, then shook her head. "No."

"You don't sound too sure."

"There isn't anyone else," she repeated angrily. She tossed back her hair and eyed him defiantly. "But there could have been. And who would have blamed me? You were gone all that time. I didn't know if you were dead or alive. For all I knew, you could have had another family somewhere else. You could have been in love with someone else. You could have for-gotten all about me," she said, feeling the sting of tears threaten her anger. "I had no reason to believe you'd ever come back. Why should I have waited for you?"

"Then why did you?"

Silence. Jessica's heart pounded in her chest as his gaze held hers. His brown eyes softened, misted, looked at her the way he used to look at her, as if she was someone so very special to him. As if she was the only woman in the world for him. As if he couldn't wait to take her in his arms and hold her. Dear God, how often she had thought about that look, how often she had prayed to see it again, just one more time.

But how could she trust it now? How could she trust her own emotions when memories of the past were so strong at that moment she could almost reach out and pluck one from the air between them?

She let her anger blaze to life again. "I didn't wait," she denied. "I was busy working, raising my son, providing a stable home for us both. I was busy growing up, learning how to make my own decisions and realizing that I had no one to rely on but myself. Look around you, Pierce. I did all this *by myself.* I didn't wait for you. I've gone on with my life. Max and I are happy. We're a family. We don't need—'' She broke off, realizing what she had almost said.

His brow arched upward, twisting slightly from the scar. ''You don't need me? That's what you were about to say, isn't it? You have changed, Jessica. I remember a time when you would never have tried to hurt me like that.''

Pierce's face looked like a cold, hard mask. At that moment, he seemed more than ever like a stranger to her. A stranger who had shared her life once, who had helped create a son with her. A stranger who had walked back into her life just when she was beginning to feel good about herself again.

''Five years is a long time, Pierce,'' she countered. ''People change. I've changed. I'm not the same woman you left behind.''

''Yes,'' he agreed quietly, ''but I never would have imagined you could have changed that much.''

Jessica lay wide awake, staring at the ceiling, thinking how strangely quiet the house seemed without her son. She could hear the soft whir of the ceiling fan overhead, the chime of the Tompion grandfather clock down in the foyer, the rustle of leaves in the trees outside her window. If she listened closely enough, she could almost imagine she could hear the sound of Pierce's breathing.

She turned her head and gazed at the side of the bed that had been his. She'd slept on the same side all these years, never giving it a second thought, even when Pierce's would have been more convenient for getting up in the middle of the night with Max.

Had she unconsciously been waiting for Pierce to

come back? Had she known all along, somewhere deep inside her heart, that he wasn't dead? That he was alive…and still loving her?

Don't, she told herself harshly. Don't believe everything he says. How could he have loved her and left her like that? How could he have loved her and not gotten in touch with her all these years? How could he have loved her and forgotten all about her?

Maybe there was a perfectly logical reason to explain where he'd been all these years. Maybe he hadn't left by choice, just as he claimed. Maybe he'd been in an accident and hadn't remembered her at all until now.

Surprising how that thought gave her very little comfort. Her own husband couldn't remember her? Couldn't remember what they'd had together? Maybe because it hadn't meant as much to him as it had to her, Jessica thought with a new flash of anger. Maybe because—

Oh, God, stop it! she commanded herself. What good did it do to go over and over all the possibilities in her head? Whatever had happened to Pierce didn't change anything. Not really. Five years had gone by. Five years of her growing and maturing and taking charge of her own life. She hadn't meant to hurt him earlier when she'd said she and Max didn't need him anymore, but it was the truth, wasn't it?

She'd learned everything there was to know about Pierce's business, and it had flourished in the past few years. She'd redecorated the house to suit her own tastes, and the result was elegant and beautiful, if a little cold. She'd raised Max all by herself, with no help from anyone, and he was an adorable, well-adjusted, happy little boy.

Jessica's life was ordered now. Completely secure. For the first time, she felt in control of her own destiny. She didn't have to depend on anyone else for her security and happiness. She'd made a safe, stable life for herself and Max, and she wouldn't let anyone, not even Pierce, threaten her peace of mind.

What right did he have to come back here now?

A little thread of guilt wove through her anger as Jessica punched her pillow, then turned her back on the empty side of the bed that had once been Pierce's.

If only he didn't look so hurt, so badly in need of someone to take care of him. She sniffed, telling herself she must be catching a cold.

If only he didn't have those horrible scars to remind them both that the past five years hadn't been kind to either of them. If only she didn't have to wonder how he'd gotten them, about the pain he must have endured.

She tried to harden her heart at the rush of emotion that swept through her. She'd suffered, too, hadn't she? She had her scars, too. She'd taken charge of her life and become her own person, but not without a price. She'd grown harder, colder, even bitter at times. She seldom laughed anymore, except with Max. It wasn't a pretty image she drew of herself, she knew. Perhaps this change in character wasn't one of her finer triumphs, but it was life. It was reality.

It was just the way things were now.

And Pierce, well…Pierce would learn soon enough that you can never go home again.

It was good to be home.

Now that he was back, Pierce didn't intend to ever leave again.

He didn't care what the hell the agency said. He'd paid his dues. Five years of his life gone, and Pierce had no idea what purpose they had served. What good he might have done.

Standing in the shadows of the backyard, he let his gaze roam over the familiar, yet changed, surroundings. The cherry trees he and Jessica had planted together had grown so tall, so thick and hardy. The flower beds were neatly tended, the grass freshly cut.

With a sharp pang of guilt, Pierce wondered if Jessica hired someone to come in regularly to do the chores that he'd once done. He'd always hated yard work, but now he found himself resenting yet another usurpation of his position here at home.

His home.

He sighed deeply. He only had to look at his reflection in the mirror to know that wherever he'd been in the past five years, it wasn't a place he would have called home. The scars, the gauntness, the haunted look in his eyes suggested he'd been through hell.

He grimaced, remembering the first time he'd seen himself in the mirror. He certainly wouldn't be winning any beauty contests, that was for damned sure. No wonder Max had been so afraid of him this morning.

Max.

Pierce still couldn't believe he had a son.

He smiled into the darkness, recalling the little boy's face, the dark hair, the brown eyes, the solemn expression. He might have been looking at his own mirror image thirty years ago, Pierce thought.

His smile disappeared, replaced by a brooding frown. He hoped the resemblance ended with the physical appearance. He'd hate to think his own son might be as unhappy and lonely as he'd been at that age.

But surely Max and Jessica had fun together. Surely Jessica spent time with their son, saw to the special needs of a little boy, made him feel wanted and loved—unlike Pierce's own parents who hadn't had a clue how to raise a child, he thought bitterly.

A boy should be allowed to have friends over, Pierce thought, remembering the hours he'd spent alone as a child. A boy needed to be able to get dirty and roughhouse once in a while without being reprimanded for it. Surely Jessica understood all that. But as Pierce stood there gazing into the darkened backyard, an image of the immaculate interior of their home flashed through his mind.

The house was beautiful, but so different from the way it used to be. He missed the casual mix-and-match furnishings they'd begun their married life with. Jessica had gotten rid of all the old stuff. He wondered if she'd even kept the antique pine bed they'd found together at an estate sale.

Pierce let his gaze drift up to their bedroom window, imagining Jessica lying in that bed, fast asleep, her hair fanning across the pillow like a dark, misty veil. How he wished at that moment that he could see her, touch her...be with her.

Would it ever happen for them again?

Would he ever be able to hold her as he'd once held her, kiss her as he'd once kissed her? Would he ever be able to make love to her again?

He closed his eyes, feeling the old familiar need rush through him. She looked so different now. So sophisticated and mature and...womanly. She'd let her hair grow long, he thought. So long and lustrous... He wondered what it would feel like beneath his hands or brushing against his bare chest.

Dear God, he could remember vividly the way she tasted, the way she kissed, the way she felt beneath him. He could remember everything about the way it used to be between them, and the images tormented him now, just as her words had earlier.

It'll never be the same again.

A mild breeze drifted through the cherry trees, stirring the leaves and bringing to his nostrils the nostalgic scent of honeysuckle and clover. It reminded him of all the summer evenings they'd spent out here, planning the rest of their lives together.

He should have told her the truth about himself long ago. Maybe none of this would ever have happened. Maybe he wouldn't have left her on that fateful day five years ago.

The assignment he'd been on was supposed to have been his last, Pierce reflected. He'd given his notice to the agency. The rest of his life belonged only to himself and to Jesse and the child she was carrying. One last assignment, and then Pierce would be free.

So what the hell had gone wrong? What had happened to him? Why couldn't he remember?

As much as he hated to bring that part of his past back into his life, Pierce knew that he could never truly be free until he learned what had happened the day he'd left the house five years ago.

And there was only one way to do that.

With one last glance at Jesse's window, he turned and noiselessly slipped through the darkness, taking care to keep to the shadows. Thankfully he still knew how to blend with the night. At least he hadn't forgotten that.

Within minutes, Pierce had located the familiar phone booth on a secluded street a few blocks from the house. He'd often used it years ago, and had wondered earlier when he'd let himself out the back door if it might have been removed while he'd been gone. So many things had changed.

But there it stood, an old-fashioned glass booth where many a message had been given and received. He'd gotten a phone call in that very booth on his way to the grocery store the day he'd disappeared, Pierce recalled.

The memory shocked him. For a moment, time stood still, then reversed. The day had been cloudless and brilliant with a mild breeze stirring the leaves in the cherry trees that lined the street where the phone booth was located. Pierce crossed the cobblestone street, opened the phone-booth door and stepped inside. Within two minutes, the phone rang and he picked up the receiver.

"Hello?"

Silence on the other end. After a few seconds, Pierce began to grow uneasy. Automatically he recited the code, but the caller still didn't respond.

The sound of a car engine was Pierce's next alarm. His instincts kicked into action. He jerked open the door and dived for the street, but not fast enough. A blinding flash of light and a stunning blow to his shoulder sent him sprawling to the ground. In his last seconds of consciousness, he lay on his back and stared at the blue sky. A bird—an eagle he thought—soared against the brilliant light of the sun.

Then...nothing.

Pierce closed his eyes, trying to summon more. Memories and impressions ripped through him as sharp as a knife, followed by the echo of emotions long forgotten. Betrayal. Fear. Guilt.

And pain. Blinding pain. Pain so intense he'd had to retreat into the darkness. Into a blackness so complete that nothing else had existed for him. He couldn't let it.

That same pain slashed through him now. He put his hands to his head, pressing his temples as if he could squeeze away the hurt. But there was only one way to stop the pain, and he knew it. Only one way to save his sanity.

He had to fade to black.

Within moments, the pain inside his head subsided. The memories vanished. And Pierce was left standing in the darkness, feeling more helpless than ever. He crossed the street and entered the phone booth. Inserting the coin, he dialed the number and waited.

"Tremont House." The voice sounded as if it belonged to an old woman. Pierce had a sudden image of gray hair pulled back into a severe bun, a ramrod-straight backbone and dark, wary eyes. Had he met her before?

"I'd like to speak to the manager."

"Whom should I say is calling?" she asked curtly.

Pierce hesitated, choosing his words carefully. "Tell him an old friend is in town. Tell him I've been…away for several years. Tell him I'm in desperate need of a room."

"Wouldn't do you any good to talk to him," the old woman answered coolly. "We're booked solid."

The line clicked, then went dead, but Pierce had his answer. He gazed bleakly down the remote, empty street.

Help would not be forthcoming as he'd hoped.

Hell, he couldn't even be sure the number he'd called was even a contact anymore. Things inside the agency could change within five minutes' time, much less five years. The agency itself might no longer exist, and if that were the case, Pierce might never be able to find out the truth.

It was a nightmare, he thought. He felt as if he'd been trapped in the Twilight zone for too long or, like Rip van Winkle, had fallen asleep for half a decade while the rest of the world had passed blithely by him.

No time for self-pity, though. He had Max and Jessica to think of, and the possibility that they might somehow be in danger. Maybe he had brought the danger with him, Pierce thought. Maybe the best thing he could do for his family would be simply to disappear again.

But even as the idea formed, he dismissed it. No one would take care of his family the way he could. No one could protect them the way he would.

Somewhere down the street, Pierce heard the distant hum of a car engine. His heart accelerated as the car turned the corner and its headlights caught the phone booth in their full glare. Automatically he tensed.

The car slowed as it passed by the phone booth. Pierce glanced around. The car was a dark green Ford Taurus, but the windows were tinted so that he couldn't see the occupant—or occupants—inside. It was exactly the kind of innocuous-looking vehicle that the agency furnished its operatives.

Were they already checking him out?

Steady, he cautioned himself. By all indications, he'd been out of the mainstream for a long time now. Even though he had no memory of the past five years, Pierce couldn't imagine that he would still be a threat to anyone. The double agent he'd been after before Pierce had disappeared would have surely long since been trapped. The codes, the contacts, even the targets would have all changed by now.

Pierce Kincaid was a dinosaur. A washed-up agent without a memory. No one would want him anymore. Dead or alive.

Not even Jesse.

But even that grim thought couldn't dim the deeply ingrained need for caution. Pierce gripped the handle of the glass door, readying himself to yank it open and make a dive for cover. The car seemed to slow even more, then with a burst of acceleration, it sped down the street.

Pierce waited for a moment, watching the taillights disappear into the night. He felt a keen mixture of relief and disappointment. For a while there, with the adrenaline pumping and all his senses working precisely as they'd been trained, he could almost believe that *he* hadn't changed that much. That there was still something left of the man he'd once been. The man Jesse had once loved.

But that man had been a lie. That man hadn't really existed. If Jesse had known the truth about him then, she might never have loved him at all.

Burdened with guilt, regret and an almost overwhelming need to return to his family, Pierce opened the glass door, stepped out into the cool night air and quickly headed for home.

The ringing of the telephone awakened Jessica at a few minutes past two. She pushed herself up, certain that a call at that time of night could only mean one thing. Something had happened to Max.

In full-blown panic, she grabbed the phone in the dark. ''Hello?''

When no one answered, Jessica first felt relief, then a strange uneasiness. Someone was on the line but wouldn't answer her. For some reason, the silence seemed eminently threatening. She could hear the soft breathing, almost sense the caller listening intently to her voice. A shiver crawled up her spine as her heart accelerated.

She swung her legs off the side of the bed and sat on the edge as if poised to flee. ''Hello? Are you there? Who is this?''

Still silence, and then very softly the line clicked dead.

Jessica hung up the phone, her hands trembling in spite of herself. She'd gotten hang-up calls before. Everyone did. No reason to be upset or frightened. No reason to suspect anything was amiss. No reason to think that call had anything to do with Pierce's return.

But what if it did?

What if someone from his past—his immediate past—had found him? What if—

Jessica got up and paced the room, wringing her hands. Dear God. What was she going to do? The unanswered questions, the suspicions, the *not knowing* were going to drive her crazy. Every little thing out of the ordinary would take on new significance for her now. She knew she wouldn't be able to stand this kind of limbo indefinitely, but what could she do? Ask Pierce to leave?

She felt guilty at even contemplating such an action, but really and truly, how could they go on like this? How could they live in the same house now that they were nothing more than polite strangers?

Perhaps not even polite, because Pierce was now someone she could no longer trust.

After crawling back into bed, Jessica huddled beneath the covers, unable to fall back asleep. Images, both of the past and the future, crowded her mind. She tried to tell herself that things had a way of working themselves out, but Jessica had never been much of an optimist. Pierce's glass was the one that had always been half-full.

There was only one thing she could do. Only one way to handle such an impossible situation. She had to think of her son, after all. His emotional, as well as his physical security had to be her first priority. She had to do what was best for him.

And the sooner she let Pierce know her decision, the better it would be for all of them.

Chapter 5

"I'll give you a month." Jessica said the words aloud in her bedroom, testing the way they sounded as she tried to decide exactly what to say to Pierce when she saw him this morning. "I'll give you a month. Not one day longer."

"A month should be long enough to get your affairs in order." Jessica flinched at the prissy formality of her words. There was just no easy way to say it, she decided, but the fact remained that she wanted him out of here. They couldn't possibly go on living in the same house indefinitely. Not after all these years.

A month seemed reasonable to her. More than reasonable, actually. Perhaps a little foolhardy, considering that for all she knew, he could be a common criminal now.

She sat up in bed. Hugging her knees, she chewed on her lip. A thief on the run. That would explain a lot. The scars. His appearance. What if he'd been in prison or...

But wouldn't she have known that? Wouldn't she have been contacted? Maybe he used aliases. Maybe he was like one of those men she'd seen on Oprah who had different identities and different families in several cities. Maybe she should call Jay and have him do some kind of a check, run Pierce's fingerprints through a government computer or something.

It was strange how that idea made her feel just the tiniest bit like a traitor when she had absolutely no reason to. Yet she'd be a fool not to do everything in her power to protect herself and her son. She'd be a fool to trust Pierce again after all these years.

"Mo-o-m? Mom, where are you? I'm home!"

The sound of her son's voice startled Jessica into action. She swung her legs off the bed and reached for her robe just as her door flew open and Max launched himself toward her.

"Why are you still in bed?" he demanded. "You have to find me clean clothes for school. I had a bath at Allie's house, but I didn't have no clean clothes to put on," he said accusingly. "Hurry, Mom. I'll be late."

Still functioning at only half speed, Jessica let her son pull her to her feet and drag her down the hallway to his bedroom. Rummaging through his drawers and closet, they managed to come up with a pair of denim shorts—the only kind he would wear—and his favorite Superman T-shirt. Mollified somewhat, he dutifully brushed his teeth and combed his hair without complaint.

Jessica watched as he bent over his black high-tops, laboriously tying the laces. She resisted the temptation to help him, knowing that the best gift she could give to her son was the ability to be self-reliant.

Oh, but how she wanted to take him in her arms at that moment, to shield him from the hardships of the world. How she wished that she could turn back the clock and make this morning as peaceful and unthreatening as she had tried to make all his other mornings.

Seeming to read her thoughts, Max looked up at her. His dark eyes, eyes so like Pierce's, narrowed slightly as if he was concentrating on something he didn't quite understand. "Why is that guy still here, Mom? I saw him downstairs. He's in the kitchen making coffee."

The image jolted Jessica. Obviously Pierce was making himself at home, but then to him, this was still his home. Jessica ran her fingers through her mussed hair. "He spent the night in the guest room, Max. He had nowhere else to go." She winced, realizing how lame her answer sounded. She'd have to do better than that.

But Max, as usual, was one step ahead of her. His frown deepened. "I been thinking," he said. "That guy—he's the one in the pictures you showed me when I was a little kid, isn't he? He's my dad, right?"

Jessica's heart pounded more rapidly. She and Max used to look at Pierce's pictures together. She'd tried to instill in her son a sense of his father, tried to make him understand that Pierce would have loved him just as much as Jessica did, if he had lived.

But what did she tell him now? she wondered desperately. How did she explain Pierce's resurrection? How did she keep Max from hating his father because there was no plausible explanation for his absence from their lives?

She took a deep breath and said simply, ''Yes, Max, he is.''

''Then why isn't he dead?''

''I don't know. Something happened to him. He…might have been in an accident. He doesn't remember anything about the years he was away.''

''You mean he's got anesia?''

Jessica stared at her son, amazed. ''*Am*nesia and where did you learn that word?''

Max shrugged. ''From Superman.'' His tone implied ''Where else?'' Aloud he added, ''Once, Lois Lane couldn't even remember who Clark Kent was 'cuz she got conked on the head by these bad guys.'' Max scratched the side of his nose. ''That guy downstairs—my dad—does he remember you?''

''Well…yes.''

''Does he remember me?''

''He never knew you, Max. You hadn't been born when he le—disappeared.''

Max seemed to mull over the information, but something in his eyes made Jessica uneasy. A glint of excitement that made her stomach flutter with dread. Already, she thought. Already Max was starting to think of Pierce as his father. Already Jessica could feel just a tiny bit of her son slipping away from her.

''Is he gonna stay here with us?''

''I'm…not sure what his plans are.''

''Does he know how to play baseball?''

Jessica's heart sank. ''I don't know.''

Max's dark eyes lit up. ''That would be great, wouldn't it? Because then you wouldn't have to get your clothes all dirty. Girls don't like that, do they?''

''Some don't, I guess. I've always enjoyed our time together, though.''

"Yeah, but you can't catch the ball very good, Mom. I bet he knows how to play baseball," Max concluded. "I bet he knows how to fight, too, just like Superman. I bet that's how he got all those scars. Marcus Tate's father's an accountant. He sits in an office all day behind a great big desk. He don't have no scars." Marcus Tate's father, the T-ball coach and once one of Max's heroes, had certainly been cut down a peg or two. Jessica didn't like the way the conversation was going.

She brushed her fingers across Max's silky hair. "Honey...." She trailed off, grasping for words. "I don't think you should get your hopes up too much about, well, about baseball and all that. I told you, I don't know what Pierce's plans are."

"But if he's my dad," Max said, frowning, "don't he have to stay here with us? Isn't it a law or something like that? Maybe I should ask Uncle Jay. I bet he'd know." Max's Uncle Jay was another point of pride with him. He was sure his Uncle Jay was a super-duper agent of some sort. Jessica had tried to explain that just because Jay worked in the Pentagon didn't mean he was a spy, but Max wouldn't hear of it. "Mom," he'd complain, "haven't you ever heard of a cover?"

Jessica sighed, bringing her thoughts back into focus. "Can we talk about this later? The bus will be here any minute, and I don't want you to miss it again."

"Okay." Max shrugged into his leather backpack, then looked up at her, his gaze solemn. "Can I ask you a question, Mom?"

"Sure, sweetie."

Sudden tears glinted in Max's dark brown eyes.

Most of the time he tried to act so cool and grown up, but he was still just a little boy with a whole list of questions Jessica didn't know how to answer. "Don't you want my dad to stay here with us?"

"Oh, Max." Jessica knelt and folded him in her arms, and for just a while, he was once again her baby, the one person in the world whose love she had been able to count on. Jessica tightened her arms around him, holding him close, trying to blink back the hot tears before they could spill down her face. At that moment, she didn't know what she wanted. "It's not that easy," she whispered. "He's been gone for five years. Things…change."

"Carly Wilson went away to her grandmother's house for two whole weeks," Max said, tolerating Jessica's embrace for only a second or two longer before he pulled away. "When she came back, she'd lost her two front teeth." He grinned, tapping his own front teeth with his finger. "She looked real funny. Is that the kind of change you mean?"

Jessica managed a smile, ruffling his hair. "Not exactly," she said. "But we'll talk some more later. Now get a move on before you miss that bus."

Jessica quickly dressed, too, slipping on blue jeans and an old faded shirt. Hand in hand, she and Max walked to the bus stop and greeted the other children and mothers who were already waiting for the bus.

Sharon, dressed in a light blue sundress, her blond hair glistening in the sunlight, gave Jessica a knowing look.

"Didn't get much sleep last night, eh?"

Jessica grimaced. "How can you tell?"

"The dark circles are a dead giveaway." She tugged at one of Jessica's rolled-up shirtsleeves. "And

I haven't seen you wear this lovely ensemble out on the street before.''

"I dressed in a hurry this morning," Jessica murmured. "I...overslept."

Sharon's brows soared. "You? I've never known you to be anything but disgustingly punctual in your whole life."

"I never claimed to be perfect," Jessica snapped, then immediately regretted her bad temper. Sharon McReynolds was the best friend she'd ever had. She and her husband, Frank, had helped Jessica with Max on more occasions than she cared to remember, and she owed them a lot. She gave Sharon an apologetic smile. "I not only overslept, but I got up on the wrong side of the bed this morning. I'm sorry."

Sharon studied her thoughtfully. "Don't worry about it."

Jessica gazed at the children playing at the curb. "I hope he behaved himself last night," she said.

"Who, Max?"

Jessica shot her a look. "Of course Max. Who else?"

"Max was a perfect angel, as always." Sharon hesitated, then said, "You aren't going to say a word, are you?"

"About what?"

Sharon shook her blond head. "I have never known anyone as infuriatingly closemouthed as you are. Don't you know I'm positively *dying* to know why you overslept this morning and why you got up on the wrong side of the bed? And who, for God's sake, is that gorgeous man standing on your porch?"

Jessica whirled. Sure enough, there he stood on her front porch, in broad daylight, for all the world to see.

Dressed in faded jeans and a white T-shirt, Pierce leaned against the railing with a proprietary casualness that instantly brought a frown to Jessica's brow.

When he saw her looking, he lifted his arm and waved as if nothing in the world was amiss. Jessica had to keep reminding herself that for him nothing was wrong. Everything was just the way it had been five years ago when he'd left the house to go get ice cream. When they'd still be in love.

She whipped her head around, looked at her friend, then glanced away.

"Well?" Sharon demanded. "Is that the strange man Max told me about? The one who obviously spent the night at your house last night?"

Jessica gave her a nervous smile. "It's not what you think."

"It never is. But you'd better explain real quick," Sharon warned, "because he's coming this way and I might just be inclined to ask *him* instead."

Coming this way? What in the world was he thinking? How was she going to explain his sudden appearance to all her neighbors? Jessica had told them long ago that her husband was dead, and now here he was, obviously not a ghost, but a real flesh-and-blood man.

Obviously a man.

Too obviously.

The group of chattering mothers fell silent as Pierce approached the group. There was something different about him this morning, Jessica thought. In the bright sunlight, he looked taller. Broader. Tougher. More confident.

More like the old Pierce.

She felt her heart stop for a moment.

The sunlight caught the scar on his cheek, high-lighted it, but somehow the effect was less daunting than when she'd first seen it. He didn't look like a man who needed taking care of at all this morning.

What he looked like, Jessica thought with a catch in her throat, was a man very much in control.

Their eyes met and clung, and Jessica's heart started beating again, almost painfully. No, she silently de-nied. I don't feel anything for him. Nothing at all. I *can't*.

But the butterflies in her stomach wouldn't listen to her. They were going crazy. They were making her feel weak and helpless and out of control, and Jessica wouldn't stand for that. Not anymore. She lifted her chin and eyed him with chilly annoyance.

That's when she realized that the whole group of mothers and children were still silent and staring at the scene unfolding before them with avid curiosity.

Out of the corner of her eye, Jessica saw Max move away from his friends and start toward them. Oh, no, she thought. Not here. Not like this. What would this kind of scene do to him? Pierce should have known better. What if Max got upset? What if he started to cry in front of his friends? He'd hate that later.

But it was too late to head off disaster now, because Max was already standing beside her. He slipped his little hand in hers and squinted up at Pierce, his ex-pression as inscrutable as his father's as they stared at each other for a long, tense moment.

Max bent and scratched a scab on his knee. He kicked the dirt with the toe of his new running shoe. He looked Pierce straight in the eye. "Hi, Dad," he said, and smiled.

* * *

The group had been silent before, but now everyone looked stunned. Max had spoken right up so that everyone at the bus stop had no trouble at all in hearing what he'd said.

Pierce felt his heart give a funny little twist. He stuck his hand casually into the pocket of his jeans. Then he grinned. "Hi, Max."

Dad. Max had called him Dad. Pierce couldn't believe it. It was too much to ask for, this soon. It was too good to be true....

And then he turned and glimpsed Jessica's thunderstruck expression. She looked as stunned as he felt, but not in the same way. There was no elation in Jessica's eyes. No joy in her face. Just a rigid determination to see this scene through with as much dignity as she could muster. He couldn't help but admire her resolve because Max's easy acceptance of him must have been like a slap in the face to her.

He tried to catch her eye, wanted to smile at her in reassurance, but Jessica wouldn't look at him. Instead she turned and watched their son as he boarded the school bus.

As Max climbed the steps, the little boy behind him said loudly, "Wow! That's your *dad?*"

"Yeah," Max said. "Did you see all his scars?"

"Yeah! How'd he get 'em?"

"Fightin' bad guys, a course."

"Cool," the little boy said with reverence.

Pierce grimaced. He was afraid Max's assessment had hit a little too closely to the truth, but he hardly had time to worry about that now. As the bus lumbered down the street toward the next stop, the crowd of mothers reluctantly began to disperse. Several of them smiled and waved at him as they turned in various directions toward their homes. A tall, attractive blonde, who stood just behind Jessica, glowered at him with open distrust.

"Jessica," the woman said, "are you all right?"

"I'm fine, Sharon," Jessica said quietly. "I'll call you later, okay?"

"Please do." The blonde gave Pierce one last disapproving look before she turned and strode up the sidewalk of the house next door to theirs.

Without a word, Jessica started down the cobblestone walkway. Pierce caught her arm as she tried to brush past him. "Jesse—"

The look she gave him stopped him cold. Her gray eyes frosted over as she glared at him. "Are you satisfied?" she demanded. "Do you see what you've done?"

"I didn't do anything," Pierce said. "I came out here to say goodbye to our son. What's so wrong with that?"

"What's *wrong* with it? Oh, please. You can't be that dense." Impatiently Jessica brushed the windblown curls from her forehead. Her manicured nails flashed pink in the sunlight. "Don't you see what you're doing to him?"

Pierce kept an easy pace beside her as they headed for home. "Why don't you tell me what I'm doing to him? I've barely met him."

"My point exactly. You just met him." Jessica turned on the top step of the porch to face him. Her hands went to her slim hips as she stood there glaring at him. Anger had warmed the chill in her gray eyes, and now they sparked with silver fire. Two rosy spots of color tinted her high cheekbones, and her lips— those gorgeous lips—trembled with indignation.

Standing on the top step put her at an even level with him. Their eyes were flush, their mouths only inches apart. Even in anger—perhaps even more so in anger—she was still the most beautiful woman Pierce had ever known. He had to resist the urge to reach out and cup the back of her neck and pull her to him, not gently, until he could claim her lips with his. He wanted to kiss her, hold her, touch her in such a way that she would have to remember she belonged to him.

Only to him.

Something of his thoughts must have shown on his face, because Jessica's eyes turned wary, almost frightened. She reached out a hand and grasped one of the white porch pillars for support.

"Your son is five years old and you just met him, Pierce." She took a deep breath, her eyes filling with tears, but Pierce didn't reach for her or try to comfort her. He didn't dare. "Max has always wanted a father like all his friends have. Someone to play baseball with, someone to take him swimming, someone to teach him the things all the other little boys know how to do. And now suddenly here you are, after all these years, ready to step in and make all his dreams come true. You're setting him up for a big fall, and I'm the one who'll have to pick up the pieces."

"What are you talking about?" Pierce demanded angrily. "I would never do anything to hurt our son. Why can't I do all those things with him? Why can't I be the father he always wanted?"

"Because I don't even know if you're going to be here," Jessica burst out. She seemed stunned by her own words, her own anger. Her fingers trembled as she lifted her hand to her mouth.

Pierce had a sick feeling in the pit of his stomach.

He took a step toward her, and when she would have backed away, his hand shot out to grasp her arm. Reluctantly her gaze lifted and met his. "Are you asking me to leave, Jessica? Is that what all this is leading up to?"

Her gaze flickered. "I don't...not exactly," she faltered, but she could no longer meet his eyes. She made a helpless gesture with her hand. "This is an impossible situation, Pierce. We have to talk, decide what's best for...all of us."

"I thought we talked last night," Pierce said, frowning. He didn't like the way she kept dancing around his question. *Did* she want him to leave?

"Things got a little too tense last night," she said.

He smiled sardonically. "No kidding. It's not every day I return from the dead, you know."

"It's not every day my long-lost husband walks through my back door," she countered, her gaze leveling on him once again. But her eyes softened just a hint. Pierce felt enormously encouraged. "We do have to talk, Pierce, but not out here. I think we've given the neighbors enough to gossip about for one day."

"Worried your reputation will be tarnished, Mrs. Kincaid?" he teased softly.

Jessica gave him a defiant look as she tossed her dark hair over her shoulder. "How do you know it wasn't already?" she asked.

Then she turned and left him standing on the porch, swearing beneath his breath.

Jessica decided she didn't want to have such a serious discussion with her husband while she looked like the waif he'd once rescued. That insecure young woman was long gone, thank goodness. Jessica wanted to make sure Pierce knew they were on equal footing now. She gazed critically at her reflection in the mirror.

The narrow black skirt and white rayon blouse she chose were simple yet elegant, and the French twist that tamed her hair made her look sophisticated and businesslike. Jessica decided she looked like a woman ready to face the world. Or, as Pierce had said, a husband who had just returned from the dead.

When she talked to him this time, Jessica didn't want to let her anger get the better of her. She wanted to present her plan to him clearly and concisely in as straightforward a manner as she could muster. She wanted to make him see that she had thought it all out, and it really was the only viable plan for their rather peculiar situation. She wanted to make this as painless as possible—for all of them.

Pierce would cooperate. How could he not? What reasonable alternative could he possibly come up with?

Yet that reassurance didn't calm her nerves in the least as she walked down the stairs. It annoyed her to find that her palms were sweating and her throat was suddenly, achingly dry.

The aroma of freshly brewed coffee greeted her as she shoved open the swinging door and stepped inside the kitchen. She let the door swish shut behind her. It barely made any noise, but Pierce, who had been standing at the sink, whirled around as if she'd just fired a gun.

It wasn't that he was startled, she noticed. There was no look of surprise in the dark gleam of his eyes. No jumping pulse in his throat. He eyed her with what she could only call steely readiness. A determination to face...whatever he had to face.

Her own heart leaped to her throat. Jessica's hand went to her neck, as if to quiet her own rioting pulse. As she stood there, Pierce's gaze softened and moved over her.

"Is that the way you always dress on your day off?" he asked approvingly. "At least, I assume the shop is closed today. I always closed it on Mondays."

Jessica cleared her throat, stepped across the room to the counter and poured herself a cup of coffee, somehow managing not to spill the steaming liquid as she clutched the cup with hands that still trembled. "I don't do everything at the shop the way you used to, Pierce." She shot him a challenging glance. "In fact, I have my own policies now. My own rules and regulations."

"I see."

Jessica shrugged. "You used to complain yourself that the way your parents ran the shop was archaic and inefficient. You just never took the time to implement change. In fact, in many ways you were a very lax businessman," she said with cool disapproval.

"Is that so?" He didn't seem perturbed in the least by her criticism. "And you are the very epitome of efficiency, I imagine."

Jessica fought the flash of hurt his flippancy brought on. "Yes, as a matter of fact, I am. Is that so hard to believe?"

"A little," he admitted. "I never thought of you as a businesswoman, Jesse."

"I used to work for you," she observed, annoyed. "That's how we met."

His gaze softened. "I remember. But you seemed

happy to quit when we bought this house. You wanted to be a wife and mother. You had no interest in the business.''

''Things change,'' Jessica said.

''So you've said.''

''In fact,'' she continued, ''I think you'll be quite surprised by the margin of profit The Lost Attic now enjoys.''

''Are you going to show me your books?'' Somehow he managed to make the innocent question sound like a sexual proposition.

Jessica frowned as she carried the cup to the table and sat down, crossing one leg over the other and then carefully smoothing her napkin across her lap.

''So,'' Pierce said as he leaned back against the sink. His eyes lingered on her legs for a moment, then lifted to meet her gaze. ''*Are* you going to work today?''

''Actually, no,'' Jessica admitted. ''I still close on Mondays.''

''Aha. Something that *hasn't* changed around here.'' He made it sound like some kind of marvelous discovery.

Jessica decided she'd better nip that train of thought in the bud right now. ''Why don't you sit down?'' She gestured toward the chair across from her. ''I have a few things I'd like to say.''

He ignored the chair she'd indicated and pulled out the one next to her. His knees brushed hers under the table, and Jessica quickly shifted hers aside.

She lifted her chin, ignoring the tiny thrill that raced up her spine. ''I think what we should do first is set some ground rules for our…cohabitation.''

Pierce's brow rose almost imperceptibly. ''Cohabition?'' he said in a voice that was faintly mocking. ''Is that what we have here?''

''For lack of a better term,'' Jessica said. She took a deep breath, throwing him a defensive glance before averting her gaze to her coffee cup. ''In fact, I have an ultimatum for you. Sort of a two-part one, you might say.''

''Let's hear the first part.'' His voice was oddly devoid of emotion. Jessica gave him another glance. Then a second one. He looked so…clean this morning, she thought fleetingly. She could smell the barest hint of soap on his skin, and his dark hair gleamed in the morning sunlight, begging to be touched. She could still remember the texture of his hair, she realized. Could almost feel the softness as she ran her fingers through it while they—

Stop it, Jessica! she admonished herself as she tore her eyes from his rugged profile. He's a stranger now. Worse than a stranger—a counterfeit.

A counterfeit husband, that was a good description for Pierce Kincaid.

''Well?'' Pierce prompted, jerking her thoughts to the present.

''I'd like you to see Dr. Prescott,'' she said. ''Today, if possible.'' Dr. Prescott had been their family doctor ever since he'd administered Pierce and Jessica's blood tests before they got married. A few years later, he'd delivered Max. Seeing him seemed like the logical first step to Jessica.

''You think Dr. Prescott can prescribe some miracle drug that will cure me, Jesse?''

''I don't know what he can do,'' she said. ''But I certainly think you should have a thorough examination. All those scars….'' Her voice trailed off as her gaze lit on the jagged line that marred the left side of his face. "I...think you can understand why I would want you to see a doctor," she said uneasily.

Pierce smiled. "I understand more than you think," he said softly. "If it'll make you feel any better, I'll go see Dr. Prescott. Just don't expect too much. Don't get your hopes up."

Jessica looked him straight in the eye. "I never do that."

Pierce's gaze flickered with something Jessica thought looked a little too much like pity. That was the last thing she wanted from him. She cleared her throat. "The second part of my ultimatum is this. I'll give you one month."

His scarred brow twisted. "To do what?"

"To stay here. To come up with the right answers. To explain to me why you left five years ago and why you haven't been in touch since. I think a month is more than reasonable. Don't you?"

Pierce shrugged. "I'm hardly in a position to bargain." He sat back, staring at her. "All right, supposing at the end of this month, I still don't have any answers for you. Supposing my memory still hasn't returned. What then, Jessica?"

"Then...I don't see that there can ever be any hope for us. Maybe you didn't leave me on purpose, Pierce. Maybe there were extenuating circumstances. But if you never get your memory back, then we'll never know for sure, will we?" She locked her hands together in her lap, trying to stop the trembling. Might as well face the truth, hadn't they? Get it all out in the open? No use pretending that things could ever be as they used to be.

Pierce's chair scraped against the tile floor as he

shoved it away from the table and stood. Jessica jumped at his sudden movement, at the look he gave her. His dark eyes glittered like black diamonds as he placed his hands on the table and leaned toward her. His face was only inches from hers. His lips only a breath away...

Jessica's heart thundered in her chest. What was he doing? What right did he have to look at her like that? As if he wanted to...

Surely he didn't think she would let him kiss her? Not after the discussion they'd just had.

But he was so close she could hear the slight quickening of his breath, could see the warmth of desire in his eyes. His lips were moving closer and, dear God, it had been so long. So very long since he'd kissed her. Jessica's eyes fluttered closed....

"One month," he said, his voice low and seductive. "I'll give *you* one month, Jesse."

Jessica's eyes flew open. She gazed up at him, and the hint of amusement she saw on his face made her anger flare to life once again. "What are you talking about?" she demanded, her face heating in embarrassment at his rejection.

He smiled. Slowly. Mysteriously. He smiled just like he used to. "I'll give you one month to fall in love with me again," he said softly.

Then he turned and strode from the room, leaving Jessica sitting alone with an open mouth and a pounding heart.

Jessica fumed all the way to the bank. What nerve! How dare he challenge her that way? Fall in love with him again? Not bloody likely. What kind of fool did he take her for?

She should just turn the car around, drive back

home, march inside the house, and demand that he leave the premises immediately. Letting him stay a month was just prolonging the agony. Both she and Max would be better off making a clean break now.

At the thought of her son, Jessica sighed. How would Pierce's return affect her relationship with Max? She'd never had to share him with anyone. Their devotion to each other had been complete and uncomplicated. Max's love was the only love Jessica had ever been able to depend on. To trust. The thought of sharing it, of losing even a little bit of his affection, was more than she could bear.

Why? she asked herself bitterly, biting her lip to hold back her emotions. Why did Pierce have to come back?

You sound disappointed, Jesse.

Unbidden, his accusation came back to her, and Jessica realized with a sinking sensation in her stomach that it wasn't disappointment she felt at that moment. It wasn't anger or resentment or even confusion.

What she felt was fear. Cold, mind-numbing terror.

I'll give you one month to fall in love with me again.

Jessica parked the car in front of the bank, then sat staring out the window. There was no way, she promised herself. No way on earth she would ever let herself fall in love with Pierce Kincaid again. She was over him. She'd been over him for a long time.

But things change, a little voice in the back of her mind taunted her.

Pierce wouldn't let himself consider the possibility that it might really be over. For just a moment this morning, for just a split second of time, he'd seen the hint of desire in her eyes. The flicker of memory that told him she hadn't forgotten how it used to be between them.

It wasn't love, he admitted grimly. It wasn't even affection, but it was something. Something he could hold on to while he grappled with all the other losses.

She'd given him a month. Not much time when you considered the five years in which he'd lost ground. He could almost smile at the image of her sitting beside him, dressed so prim and proper, issuing her two-part ultimatum with what seemed like all the confidence in the world.

How she'd changed, he thought in wonder. How she'd matured.

There was hardly anything left of the woman he'd fallen in love with and married, of the woman who had once looked up to him with a hero worship that had made him feel ten feet tall. Jessica had grown into her own woman, as he always knew she would. What he hadn't counted on in those days was that she might one day outgrow her need for him.

Of course, he had to admire what she'd done. Running a business and raising their son single-handedly couldn't have been easy. He admired and respected her more than ever, but when he thought about the way she used to be, he couldn't help feeling something of the loss she must have felt when he disappeared five years ago.

One month, he reminded himself grimly. He had one month to counteract all the negative feelings the past five years had generated inside her. He had one month to win back his wife. One month to regain his memory.

One month to fight for his life.

Chapter 6

"Doctor, can a person pretend to have amnesia when in fact he really doesn't?"

Dr. Prescott raised an eyebrow as he settled back in his leather chair. "Are you saying you think that's the case with your husband, Jessica?"

Jessica squirmed under his unwavering stare and tried to settle more comfortably into her own chair. She'd been in Dr. Prescott's office for several minutes now while Pierce waited in the examination room. She wondered if he was as nervous as she was.

She made an aimless gesture with her hands. "I don't know what I'm saying, Dr. Prescott. It just seems so strange to me that he could leave one day, be gone for five years, then show up out of the blue thinking he'd only been gone for thirty minutes. I mean, is that really possible?"

"I'll admit it seems a bit…extreme, but selective amnesia— if that's what he's suffering from—is a

complicated illness, Jessica. There's still a lot about it
we don't understand. I know of several documented
cases, not unlike Pierce's, where the amnesia victim
loses an entire block of time from his memory, nothing
else, just a particular period of time. The rest of his
memory remains intact.''

''What would cause that?''

Dr. Prescott leaned forward and folded his hands on
the top of his desk. ''Any number of things, actually.
An accident. A serious illness. Sometimes a blow to
the head is all it takes to bring on some form of amnesia. Selective amnesia, however, is a bit trickier.
Sometimes the cause can be more mental than physical, the result of a severe shock or trauma. Something
so painful the victim has to block it from his or her
memory in order to deal with it. Sometimes in order
to survive.''

Jessica thought about the scar on Pierce's face and
on his arm. Would his wounds have been traumatic
enough to make him block the memories? Or had it
been something else? A different kind of shock? Jessica took a deep breath, avoiding Dr. Prescott's kindly
stare. ''During this five years, could...could he have
been leading another life? Could he have forgotten
about...you know, his real life during that time?''

''It's entirely possible,'' Dr. Prescott said. ''You
see, sometimes when a person recovers from total amnesia, he won't remember anything about the interval
of time when his memory was gone, not even the people he met or the places he went to. His mind simply
reverts to the person he was before he lost his memory.
Do you follow me, Jessica?

''What I'm saying is that something could have
happened to Pierce five years ago to bring on a com-

plete memory loss. He might not have even known his own name. Then five years later, something might have triggered the recall. Gradually his memories returned, but the period of time in which he suffered from amnesia, the interval, could be gone forever.''

"You mean…we may never know what happened to him?''

Dr. Prescott must have read Jessica's distressed reaction, because he added softly, ''That's not necessarily conclusive, Jessica. I'm merely reciting some textbook cases. As I said before, there's still much about amnesia we don't understand. Each case is different. Sometimes memories will manifest themselves in dreams. That can be extremely helpful.'' He stood and picked up the folder on his desk. ''We can talk some more later if you like. I know it sounds complicated and confusing, but right now I think I better get to our patient.''

The sound of the office door closing behind Dr. Prescott barely registered with Jessica. She sat staring straight ahead, her mind reeling with all she had learned.

Something could have happened to Pierce five years ago to bring on a complete memory loss. He might not have even known his own name.

Jessica closed her eyes, letting the impact of the doctor's words sweep over her. It was entirely possible that everything Pierce had told her was true.

One thing I do know. I didn't leave you because I wanted to.

Jessica put her hands to her face, overcome with emotion. Did she dare believe it? Did she dare believe that Pierce hadn't left her because he wanted to? That he hadn't just abandoned her because he didn't love her anymore?

And if it was true, if she did accept it, where did that leave them? Five years had gone by. Five long years of learning to live without him, of being happy with the person she had become. She wasn't the woman Pierce had left behind, no matter what his reason for leaving had been.

Jessica knew she would never be content again to stay at home and be the perfect wife for him. She would never be able to tolerate his overprotectiveness, his treating her as if she were some rare and fragile flower.

She was older, stronger, more mature now. She was capable of taking care of herself and her son, and if truth be told, she had no idea where Pierce, with or without his memory, was going to fit into her life.

"My God, son, what the hell happened to you?"

"If I knew that I probably wouldn't be here," Pierce said dryly as he sat, shirtless, on the examination table. He knew Dr. Prescott was staring at his back. He could see the shock on the nurse's face beside him as she glanced around, then hastily averted her eyes.

It had been quite a shock to Pierce last night, too. After his shower, he'd studied himself in the mirror—not out of any particular sense of vanity, far from it—but to try to reacquaint himself with a body that seemed very much a stranger's to him.

The mass of thin, crisscrossing scars on his back had only served to confuse him even more. When he'd tried to remember how he'd gotten them, he had experienced a headache so severe, so blinding, Pierce had feared he might black out.

Dr. Prescott whistled softly. "You know what this puts me in mind of? Some of the POWs I saw as an army doctor during and after Korea." He hesitated for a moment, then said, "Step outside for a minute, will you, Sue?"

The nurse nodded and quietly left. Dr. Prescott came around and took a seat in front of Pierce. "Has Jessica seen your back?"

Pierce flinched, reaching for his shirt. "No, and I'd just as soon she not know about it."

Dr. Prescott raised a brow. "She'll have to sooner or later, won't she? That is, if you two plan to resume a normal married life."

"That doesn't seem too likely at the moment," Pierce muttered, buttoning his shirt.

"Pretty emotional time for you two, I would imagine," Dr. Prescott observed kindly. "Five years is a long time to be separated from one another. A lot can happen. Things change. People change. If I was inclined to offer something other than medical advice, I'd say it's not the time for anything but complete honesty."

Pierce frowned at the terrazzo floor. "If I was inclined to accept unsolicited advice, I'd say you could be right. But complete honesty is not always all it's cracked up to be, Doctor."

"I wouldn't share that bit of wisdom with Jessica if I were you. She…well—" he searched for the right words, gesturing with his hand "—let's just say she has her doubts about your condition."

"She doesn't believe I have amnesia."

"She's skeptical."

"And you?" Pierce asked bluntly.

"Now that I've examined you? No. Judging from your back alone, I'd say you've been through enough trauma in the past five years to want to block it from your memory in any way possible." He paused, eyeing Pierce with an understanding but not pitying look. "Make no mistake, that's purely a gut instinct from someone who's been there, and not the professional opinion of a medical doctor. I'll reserve that judgment until we have all your test results in."

"Fair enough," Pierce said, shoving himself off the examination table. "But one more thing, Dr. Prescott. I don't want you to mention the scars to Jessica. The one on my face is bad enough. I'd like to tell her about the others myself, when the time is right."

When he thought she could handle it without looking at him in pity and disgust, Pierce mentally added.

When the door to the office opened again, Jessica jumped to her feet, a testament to her agitation. Her gaze went first to Dr. Prescott, then to Pierce who followed just behind the doctor.

"Have a seat, you two," Dr. Prescott began. He seated himself behind his desk and opened Pierce's chart, studied it for a moment, then closed it and laid his folded hands on top of it. Jessica wasn't sure why but the gesture seemed fraught with symbolism. An open-and-shut case. Nothing more to be done.

Reluctantly she sat down again, and Pierce took the seat next to her. She cleared her throat and stared ahead at Dr. Prescott, but it was Pierce who dominated her thoughts. She could *feel* him beside her, and her overwrought nerves seemed to scream with awareness.

"As I just told Pierce," Dr. Prescott explained, "I

want to withhold my final opinion until we have all the test results in, but I do have one recommendation I'd like to make at this time.''

''What is it, Dr. Prescott?'' Jessica asked nervously. Pierce remained silent as if he, too, was withholding final judgment.

''I'd like to give you the name of another doctor, a psychiatrist, I think you should see.''

Jessica wasn't looking at Pierce, but she felt his almost violent reaction to Dr. Prescott's suggestion. Dr. Prescott scribbled the name and number on a piece of paper and handed it across the desk. When Pierce made no move to accept it, Jessica reached out and took the paper from the doctor's hand, glancing at the Georgetown address.

''His name is Dr. Layton. He just moved here recently from Chicago. He's cut back on his patient load, but I think he'll be willing to see you with my recommendation. His work with amnesia victims is well-known and respected in the medical community. I really hope you'll go see him, Pierce. At the very least, he can help you cope with the stress.''

''We'll call him,'' Jessica promised as they all stood, concluding the meeting.

Pierce said nothing. He opened the door for her and they walked out of the office together, but still he remained ominously silent. When Jessica tried to question him about the examination on the drive home, he answered her questions as curtly and evasively as possible. Once home, he went straight to the guest room. He was still there when Jessica left to go pick up Max at the baby-sitter's.

Jessica pondered his reaction on the drive to Mrs. Taylor's house. It seemed to her that Dr. Prescott's suggestion that Pierce see a psychiatrist had brought on some sort of anxiety attack, but why? Why would he be so reluctant to see a psychiatrist, someone who could help him, unless…

Unless…he was afraid of what he might reveal.

Jessica blocked that idea from her mind. She wouldn't think about it now. Not when her son was hurling himself at her like a speeding bullet. She caught him up and spun him around. It felt so good to hold him in her arms today.

"Do you have a kiss for me?" she asked.

"Uh-huh." He dutifully pecked her cheek. "Did you bring my cape?" he demanded.

"It's in the car, Mr. Kent."

"Good." He wiggled out of her arms and looked up at her, squinting one eye. "Can we go see my dad now?"

Jessica said nothing as she and Max climbed into the car. All the way home, Max kept up a running commentary on the day's events. Alan Michael had brought a dead turtle to school that morning which had greatly impressed Max. By lunchtime, though, it had started to smell so the teacher made them give it a decent burial in the playground.

"It was real cool," Max said. "Cari Thompson cried but everyone knows she's just a big baby, anyway."

Jessica murmured the proper response, and Max launched into a new topic. "I made a new friend today," he informed her. "I think his family's gonna move into the house next to Mrs. Taylor's. At least I hope so. He was real cool."

Jessica made a mental note to check with Max's

baby-sitter about her potential new neighbors. "Is he about your age, Max?"

Max thought for a moment. "He's older, I think. But we played a really cool game called secret mission."

"Secret mission? What kind of game is that?"

Max instantly clammed up. He locked his lips together and stared out the window as if he'd said more than he should have. "It's just a dumb kid game," he muttered. "No big deal."

"You mean like the superhero games you and Marcus sometimes play?"

Max brightened. "Yeah. Like that."

"Well, don't get too carried away with it, okay? Remember, it's just pretend."

"Okay, Mom. Are we almost home? I promised Allie I'd help her build a house for Snowflake today. Course, cats don't like houses, you know. Dogs do, though."

Jessica ignored the bait. Her mind was still on their previous conversation. She hoped Max's imagination wouldn't get the better of him with this new game. She supposed she should be relieved that his obsession with superheroes might be waning, but secret missions? What would he come up with next?

She slanted him a look as she braked for a traffic light. Was it her imagination, or did he seem a little secretive tonight? A little evasive? Oh, he was talking ninety to nothing as usual, but there was something about the way he almost skillfully led the conversation onto topics he knew Jessica wouldn't object to that bothered her. Made her just a tad suspicious.

He reminded her a little too much of the way Pierce used to be when he came home from one of his buying trips, she thought with a start. Pierce would dazzle her with attention from the moment he walked in the door until Jessica would soon forget all about the questions she'd intended to ask him when he got home.

Maybe she was just being overly suspicious in hindsight, she concluded, but her gaze strayed back to her son.

He's only a little boy, she reminded herself. It was only natural he'd have secrets from her. Nothing sinister in that. Probably had a frog stashed somewhere up in his room. Or dirty underwear stuffed under his bed.

He caught her looking at him and smiled Pierce's smile. "I love you, Mom," he said sweetly.

"I love you, too, son."

Oh, dear. Something was definitely up. Jessica had a feeling that the next time she cleaned his room, she was in for some nasty surprises.

"Why don't we just order a pizza?"

Jessica stared at the meager selection in the refrigerator, trying to ignore Pierce and his comment as he hovered over her shoulder.

"You love pepperoni."

Jessica slammed the refrigerator door, annoyed with herself for not having gone to the grocery story after leaving the doctor's office and annoyed with Pierce for being…well, for being Pierce. She couldn't seem to get his reaction to the suggestion of his seeing a psychiatrist out of her mind. It seemed to her that he should be willing to do whatever it took to restore his memory. She didn't understand his reluctance.

"For your information," she said, turning to confront him, "I haven't eaten pizza in years. It's loaded with fat and cholesterol. Max is a growing boy. He needs proper nutrition.''

"Just trying to help," Pierce said, throwing up his hands. "Why don't we go down to Kelly's," he proposed, referring to a cafeteria where they used to eat once or twice a week.

"Kelly's went out of business three years ago," Jessica said. "I'll just have to go to the grocery store."

"But, Mo-o-m," Max complained as he materialized in the doorway. His red cape fluttered behind him. "I'm starving!"

"Surely pizza just this once wouldn't hurt," Pierce murmured.

"Pizza?" Max's spirits immediately perked up. He tossed his cape over his shoulder. "Do we get to have pizza for supper, Mom?"

Jessica could almost see the little boy's mouth watering. Even though she'd always worked, Jessica had tried to give Max balanced meals, at least at dinnertime. It was a point of pride with her. But her head was hurting tonight, her stomach was clenched with tension, she was tired, and she had to go to work tomorrow. A trip to the grocery store was the last thing she wanted to make.

"Oh, all right. I'll call in the order," she conceded, giving Pierce an exasperated look that said "You may have gotten your way this time, but don't try it again" as she brushed past him to reach the phone.

Max clapped his hands in glee. "Yippee! Pizza! Get a real big one, Mom. I can eat five hundred pieces all by myself."

The sound of Pierce's laughter drew Jessica's gaze. The quality of his laughter had always affected her so strongly. She realized now how long it had been since she had heard it. How much she had missed it.

Pierce ruffled Max's hair affectionately. "That's quite an appetite you have there, Superman."

Max beamed proudly. "Mom said I got that from you. She said I got your smile, too." He grinned broadly. "Didn't you, Mom?"

Jessica could feel Pierce's eyes on her as she avoided his gaze. "I...I don't remember."

"Sure you do. We were watching the wedding movie, remember? The part where you were feeding each other cake. Mom said you could've eaten that whole cake all by yourself on account of your teeth are sweet or something like that. We used to watch that movie all the time, didn't we, Mom? 'Cept we had to stop, 'cuz it always made her cry."

Max rattled on, oblivious to the tension in the room. He twirled his cape over his arm. "'Specially that part where you put the ring on her finger and said you would always be together till death has a party or something like that. Didn't you always cry, Mom?"

Jessica could feel Pierce's stare, and almost against her will, she lifted her gaze. His eyes were deep and dark and liquid with emotion. *I'm sorry,* they seemed to tell her. *I'm so sorry for your pain.*

And at that moment, all Jessica wanted to do was drown in those eyes, melt inside his arms, and rejoice in the miracle that had brought her husband back to her. He was *alive.* Dear God, Pierce was alive. All those years of agony. All those days of uncertainty. All those nights of loneliness.

Pierce was alive.

Shouldn't that be all that mattered?

But it wasn't, Jessica thought with a pain deep inside her heart. There were too many unanswered questions. Too many memories. Too much time between them. Too much doubt and suspicion.

Nothing would ever be the same again.

Jessica dropped her gaze and turned away. "I'll place the order," she murmured, reaching for the phone.

"Come on, Max," Pierce said quietly. "Let's make ourselves useful. Do you know how to set the table?"

"Sure I do," Max readily agreed. "I learned when I was about...four."

"You can probably teach me a few things," Pierce said wryly, casually putting a hand on the little boy's shoulder. Jessica's heart almost stopped when she saw the way Max gazed up at his father.

"Okay," he said, grinning. "I bet we could teach each other a lot of things. I got lots of comic books. You can borrow them if you want. Maybe you could even read them to me sometime on account of I can't read yet. I like to look at the pictures, though."

Pierce smiled back, then glanced at Jessica. For a moment back there, he'd almost imagined he'd seen a glimmer of warmth in those gray depths. A trace of some of the joy he'd felt this morning, but it was all gone now—if it had ever been there in the first place. Her eyes were like twin glaciers. Frozen. Hard. Impenetrable.

And they seemed to be saying, *One month, Pierce. You have one month.*

He felt Max's little hand in his, and he looked down at his son's earnest face gazing up at him. Dear God, he thought, how would he ever be able to leave them now?

* * *

While they waited for the pizza, Jessica went upstairs to change into jeans and a sleeveless cotton blouse. After dinner, she planned to do some work on the games room before bedtime. Her goal was to have it completely remodeled by Max's birthday in July, but work at the shop had taken up most of her time lately, plus she had a buying trip planned in two weeks, which would throw off her schedule even more.

At the thought of the trip, she frowned as she climbed the stairway to the third floor and stood in the doorway. She'd have to postpone it now. There was no way she could leave Max at a time like this.

Actually, Jessica had always hated leaving Max at any time. Since he'd started kindergarten, she couldn't take him with her as she used to, so she had come to rely more and more on Brandon Chambers, an antiques buyer who traveled extensively all over the world. Brandon was good and he was reliable, but he'd never had quite the nose for the unique, as Pierce did. Jessica scowled. As Pierce had once had, she amended. She had no idea where her husband's talents lay these days.

Nor did she care.

But why did he still have to be so handsome? she thought morosely. So…masculine? The scars on his face and arm didn't diminish his good looks at all. In fact, in some strange way, they only added to his appeal. Made him seem invincible somehow. Strong and solid and…permanent.

For God's sake, hadn't she learned anything in the past five years? What was the old adage? You shouldn't judge a book by its cover? How a man looked wasn't important. It was what he was like *in-*

side that mattered. It was how trustworthy he turned out to be that counted. And she'd learned the hard way that Pierce was not to be relied upon.

Take Brandon, for instance. He was nice-looking, but not handsome like Pierce, and not nearly so tall. Silver accented his brown hair and his hazel eyes were light, open and honest. Not mysterious and soul-stabbing dark like Pierce's.

But what mattered to Jessica was that Brandon Chambers had been extremely kind to her. He'd helped her out when she'd been at her wit's end. He'd stepped in and taken over the buying trips from her when she had almost had to close the shop because she couldn't be both entrepreneur and mother at the same time.

Of course, she paid him a healthy commission for his finds, and she wasn't the only dealer in the D.C. area he bought for. But it seemed to Jessica that he always gave her a more than fair deal, and even more importantly, she trusted him completely.

So why didn't she feel anything else for him? she wondered forlornly. She knew Brandon would like for their relationship to evolve into something more than the friendly business arrangement they shared now, but Jessica had been reticent to encourage him and she didn't know why. He was perfect for her—successful, attractive, trustworthy and kind. What more could she want in a man?

Sparks, she thought immediately. A racing heart. Sweaty palms. The whole nine yards of falling in love again. That's what she wanted and what she didn't have with Brandon.

That's what she'd had with Pierce, and look where it had gotten her, she thought bitterly, kicking at a piece of broken tile. She almost wished she could get down on her hands and knees now and start chiseling away at the tile floor. The physical exertion she had to put into the project might ease some of her mounting frustration at the impossible situation she found herself in.

Instead she crossed the room and made sure the French doors to the balcony were secure. Yesterday she'd noticed that some of the railing had rotted through, and she'd cautioned Max to stay away from this room until she could get a carpenter in to replace the railing. Just to be on the safe side, she'd also shoved a sawhorse in front of the doors.

With the toe of her tennis shoe, Jessica sent another piece of white tile flying toward the opposite wall. Memories of the plans she and Pierce had made for this house came rushing back to her. Turning the converted attic into a game room had been Pierce's idea. When the children had company over, the little beggars could all go upstairs and Mom and Dad could still have their privacy, he'd said.

Children. They'd planned to have several to compensate for both their lonely childhoods. Jessica had long ago given up that dream, but at least she had Max.

No one could ever take him away from her.

When Jessica returned downstairs, the table had already been set and the pizza waited in the center. Pierce had lit candles and turned down the lights, and the room looked beautiful, soft and romantic with the panes in the stained-glass window sparkling like rubies and emeralds and aquamarines and the crystal candelabra flashing like diamonds. The dining room no longer seemed cold and perfect, but vibrantly alive and rich with color. Jessica realized with a start that it was the first time she'd seen the room by candlelight since she'd redecorated a few years ago.

She'd given up all the little luxuries that she and Pierce had once indulged in. It seemed too frivolous for just her and Max, and besides, she was always short on time. Most nights it took everything she had just to get a decent meal on the table after working all day, but somehow Pierce had managed to turn pizza and Coke into an elegant feast for three.

"Why is it so dark in here?" Max asked curiously. "Are we gonna tell ghost stories?"

"Eating by candlelight is a tradition," Pierce explained. "It's considered refined and…romantic."

"You mean like kissy face? Yuk!" Max screwed up his face in distaste.

"I thought your mother might enjoy it. She used to like to eat by candlelight."

"Why?" Max demanded, climbing into his seat. "That's girl stuff."

"Your mother is a girl. A woman," Pierce said slowly, his eyes on Jessica.

Jessica cleared her throat. "It's…very nice," she said. "Shall we sit down?"

Pierce pulled out her chair and Jessica sat down. She reached for her napkin and unobtrusively wiped her damp palms on the linen.

"Can I have the first piece, Mom? That one," Max said, reaching across the table to stick his finger into the center of a fat, gooey slice.

Jessica put the choice slab of pizza on his plate. "Max, your napkin," she reminded him quietly. She may have forgone the amenities during the past few years, but she'd at least taught Max basic table manners. It just didn't always show.

"I can use my cape," Max informed her.

Jessica shook her head. "I don't think so."

Max shrugged and stuffed his napkin into the neck of his T-shirt, and Jessica winced. "In your lap, Max."

"This is the way Nicky Perrelli's grandfather does it," Max explained. "That way, he never gets s'ghetti on his shirt." With both hands, he picked up the pizza slice, took a huge bite, then held it out as far as his arms could reach, trailing cheese across the antique white lace tablecloth. Her best one. Jessica grimaced but didn't comment. Obviously Pierce had never eaten dinner with a five-year-old.

Smiling and looking pleased with himself, Pierce placed a huge slice of pizza on Jessica's plate, then took one for himself. Jessica took a tentative bite, then sighed. *Heavenly.* She'd forgotten how divine pizza could be. It was almost a religious experience. She ate the rest of her piece with almost as much gusto as Max did, and had to restrain herself from reaching for another one.

Especially when Pierce kept urging her to eat more. "Come on," he said. "You haven't eaten enough to keep a bird alive."

"Better not," she said, sipping her drink. It wasn't even a diet Coke, she noticed. It was good. What a shame Pierce had to remind her in just one meal of everything she'd been missing lately.

"You can't be watching your weight," he commented innocently. "You look wonderful, Jesse. I like your hair that way."

In spite of herself, Jessica warmed to the compliment. What woman wouldn't? It had been so long since she'd felt attractive. Since she'd felt like a woman.

But she reminded herself just as quickly that Pierce had always known how to charm the socks off her. She wouldn't let him get away with it this time. It would take more than a few pretty phrases to sway her from her decision.

Pierce had a month, and not one day longer.

Their gazes met in the candlelight and suddenly, without warning, Jessica's mind swept her back in time, to another candlelit table, but this one in Paris. Pierce had seemed just as mysterious to her then. Just as handsome and charming, and when he'd proposed to her, Jessica had accepted wholeheartedly. She had been willing to take a chance then because she had loved him so much....

But what about now? What did she feel for him now?

With an effort, Jessica tore her gaze from Pierce, and the memories drifted away. She tried to turn her attention back to the meal, but a chill was in the air, an emptiness, as if she'd lost something precious. Jessica didn't understand it. Didn't understand why, at that moment, she should miss Pierce more than she had in years.

She gazed around the table, her husband at one end, her child at the other. She sat between them. It was such a homey scene, she thought. So innocent and normal-looking. Anyone eavesdropping on them would never have suspected the undercurrents flowing around the table.

How many times had she prayed for such a night? Jessica wondered. How many times had she wished that Pierce would come home so they could be a real family?

But Pierce hadn't come home. At least, not when she'd wished for it. Now didn't count, she thought bitterly. Now was too late.

Losing interest in his second piece of pizza, Max stared at the candles in fascination. He waved his hand, making the flames dance wildly. "Do we get to blow them out when we're done?" he asked hopefully.

"Not like you mean," Jessica told him. "These are not like birthday candles."

His expression was crestfallen. "We don't get to make a wish?"

"Yeah," Pierce echoed, his eyes darkening in the flickering light. "We don't get to make a wish? I know exactly what I would wish for."

Jessica's heart thudded against her chest at the look he gave her. "You," his eyes seemed to be saying. "I'd wish for you again, Jesse."

And what would she wish for? Jessica asked herself sternly. For yesterday? Might as well wish for the moon, because yesterday was gone forever.

"I know what I'd wish for, too," Max chimed in. "I'd wish for a dog. A real big one. Like a sheep dog, or something like that. Every kid in my class has a pet 'cept me," he mourned. "I don't even have anything to bring to the pet show next week, and Alan Michael says it's because I'm still a baby. I'm not a baby, Mom. I could take care of a dog."

"We've been all through this," Jessica said with a sigh. "I know you're not a baby, Max, but you're too young to take care of a pet all by yourself, and I just don't have the time. I'm sorry."

"Maybe I could help."

"You?" Jessica's and Max's voices piped up at the same time, hers edged with suspicion, Max's with hope.

Pierce shrugged. "I like dogs. I wouldn't mind giving Max a hand. You wouldn't have to worry about it at all, Jesse."

And what happens when you leave? Jessica wanted to scream at him. Then I'll be stuck with your responsibility, just like I was the last time. Only she had never felt that she was stuck with Max. Quite the contrary. He'd been her lifeline. Her salvation.

But he still couldn't have a pet.

She said with quiet determination, "I've already made my decision."

"But Mo-o-m!"

"I don't want to hear any more about it, Max. If you're through eating, you may be excused."

Sullenly he pushed back his chair, but as he did so, his arm dragged across the table, upsetting his glass. Dark, sweet liquid poured out all over the antique lace tablecloth.

"How many times have I told you not to set your glass so near the edge of the table?" Jessica admonished as she jumped up and began dabbing at the puddle with her napkin.

Max's lips quivered as he stood beside his chair. "I'm sorry."

"It's all right," Pierce said, coming to stand beside them. His hand reached out, but Jessica noticed he restrained from touching his son. "Everyone makes mistakes."

Gritting her teeth, Jessica ignored him. "Go on upstairs, Max, and start your bath. I'll be up there in a few minutes."

His little shoulders slumping, Max left the room. Even his cape looked wilted.

"It was just an accident," Pierce said again. "Why are you making a federal case out of it, Jesse?"

Jessica whirled on him. "That particular accident has happened almost every night for the past two weeks. He wasn't paying attention to what he was doing. He was being careless."

"He's only five years old," Pierce said, clearly annoyed.

Jessica threw the napkin onto the table. "You don't have to tell me how old my son is. I was there when he was born, remember? And for your information, five years old is not too young to begin learning about responsibility."

"Then why not let him have a dog?" Pierce countered. "What better way to teach him about responsibility?"

"And what happens when he gets tired of the animal?" Jessica flared. "The responsibility would end up being mine, and I have more than I can handle at the moment."

"All the more reason why you should let me help you."

"And what happens when you leave?" she asked coldly. "What happens if you get tired of your responsibilities? I'd have to pick up the pieces for both Max and me, and I won't do that again, Pierce. I can't." Eyes stinging with tears, Jessica turned her attention to the table and began scrubbing fiercely at the stain.

"Let me do that," Pierce said softly, putting his hand on top of hers. "It's my fault. I shouldn't have used this tablecloth. I remembered it was always your favorite. We got it in Brussels, remember?''

"Stop it."

"Stop what?"

"Stop trying to make me remember. I know why you used this tablecloth. Why you lit candles. Why you made such a production out of a simple meal." She gazed at him with cold contempt.

Pierce shrugged. "I just wanted to make our first meal as a family special."

Jessica sniffed, turning away from him. "I know exactly what you were trying to do. You were trying to make things the way they used to be. You were trying to become a part of our lives again, trying to win over Max by taking his side against me. Well, it won't work, Pierce. I won't let you use my son that way. I said you could stay here a month, and I won't go back on my word. But don't think that means I'll let you insinuate yourself into our lives any more than you already have. I won't let you take my son away from me. Max is mine.''

Pierce stared at her in shock. "Is that what you think I want to do? Max is *our* son, Jessica. I don't want to take him away from you. I just want to share him with you. I want to be part of his life. And yours, too, if you'll let me."

"Then tell me where you were for the past five years," she demanded.

"You know I can't do that."

"Can't or won't?"

It was Pierce's turn to throw down the napkin. His dark eyes blazed with anger. "You think I'm lying about this?''

"That thought has crossed my mind," she admitted.

"Why else would you be so unwilling to see a psychiatrist?"

His eyes glinted dangerously. "This is crazy, Jessica. You're being unreasonable."

"*I'm* being unreasonable! If I had amnesia, I'd try every way possible to get my memory back."

He shook his head. "This isn't you talking, Jesse. This sounds like Jay."

"No, it *is* me," she insisted. "You just don't know me anymore. Of course I have suspicions. I can't help it. I can't just ignore the years you've been gone. I can't pretend you've been here all along because that's the way it is for you." She paused for a breath. "I can't turn back the clock, Pierce. I can't be the woman you left behind. I don't want to be."

"I'm not asking you to be," Pierce said. He turned away, frowning. "Look, I know this is hard for you. It is for me, too. All I'm asking is for you to give me a chance to prove to you how much I love you and Max. How much I want to be a part of this family." He turned to look at her, his gaze earnest. "Isn't that all that matters?" he asked quietly.

Jessica refused to answer. She walked over to the window and crossed her arms as she stared blindly into the darkness. I don't know, she thought. I don't know what matters anymore.

"I'm not trying to threaten your independence, Jesse." His voice lowered. "I wouldn't want to diminish anything you've accomplished."

What she'd accomplished. Images of the past five years flashed through her mind. The long nights spent walking the floor with Max when he couldn't sleep. The grueling hours at the shop the next day when she was dead on her feet. The endless juggling of hours when there were never enough in one day.

What she'd accomplished, Jessica thought, was to feel like a robot half of the time. Hardly ever like a woman. Why, after all these years, did that fact bother her so much?

She sensed Pierce's presence behind her. Could almost imagine his arms steadfastly around her. Her heart began to beat a little faster. His hand touched her arm, a tentative caress, and Jessica closed her eyes.

Please, she thought, don't make me care again. But her pulse was racing at even so slight a touch.

"Jesse." His breath warmed her cheek. "Don't you see? I'm not a threat to you. You're the one who holds all the cards now. You're the one who's in control."

But you're wrong, Jessica cried inwardly.

She had never felt less in control.

Both of Pierce's hands were on her arms now, and he pulled her back until she was leaning against him, her head nestled against his shoulder. For just a moment, Jessica let herself relish the support, allowed herself the luxury of his strength, but then she remembered that he was the man who had left her without an explanation, and she stiffened, tried to move away.

But Pierce held her. He whispered against her ear. "Let me hold you. Just for a minute."

The ragged desperation in his voice made Jessica's eyes sting with tears. Almost unwillingly she felt herself relax against him, and Pierce's arms tightened around her. In his embrace, it was almost too easy to remember how much she had once loved him, needed him.

Desired him.

Dear God, she prayed. Don't make me want him again.

"Have you been lonely, Jesse? Did you miss me?"

His hands were so warm and comforting against her bare arms, but his words brought the past back to her, made her remember the hurt and the doubts and the endless tears.

She pulled herself away from him and stared bleakly out the window. "The first few weeks after you were gone, I wanted to die. I didn't think I could go on without you. I wanted to give up." Jessica sensed his reaction to her words. His despair. She turned to face him. "But I couldn't give up," she said. "I had our child to think of. Max was born exactly two months after you disappeared."

"Were you alone?" His dark eyes flickered with pain.

He'd asked the question as if dreading to know the answer, but Jessica didn't try to shield him. Why should she? She lifted her chin and looked him in the eye. "Yes. Jay was out of the country. There was no one."

Pierce was silent for a moment, then he said, "You'll never know how much I wish I could have been there with you. God, Jesse, I've lost so much more than just memories. I've lost a part of our life together that I can never get back. I'm so sorry. I'm sorry I let you down."

"Sorry is an easy word, Pierce," Jessica said, forcing back the tears. She wouldn't let him get to her. No matter what he said or did, she wouldn't allow herself to forget what he had done to her.

"But what else can I say?" he asked with an edge of desperation in his voice.

"Nothing. There's nothing you can say," she said, but there was a numb, hollow feeling inside her. "What's done is done. I can't help feeling the way I feel."

"Do you hate me that much, Jesse? Are you that bitter? Can it be," he asked softly, his eyes dark and intense, "that you would forgive me for dying but not for living?"

Chapter 7

"And they lived happily ever after."

Jessica closed the book she'd been reading to Max and bent to kiss his satiny cheek. "I'm sorry I yelled at you earlier, sweetie. I've had a lot on my mind lately, and I took it out on you. That was unfair of me."

Max yawned widely, his eyes starting to droop. He snuggled under the covers. "It's okay, Mom. I forgive you. Everyone makes mistakes." His tone mimicked his father's perfectly, and Jessica's heart turned over.

She couldn't get Pierce's accusation out of her head. It echoed through her mind and pounded against her temples as relentlessly as a drumbeat.

Can it be that you would forgive me for dying but not for living?

Jessica closed her eyes, feeling the pain of his words deep down inside her. She hugged Max tightly, tucked him in, then walked down the hall to her own room.

But she knew she wouldn't be able to sleep. Pierce's words, the pain in his voice wouldn't let her.

"It's not true," she whispered into the darkness.

But even as she denied it, deep in her heart she knew that Pierce was right. She couldn't forgive him for being alive because that meant that he'd deserted her, just as everyone else in her life had. She couldn't forgive him for being alive because that meant he'd stopped loving her, just as all the others had. She couldn't forgive him for being alive because that meant he could leave her again.

And Jessica was very much afraid she wouldn't be able to stand it a second time.

Voices. He heard voices.

Were they coming back? Would he have to endure their torture all over again?

In some ways, Pierce welcomed their return because that meant they hadn't gotten what they wanted yet. That meant he hadn't succumbed to the pain. The intense psychological training he'd undergone early in his career had worked. He could fade to black and the secrets he carried in his head would remain protected. Pierce knew that he would die before revealing them. That was what he was trained to do. That was what the agency expected him to do.

The door to his cell slid open and two men entered. They grabbed Pierce by the arms and jerked him up off the damp stone floor. He could barely walk, but they didn't seem to notice. They dragged him across the filthy floor, shoved him out into the murky corridor, and when he fell to his knees, one of them kicked him in the side, where at least two of his ribs had already been broken.

They spoke in low, covert tones. In spite of the fact that Pierce was fluent in Spanish, he lost much of their rapid-fire dialogue. One word kept cropping up. *Traidor.* Traitor. Were they talking about him?

They hauled him down the corridor and into a small office where they shoved him down onto a straight-back wooden chair, blindfolded him, and secured his hands and feet to the slats and rungs of the chair. The room grew silent as the men left. Pierce was in complete darkness. He knew better than to struggle against the ropes. The men were experts, just as he was. The more he moved, the tighter the bindings would become, and when at last they released him, the pain would be excruciating.

But the pain was the least of it. He could tolerate the pain. What he couldn't stand was the not knowing. The uncertainty of his position. Jessica must be going crazy by now. What had they told her? Did she know the truth about him now?

Pierce groaned, wishing he could have told her himself. She must feel so betrayed, he thought. So angry. He had to get away from here and somehow make it right with her again.

But where the hell was he? What had happened to him? What had gone wrong? One moment he'd been standing in the sunshine, the next thing he knew he'd awakened in a dark, stinking cell with a lump the size of a baseball on the back of his head.

That had been three days ago, the best he could tell.

Since then he'd been beaten twice, and each time the previous wounds had reopened. Pierce suspected that infection had set in. He was very much afraid he would die in this place, that he would never see Jesse again. Never see his child.

The door opened and closed. Automatically Pierce turned his head toward the sound. Two men stood talking in low voices at the door, but it wasn't the same two who had brought him here. Though he couldn't distinguish any of their words, he could tell by their tone that they spoke with authority. They were men in control, used to giving orders and having them obeyed. They both spoke in Spanish, but one of them had an accent. An American accent. Pierce strained to hear. Did he recognize that voice?

He sat listening to the slow, measured footsteps as one of the men crossed the wooden floor toward him. The steps paused in front of him, and Pierce tensed.

"Are you ready to talk?" a voice asked. But it wasn't the American. This man's English was flavored with the barest hint of a Spanish accent. Cuban to be precise. Pierce's predicament was beginning to make a grim sort of sense.

"I don't know what you want," he said.

"Then you are a very stupid man," the voice said. "How long do you think you can hold out to our... questioning? Sooner or later you will have to tell us what we wish to know."

"When hell freezes over," Pierce said.

"As you wish."

The American laughed. Again Pierce wondered if he recognized the voice. If he knew the man.

The Cuban's footsteps beat a staccato against the wooden floor as he crossed the room and opened the door. He barked an order, and then Pierce heard more footsteps. Two other men entered the room, the two goons who had manhandled him earlier, he guessed.

"Do what you want with him," the man in charge

told them. "But don't kill him. Yet." Then the door slammed as he and the American left the room.

Pierce knew what was coming. He'd been through it before. As he mentally braced himself for the pain, a picture of dark hair, gray eyes and a shy smile flashed through his mind, and Pierce knew that he could endure just about anything if it meant he would some day be able to see Jesse again.

He savored her image for just a moment, then he gave himself the command that would make his mind shut down.

"Fade to black," he whispered.

"Fade to black. Fade to black," Pierce mumbled over and over.

Jessica sat down on the edge of his bed and grabbed his shoulders. His skin felt red-hot to her touch. His head thrashed against the pillow, and he was trembling all over. Jessica tried to shake him awake, but he flinched away from her touch as if she had hurt him.

"Pierce, wake up," she said. "You're having a nightmare."

At the sound of her voice, he seemed to calm down for a moment. His eyes flickered but didn't open. "They're coming again, Jesse. I can hear the footsteps."

"It's all right," she soothed. "It's only a dream."

He clutched his head with both hands. The grooves around his mouth and eyes deepened. "I have to forget you now, Jesse. I'm sorry, but I have to forget everything. I have to fade to black."

"Pierce, wake up," Jessica said, more firmly this time. She reached out and shook his arm. Pierce's eyes flew open as he grabbed her. Jessica gasped, frightened. She tried to scramble away from him, but Pierce's hand pinned her to the spot.

His hair was all mussed and his eyes gleamed in the dim light from the hallway. He looked savage and dangerous as he glared at her like a wild animal caught in a trap.

Jessica's heart pounded with fright. His hand seared her arm, branded her. Made her all too aware of the flimsy nightgown she wore, the state of his own undress. His chest and arms were bare, thinner than she remembered, but still strong. Still muscular. Still able to hold her, even if she should struggle.

But Jessica wasn't struggling. She was staring at her husband, at the stranger who looked for all the world like a man who could just as easily kill her as kiss her. She wondered wildly if he had the notion to do both.

"What are you doing in here?" His voice was dark with suspicion. His eyes flashed deadly in the pale light. Jessica shivered, unable to tear her gaze away from him.

"I heard you call out. You were having a nightmare," she said. "Wh-what were you dreaming about?"

"I don't remember." He cocked his head, listening. "What's that noise?"

"It's just the rain," Jessica said, nodding toward the window. "A storm blew in awhile ago." She felt his hold on her arm ease, but he didn't release her. She looked down at his hand, then back up at him. "You said my name in your sleep. You said, 'I have to forget you now, Jesse.' What did you mean, Pierce? Why did you have to forget me?"

His hand dropped from her arm. He lifted both his

hands to his temples, much as he'd done in his sleep. "I don't know."

Jessica leaned forward. "What does fade to black mean?"

He dropped his hands and looked at her. "What?"

"You said 'I have to fade to black.' What does that mean, Pierce?"

He was looking past her toward the window, staring blindly into the wet darkness. Something flickered in his eyes, a flash of recognition. Then he shook his head. "I don't remember."

"But you have to," she said desperately, reaching out impulsively to touch his arm. "Dr. Prescott said that sometimes memories manifest themselves in dreams. If you were dreaming about what happened to you, then you must remember something. Think about it, Pierce. Try to bring back the dream. Try to remember why you had to forget me."

"I can't, dammit," he exploded, shoving her hand away. "Don't you understand? I don't remember anything. Beyond two days ago, my mind is a complete blank for the past five years."

"But you remember things that happened *before* five years ago."

"Obviously." His gaze roamed over her with the same possessive gleam she was beginning to recognize.

Jessica ignored the insinuation. She didn't want to get sidetracked from their conversation. It was too important. Too crucial to her peace of mind. "Then you must be purposefully blacking out those five years. For some reason, you don't want to remember."

"You don't know that."

"I'd say it's a reasonable assumption," she said.

"Look at all the scars you have, Pierce. On your face and on your arm. You must have been in terrible pain at one time. Maybe that's why you can't remember. Maybe you're trying to block out all that pain. A psychiatrist might be able to help you," she said. "Pierce, you have to go see Dr. Layton. The sooner the better."

"Do you think I'm crazy?" His tone was bitter, almost mocking, but Jessica sensed something deeper in his voice, an uncertainty that matched the flash of fear in his eyes. Then he shuttered his expression, once again closing her out.

"I think we both need help in dealing with this situation," Jessica said helplessly. "We can't go on like this indefinitely."

"I didn't think we were. You gave me a month, as I recall." Pierce sat up in bed and the cover slipped even lower. Jessica tried to keep her eyes on his face, but light from the hallway pooling on his shoulders and chest drew her gaze downward, where the dark hair narrowed and disappeared beneath the quilt. She could remember with vivid detail—

Her gaze flew back up to his. Her face flamed. What was she doing, ogling him like an infatuated teenager? Like a...a love-starved widow? What in the world was *wrong* with her?

Nothing, Jessica thought. Nothing was wrong with her, and that was the problem.

"Would you like to reopen negotiations?" Pierce asked, sensing her reaction. His voice was low and deeply sensual. His eyes darkened, burned with an intensity that made her tremble. His lips curved into the barest hint of a smile. "A month isn't much time, Jesse."

It might be too long, she thought. "Pierce...." Her

voice trailed off as his hand lifted and caressed her cheek. Jessica closed her eyes at the tenderness. At the quiver of emotion inside her. "Pierce?"

"I'm right here, Jesse." His fingers wove through her hair and lifted the curls as if carefully testing their weight. He let the silky strands slip through his fingers, and Jessica heard the sharp intake of his breath just before he pulled her to him.

The moment his lips touched hers, the tenderness vanished, replaced by a deep, aching need that slashed through Jessica's defenses with stunning velocity. With his hands on her arms, Pierce urged her up, until they were both kneeling on the bed. His pajama bottoms were cotton, almost as thin and revealing as the satin nightgown she wore. They both might as well have been naked.

The heat scorched through the fabric of their nightclothes and fused their bodies together until Jessica could no longer distinguish her own heartbeat from Pierce's. She clung to him, letting him part her lips with his tongue, allowing him to delve into the velvet recesses of her mouth, permitting him to touch her wherever and whenever he wished. Her body came alive beneath his hands.

Five years, she thought. Five years she had waited for this kiss. She would have waited an eternity, she realized. No one could ever have made her feel this way. No one but Pierce...

He lifted his mouth from hers, and Jessica sobbed a breath. She was trembling all over, her body on fire with need. Pierce's hands tunneled through her hair, holding her face still as his eyes caressed her every feature.

"Again," he whispered heatedly, dipping his head

to hers. This time Jessica was ready for his kiss. This time it was she who parted his lips, tangled her tongue with his until Pierce groaned. He cupped her bottom with his hands, pulled her even more tightly against him as the second kiss turned into the third and then the fourth....

His hands were all over her, making her burn with a passion she had buried for so many years. Making her want him as she had never wanted anyone. Making her lose control and loving it. His hand found her breast, massaged the swollen peak until Jessica arched against him.

"My God," he groaned. "It was never this way before."

Jessica barely heard him. Her lips ached for his kisses and she reached for him, but Pierce's hands closed around her wrists, stopping her.

"Wait a minute," he said.

His tone had changed. Something was wrong. Confused, Jessica gazed up at him. His eyes, hot with desire only moments before, now gleamed with cold suspicion. Her own passion cooled as a chill of dread crawled up her spine.

"It was never this way before," Pierce repeated slowly, still holding her wrist. "*You* were never this way."

"I don't know what you mean." Jessica glanced away, embarrassed. She was all too conscious now of the way they were dressed. All too aware of the echoes of passion still throbbing inside that room. Dear God, what was the matter with her? Had she completely lost her senses?

"You were never that easily aroused." He made it

sound like an accusation. As if there was something wrong with her.

Hot anger poured over her at his insinuation. Jessica jerked her hands from his hold and jumped from the bed. "Just what are you accusing me of, Pierce? What right do you have to talk to me that way?"

"I'm your husband," he said with icy calm. "I have every right to know what you were doing while I was gone. Who taught you to kiss like that, Jessica? Who showed you how to lose control? God knows, it wasn't *me.*"

"How dare you?" she screamed. "How dare you accuse me of being unfaithful to you? And what if I was? You were the one who left *me.* You have no claim on me anymore."

"Don't I?" The look in his eyes frightened her. Made her tremble all over again.

"No," she said uncertainly. She backed away from him, shoving her hands in her hair. "I can't believe I let you kiss me that way," she whispered, tears scalding her eyes.

"Which part can't you believe?" Slowly Pierce got up and stalked her across the room. "That you let me kiss you or that you enjoyed it?"

"I didn't enjoy it." She was lying and they both knew it. Jessica felt the wall behind her back and realized she had nowhere else to run. Pierce knew it, too. He planted his hands on the wall on either side of her face and entrapped her until she was forced to look up at him, forced to meet his suspicious eyes.

"You're mine," he said, not tenderly. "Make no mistake about that."

"You're the one who's mistaken," Jessica told him. Her voice shook with anger and frustration and a thousand other emotions she didn't dare name. She brushed the tears from her face with the back of her hand. "I've changed, Pierce. I don't need you to tell me what to do anymore. I don't need you for anything."

"Not even for this?" His finger traced the outline of her lips, and Jessica sucked in her breath. Even so light a touch could send thrill after thrill spinning through her. She shoved his hand away.

"No," she denied, as much to herself as to Pierce. "Especially not for that."

"Because there's someone else?"

"I told you last night there's no one else."

"But there has been. You don't kiss the way you used to kiss, Jessica."

"I don't do a lot of things the way I used to do them."

His eyes hardened. "Such as?"

"I don't owe you any explanations."

She tried to brush past him, but Pierce caught her arm and stopped her. "This isn't over yet, Jesse. Not by a long shot."

"Yes, it is," she said, trying to jerk her arm from his grasp. "You just don't want to believe it. Now let go of me."

"Not until—"

"You leave her alone!"

Pierce and Jessica whirled in unison. Max stood in the doorway, his little hands doubled into fists at his side as he eyed Pierce with all the bravado a five-year-old boy could muster. He wore his Superman cape over his pajamas, and the cowlick at the crown of his head stuck straight up, giving him a comical yet vulnerable appearance. But his eyes—his father's eyes—

were dark and steely with disapproval. His bottom lip quivered but remained defiant.

"It's okay, Max," Jessica soothed. Both she and Pierce started across the room toward their son, but the little boy backed away. His angry gaze focused on Pierce. His fists tightened at his side.

"I thought you were my dad," he said, his voice trembling with tears. "I thought you were a good guy, like Batman or…or Superman. But you're not. You're a bad man. You tried to hurt my mom."

"I didn't, Max," Pierce denied, spreading his hands in supplication. "I would never hurt your mom. I promise."

"Yes, you did," Max accused, standing his ground. He trailed his pajama sleeve across his nose. "I saw you. You made her cry. You're not a hero at all. You're a bad guy," he shouted. "I hate you! I wish you'd never come back here! I wish you were dead again, that's what I wish!"

Max turned and raced down the hallway as fast as his little legs would carry him. An awkward silence fell over the room. Stunned, Jessica looked over at Pierce and started to say something—she wasn't sure what—but the stricken look on his face stopped her.

Behind her, she heard her son's footsteps on the staircase, heard his bedroom door slam shut.

But still she hovered in the doorway, torn between her husband's pain and her son's fear. Max needed her. She had to go to him, but the look on Pierce's face, the agony in his eyes—dear God, how would she feel if Max had turned against her like that? What would she do if her son didn't love her, didn't want her, didn't need her?

"He's just a little boy," she whispered. "He didn't mean it."

"He meant it," Pierce said, his eyes distant and bleak. "He meant every word of it. But you know what hurts the most, Jesse? I've seen that same look on your face. I've seen that same wish right there in your eyes."

Without another word he turned, grabbed the jeans that had been draped across a chair, went into the bathroom and closed the door.

Jessica took a deep breath, opened her son's bedroom door and stepped inside. The room, with its crowded shelves and toy-strewn floor, had a forlorn look to it. Superman, Batman and a host of other human and superhuman heroes stared down at her accusingly from the walls. She'd failed him, they seemed to be saying. She'd failed her son.

On the floor at her feet, Max's cape lay in a red puddle. Jessica stooped and picked it up, smoothing the satiny cloth beneath her fingers. He must really be upset to have abandoned his cape, she thought.

She turned toward the bed with trepidation. What in the world could she possibly say to him? Naturally it was all her fault. She'd always thought Max's fascination with superheroes a harmless game, but now she saw it for what it really was.

Max had been looking for a father in these men. He'd been looking for someone to look up to, someone to admire. A role model. He'd been looking for Pierce, and he'd learned the hard way tonight that his father was only a man. A man who made mistakes.

You're not being fair, Jessica told herself. You can't blame all this on Pierce.

But if he'd never come back—

If he hadn't made her want him—

She put her hands to her face. If only she could turn back the clock, wake up yesterday morning and find the world normal and safe again. If only she could protect her son not just from this hurt but also from all the pain he was bound to experience throughout his life. She didn't have the power to do that, though. No one did.

Jessica walked over to his bed, holding his cape. He'd pulled the cover up over his head and was trying to ignore her. He lay perfectly still, not making a sound. They'd been through this routine before.

"Max? Can I talk to you for a minute? Honey, I know you're upset...." She sat down on the edge of the bed and reached for her son. She found only a pillow. Frowning, Jessica jerked back the covers. The bed was empty.

She jumped up and looked anxiously around the room. "Max? Where are you? Come on, sweetie. I want to talk to you."

No answer.

Jessica crossed the hall to the bathroom. The night-light revealed the sink, the toilet, the bathtub—but no Max.

"All right, Max, I know you're upset, but you get out here this instant." She tried to keep the panic out of her voice, but her concern was growing by the minute. Jessica hurried up and down the hallway, opening doors and turning on lights.

She stood at the top of the stairs, her hands planted on her hips. How could he have just disappeared like that? She couldn't have been more than two or three minutes behind him. He couldn't have come back down the stairs without her seeing him. He had to be hiding someplace up here.

But she'd looked everywhere except the unfinished game room on the third floor, which was off-limits to Max. He wouldn't have gone up there. He wouldn't have deliberately disobeyed her. But what if he had? What if he'd somehow managed to open the balcony doors...

Jessica whirled and ran down the hallway and bounded up the stairs that led to the third floor. She threw open the door, flipped on the light and searched frantically for Max. But the French doors were still closed, the sawhorse still in place, and Jessica let out a breath of relief. She turned and started to switch off the light when she heard a muffled noise. A very slight sound but it lifted the hair on the back of her neck.

"Oh, God." Jessica was across the floor in one second. She shoved the sawhorse out of the way and reached to unlock the French door, but the latch had already been turned. Max had used the sawhorse—her barricade—to stand on in order to reach the lock. He'd opened the doors and gone outside.

Jessica ran out onto the balcony, almost slipping on the rain-slick boards. Thunder crashed in her ears, and lightning blazed a fiery trail in the eastern sky. Then all was black again. But in the instant when the night was lit up, Jessica had seen what she had feared the most. Her heart stopped in midbeat. A whole section of the railing had fallen away at the end, revealing nothing but a gap of darkness and a thirty-foot drop to the stone terrace below.

"Max!" She screamed his name into the wind.

His pitiful little voice weakly answered her. "Mom? I fell down, Mom."

"Oh, God." Jessica was on her hands and knees, peering over the balcony. A part of the railing was still fastened to its support, but the other end hung freely, and this flimsy hold was all that kept Max from falling to the stones below.

Another flash of lightning revealed his form to her, and Jessica caught her breath in terror. His legs dangled in midair, and when he turned his face up to her, she saw his hands slip on the board.

"Hold on, baby," she said. "Please, Max, hold as tightly as you can until I tell you to let go. I'm going to grab hold of you now, okay? Don't be frightened."

"I'm falling, Mommy!"

"No, you're not, Max. You're very strong, remember? I know you can hold on." Jessica continued to coach him as she lay on her stomach on the wet balcony. She stretched her arms down toward Max. Inches remained between them. She slid more of her body through the opening, but the slippery floor was treacherous. She had to be careful.

"Think what Superman would do if he were here. He'd hang on, wouldn't he, Max, until someone could reach him? He wouldn't let go for anything."

She still couldn't reach him. The board creaked beneath his weight. The railing slipped even farther away from its remaining support. Jessica was hanging so far over the edge now that she feared even if she could grab her son, she wouldn't be able to hold his weight. They both might fall. She tried again, making a desperate attempt as her body slid dangerously close to the edge.

Dear God, she prayed. Help me.

"Move out of the way." Strong hands grabbed her, pulled her back from the edge. She rolled away as

Pierce took her place on the balcony floor, stretching his long arms through the opening to find his son.

"I've got you, Max," Jessica heard him say calmly. "Let go, son."

"No! You'll drop me!" Max cried. Jessica heard the ominous squeak of the support as it pulled farther away from the balcony.

"I won't drop you," Pierce said. "I promise."

"No!" Max cried again, wrenching his arm free.

Jessica scrambled to her feet and leaned over the balcony, until she could see Max. The part of the railing he clung to was slipping farther and farther away. Pierce's hand was reaching out to him, but every time Pierce tried to grab him, Max would move away, causing the board he clutched to swing precariously.

"Max," she called, trying to keep the terror from her voice, "listen to me. Let Pierce take your hand, sweetie. It's okay. Let him take your hand, Max."

Max shook his head, but when Pierce's hand closed around his arm again, he didn't try to move away. He still clung to the broken railing with all his might.

"Let go of the railing, Max," Jessica urged. "Pierce has you. He won't let you fall, I promise."

"Trust me, son. I won't let you fall," Pierce coaxed quietly.

Max hesitated, then with a pitiful "Mommy!" he let go of his handhold, and Pierce lifted him up to safety.

A split second later, Max was in Jessica's arms. Small, cold hands came up and clung to her neck. "It's okay," she whispered. "You're safe." He was shaking so badly Jessica could hear his teeth chattering. She wrapped her arms around him, holding him close.

Over Max's shoulder, she looked up at Pierce. Rain lashed his face and ran in rivers down his skin. Jessica could barely distinguish his features in the darkness, but she knew, somehow, that he was as shaken as she was.

"Thank you," she said. "If you hadn't been here—"

"Don't think about that," he said. He knelt and put his hand on Max's head. "I *was* here. That's all that matters."

"But I couldn't reach him—"

"And I couldn't make him let go. He needed us both tonight, Jesse," Pierce said quietly.

If Pierce hadn't been there—

Jessica closed her eyes, feeling her body tremble all over. She was still in the throes of shock and couldn't seem to shake it. Max could have been killed tonight, she thought. Her baby could have died because she couldn't reach him. Couldn't save him.

If Pierce hadn't been there—

Her legs refusing to support her, Jessica sank onto the floor beside Max's bed and watched her son sleep. Only moments earlier, she'd helped him change into dry pajamas, then fixed him a cup of hot chocolate. Max had gulped down the drink, eaten the last of the marshmallows from the bottom of the cup, then promptly fell asleep.

But Jessica couldn't bear to leave him. Not yet. She had to be able to look at him whenever she wanted, to touch him if she needed to in order to reassure herself over and over again that he was really safe. That everything was all right.

But if Pierce hadn't been there—

She would have found a way to reach him, Jessica tried to convince herself. She would have found a way to save her son. She had always been able to take care of him by herself. They'd never needed anyone else.

He needed us both tonight.

Dear God, tonight she hadn't been enough. She *had* needed someone else. She'd needed Pierce, and he'd been there. He'd been there for her when she'd needed him the most.

Shouldn't that be all that mattered?

Jessica felt a tear slip from the corner of her eye and trail down her cheek. She wrapped her arms around her knees and hugged them tightly as she rocked herself back and forth beside her son's bed. Not since that awful day when her sister had left her at the orphanage could Jessica remember feeling so lost and confused.

And so terribly frightened because she knew, without a doubt, that tonight her world had been changed forever.

Chapter 8

"*Punished?* You mean I gotta be punished?" Max glared at Jessica in disbelief as he shoved the last bite of his blueberry waffle into his mouth. "But, Mom, I coulda been killed last night. I coulda been smashed into a million pieces on the terrace. My head coulda been knocked off." He grabbed his throat dramatically. "There woulda been blood everywhere—"

"Enough," Jessica said, putting up her hand to halt the gruesome tirade. The image of her son dangling from the balcony last night was still too fresh in her mind to appreciate Max's graphic embellishments this morning. But at least he didn't appear any the worse for wear, she noticed in relief. In fact, he looked pretty happy with himself this morning. Almost glowing.

Until she'd mentioned the little matter of punishment, of course. Now he scowled at her with dark, disapproving eyes. "What do you think a reasonable punishment would be for your disobedience, Max?"

"My what?"

"For your having gone out on the balcony last night after I told you, more than once, to stay away from the third floor until I could get that railing fixed."

"Oh, that." Max swirled the syrup on his plate with his finger, then lifted it to his mouth.

"Yes, that," Jessica said. "I was thinking no TV for a week. What do you think?"

Max eyed her in horror. "Starting when?"

"Immediately."

"But Mo-o-m. Superman comes on tonight."

Jessica sipped her coffee. "Sorry. You should have thought about that last night."

"But a week's a long time," Max wailed. "I'll be thirty-eight by the time I get to watch Superman again."

"Could be," Jessica agreed, "if you don't stop arguing with me. One week without TV and that's final. End of discussion."

Max's bottom lip jutted out in defiance, but then his eyes lit up as he gazed past Jessica's shoulder.

"Good morning."

The sound of Pierce's voice startled her. He always entered a room so quietly, she thought, almost as if he were sneaking up on her.

Jessica's heart raced as she turned toward the door. He stood with one hand propped against the frame as he smiled across the room at Max. Then at her. And her heart beat even faster.

He was dressed in jeans and a navy cotton sweater with the sleeves pushed up, and Jessica's first thought was that he looked good this morning. Real good. Except for the fact that the clothes hung a little too loosely on his lean frame, he looked almost like his old self.

She smiled timidly at him. "Good morning," she answered. "Did you manage to get any sleep last night after the excitement?"

He grinned, and she realized too late that he'd deliberately misinterpreted her words.

"Not much," he murmured.

A memory of that kiss they'd shared instantly popped into her head, and Jessica's face flamed as she stuttered, "I—mean after the—the rescue and all. I want to thank you again for everything you did."

His eyes darkened for a moment as he stared at her. "Don't thank me, Jesse. Max is my son, too, you know."

"Yes, I know." Her gaze dropped, and she toyed with the topaz ring on her finger. It was a fact she had grappled with for days now.

"Did you save my life last night?" Max chimed in.

"I don't know," Pierce said, straightening from the doorway. He crossed the kitchen and sat down at the table with them. "What do you think?"

"I think you did," Max said, bursting with excitement. "Wait'll I tell all the guys. You were just like Superman. Can you fly?"

Pierce laughed. "Only in my dreams."

"Know what? Me and Marcus Tate already figured out how you got all those scars. I bet it was from fightin' bad guys, right? 'Specially that real big one on your face."

"Max!" Jessica was appalled by her son's lack of tact.

Max's eyes widened guilelessly. "What'd I say wrong? I like scars. I want a bunch of 'em all over.

Maybe even a tattoo someday.'' He rubbed his nose with his sticky finger. "Do you have any more scars? Can I see them?''

Jessica cringed but Pierce appeared undaunted. He said, "Not at the breakfast table, I'm afraid. I don't think your mom would approve.''

He grinned at Max, man to man, then turned and met her gaze. For a moment, for one split second, their eyes held and something special passed between them. A mutual affection for their son that created an undeniable bond. No matter what happened in the future between them, Max would always be there to remind them how very much they had once loved each other.

Jessica felt a knot form in her throat, and she had to look away. Had to sever the hold Pierce had on her this morning, because no matter how grateful she was to him for last night, she was still very much afraid of him. Afraid of the man he might have become.

"I can't watch no TV for a whole week," Max moaned, eyeing Pierce hopefully. "Can you believe that?''

"I can't watch *any* TV," Jessica corrected.

"Yeah, but you don't even like it," Max said. "A week's a long time, isn't it?'' He turned his big, dark eyes on Pierce. Jessica was familiar with the tactic. She felt her own resolve weaken, but instantly hardened it. She couldn't let Max charm her out of this one. His disobedience could have gotten him killed last night. She shuddered, remembering the close call.

Unfortunately Pierce hadn't had as much experience dealing with their son's devastating appeal. "Well....'' he hedged, eyeing Jessica doubtfully.

Don't say it, she thought. Don't you dare say it.

"It *does* seem a bit harsh.''

He said it. Jessica pursed her lips. All the good feelings she'd had for Pierce last night and this morning evaporated in the twinkling of an eye. She folded her napkin precisely, creased it, and set it on the table. ''I told you earlier the subject is closed, Max,'' she said, trying to keep a firm rein on her anger. After all, Max was only a little boy. She could hardly blame him for trying to capitalize on his newly forming relationship with his father. Kids always played one parent against the other when they could get away with it.

It was Pierce she blamed. He should have known better. ''If I hear another word about it, I'll make it two weeks.'' She looked up and defiantly met Pierce's gaze. Instead of looking contrite, he merely stared back at her.

Incensed, Jessica pushed her chair back and stood. ''Time to catch the bus, Max. Go find your backpack.''

Dutifully Max left the room. As soon as the door swung closed behind him, Jessica whirled. ''How dare you undermine my authority like that? What do you think you're doing?''

Her attack seemed to catch Pierce off guard. He gazed at her thoughtfully for a moment, then shrugged. ''You're right. I shouldn't have said anything in front of Max. But you know, Jessica, you really should have discussed his punishment with me first.''

Jessica's mouth flew open. ''Discussed it with you? Why would I do that?''

''Because I'm his father. Because I should have a say-so in these kinds of decisions. I happen to think the punishment is too harsh, considering the circumstances.''

Jessica planted her hands on her hips. ''No TV for

a week is too harsh for deliberately disobeying me? He could have been killed last night. At the very least, seriously injured. I can't let him think that kind of behavior is acceptable."

"Yes, but you set awfully high standards, Jessica."

Jessica couldn't believe what she was hearing. "Are you saying you *condone* what he did?"

"No. But I'm saying there were extenuating circumstances. He'd seen us fighting. He was upset and confused, and he did something he knew would get our attention."

Jessica turned away and started clearing the table. He might have a point, but she didn't want to see it. "Extenuating circumstances is always a convenient excuse for doing something we know we shouldn't."

"Are we talking about Max now or me?"

Jessica set down the stack of dishes and turned. "All right," she said, "let's talk about you. You've been back in this house for less than three days and already you expect to be included in the decisions I make regarding my son. You've undermined my authority with him more than once. You've made it seem as if it's you and him against me. You're trying to bribe him into loving you, but what happens when you leave, Pierce? What happens when you're no longer here for him to count on?"

"You mean what happens when my month is up?" he challenged. Anger sparked in the dark depths of his eyes.

"Yes," Jessica said, "that's exactly what I mean."

Pierce's gaze narrowed. "Let's get a few things straight, Jessica. You're the one who set the deadline, not me. You're the one who seems obsessed with my leaving. If and when I do leave, it'll be because *you* want me to. Our relationship may end, if that's your choice, but I won't give up Max. He's my son, and now that I've found him, not you or anyone else will ever take him away from me. Is that clear?''

Crystal clear, Jessica thought, stunned. She watched Pierce turn and exit the room as she sat back down at the table, her legs shaking. Would it come to that? she wondered desperately. Is that how it would finally end between her and Pierce? In a bitter battle over their son?

Memories drifted through her mind—the day she'd told Pierce she was pregnant, the elation he'd felt, the elaborate fuss he'd made over her. They'd looked forward to the arrival of their first child with such joy and anticipation. A child had seemed the perfect way to cement their union. A precious gift that only they could give to one another.

Now everything seemed like such a mess. What if Pierce decided he wanted more of Max than Jessica was willing to share? What if he decided he wanted to raise their son himself? What if he tried to take Max away from her?

Panic mushroomed inside her at the thought, along with a determination so fierce it almost took her breath away. Jessica clutched the edge of the table so tightly her knuckles whitened.

There was no way she would ever allow that to happen. Max was hers, and the sooner Pierce realized it, the better off they'd all be.

But over the next few days, Jessica began to feel her old life slipping further and further away from her grasp. Gone were the quiet, routine, uncomplicated days of the past. Now all her waking thoughts centered on Pierce, her mixed feelings toward him, and her concern about his growing closeness with their son.

Much to Jessica's chagrin, every day Max seemed to become more and more attached to Pierce. In the evenings before dinner, they took to playing baseball together in the backyard. Sometimes Sharon's daughter, Allie, would join them, and the yard would be filled with shouts of laughter and childish squeals of triumph.

Reluctantly Jessica had to admit that Pierce was wonderful with the children. Sometimes she would watch them from the kitchen window, and a bittersweet tightness would form in her chest. How often she had dreamed of such a scene.

But all she could think of these days was how more and more Max was turning to Pierce for attention instead of her. How more and more her son wanted to spend all of his free time with his father instead of her.

The first time Max had asked her if Pierce could read him his bedtime story had nearly broken Jessica's heart. Story time had always been her and Max's special time together. They would cuddle in bed at the end of the day and enjoy an adventure together.

Not so anymore. Now Max wanted Pierce to tell him "real-life" stories, as he called them. He wanted to know everything there was to know about his father. His interest in Superman waned, then disappeared altogether. His little cape remained discarded on his closet floor, forgotten and abandoned for a "real-life" hero, as Jessica knew he had begun to think of Pierce.

And what made matters even more difficult was the fact that everyone in the neighborhood had seemingly accepted Pierce back into Jessica's and Max's lives just as easily as her son had. Pierce had become a regular fixture at the bus stop in the mornings. Once, when he was late coming out, Jessica saw several of the women watching her house expectantly, waiting for his imminent arrival. And just yesterday morning, Jessica had noticed, rather in disgust, how many of the mothers had started putting on their makeup and doing their hair before they brought out their children.

Obviously the added primping was for Pierce's benefit, and Jessica couldn't help feeling just the tiniest twinge of jealousy. She began getting up a little earlier to spend extra time on her own appearance, though she wouldn't allow herself to analyze the reason why.

Only Jessica's friend, Sharon, remained reticent toward Pierce. Only she seemed to understand Jessica's qualms about Pierce's return.

"Doesn't it drive you crazy?" she asked Jessica one day. "How can you stand him living in the same house with you and not knowing where he's been for the past five years? Or who he's been with," she added slyly. "Watch yourself, Jessica. There's something about him...something in his eyes...." She paused, then said, "I have a feeling there's a lot more to that man than any of us can imagine. Even you, Jessica."

Jessica hardly needed Sharon's warning. She was consumed with her own doubts and suspicions. She thought about Pierce all the time. She couldn't even forget him in her sleep. The kiss they had shared a few nights ago filled her dreams except, in these dreams, they didn't stop with the kiss. They made love over and over and over again until Jessica would wake up in the middle of the night, so aroused and frustrated and confused she would sob into her pillow.

How much longer could she go on like this? she would ask herself helplessly. How much longer could she live in the same house with Pierce, sit across from him at meals, see him with their son, imagine him downstairs in his bed—and not succumb to the mounting need inside her? How much longer could she bear not to have him touch her again, to have him hold her again?

Twenty more days, Jessica thought, as she x-ed through yesterday's date on the calendar in her office. That's how long she would have to fight this yearning inside her. This…desire, she thought, putting a name to it. She closed her eyes for a moment as a wave of panic washed over her.

"Sleeping on the job, Jessica?"

At the sound of the masculine voice, Jessica's eyes flew open. She cleared her throat, straightened some papers on her desk, and smiled self-consciously at Brandon Chambers as he stood in front of her desk.

"Penny for your thoughts," he said, smiling down at her.

Jessica felt her face warm. She closed the ledger on her desk and stood. "You might feel shortchanged," she tried to say lightly. "When did you get back from Europe?"

"Yesterday afternoon. I have some real treasures for you this time. The bulk of the shipment won't arrive for a few more days, but in the meantime, feast your eyes on this." He pulled an intricately designed gold and aquamarine necklace from his pocket and displayed it on the desk in front of Jessica. "Lovely, isn't it?"

"It's beautiful," Jessica breathed. "Am I going to be able to afford this?"

"It was a steal," Brandon assured her. "I knew it was perfect for you the moment I laid eyes on it. And there's even a story behind it. I'd love to tell you about it over dinner tonight."

Jessica fingered the necklace, avoiding Brandon's gaze. "Sounds very intriguing," she murmured evasively.

"Shall I make reservations at Justine's? How does eight sound?"

"I'm afraid I can't make it tonight," she said. "Perhaps another time...." Honestly, Jessica chided herself, she and Brandon had had dinner countless times together. Why, all of a sudden, did she feel the need to put him off? To make sure he knew their relationship was strictly business?

Because of Pierce, that's why.

Everything had changed since he'd returned. Even her feelings toward her friends.

Brandon reached over and caressed the necklace. "This would make a handsome addition to your collection, Jessica. You could even feature it in the ads you were telling me about."

"That's a wonderful idea," she agreed, anxious to return their conversation to a less awkward subject. Mentally she changed the layout for her full-page spread in *Antiques Quarterly* to incorporate the necklace. She wished Brandon would just go ahead and tell her the story behind the necklace instead of dangling it in front of her like bait.

The history, even more than the age of a piece, was always an irresistible lure to potential customers and an invaluable selling tool once you got them into the shop. Pierce had taught her that.

Pierce had taught her a lot of things, she thought

with a funny little catch in her throat. But that was a long time ago. A lifetime ago.

"You could even model it yourself," Brandon suggested. "You've certainly got the looks for it. Try it on. Here, let me help you." He took the necklace from her fingers and, standing behind her, draped it around her neck as Jessica lifted her hair.

"How does it look?" she asked, turning to face him.

"Lovely," Brandon said softly, reaching to touch one of the stones. "Exquisite."

Jessica's first reaction was to pull back from his touch, but before she could, a movement at the doorway drew her attention. Pierce stood scowling at them both, his dark eyes flashing with anger. His gaze dropped from her face to the necklace, then back up to her eyes. Jessica felt herself blushing guiltily, even though she hadn't done anything wrong. She lifted her chin and stared back at him. He didn't say anything, just walked slowly into her office.

Brandon said, "Can we help you?"

Pierce's gaze shifted, very briefly, to the other man. "I seriously doubt it."

"Then perhaps you'd care to wait outside," Brandon said stiffly. "This is a private office."

"Uh, Brandon," Jessica began, putting her hand on his sleeve, "it's okay. I know him. I mean he's...this is Pierce. Kincaid."

"Kincaid?" Something flickered across Brandon's features. Something that looked like recognition. Or fear, Jessica thought, though she couldn't imagine why he would be afraid of Pierce. Brandon said in a disbelieving voice, "You mean, he's your *husband?*"

Jessica refused to look at Pierce. She took a deep breath. "Yes."

Brandon's gaze darted to Pierce. "But I thought—"

"That I was dead? That seems to be the general consensus around here." Pierce smiled lazily, but there was no humor in his eyes. Quite the contrary. Jessica felt a tremor of fear in her stomach. She didn't like the way he seemed to be sizing Brandon up.

Pierce walked around the desk and stood directly behind her, putting a hand on her shoulder in a deliberately casual but unmistakably familiar gesture. Jessica resisted the temptation to shake it off.

"Well, I...hardly know what to say," Brandon said, straightening the knot in his tie. He looked thoroughly disconcerted.

Pierce said, "How about 'welcome back'?"

"Yes, yes, of course." Brandon extended his hand. "Brandon Chambers. I'm an associate of Jes—of your wife's."

"Really?" The two men shook hands, then Pierce placed his hand back on Jessica's shoulder.

"So...where've you been?" Brandon asked awkwardly.

"It's a long story," Pierce murmured. He bent and kissed Jessica's neck. "Is that a new necklace, sweetheart?"

Jessica jumped. Her hand flew to her throat. She felt as though she had been stung by a wasp. Burned by a fire. Kissed by a lover. Her heart was beating all over the place as she carefully removed herself from her husband's grasp and retreated a few steps away.

"It really is a beautiful piece," she told Brandon. "If the price is right, you have yourself a buyer. In the meantime, I'd better return it to you.'' She lifted her hands to unclasp the necklace.

"Let me help you,'' Brandon said quickly.

At the exact same time Pierce said, "Turn around, Jesse.'' It didn't surprise her to find Pierce's hands at her throat as he undid the chain, lifted it away, and held it out to Brandon. The aquamarines sparkled in the overhead lighting as Pierce let the necklace slither into Brandon's open palm.

The two men eyed each other for a moment with open hostility, then Brandon smiled. He placed the necklace very carefully on Jessica's desk. "The price is immaterial, Jessica. The moment I saw that necklace, I knew it had to be yours.'' He flashed Pierce a brief, dismissing look as he paused significantly at the door. "I'll phone you later?''

"Please do,'' Jessica murmured, sinking down into her chair. She toyed with the necklace for a moment until Pierce reached out and took it from her hands. He perched on the edge of her desk and examined the necklace in the light.

"Circa 1920, I'd guess. Ten karat gold. At least two of the aquarmarines are chipped, and the clasp has obviously been replaced. Not a quality piece, but it does have a certain...pretentious appeal, I suppose.''

Annoyed, Jessica reached out and snatched the necklace from his fingers. "I happen to like it,'' she snapped. "And for your information, big, intricate pieces are very popular right now.''

"I noticed you'd added a jewelry case out front. I never could muster much interest in it myself. Except for the ring I bought you, of course.'' His gaze flashed to her left hand and her bare third finger.

Jessica folded her hands together, feeling naked.

"Yes, well, truth to tell, you never mustered much interest in the shop at all, Pierce. Except for the travel, of course. You always loved that."

"Only when you went with me," he said softly. "We had some good times, didn't we? Remember Venice and that little hotel we stayed in right off the—"

Abruptly Jessica stood, shutting off the memories. "I don't have time for this. I have work to do. Three crates of Austrian crystal came in this morning and it all has to be unpacked, cataloged and shelved. So if you'll excuse me—"

"Who is he?"

Jessica glanced up. "Who?"

Pierce lifted one brow at her obtuseness. "This Chambers guy. What's he to you?"

"He's an independent buyer," Jessica said, not liking Pierce's tone.

"Having a middleman must eat into the profits," he said, still fiddling with the necklace.

"Yes, but it cuts down on a lot of traveling for me. Brandon's been very helpful, and he's given me some really good deals."

"Oh, I'll bet he has."

Jessica planted her hands on top of her desk. "And just what does that mean?"

"Is he the one?"

"Is he the one what?"

"The one who taught you to kiss the way you kissed me a few nights ago."

Heat flooded over her at Pierce's words and at the memory. Jessica crossed her arms as if to stave him off. "I have no idea what you're talking about. My relationship with Brandon is strictly business," she said primly. Then realizing how defensive she looked, she immediately dropped her arms to her sides.

Her nervousness didn't go unnoticed by Pierce. His gaze narrowed on her. "Relationship, huh? Interesting choice of words, Jessica. Was his dinner invitation a part of this *business* relationship? Do you go out with him often?"

"That's none of your concern," Jessica snapped. "I'm getting awfully tired of these innuendoes, Pierce."

"I'm getting tired of making them," he said. "So why don't you convince me that I have nothing to worry about?" Somehow his tone had changed in no more than a heartbeat. His voice had lowered, deepened, become even more sensuous.

Jessica's heart started to pound a warning. Don't let him do this to you, she cautioned herself. Don't let him sidetrack you as easily as he used to.

But from his perch on the desk his hand was already closing around her wrist. He exerted just the tiniest bit of pressure until he had pulled her toward him and she was standing between his thighs. He lifted her hand to his lips and kissed her palm.

Jessica closed her eyes and clenched her fist. "Don't," she breathed.

"Why? Because of him?"

Her eyes flew open. "Why must you always think the worst of me?"

"Maybe I could ask you the same question." His thumb lazily caressed her wrist. "We've been apart too long, Jesse. We don't know how to act with one another anymore. We're afraid to trust each other. Afraid to trust our instincts."

"I don't know what you mean."

"Sure you do." He tugged her even closer, until he could slip his arms around her waist. Jessica's hand was free now, but instead of using it to push him away, she rested it lightly on Pierce's shoulder. "You want to kiss me right now, almost as much as I want to kiss you, but you're afraid to, aren't you?"

"You…want to kiss me?" Her own timidness confused Jessica.

"More than anything."

"But Pierce—"

"I know," he said, his deep gaze searching her face. "You've changed. You're not the same woman I left behind. You're independent now. You have a career. You don't need me anymore. And I still want to kiss you, Jesse. More than ever."

"But I don't think—"

"Don't think, sweetheart," he whispered. Their gazes clung for a moment, then he cupped her neck and brought her head forward until their lips slowly merged.

Jessica felt quivery all over. Where the kiss had been desperate and almost violent a few evenings ago, today the joining was soft and tender and fraught with emotion. Her lips trembled beneath his.

In that exquisite moment, Jessica remembered how it felt to be loved and wanted and utterly protected. She remembered how it felt to be Pierce's wife.

When they broke the kiss, she rested her head against his shoulder, unable to look at him, afraid of what he might read in her eyes.

His hand slipped beneath her hair to caress her neck. "You see, Jesse?" he whispered. "It's still there. What we had, what we felt for each other is still there. We just have to give ourselves time to find it again."

Jessica turned her head so that she could look up at him. She resisted the urge to trace the scar on the side of his face with her fingertip. She fought the temptation to wrap her arms around him and kiss him again, but long and deep and hard this time. Her emotions were in a jumble right now, and Jessica knew she had to be very, very careful.

With an effort, she lifted her head from his shoulder and pulled herself free of his arms. "Please don't read too much into what just happened," she said.

"It's hard not to," he said, "when it's something I'd like to believe so badly."

"But it doesn't mean anything," she protested. "Not really. We were married, Pierce. We have a son together. We're bound to still have feelings for one another. I don't deny that. But that doesn't mean I'm willing just to forget everything that's happened. I still need answers. I have to know what happened before I can even begin to think about a future…together."

"You have to learn to trust me again. I understand that," Pierce said. He eyed her steadily. "I know all this is scary for you, Jesse. It is for me, too."

Jessica looked at him in surprise. "You're scared?" She'd never known Pierce to be afraid of anything. He thrived on risk. Or used to.

He smiled. "Of course, I'm afraid. What do you think this is like for me, losing five years of my life? It scares me to death to think of those missing years, but it frightens me more to think of losing even another day with you and Max."

At the mention of their son, Jessica's gaze hardened, became defensive, but before she could speak, Pierce put up his hand to halt her words. "I know where part of your fear is coming from, Jesse, but believe me,

I'm not trying to take Max away from you. I would never do that. He loves you. He needs you. I couldn't take your place even if I wanted to. You've done a fantastic job, both at home and here at the shop, and I'm proud of you.''

In spite of herself, Jessica felt a small glow of pleasure at his words. High praise from a man like Pierce. She tried to warn herself that she was setting herself up for another fall, but Jessica's heart had already made up its mind.

Pierce got up and came to stand behind her at the window. He slipped his arms around her, holding her close. She tried to quiet the trembling inside her, but it felt so good to be in his arms again.

To be held by the only man she had ever loved.

He said softly, ''I don't expect you to be the woman you were five years ago, sweetheart. I did at first, naturally, because the time hadn't passed for me. But I understand now how you feel, and you can relax about all that. I'm not trying to take anything away from you. I know I've tried to rush you into something you weren't ready for. I know I've tried to make things the way they used to be when that's impossible. You were right that first night. Things will never be the same again. I understand that now.''

A feeling of loss settled over Jessica at his words. She had to close her eyes to blink back sudden tears.

''But just because things have changed, just because *we've* changed doesn't mean the feelings we had for one another are all gone.''

Jessica cleared her throat and attempted to strengthen her resolve. ''What are you trying to say, Pierce?''

''I'm saying we should give each other another

chance. I'm saying we should try to get to know each other again without any promises and without any pressure. We have over two weeks left in your thirty-day ultimatum. If at the end of that time you still want me to leave, I will. I'll fade quietly out of your life.''

''And Max's?''

She felt him stiffen at her challenge, but he didn't release her. If anything, he tightened his embrace. ''Max will always be my son. Just as he is yours. But no matter what happens between us, I would never try to take him away from you. You can trust me, Jesse, whether you realize it or not.''

At that moment, Jessica wasn't even sure if she dared to trust herself.

''Tremont House.''

''I'd like to speak to the manager.'' Pierce shifted the receiver to his other ear as he glanced around. It was just after five, and the traffic on Jefferson Avenue was starting to bunch up. As the line of cars crawled by, Pierce suddenly felt exposed at the open-air pay phone.

The voice, the same one he'd spoken to the other night, asked, ''Who's calling, please?''

''A friend who needs a room.''

''We're booked solid,'' came the standard reply.

''Look, damn you, I want to talk to the manager, and I want to talk to him now.'' Pierce's voice was low and calm but deadly insistent. This time, he wouldn't be put off. He wanted some answers, and he'd do what he had to do to get them. ''If he's not on the line in, let's say the next five seconds, I'll take my story to the press.''

There was a brief pause, maybe all of two seconds, then another voice said tersely, "This is Walker."

Pierce smiled grimly. The man had been listening all along, as he'd suspected.

"Are you the manager?" Pierce asked, sticking to the routine.

"Are you the same *friend* who called a few evenings ago?"

When Pierce responded in the affirmative, the man who called himself Walker said, "I got the message. I've been wondering when you'd make contact again. Welcome back, Kincaid."

The friendly exchange shocked Pierce. He said uncertainly, "Do I know you?"

"We've met. Actually we worked together five years ago on the Alpha project."

Flashes of memory were starting to dart around in Pierce's head. "Alpha—"

"Code name for a certain operation in the Caribbean. Is it coming back to you now?"

"Not exactly. I need a few more details filled in. I want to talk to someone," Pierce said. "Face-to-face. I need some answers, and you damn well better give them to me."

Walker paused, then said, "That can be arranged at a later date."

"Why not now?"

"Security reasons," he said evasively. "Certain precautions have to be taken where you're concerned. You understand."

Pierce didn't understand a damn thing. He said angrily, "Just what the hell am I supposed to do in the meantime? I've lost five years of my life, Walker, and I don't even know how or why. But I'm willing to bet the agency's behind it. At the very least, you people owe me an explanation.''

"'You people,''' Walker repeated. "You sound as if you think we're the enemy, Kincaid."

There was something in the man's voice that sent a chill of warning through Pierce. He was treading on dangerous ground, and he knew instinctively he had to proceed with caution.

As if to reiterate that point, Walker said, "For the time being, I suggest you sit tight, and don't talk to anyone. I mean anyone. It's a matter of national security. At the highest level."

Pierce expelled a vicious curse. "If my family's in danger, I want to know it, you son of a bitch."

"They're not," Walker said immediately. "You don't need to worry about that."

Pierce wasn't convinced. "I'll give you forty-eight hours," he said. "If I don't hear from you by them, I'll start looking for the answers myself. And believe me, no stone will be left unturned until I find them."

"You still work for the agency," Walker warned. "I'm advising you to stay put and keep your mouth shut until further notice. When the time is right, you'll be contacted. You have your orders."

"And you have yours. Forty-eight hours," Pierce said and hung up the phone. He drew a long breath and looked around, feeling the invisible eyes of the agency tracking his every move. What Pierce couldn't figure out was why those eyes felt so unfriendly. And so dangerous. He was supposed to be one of the good guys.

Wasn't he?

Chapter 9

Forty-eight hours had come and gone, and Pierce was still as much in the dark as he'd ever been. The agency had ignored his ultimatum. At least, the man calling himself Walker had.

Pierce realized he had taken a big chance, laying all his cards on the table, not just with Walker but with Jessica as well. She could easily have turned even further away from him, but at that point he hadn't known what else to do. He couldn't stand seeing the fear in her eyes every time he and Max were together. It seemed to him the only thing he could do was to try to allay her worries. Let her know that he wasn't a threat to her. In any way.

But was that true?

Pierce hadn't overtly heard from the agency, but at times he had the distinct feeling that he was being watched, followed. Yet no one made contact.

Sometimes, especially in the dead of night when he

lay in bed wide-awake, trying to remember, trying to sort out the fragmented pieces of memories floating around in his head, he had to wonder if he should just leave again. If he should disappear from Jessica's and Max's lives until he could sort out what had really happened to him. Until he could find out the truth.

But Walker had warned him to stay put, and even though Pierce had no reason to trust anyone from the agency these days, he had to agree with that course of action. The thought of leaving Jessica and Max alone and unprotected sent cold chills through him. In spite of what Walker said, Pierce had a very strong feeling of danger, and somehow he knew that if he left his family now, they would be vulnerable to that danger. Only he could protect them. Only he could keep them safe from the threat that he had brought with him. A threat he didn't even recognize.

Meanwhile, Pierce was following through on his own threat. He'd very quietly set the wheels of his own investigation in motion. He'd even broken down and called his brother-in-law at the Pentagon.

"What do you know about Brandon Chambers?" had been his first question.

After a couple of seconds of stony silence, Jay had said, "Is this personal or professional?"

"What do you think?"

It took a few minutes of wangling before Jay finally conceded. "All right, I'll tell you what I know. He showed up at the shop a few months after you'd disappeared. I was suspicious myself at first, but his credentials all checked out. He buys for dozens of antique shops all over the area. As far as I can tell, he's on the up-and-up. And Jessica certainly seems to trust him," he added slyly.

Pierce had hung up the phone, not feeling a damn bit better. Regardless of what Jessica and Jay thought, Pierce *didn't* trust Brandon Chambers. There was something about the man's eyes, the way he had looked at Pierce as if—

"D-a-ad! Keep your eye on the ball!" Max admonished as the baseball went whizzing by Pierce's head.

Pierce nodded and grinned, returning his attention to the game. "Sorry, Max. I'll try to do better."

"Here, Mr. Kincaid." The little girl from next door came running up to him, holding out the ball. "I catched it for you."

"Thanks, Allie. That's quite an eye you have there."

She beamed and squinted up at him. "My mother says you're strange," she said, bending to scratch a scab on her knee, "but you look okay to me."

"Thanks. I think."

"Are you coming to our party tonight?"

"Well, I'm not sure," he said, tossing the ball back to Max. "I'll have to check with Max's mother."

He nodded toward the picnic table where Sharon and Jessica sat talking quietly in the shade. The morning breeze lifted Jessica's curls and settled them around her face, setting off her creamy complexion and her wide gray eyes. She wore white shorts and a sleeveless yellow top, and Pierce felt a tenderness well inside him as he stared at her. She looked so young and relaxed this morning.

She looked exactly the way he remembered her.

And maybe it was his imagination or wishful thinking, but her attitude seemed to have lightened since their conversation at the shop. The hostility was gone from her eyes as if she was genuinely making an effort to keep an open mind. To get to know him again.

And once or twice he could have sworn he'd seen a flicker of interest in those gray depths. Maybe even a spark of desire, Pierce thought hopefully, feeling his pulse quicken just looking at her.

"Jessica's pretty, isn't she?" Allie said, following his gaze.

"Very."

"She's nice, too."

Pierce grinned. "She sure is."

Allie giggled. "I bet I know what."

"What?"

"I bet you'd like to kiss her."

Pierce felt his face redden. Since when did five-year-olds get so wise?

Allie clapped her hands to her mouth, suppressing more giggles.

Max called crossly, "Move out of the way, Allie. No girls allowed in this game."

"Hey, young man," Jessica admonished from the sidelines. "Since when did you get to be such a chauvinist?"

"Since he wants to have his father all to himself," Sharon suggested. Her blue eyes regarded Jessica thoughtfully. "I must say, you're certainly taking all this in stride, Jessica."

"You think so?" Jessica smiled, tucking a stray lock of hair behind her ear. She stared at her sandaled feet for a moment. "I'll let you in on a little secret. The first few days Pierce was back, I was terrified he might try to take Max away from me. But I realize now I was just overreacting. I was projecting my past into my feelings."

"You sound so wise," Sharon commented, sipping her iced tea. "So analytical. Now tell me how you really feel."

"What do you mean?"

"Are you in love with him?"

Jessica looked up, surprised by her friend's bluntness. "I—I'm not sure. I still have feelings for him," she said reluctantly, "but I'm not sure how much of that is just memory."

Her gaze went to Pierce as he pitched the ball to Max. Over the past couple of weeks, he'd filled out a little. His jeans were beginning to fit him more snugly and the lines in his face had softened a bit. That dark, haunted, hungry look in his eyes had vanished. When he laughed, he looked ten years younger, and he laughed a lot when he was with his son. They both did.

It hurt Jessica to realize how little laughter there had been in her and Max's life. She'd concentrated so hard on being a success at work and being the perfect mother all round that she was very much afraid she had never learned how to be a mom, the kind who relaxed and enjoyed life.

But Pierce was teaching her that.

He was teaching her and her son how to have fun.

"It doesn't bother you that you may never know what happened to him all those years ago?" Sharon asked softly.

"It bothers me," Jessica admitted. "But what can I do about it?"

Sharon shook her head. "You amaze me, Jessica. You're always so levelheaded. It doesn't worry you that you'll be alone with him for the next few days?"

Jessica whipped her head around. "What?"

Sharon's blond brows rose slightly. "Don't tell me you forgot. Max is supposed to go camping with us this week, remember? We're leaving tomorrow."

Jessica had completely forgotten the plans she'd made with Sharon over a month ago. It seemed impossible that Memorial Day weekend was already here. It seemed impossible that Pierce had already been home over two weeks and that they had only a little more than a week left of the ultimatum she'd given him.

What then? Jessica wondered. Where did they go from there?

He'd said he wanted to get to know her again, without promises and without pressure, and true to his word he'd been nothing more than casually friendly since their conversation at the shop. He hadn't so much as come near her.

Much to her disappointment, Jessica acknowledged to herself.

Her gaze strayed back to Pierce, and suddenly she couldn't help remembering the way it felt to be in his arms.

It was never this way before.

A wave of warmth washed over her as she remembered the night she'd gone to his room, the way he'd kissed her and the way she'd kissed him back.

It was never this way before.

Who had changed? Her? Pierce? Or both of them? And if a kiss had done that to her, what would it be like to make love with him now? Would that be different, too? Would it be even more passionate than before? More intense? More powerful?

Jessica felt a tingle of anticipation in the pit of her stomach. Pierce glanced her way and their gazes met.

Fade to Black

Something electric passed between them. Something purely sexual. It seemed as though he could read her every thought. Jessica's face reddened as his gaze moved over her, lingering for a long moment on her bare legs.

"...and I know the kids would be disappointed if Max didn't get to go. What do you say, Jessica?"

Jessica tried to turn her attention back to Sharon. "What?"

Sharon gave her an odd look. "Can Max come camping with us or not?"

Alone with Pierce for a whole week. Jessica's heart began to pound like a drum. She felt her palms moisten. "I—I'll have to check with Pierce," she stammered.

Sharon's brows soared, but she refrained from comment. "Okay," she agreed. "Can you come over early tonight and help me set up? The others guests will be arriving at six, so if you could come around five-thirty, that'd be great."

"Sure," Jessica said absently, fanning herself with her hand. Was it her imagination or had the temperature suddenly gone up a few degrees, even in the shade?

Sharon stared at her for a long moment, then grinned. "Gee, I'm worried about you, Jessica. A decreasing attention span, glazed look in your eyes, red cheeks, shortened breath. Sounds like a heat stroke to me." She stood to go but then turned and said softly, "Or is it just love?"

Or is it just love?

Jessica felt a little tremor of fear in her stomach as she contemplated Sharon's question. Could she be falling in love with Pierce again? So soon? In spite of all the unanswered questions?

You amaze me, Jessica. You're always so level-headed.

Jessica didn't feel levelheaded now. Not at all. She felt all trembly inside and out of control. She felt like a woman on the verge of falling in love who didn't give a damn about responsibility. Didn't give a damn about the future, only the present.

Except that Jessica couldn't afford the luxury of acting on impulse, of letting her emotions rule her life. She had a son to think about. She had their future to worry about. She didn't want Max to get hurt because of a decision she had made in a moment of passion.

It was all so confusing, she decided. With the palm of her hand, she tested the cake cooling on the rack. She found a can of frosting in the pantry, opened it and sampled a bit on the tip of her finger, shrugging. Not as good as homemade, but not bad, especially considering she was in a hurry. It was after four, and she still had to bathe and get ready for Sharon's party.

Feeling the time slip away, she sighed as she slathered the frosting on the cake. She hoped that Max was already in the bathtub, scrubbing off the grime from his and Pierce's baseball game, but you could never tell with him. Her son was easily diverted when it came to bath time.

Pierce came in just as she was putting the finishing touches on the cake.

"Looks good," he said, his eyes raking her up and down.

"Where's Max?" Jessica asked, trying to ignore the suddenly close confines of the kitchen.

"Outside with one of his friends. They found a dead lizard, last I heard."

Jessica groaned. Dead animals were always an irresistible lure to her son. "He's supposed to be in the bathtub. I'll never get us both ready in time now. Sharon wants me to come over early, and I still have to make a salad—"

"Relax," Pierce said, putting his hands on her arms. "I'll go and find Max and make sure he gets his bath. You do what you need to do in here, and then go get yourself ready."

"But I—"

"Jessica," Pierce said in an admonishing tone. "You don't have to do it all by yourself anymore. I'm here now. I want to help you if you'll let me."

"But—"

He swiped her mouth with his fingertip. "There. See?" He held up his finger, showing her a streak of chocolate across it. "I'm already helping you out. Wait a minute. I missed a spot." Before she had time to realize what he was doing, Pierce bent and retrieved the rest of the chocolate from her lip with his tongue. "Mmm, delicious. Tastes even better than it looks."

Jessica froze. "What are you doing?"

"What does it feel like I'm doing?" Pierce murmured.

"But you said no pressure. You said...."

His arms slipped around her waist, and Jessica's protest died on her lips. The look in his eyes sparked too many memories of too many nights spent in his arms.

She drew a long breath, telling herself her heart shouldn't be racing and her pulse shouldn't be jumping so erratically just because he had touched her. Just because she was remembering something they had once shared.

And because she knew he was remembering, too.

And because it felt so good to be in his arms again.

"Remember the last time I did that? It was at our wedding," he said softly. "I was in such a hurry to get the reception out of the way that when I fed you your cake, I got frosting all over your mouth."

"You barely gave me time to throw the bouquet," Jessica reminisced.

"I was in a hurry to start our honeymoon," he admitted with a grin. "I'll never forget our wedding night, Jesse. You looked so sweet in that white frilly thing you wore to bed. I had the devil of a time getting it off, though. Probably because I was so damned nervous."

Jessica gazed up at him, enjoying the closeness. The comfort of shared memories. "You nervous? I don't believe it. You always seemed so experienced to me. So sure of yourself."

"An act," he confessed, his arms settling more possessively around her. "I was nervous, all right. I'd never been with a virgin before."

Jessica blushed as she always did when that particular subject was mentioned. She pushed at his arms but not forcefully enough to push him away. "Do you have to remind me of that? A twenty-year-old virgin must have seemed pretty weird to someone like you."

He smiled down at her, his eyes deep and intense. Incredibly dark. "You seemed very special to someone like me. You seemed like the woman I'd been waiting for all my life. Do you know what it's always meant to me that I was the first for you, Jesse? It was like the rarest, most precious gift you could ever give me.''

Jessica began to relax even more, basking a little in the glow of their shared past. It had been so long since they'd reminisced together. And Pierce had always had a way of making her feel good about herself, in spite of her childhood.

She lifted her hands to his shoulders, feeling the hard definition of his muscles beneath his shirt. ''Do you know what I thought the first time I ever saw you?'' She teased him with a smile. ''I thought you were the most dashing, the most sophisticated, the most handsome man I'd ever seen.''

''You were such a naive little thing.''

''You always seemed so mysterious to me. As if you had done things you couldn't share with me. As if there were secrets from your past you couldn't reveal even to me. That made you even more irresistible,'' Jessica said, laughing softly.

Something flickered in Pierce's eyes. A flash of regret?

He said, ''I don't want to have secrets from you, Jesse. I want to share everything with you now. There are so many things I want to tell you, but I can't. I...can't.''

''I know,'' she said softly. ''Because you don't remember.''

His smile seemed rueful. ''I don't deserve you, you know. I never did.''

Jessica started to protest, but his eyes stopped her. They were so dark and unfathomable. So intense. So deeply probing she could feel his gaze all the way to her soul. She knew she should move, break the spell, remember that this was the man who had hurt her so badly. But a sweet contentment was slipping over her. A languor that made her want to remain exactly where she was. In Pierce's arms. Forever.

She closed her eyes and whispered his name.

"I'm here, Jesse," he murmured as he threaded his fingers through her hair. "I'll always be here. If you'll let me."

For an eternity it seemed, he just held her, giving her the comfort she needed. Jessica wasn't sure when their bodies began to shift, edging beyond comfort to something else—something that bordered on sexual awareness. But suddenly she was conscious of a dozen different sensations. The feel of his jeans against her bare legs. The flicker of desire warming his dark gaze. The delicious torment of his fingers in her hair. And his mouth. His mouth only inches from hers.

She closed the distance, parting her lips in anticipation.

She heard Pierce's breath catch, then he groaned as his hands fisted in her hair and he drew her mouth the rest of the way to his. She opened for him immediately, and Pierce sent his tongue deep inside her mouth, shocking Jessica and then thrilling her.

The kiss was deep and hard and electric, and it made Jessica remember exactly what she had been missing for five years. Abstinence had never been a problem for her, but now she was suddenly, achingly aroused to the point of desperation. To the point of not caring. To the point of no return.

She rubbed against the front of his jeans, feeling the heat of his erection through their clothing. Jessica's legs began to tremble. It would be so easy, she thought. So easy just to give in to her need, allow

Pierce to lead her upstairs and undress her, make her want him until she begged him for release.

Her thoughts shocked her. Was she that desperate? That aroused?

It was never this way before.

Pierce broke the kiss and stared at her with a look so hot and so hungry that Jessica felt a thrill of alarm race through her. What had she done? she wondered. What had she started?

"Sweetheart," he murmured, letting out a long, ragged breath. He reached for her again, but this time Jessica managed to put up a token resistance.

"Pierce, it's broad daylight and we're standing in the middle of the kitchen."

"I don't give a damn where we are."

His lips nipped hers, sending a sensuous shiver down her spine. "But there's no time…I mean, I still have to get dressed and all…." Jessica knew she was babbling, but she couldn't seem to string two coherent thoughts together. Not when Pierce was looking at her the way he was looking at her.

He lifted a hand and raked it through his hair, sighing deeply. "You sure as hell can kiss, Jesse. See what you've done to me? In broad daylight. In the middle of the kitchen."

Jessica's gaze slid downward to the front of his jeans. There was no mistaking his meaning. "I'm… sorry."

"Don't be. I just wish we had time to pursue this elsewhere. Or…do we?"

Jessica tried to shake off the lingering remnants of her arousal. "We don't. And besides, I don't think it's a good idea to rush into anything. I think we should wait until we're both sure we're ready."

"In case you haven't noticed, I'm as ready as I'll ever be," he said in a pained voice. "In fact, if I was any more ready—"

The back door slammed, and they both jumped apart like guilty teenagers. Max appeared in the doorway, eyeing them with avid curiosity. Jessica put up a hand to smooth her hair. Max's dark eyes didn't miss a move.

She said nervously, "Where've you been, sweetie? It's time for your bath."

Max gazed first at Jessica, then at Pierce, then back to Jessica. She had the feeling that they hadn't fooled him at all. He knew that something was going on. He held up a dead lizard and dangled it by the tail. "Can I keep this?"

Automatically Jessica stepped back, right into Pierce's arms. His hands went around her waist, steadying her against his body and making Jessica all too conscious of what had just gone on between them. "Please get that thing out of my kitchen," she said, her voice not quite as steady as she would have liked.

"But, Mom—"

"No buts. Get it out of here this second," Jessica ordered.

Max turned around and left without further protest.

Behind her, Jessica heard Pierce laugh. She spun around to face him. "What's so funny?" she demanded.

"Nothing," he said. "But for a minute there, I was afraid you might be talking to me."

Chapter 10

"Can I go camping with Allie and her mom and dad? We'll only be gone till Saturday."

Pierce sat on the edge of the bottom bunk bed in Allie's room as he tucked the covers around Max. Allie hung halfway out of the top bunk, listening avidly to Pierce and Max's conversation. The sounds of the party outside drifted in through the open window, making the children too restless to sleep.

"We got enough food and bug spray and toilet paper for everybody. You don't have to worry about anything, Mr. Kincaid," Allie said solemnly, her blond hair swinging back and forth like a silk curtain in a stiff breeze. "Can he go with us? Please, can he?"

"Can I, Dad? Please, can I?"

Pierce's heart skipped a beat or two. It never failed to thrill him every time Max called him Dad. He had to resist the temptation to give in to his son's every whim, but that urge had gotten him in trouble with

Jessica more than once. Not that her anger wasn't justified. It was. But it was just so damned hard not to want to make up for all those years he'd missed with his son.

Pierce said cautiously, "What did your mother say about this camping trip?"

"She said she'd have to talk to you about it. Did she?"

Talk to him about it? Pierce stared at his son in surprise. Jessica was asking for his opinion? His advice? He didn't want to read too much into it, but he couldn't help feeling encouraged by this latest development. Maybe his talk with her had helped, after all.

He ruffled Max's hair and reached up to tickle Allie's ear. "I tell you what, you two. I'll talk to Jessica about it tonight, and we'll let Allie's mom and dad know before we leave the party. How's that?"

"Okay, but will you come and tell us?" Max demanded. "I won't be able to sleep until I know."

Pierce grinned. "You got it."

Max grinned back. "Thanks, Dad. I love you."

Pierce felt his throat tighten with emotion. Keep it light, he advised himself. Don't embarrass him in front of his friend. He said, a little too gruffly, "I love you, too, son."

Allie's blond head popped up over the railing again. "I love you, too, Mr. Kincaid."

Then she collapsed on her bed in a fit of giggles, but the tension inside Pierce eased up. He and Max met each other's gaze in conspiratorial silence, shaking their heads in a man-to-man agreement about the incomprehensible behavior of women in general.

The pool glistened aquamarine in the glow of the torches Sharon had planted around the edges of the yard, and citronella candles flickered on the tops of picnic tables lining the covered terrace. Everyone had abandoned the water in favor of the tables once dinner had been served, and now soft music was playing on the stereo and a few couples were dancing. Jessica sat away from the crowd at the dark end of the pool, enjoying the cool evening breeze and the pleasant drone of the distant chatter.

She nursed a glass of wine in one hand as she dangled her feet in the water. It had been a pleasant evening, and she felt content and mellow and just a little bit lazy. Pierce had put Max and Allie to bed upstairs in Allie's room a little while ago, and now all Jessica had to do was relax and enjoy the rest of the night. Automatically she searched for Pierce in the crowd.

She spotted him at the other end of the yard, where the light of the torches hardly reached. Like her, he was all alone, standing apart from the crowd. She remembered a time when Pierce would have been the life of the party. Not that he'd ever been loud or boisterous or sought attention, but back then, people had just naturally gravitated toward him. Now he seemed to shy away from crowds as fervently as Jessica did. It wasn't like him to be such a loner.

But he'd been acting strangely toward her all evening, Jessica reflected. Ever since that scene in the kitchen, he'd made it a point to keep his distance from her. In fact, he hadn't even sat by her at dinner, choosing to sit with Max and his friends, instead. He didn't seem angry, just reserved. Pensive.

Jessica couldn't help wondering what he was thinking about.

See what you've done to me? In broad daylight. In the middle of the kitchen.

She flushed slightly as his words came back to her. His arousal may have been more apparent, but it had been no more thorough than hers had been. No more intense. She shifted, feeling her body tingle in all the places that had been too long ignored.

The wine was making her have thoughts she oughtn't to be having, Jessica decided, and it was making her feel a little too warm. Perhaps she should jump into the pool and cool off. Maybe Pierce would come and join her—except he hadn't been swimming all evening. He was wearing trunks, an old navy blue pair he'd had years ago, and a white T-shirt, but even when Max had asked him to come into the water earlier, Pierce had declined. He'd sat at the edge of the pool instead, enthusiastically applauding his son's swimming ability. He hadn't even taken off his shirt when the kids' splashing had gotten him soaking wet.

Curious, Jessica thought. Pierce had never been the modest type before. Of course, he had lost some weight, but he still looked better by far than any man at the party. Jessica could feel the warmth easing over her again as she watched him from a distance, willing his gaze to hers.

Pierce sat in the shadows, trying to keep his gaze off Jessica, but it was damned near impossible, the way she looked tonight. The way she'd kissed him earlier.

It had never been that way before, that instant arousal, that almost overpowering need. Jessica had always been a little reticent about lovemaking, a little reluctant to take pleasure from the physical side of their relationship. Pierce had always tried to be gentle with her and as understanding as he could be under the circumstances, but he'd always had the disquieting feeling that there was a part of her he had never been able to touch.

But she'd changed, he reflected. The way she kissed, the way she moved against him led him to believe that she was now as eager for their lovemaking as he was. The question that bothered him, though, was *why?* Why had she changed?

Or more to the point—*who* had caused her to change? Who had taught her the things she would never allow him to teach her?

She'd said there was no one else, but in five years? Had she abstained from sex for five whole years? Maybe that explained this new boldness in her. God knows what five years of celibacy had done to him, he thought with a grimace.

How can you be so sure there wasn't someone else in all that time?

Jessica's question returned to haunt him, and Pierce didn't have an answer, just a feeling. Just a certainty deep inside him that there had never been anyone else for him since Jessica. And there never would be.

He watched her with a brooding frown as she lifted the glass to her mouth, and he suddenly wanted to taste the wine from her lips. To let his tongue continue the exploration he had begun in the kitchen earlier that day. To see just how much they had both changed.

She trailed her feet in the water, then lifted her hair from her neck. The innocent action accentuated the line of her breasts in the white one-piece swimsuit she wore. The cut of the suit was no less tantalizing because it was modest. Her body had filled out in all the right places since he'd been gone. Not that she hadn't looked great before. But now...

Pierce took a long swallow of his cold beer, suppressing a groan. She looked so damned sexy it was all he could do to keep his hands off her.

I'm saying we should try to get to know each other again without any promises and without any pressures.

Pierce muttered a curse under his breath. What the hell had he been thinking? No promises? No pressure? No sex?

That wasn't what he wanted at all. The longer they kept their intimacy at bay, the easier it would be for Jessica to walk away from him at the end of the thirty days. And Pierce had no intention of letting that happen.

He studied her now, so cool and aloof, so prim and proper, but he remembered the way she'd been this afternoon. Warm and trembling and ready.

For him.

He got up, tossed the beer can into the trash and slowly walked toward the pool.

Jessica watched him. The pool lights had been turned off, and the torches cast dancing shadows across the surface of the water. Standing at the opposite side where the light barely touched him, Pierce stripped off his shirt and dived into the cool water. He surfaced at her feet, his hand coming up to snare her wet ankle.

"Why don't you come in?" he invited. "The water's great."

"I went in earlier," she reminded him. "But I was beginning to think you didn't like to swim anymore."

"I just don't like crowds."

"Seems as though I'm not the only one who's changed," she said pointedly.

Pierce shrugged. "I've never denied that. Sometimes when I look in the mirror, I hardly recognize myself."

"I'm not talking about the physical changes, Pierce," she said quietly.

"I know. But I guess what I'm trying to say is, I realize I look different, Jesse. I know I'm not exactly easy on the eyes. If you don't want to be with me, if you can't stand—"

"Don't say that," Jessica whispered. "Please don't think that."

Impulsively she slipped into the pool. It was cool and dark and gave them an instant illusion of privacy. The music and laughter faded into the background as Jessica stood in shoulder-high water facing Pierce.

"The scars don't matter to me."

"They matter to me," he said, "because I don't know how I got them." He hesitated, then said, "I probably should warn you. There are others."

Jessica looked at him, feeling the impact of his words all the way to her heart. She asked hesitantly, "Worse ones?"

"Yes."

"I'm sorry," she said, her voice tremulous. "I'm so sorry for what you must have gone through. I can't imagine what could have happened to you, but I...." Her words trailed off and she took a shuddering breath. "Is that why you didn't want to go swimming earlier? Because you didn't want to take off your shirt?"

"Yeah. It's not a pretty sight. I'm sorry, Jesse."

Jessica couldn't help herself. She lifted her hand and

trailed her finger down the scar on the side of his face. "You're still the most attractive man I've ever met, Pierce."

Even though he wasn't touching her, she could sense his reaction to her words. His pleasure. "And you are undoubtedly the most beautiful woman I have ever seen. You take my breath away."

It was so easy to let the water carry her toward him. The darkness hid them, wrapped them in a blanket of intimacy that made Jessica feel daring and desperate, a very dangerous combination.

Pierce's hands rested lightly on her shoulders, then slid beneath the water till he found her waist. He pulled her toward him and Jessica floated against him without resistance. The water felt cool against her skin, but inside she was burning up. She wanted Pierce to kiss her in the worst way and she wanted it now, this instant....

Pierce's lips found her neck, teased her ear, then trailed across her cheek, barely skimming her mouth. She tasted like wine and chocolate and something a little more decadent. More sinful, except that it wasn't sinful because she was his wife, and that notion excited Pierce even more. She was his. And she always would be....

As if to prove it to her, Pierce kissed her more forcefully, angling his head so that he could part her lips even farther. He wanted in. Now. And Jessica offered no resistance.

Her mouth was so sweet and hot and wet that it reminded him of other areas he would like to explore. Other places he wanted in. His hands slipped through the water to skim the edges of her swimsuit. Even in the water, she felt warm to his touch.

He broke the kiss, his fingers still gently exploring under the water. Jessica's head dropped forward to rest against his chest. He could feel her trembling, shuddering as his fingers probed more deeply, more thoroughly. She clung to him desperately, her breathing deep and ragged. He shot a glance across the yard toward the terrace. If anyone looked over here, they would just see shadows. At the most, a kiss. He'd break things up in a minute, but not quite yet. Not when she felt so delicious against his fingers. So hot. He drove deeper and felt her shudder against him. Just a minute more—

A peal of laughter rang out across the yard, an irritating intrusion into their little island of privacy. Pierce let out an unsteady breath, forcing his hands away from Jessica as he realized how far he'd let things go. The wine and, he hoped, the kiss had lowered Jessica's inhibitions, but he never should have taken advantage of her vulnerability. She would hate herself for her loss of control, and she'd very possibly hate him, as well.

He lifted his hand out of the water and smoothed her hair. She remained against him, but Pierce could tell that she had withdrawn from him. She was gathering her poise, he suspected, before she could face him, let alone the crowd of people on the terrace. He heard her draw a breath that sounded almost like a sob.

He forced a casual note into his voice. ''Looks like the party's winding down. Maybe we should collect Max and be on our way, too. If you'd like to go on ahead, I'll make our goodbyes.''

Jessica lifted her head from his shoulder, but her

eyes didn't quite meet his. "No, it's okay. I'll tell Sharon we're leaving."

Pierce watched her pull herself up out of the pool and grab a towel from a nearby lawn chair. She walked across the yard toward the terrace, not once looking back at him.

Jessica followed Pierce up the stairs as he carried Max to bed. They hadn't said two words on the way home from Sharon's, and the silence between them was rapidly turning into awkwardness. She suspected they were both reflecting on what had almost happened between them a little while earlier.

How could she have done it? Jessica asked herself over and over.

How could she have lost control like that?

How could she have behaved so... wantonly in public?

And now what would Pierce think of her? What would he expect from her? And what did she want from him?

Tonight had changed everything. After what had almost happened in the pool, Jessica knew they could never go back to being polite strangers. They would no longer be satisfied with casual dinner conversation or a few chaste kisses. The question now wasn't so much if they would have sex, but when. And not if it would change her life, but how much?

And was she ready to face such a change?

Jessica leaned against the door frame and watched Pierce with their son. He was so gentle with Max, so tender and so loving that it made her heart ache just to watch them together. Max trusted Pierce wholeheartedly. He had no reservations at all about letting him back into their lives. Jessica wished she could be so sure. She wished her own feelings for Pierce were so uncomplicated.

Max stirred in his sleep as Pierce tucked the covers in around him. "Dad?"

"I'm here, son."

"Did you ask Mom about the camping trip?"

"Why don't we both ask her now?"

Max sat up in bed, rubbing his eyes as he looked around the dimly lit room. "Is it okay, Mom?"

Jessica crossed the room and stood beside the bed. Pierce was sitting on the edge, and he and Max were both gazing up at her. They looked so much alike that Jessica felt a tenderness for them both well up inside her. She said, "You know you'll be gone until Saturday, sweetie. That's five whole days. Almost a week. Are you sure you want to be away from home that long?"

"Are you afraid you'll get lonely for me?" Max asked solemnly.

Jessica smiled. "A little."

"But I know a trick," Max said. "If you think about me every night before you go to sleep, then you won't be so lonely for me."

"I know that trick, too," Jessica said, bending to kiss his cheek. "And I will think about you every night before I go to sleep."

"I'll think about you, too, Mom," he promised. "Just like I used to think about my dad every night until he came back home."

Jessica met Pierce's gaze. She could see his eyes shining in the moonlight and knew that he was as moved by their son's revelation as she was. Jessica wanted to take his hand and tell him how she used to think about him, too, every night before she went to sleep. She wanted to tell him how she used to pray for his safe return, wish with all her might that she could see him just one more time.

She felt a tear trickle down her cheek as waves of emotion swept over her.

"I guess it's all settled then," Pierce said. His voice was strangely subdued. "I'll help you pack in the morning, Max. How's that?"

"Good," Max said contentedly. He settled down under the covers, but almost instantly bolted upright again, his eyes wide with alarm. "When I get back from camping, you'll still be here, won't you?"

"I'll always be here, son. I'm not going anywhere."

"Never again?"

"Never again. I promise." His words were reassurance for Max, but his eyes were on Jessica. Something settled inside Jessica, a feeling of peace that at least one obstacle had suddenly been cleared from their path. She believed Pierce. She trusted him. And she wanted him to stay.

She wanted to tell him so much of what she was feeling and more, but Max was clinging to his hand as if he, too, was suddenly aware of how much he meant to him.

"Will you stay with me until I fall asleep?" he asked.

A few days ago, such a request would have torn Jessica up inside because her son was turning to someone else for comfort where he had once turned to her. But now as she watched Pierce stretch out beside their son and pull him into the protection of his strong arms, Jessica knew only a feeling of deep contentment.

Yet another barrier had fallen between them.

* * *

Jessica expected the knock on her bedroom door, but when it came, her stomach knotted in apprehension just the same. She laid the hairbrush on the dressing table and stood, then tightened the belt of her robe as she crossed the room to open the door.

"I just came to say good-night," Pierce said, when she drew open the door. "Max is finally sleeping."

"Good."

Their eyes met in the lamplight, and in that instant, awareness leaped across the space that separated them. Pierce leaned one arm against the door and took a moment to gaze around the room, his eyes lingering just a fraction too long on the king-size bed they had once shared.

She should have gotten rid of it a long time ago, Jessica realized. It held too many memories for them, and she wasn't sure it was a good idea to have such an intimate reminder of what they'd once shared. Maybe it would have been better to start new memories where old ones didn't exist. Where comparisons weren't inevitable.

His gaze returned to her and he smiled a little half smile that sent her heart racing. "You know, Jesse, of all the things we've talked about since I've been back, there's one subject we've pretty much avoided."

"What?" Her voice sounded breathy, a little too excited.

"We haven't talked about sex. I think maybe it's time we did."

Jessica let out a shaky breath. "Don't you think it's a little late for conversation? I mean considering...what almost happened earlier...." She glanced away, embarrassed.

Pierce walked into the room and closed the door.

The sound of the latch clicking shut made Jessica even more nervous. The room suddenly seemed too small and intimate, the bed too large and overpowering.

''I think the timing's perfect,'' he said softly. ''It occurred to me earlier that you're afraid of me. Afraid to let yourself go with me. I can't help wondering why.''

''Five years is a long time,'' she said, fiddling with the top of her robe. ''We've both changed. And everything.''

''Yeah,'' he agreed, his eyes darkening suspiciously. ''It's that 'everything' I want to talk about. You said there was no one else in your life, hasn't been anyone else. Does that mean you've abstained from sex for five whole years? Is that why you're so reluctant to be with me now?''

''I could ask you the same question,'' Jessica said. ''Only, you don't remember, do you?''

His eyes were deep and probing as he searched her face. ''I was never unfaithful to you.''

Jessica knew the wave of relief flooding through her was ridiculous under the circumstances. She tried to fight it off, tried to think more rationally with her brain instead of her heart. ''How can you be so sure? How can you say that when there are so many things you can't tell me about the past five years?''

''Because I am sure. Because I know, right here—'' he touched his hand to his heart ''—that there was never anyone but you. Can you tell me the same thing?''

She lifted her gaze to his. ''Yes,'' she whispered. ''I was never unfaithful to you, Pierce.''

For just a moment, the darkness in his eyes lifted, and Jessica glimpsed an emotion so powerful, so intense, it took her breath away. "My God," he breathed, "I've been so afraid. I knew I had no right to ask, but I had to know. Jesse...."

He pulled her into his arms so fast, Jessica felt as if the floor had given way beneath her. She grabbed his arms for support, letting him guide her back against the wall until he could press against her, his body hot and hard and insistent.

"It's been so long," he whispered. "We've been apart for so long. Sometimes I wonder how I survived at all without you."

"Because you had to," she said. "And so did I."

"Yes," he agreed, "but I don't think I can survive another night without making love to you. When I'm close to you like this, I can't stand not touching you. My God, I remember everything about you. How silky smooth your hair feels beneath my fingers."

As if to demonstrate to himself the truth of his words, he wove his hands through the dark cloud of her hair. "And your mouth..." He took a deep breath. "Your mouth is so damned sexy, sweetheart. I want to kiss you deep and hard every time I look at you." He rubbed a thumb across her lips, a prelude to what she really wanted. "We've been leading up to this all day. You know that, don't you?" he asked softly.

Jessica closed her eyes and leaned back against the wall, her breathing deep and uneven. He was quickly seducing her, with his hands and his mouth and his words, and she didn't know if she had the will to stop him this time, because she was remembering, too. She knew the feel of his hands against her flesh, the hardness of his body on hers. She knew what it was like, the exquisite thrill, the moment he plunged inside her....

"I remember what it's like, seeing you lying on that bed, waiting for me." He slid his knuckles down her face, traced the line of her chin with one finger, then found the pulse point in her throat. His hand dipped lower. "You have the most beautiful breasts," he murmured. "So round and firm and just the perfect size for my hands. And my mouth," he added, watching her. His hands smoothed down her sides, barely skimming her breasts, but Jessica felt the sensitive peaks tingle and swell, aching for a deeper, more thorough touch.

"This is crazy," she breathed, trying to control the mounting sensations inside her.

"Insane," he agreed.

His hands were at her waist, pulling her toward him until he could lock his arms around her, holding her against him so tightly, Jessica had no doubt at all about his own state of arousal. Their mouths joined and he shot his tongue deep inside her, thrilling her with the urgency of his thrusts.

Jessica shifted, automatically adjusting her position to accommodate him. The feel of his erection caused something to gush inside her. Nerve endings quivered with sensation. Deep inside, she could feel her body start to clench and unclench, clench and unclench. Desperate now, she pressed herself against him, molded herself to him until only their clothing prevented penetration.

"Sweetheart," Pierce groaned, "let me get us to the bed."

He started to lift her, but Jessica pushed aside his hands. "No."

He hesitated. "Not the bed?"

Jessica shook her head, drinking in great gulps of

air to try to calm her racing heart. "Not...this," she gasped. "Not sex. We can't."

His hands froze. "Why not?"

Jessica glanced away, her face flooding with color at the reality of the situation. He was her husband, for God's sake. No need to be embarrassed, but for some reason she suddenly felt unbearably shy. "Because I'm not...I'm not protected, that's why." Speaking her fears aloud effectively doused Jessica's passion. She retreated a few inches away from him, securing the belt of her robe. "I should have thought about it earlier, but I...I wasn't thinking at all."

Pierce just stared at her for a long, tense moment. He looked as if he couldn't quite believe what he was hearing. "You mean if we make love, you could get pregnant?"

"Surely you haven't forgotten the way that works," she said shakily. "Of course I could get pregnant."

Another pause. His gaze softened. "Would that be so bad?" he asked quietly. "We always wanted a big family."

"Yes, it would be bad," she practically shouted. "It would be horribly irresponsible of us. We can't bring another child into this world until we know...that is...until we're sure that...."

Pierce helped her out. "Until we're sure we'll stay together?"

Jessica ran a trembling hand through her hair. "Yes. It's the only sensible decision. The only mature one."

"Yeah," Pierce said, scrubbing his face with his hands. "But I'm not feeling too damned mature at the moment."

He brushed his lips against hers, an agonizingly brief contact, then he turned and strode out of the bedroom.

Chapter 11

"Max, I don't think you're going to have room for all those toys," Pierce said as he lifted a stack of T-shirts from one of Max's drawers and placed them inside the open suitcase.

Max struggled across the room, carrying a box of superhero figures. He eyed his suitcase warily, took out the stack of shirts Pierce had just carefully packed, then dumped the toys inside.

Pierce shook his head. "I think we're going to have to come up with a compromise here, or else your mother will have both our heads. How about just a few of those figures?"

Max shot him a glance. "How many is a few?"

"Five," Pierce said, then seeing Max's outraged look, quickly bargained. "Okay, ten. But we have to make room for your clean clothes somehow."

"How about we leave out my toothbrush?" Max suggested helpfully, digging under the pile of toys to find it. "I probably won't need it, anyway. I'm just going to be gone until Saturday."

Pierce smothered a grimace. "Well, a toothbrush doesn't take up all that much space, and the Mc-Reynoldses would probably appreciate it if you could somehow find the time to use it."

"Okay," Max agreed reluctantly. "Then what else can I leave behind? I need this stuff, Dad."

"How about Freddy?" Pierce pulled the bedraggled bear from Max's suitcase and held it up.

Max bit his lip, eyeing the stuffed toy longingly. "What if he gets lonely for me while I'm gone?"

"Remember what you told your mother last night? Freddy can think about you every night before he goes to sleep. And just to make doubly sure he doesn't get lonely, you can think about him, too. How's that?"

Max considered the suggestion. "That could work, I guess. Will you…think about me, too?"

"You bet."

"And will you keep Mom from getting too lonely for me?"

Pierce smiled. "I'll sure do my best."

Max looked up at his father, his eyes wide and dark and solemn. "Can I tell you a secret? Promise you won't tell?"

Pierce crossed his heart with his finger.

Max nodded, satisfied. "I used to hear Mom crying sometimes at night when she thought I was asleep. I think she was lonely for you."

Pierce closed his eyes for a moment, feeling a wave of guilt wash over him. "I'm going to try to make sure that your mother never has a reason to cry again. That's a promise, Max."

Max grinned. "You always keep your promises, don't you, Dad?"

"Yes," Pierce agreed grimly, remembering the oath to the agency he'd taken years ago. "I always do."

Max took Freddy from Pierce and sat down on the edge of the bed, cradling the bear in his arms. He was silent for a moment, then he looked up at Pierce, his gaze serious. "If someone told you their secret, it wouldn't be right to tell someone else about it, would it?"

"Not usually," Pierce said. "But it would depend on what the secret was. There are times when you should. For instance, if the secret was one that might cause harm to someone else, then you'd have to tell. Or there are secrets like the one you just told me about your mother. You thought that was something I needed to know. Is there something else you want to tell me, Max?"

Max shook his head. "I promised I wouldn't tell, and I want to be like you. I want to always keep my promises."

This conversation was making Pierce feel uneasy. "Is this promise going to cause harm to someone if you don't tell? Is it dangerous?"

Max shook his head. "No. It's just about a dumb game me and my friend play."

Pierce let out a relieved breath. "Well, if it's a promise you made to a friend, and there's no harm to anyone else, then I guess I'd have to agree. I guess you'd need to keep your friend's secret. Otherwise he might not think he could trust you. But if you ever do need to talk to me about anything, I'm here, son."

"I'm here, too, Dad, if you ever need to talk to me," Max said soberly.

"Thanks, Max. I'll remember that."

A little while later, Max was all packed up, and he and Pierce and Jessica stood out in the front yard as Frank McReynolds loaded the rest of their gear into the back of the van.

Jessica bent down and gave Max one last hug. "Now you call me whenever you get a chance," she instructed.

"There won't be no phone in the woods, Mom," Max admonished her, but his arms clung to her neck a little longer than usual.

"Don't worry, Jessica. We'll call," Sharon assured her. "Ready to hit the road, Max?"

He nodded, pressing his face against Jessica's one last time. Then he climbed into the van, and Jessica felt the beginnings of tears as she watched him and Allie hopping up and down in excitement. Pierce's arm came around her, and automatically the loneliness began to ease. Jessica laid her head against his shoulder, and his arm tightened around her.

Amid a barrage of goodbyes and be goods and have funs, the van slowly backed out of the driveway and lumbered down the street. Jessica and Pierce stood on the sidewalk, still waving as the van turned the corner and drove out of sight.

"So," she said, taking a deep breath and letting it out.

"So," he said, watching her carefully.

Jessica self-consciously wiped the back of her fingers across the moisture on her face. "You must think I'm pretty silly, getting this upset over a camping trip. It's just…he's never been away from me before. I always took him with me when I traveled."

Pierce lifted a finger to trace the path of a new tear

sliding down her cheek. "I don't think you're silly at all. I miss him, too."

She gazed up at him. "You do? Already? I mean, you understand," she finished softly. He nodded, and for the first time Jessica spoke what was in her heart. "I'm glad you're here, Pierce."

"I'm glad I'm here, too." They smiled at one another to mark the beginning of a new understanding, and then he said, "What we need is a diversion."

"A...diversion?"

He kept his arm around her shoulders as they turned toward the house. "To take our minds off missing our son. How about dinner out tonight? Just you and me. Kind of like the old days. Except better. I'd love to take this new, independent career woman out on the town," he teased as they walked up the porch steps. "Of course, since you're working and I'm not, you may have to pick up the tab."

Jessica tucked her hair behind her ears as they stopped on the front porch and turned toward one another. A breeze drifted through the trees, stirring the scent of honeysuckle in the early morning air. Memories teased the fringes of Jessica's mind, and she wasn't sure if they were good or bad ones. "The shop is still yours, Pierce. You still own it."

He shook his head and smiled. "The shop is *ours,* Jesse. You've made it every bit as much yours as it ever was mine. Maybe more so." He paused, then said, "There could be a place for both of us, though."

In silent consent, they sat down on the porch swing and rocked slowly back and forth. It seemed like such an innocent thing to do, uncomplicated and normal, but Jessica knew that something important was hap-

pening between them. Something that had been building for days.

She considered his suggestion as the movement of
the swing lulled her senses. She was surprised to find
that she didn't resent Pierce's proposal. Not in the
least. "You could be right," she said. "I would like
to be able to spend some time with Max. I've missed
so much, it seems."

"Not nearly as much as I have," Pierce said. "But
we have the rest of our lives to make up for it. Why
don't we start tonight? It could be a new beginning
for us, Jesse."

He stopped the movement of the swing as he turned
to her expectantly. Jessica could hear the hammering
of her heart in the early morning stillness and wondered if he could, too.

"I'm not sure I'm ready," she murmured, avoiding
his gaze.

Pierce started the swing again. "We'll start with
dinner," he said easily. "We won't plan on anything
beyond that."

He rested his head against the back of the swing
and his eyes closed. He looked completely relaxed and
unhurried, but Jessica knew his calmness was a facade.
They were both thinking ahead to after dinner, to returning home where they would be alone tonight, with
no interruptions.

"How about dinner tonight, Jessica?"

Jessica put the final touches to the jewelry display
in the glass case before looking up. Brandon had come
in unexpectedly this morning. She'd thought he was
still in Amsterdam. Or Caracas. Where *had* he told her
he was going last week?

She closed the case and glanced up. "I'm afraid I can't tonight. I've already made plans." At the thought of the promised evening with Pierce, her stomach began to flutter in anticipation. She caught herself smiling.

So did Brandon. Something flickered across his features before he tempered his expression, but Jessica felt the stirrings of an uneasiness she didn't quite understand.

"Do these plans include your ex-husband?"

"He isn't my ex-husband," she clarified. "Pierce and I are still married."

"I would have thought that situation only a temporary technicality," he said, leaning against the counter as he regarded her steadily. "After all, the man's been gone for five years. What can you possibly have in common with him now?"

Jessica thought about the way Pierce had touched her in the pool last night, and her face warmed at the memory. She brushed an invisible spot of dust from the Tiffany lamp on the counter. "You mean aside from our son? I don't know what we may or may not still have in common," she acknowledged. "Maybe that's why I want to have dinner with him tonight."

"I hope you know what you're doing." His voice was soft and concerned, but there was still something in his eyes, a hardness she had never noticed before. "I'd hate to see you get hurt," he added.

"I have no intention of getting hurt," Jessica said, but in truth she had no idea whether she was doing the right thing or not. All she knew for sure was that the feelings between her and Pierce were much too strong to ignore. God knows she'd tried. But she couldn't fight them any longer. Didn't want to.

"What did you bring me from your trip?" she said lightly, trying to return their conversation to business matters.

Brandon grinned. "Something irresistible. Something you can't possibly say no to."

"Well, let's see it," Jessica said, then caught her breath at the gold and jade earrings he withdrew from his pocket. They were the exact shade of green as the dress she planned to wear tonight. For Pierce.

The band played "Unforgettable."

Jessica remembered vividly that one detail, but on looking back later, so much about the evening with Pierce was only a hazy memory, a shimmering impression of a night destined to change her life.

She remembered that she wore her green dress and the jade earrings, and Pierce was dressed in a raw silk sport coat, a white shirt that looked irresistibly soft and inviting, and dark pleated trousers that fitted him so well she was certain they must be new. Jessica remembered thinking that he was dressed the way he used to, the casual elegance masking the soul of a man who dared to take risks, who had once thrived on living on the edge.

She remembered that the rustic, wooded setting of the restaurant Pierce had chosen made it seem as if they were miles from anywhere, and the candlelight flickering on the table made his eyes seem even darker, more mysterious.

She remembered that they danced. Close. Like lovers. And she remembered that later they strolled outside in the restaurant's garden, and that Pierce kissed her beneath a full moon.

But what Jessica always remembered most about

that night was the anticipation that, like a drug, lulled her into an almost dreamlike state of lethargy, where everything looked beautiful and romantic, and where anything seemed possible.

Even love.

The house looked dark and deserted when they pulled up into the driveway, but Jessica had left a lamp on in the living room and another one on in her bedroom. The soft glow from the upstairs window drew her gaze for a moment as Pierce wrapped his arm around her and guided her in through the back door.

She stumbled once in the darkness, and he caught her against him, his hands finding her waist and holding her for a moment longer than was necessary. Jessica gazed up at him in the darkness, unable to read his eyes or his expression, but she somehow knew that he was feeling that same sense of expectation, that trace of recklessness that had been teasing them both all evening.

"Shall we say our good-nights down here, Jesse?" he murmured softly.

His hand skimmed her bare arm. His touch was electric. And Jessica wanted more.

She curled her fingers around his lapels, pulling him toward her for the kiss she had been craving all evening. Not the light, romantic kiss he'd given her in the garden, but a deep, soul-shattering kiss that would leave not one iota of doubt in either of their minds as to how the evening would end.

"I'd rather say good morning," she said daringly, feathering her lips against his.

Pierce let out a long breath, pulled her against him and trailed his hands up and down her back. "Do you know how good it feels to hold you? God, you can't possibly know.''

"Oh, but I do," she said. "I've waited so long for you. For this night."

"Sweetheart," he breathed and captured her lips with his. He touched his tongue to hers, and Jessica felt the sensation all the way to her toes.

"Let's go upstairs," he said, taking her hand.

Jessica was floating again. She was barely aware of the stairs beneath her feet or the doors that opened at the slightest touch, but suddenly they were in her bedroom and she was in his arms again, and the king-size bed—their bed—was beckoning to them both.

Pierce swung one of the jade earrings with his fingertip. "Beautiful," he whispered. "Just like you."

"Brandon brought them to me today," she said. "I couldn't resist. I—I'd hoped you'd like them."

"I love them, but since Chambers brought them to you, we'll remove them first," he said teasingly, reaching to undo the backs. He tossed the earrings on her dresser, then reached for the zipper of her dress.

Suddenly shy, Jessica said, "Let me…I'll just be a minute." She scooped up her robe and sailed past him into the bathroom. She closed the door and leaned against it, fanning her face with her hand.

No turning back now, Jessica, she warned herself. You better make darn sure this is what you want. Away from Pierce she felt the doubts begin to sneak back in. The glow from the evening— from the wine and from his kiss—fizzled in the harsh glare of the bathroom light. She hadn't made love in five years, and Jessica had never felt very confident about her abilities to please him, even all those years ago.

What if she did something stupid? What if she did

something that would embarrass both her and Pierce and make him wish he'd never come back? Or worse, what if he didn't like the way she looked anymore? She wasn't as thin as she used to be, she thought, gazing down at her figure. Pierce had always treated her like a china doll, but Jessica had lost that fragile look a long time ago.

But when she glanced at her reflection in the mirror, saw the glow in her eyes, the color in her cheeks, the slightly swollen line of her lips from his kisses, she knew suddenly that, no matter what the night held for them, no matter what revelations came to light, this was exactly what she wanted. For the first time in five years she felt like a woman again. Pierce had not only returned from the dead but he'd also brought her back into the world of the living.

Quickly she removed her dress and stockings and underwear, and belted the robe around her. She brushed her teeth, ran a comb through her hair, and spritzed her favorite perfume on all the pulse points she could think of. Then she opened the door and went out to join her husband.

Pierce saw the doubt and uncertainty in her eyes immediately. He watched her cross the room and stand for a second too long beside the bed before she curled up beside him. She looked so young with her long, dark hair fanned out across the pillow and her gray eyes wide and shadowed with apprehension and maybe just a hint of fear. She seemed sweet and vulnerable tonight, and so fragile that he wondered if he even dared touch her.

So he just looked at her for an agonizing moment, telling himself that he could make her happy. He could be the man she'd always thought he was. Tonight he had a lot to prove, not just to her, but to himself.

Would she still want him? When she saw what he looked like now, would she still find him attractive? Or would she be turned off by what the past five years had done to him?

She was waiting for him to make the first move, Pierce realized. She was gazing over at him, and he felt a surge of tenderness well inside him. She was looking at him the way she used to look at him.

He took his cue immediately.

"We can do away with this, can't we?" he asked, undoing the belt of her robe. Jessica raised herself up as he slipped the fabric off her shoulders and down her arms, and then it was gone.

The last barrier between them.

She slid beneath the covers and Pierce reached across her to turn out the light.

"You don't have to," she whispered shyly.

"It's best," he said in a tone Jessica couldn't quite decipher. Then he said, "Come here, sweetheart," and she stopped trying to analyze anything.

His kisses and caresses quickly returned her to that floating, dreamlike state of euphoria. Jessica had never felt so relaxed. So free from responsibility.

"We don't have a thing to worry about tonight," he said, echoing her thoughts. "It's just you and me, Jesse. The way it used to be. I'll take care of you, you know. I'll take care of everything."

Jessica knew what he was talking about. She'd seen the box of condoms sitting on the nightstand when she'd come back into the room. "I thought you said you weren't planning anything beyond dinner," she murmured, closing her eyes as his hand played along her side, riding over her hip, then lingering on her thigh.

"Do you mind?" he asked, tracing her lips lightly with his fingertips.

"No," she said, and meant it. "Sometimes it's nice to be taken care of." Jessica was amazed at herself for admitting it, but it was true. Tonight she needed to be able to rely on someone other than herself. She needed to be able to trust again. She needed Pierce.

Jessica sighed, and Pierce wrapped her even more tightly in his arms.

It was so easy, after all, she discovered. So easy to let go of the doubts and fears and frustrations. So easy to let him back into her life and back into her heart. Jessica caught his face between her hands and kissed him deeply.

Instantly Pierce responded to her need. He kissed her in return, tenderly at first and then with a growing demand that left them both breathless and aching. His head moved downward, leaving a trail of hot, wet kisses as he searched for, then found first one breast and then the other. He moistened the sensitive peak with his tongue, then took it into his mouth, drawing a long, shuddering breath from Jessica. She plunged her hands into his hair and held him close.

The darkness of the room only heightened her senses. Jessica could barely see Pierce's face, but she didn't need to see him. She could feel him, feel every inch of his long, hard body as he lay against her, touching her so intimately she thought she might die from the thrill of it all.

It was never this way before.

Jessica didn't want to think about that, didn't want to make comparisons with the way it used to be, but dear God, it *was* different. It *was* better. She guided him to the places that screamed for attention, and Pierce eagerly complied. She whispered his name over and over in the darkness, entreaties that came from her heart, her very soul, and Pierce answered her.

"I'm right here, Jesse," he whispered.

He took his time with her, kissing her all over, touching her in places that made her moan softly into the darkness. Pierce had only one thought and that was to please Jesse. For the moment, he put his own needs aside and tried to concentrate on making her want him as badly as he wanted her.

But it had been so long. So very long. Five years he'd spent without her. Even though he couldn't remember the passage of time, Pierce somehow felt the unbearable loneliness of every one of those years now, the desperation and despair of the long separation.

The intense emotions rushing through him made him want to hurry the consummation, to lay claim to his wife once again, to experience that heart-pounding thrill the moment he entered her.

But not yet, he thought. Not until she was ready for him. This night belonged to her.

He felt her hand on his. Unexpectedly she changed the rhythm of his touch, and Pierce heard her breath catch in her throat. It elated him to know that she could take such pleasure in their lovemaking now, that she could unashamedly let him know what she wanted, what brought her pleasure.

It was never like this before.

Don't think about that, he admonished himself. It had always been wonderful with Jesse, but Pierce had never been quite sure of his ability to please her. She'd always been so shy about voicing her needs, about showing him what brought her the greatest enjoyment.

But not now. God, it *was* better between them now. So much better. *He* was better, Pierce realized, and he knew why. Because pleasing Jessica was so much more important—and so much more thrilling—than taking his own satisfaction.

He heard her breath quicken, felt the muscles in her legs tense and knew that she was almost there. He slid down in bed and let his mouth replace his hand. The explosion was almost immediate. Jessica's back arched and her hands grasped his shoulders as she cried out. The convulsions lasted an impossibly long time, and Pierce thought his own body would explode just watching her. Before the shudders quieted, he reached for the box on the nightstand, dealt with the necessities, then moved over her and eased inside.

Jessica's heart was still pounding from the after-shock of the powerful climax when she felt Pierce enter her. She tensed. It was difficult at first. After all this time, the passage was almost too snug, but Pierce took his time, easing in little by little, whispering to her how much he wanted her.

"It's been so long," she whispered a little desperately. "I'm sorry it's so…tight."

Pierce shuddered above her. "God, I'm not. It's like our wedding night, remember?"

The memory made Jessica smile. Made her want to experience again that closeness with Pierce, a man who had been her husband and her lover and her friend. It could be that way again, she thought. It could be that way again, only better.

His movements inside her were slow and unde-manding, so Jessica began to relax. And as soon as she relaxed, the pleasure began to build all over again. She shifted her thighs until she was able to draw his full length inside her, and Pierce stilled for a moment, letting her body adjust to his.

It was Jessica who moved against him. It was Jessica who set the rhythm, moving her hips slowly at first, then faster and harder, taking him in so deeply Pierce knew he would come apart any second now.

"God, you're good," he groaned, matching her frenzied rhythm. "So damned good."

In the end it was Pierce who took charge. No longer able to sustain the motion, Jessica collapsed back on the bed, breathing deeply as the sensations rapidly began to build and build in the lower part of her body. Pierce plunged inside her, time after time, until the release ripped through her, shattering the last vestige of her control.

Holding him close, Jessica felt Pierce's shudders, his last deep thrusts, and knew with a sense of contentment that she had pleased him. Almost as much as he had pleased her. She felt like laughing and crying all at the same time.

After a moment, he started to roll off her, but Jessica clasped him tightly. "Don't leave," she whispered, feeling the emotions well up inside her. "Not yet."

Pierce touched the tear at the corner of her eye. "Did I hurt you? Oh, God, Jesse, I didn't mean to."

"You didn't. It's just...." Her voice trailed off and her eyes closed. "It was so wonderful being close to you again, but it was...so different this time. So intense. I've never felt this way before."

Pierce smiled. "So you noticed that, too." He rolled to his side, but he kept his arms around her, kept their bodies connected as he pulled her more snugly into his embrace. They lay face-to-face. Heart to heart. And Jessica couldn't imagine being anywhere else at that moment.

"Why do you think it's so different now?" she asked, laying her head against his shoulder.

His hand lazily traced her back. "I imagine it's because of what you keep telling me. We've both changed."

"That much?"

He grinned. "It would seem so. You've grown up, become very mature and independent. You know what you want and you weren't afraid to let *me* know."

Jessica covered her face with her hands. Now that the passion had subsided, she felt a little embarrassed by her behavior. "You must think I'm terrible," she said.

Pierce pulled her hands away from her face and kissed her soundly. "I think you're wonderful," he said. "But you're not the only one who's changed, sweetheart. I think I've grown up, too. I've learned that life is more than just living on the edge. More than just one momentary thrill after another. My family is the most important thing in the world to me now, and I want to be here for you for as long as you'll have me. Because I love you, Jesse. More than anything."

Jessica felt another tear slip down her face. She reached up and brought his mouth close to hers. "Please don't leave me," she whispered, just before their lips touched.

"Never again," he vowed.

Chapter 12

He was gone when Jessica awakened. She bolted upright in bed.

"Pierce?"

"I'm right here, Jesse," came his soft reply.

It was still dark, but a soft glow illuminated the room as if dawn hovered just on the horizon. Pierce was sitting in the wing chair near the window, and he'd turned on a lamp, angling the shade so that the light fell away from the bed. Jessica saw that he'd been looking through the stack of photo albums she kept in the bookcase near her dresser.

"Can't you sleep?" she asked, shoving the hair back from her face.

"I have a lot on my mind, I guess."

His head was bent over the pictures, and his expression was shadowed, but even from across the room, Jessica sensed that something was wrong. She reached for her robe and slipped it on as she got out of bed. She crossed the floor and knelt beside the chair, then gazed down at the pictures in the album spread open on his lap. By the looks of the pile beside his chair, he'd already been through most of them.

Jessica knew what they contained. They were a catalog of Max's life from the day he was born. His first tooth, his first step, his first day of school. Jessica had been meticulous about chronicling in photographs the five years Pierce had been away. She wondered now if it was because she'd always known somehow that he'd come back to her.

"That was the day Max started kindergarten," Jessica said softly, smiling at the image of her son's solemn little face as he waved to her from the school-bus steps. The camera had captured the tears glistening on his cheeks, and Jessica remembered that she'd had a hard time fighting back her own tears as she'd watched the bus drive away. She'd felt as if she'd lost a very precious part of herself that day.

"I've missed so much," Pierce said. His own eyes were shining as he looked up and met her gaze. "I've lost so much more than just memories, Jesse, and no matter what happens, I'll never get those years back. They're gone forever."

Jessica didn't know what to say. Something unleashed inside. She felt the last of her anger and resentment melt away as she gazed into Pierce's tormented eyes. She knew, without knowing how she knew, that he hadn't left her and Max all those years ago because he'd wanted to. He'd left because he had to. Because no other choice had been given to him.

She mourned his loss now, just as she had mourned hers the day he'd disappeared.

She reached up and smoothed back the lock of dark

hair that had fallen across his brow. "I don't know how I would deal with a loss like yours," she said softly. "I can't imagine how it would feel to have missed all those years of Max's life."

"And yours," he said, gazing at her with dark, haunted eyes. "You can't know how deeply I regret losing those five years of our marriage, Jesse. Years that we can never get back. Sometimes I wonder...."

"What?"

He took her hand and squeezed it. "Sometimes I wonder if things will ever work out for us. I want them to. You don't know how badly, but sometimes I can't help thinking that we may never be able to find what we once had."

"Maybe not all of it," she said. "Some of it *is* gone forever." Jessica felt something of the loss she'd experienced the day Max had started to school. Something precious had been lost to her forever. But in a way, she and Max had grown closer after that day. She'd enjoyed immensely this new phase of his life, taken great pride in his accomplishments at school.

Her hero worship and youthful adulation for the kind of man Pierce had been was gone forever because the girl she'd been was gone. She was a woman now, and like her son, she didn't need a hero anymore. Didn't need someone to protect her from the cruelties of the world. She'd proven that she could do that for herself.

What she needed now was just a man. Someone to love her for better or worse. Jessica took a deep breath. She mourned the loss of her youth for just a moment, then she let it go. Maybe it was time she and Pierce moved into a new, more mature phase of their lives.

He was staring down at the pictures again, his expression deeply saddened, and Jessica's heart ached for him.

"Let it go," she whispered. "Let it go, love. You and Max have years and years ahead of you. You won't miss any more of his life, Pierce. I promise you."

"And what about your life, Jesse?"

Jessica didn't answer him. Instead she drew their linked hands up to her mouth and kissed each of his scarred knuckles. "It can never be the same for us again," she said softly. "I'm not the same woman you married, and you're not the same man who left here five years ago. But I do love you, Pierce. Maybe more than I ever did."

Pierce closed his eyes as if overcome by his emotions. "You don't know how I've wanted to hear you say that. I've seen the woman you've become, Jesse. I've seen the way you've raised our son. I admire and respect you more than anyone I've ever known. And if you don't need me anymore, well, that's okay." He set the album aside and stood, drawing her to her feet. "Because you see, sweetheart, I do need you. I need you desperately."

It was so easy to hold him, to offer him the comfort of her arms as he'd done so often for her in the past. For a long while they stood in the glow of the lamp, their arms around each other as they each grieved in their own way for what would never be again.

Jessica wasn't sure when things began to change, but suddenly their embrace tightened. Their bodies shifted and fitted together more intimately. She felt Pierce's lips in her hair and then at her ear and she turned her head just slightly, so their mouths were only a breath away.

"Oh, God," Pierce whispered, holding her close.

Then he kissed her, and Jessica felt the past crumble around them.

He unfastened her robe and slid it off her shoulders, then lifted her and carried her to the bed. Jessica kept her arms around him, pulling him down with her as she lay back against the pillows.

Their kisses became hot and greedy with anticipation. They knew what to expect from each other now, knew exactly how to give each other the greatest pleasure, and Jessica couldn't wait for that exquisite moment of fulfillment. She reveled now in the physical side of their love where once she had been too inhibited to fully enjoy it.

Pierce pulled away from her for a moment. "I'll turn off the light," he said.

"No, don't," she said, reaching for him again.

"But, Jesse—"

"I want to see you," she insisted. She sat up in bed and then knelt before him, still a little shy in her nakedness, but the look in Pierce's eyes made her awkwardness vanish. She let him look at her for as long as he wanted, and then, when he reached for her, she went gladly into his arms.

In the lamp glow, she could see the scar down the side of his face, and Jessica lifted her lips to kiss it. Pierce flinched beneath her touch, but he didn't move away. He remained still under her scrutiny, letting her get to know his body again as he'd done with hers.

Jessica's lips skimmed down the side of his face, tracing the length of the scar, then moved to his neck and across his shoulders. She shifted around him so that she was kneeling behind him. She bent and kissed the back of his neck as her hands caressed his arms and shoulders, and then moved to his back.

Her hands froze when she felt the mass of scars.

Pierce tensed but didn't move. He sat with his head slightly bowed as if waiting for her retreat.

Even in the soft light, the scars were horrible, worse than anything Jessica could ever imagine. The thin red ridges crisscrossed over the entire surface of his back, leaving very little skin that was unmarked. The horror of what he had gone through rose in Jessica until she thought for a moment she might be sick, not from the scars but from the suffering he'd endured and the pain she'd caused him when he returned home. It was almost too much to bear.

But no matter how badly she felt, Jessica knew she could do nothing to make him think she was rejecting him again. Far from it. If possible, she loved him even more. He'd survived incredible torment just to find his way back to her. She put her arms around him and held him close, her cheek against his scarred flesh.

Pierce felt her tears against his back, and it tore him up to realize what the sight of his scars must have done to her. He turned until he was able to take her in his arms and pull her into his lap. She clung to him, crying as he'd never seen her cry before.

Pierce didn't know quite what to do, so he simply held her as the sobs racked her body and her tears streamed down his chest.

"Jesse, Jesse," he soothed, putting his cheek against hers. "It's okay. It's all in the past, remember? We have to let it go, sweetheart."

"I'm sorry," she whispered over and over. "I'm so sorry."

Pierce held her even more tightly. "You have nothing to be sorry about. None of this is your fault."

"But it is, don't you see?" The sobs made her speak haltingly, brokenly. "You came back home... and after everything you'd been through...I made you think you weren't welcome here. I made you think...this wasn't your home anymore. That...Max and I...didn't want you or need you or...love you."

"Well, what were you supposed to do? I'd been gone five years without a word, and then I just showed up one day, expecting everything to be as I'd left it. I don't blame you for not welcoming me with open arms. You were right not to trust me, Jesse," he said, closing his eyes. There was a crushing weight inside Pierce's chest and he knew why. Because he still wasn't telling her the whole truth.

Maybe he should, Pierce thought. Maybe he should forget the oath he'd made to the agency years ago and clear his conscience right here and now with Jesse. He owed his allegiance to her now. She and Max were his only concern, but the need for complete secrecy had been too long ingrained in his makeup. He knew the life-or-death importance of discretion, and he couldn't be sure that any revelation he made now might not somehow jeopardize Jessica and Max's safety.

So he said nothing.

And he let Jessica give him her love, knowing that when she found out the whole truth, there would be hell to pay for this night that had brought them closer than they had ever been before.

Jessica lifted her tearstained face to his. "Make love

to me, Pierce,'' she whispered. ''Please. I need you so.''

''Oh, Jesse—''

Her fingertip silenced his words. ''Don't say anything,'' she begged. ''We've said too much already. Just hold me. Stay with me.''

''Yes,'' he whispered. ''For as long as you'll have me.''

Their lovemaking was more frenzied this time, more desperate and hurried as if they had suddenly realized just how long they'd been separated. Or as if they were new lovers, discovering passion for the first time.

He didn't lay her back on the bed as Jessica expected, but made her stand before him so that he could worship her body with his eyes and his hands and his lips. Jessica trembled as his mouth unerringly found the place she'd guided him to earlier. Her hands tangled in his hair as a wave of sensations raced through her. Jessica fought for breath, fought for balance as Pierce brought her in an astonishingly short time to another shattering climax.

She collapsed against him, and he caught her, then kissed her, deep and hard and thorough, his tongue thrusting in and out, in and out, in a teasing preview of what was to come.

This time it was Jessica who reached for the box on the nightstand, Jessica who dealt with the necessities, Jessica who made it a thrilling prelude to their lovemaking.

Pierce lifted her and settled her on his lap as she wrapped her legs around him. He lifted her hips, then let her slide slowly down on him, and Jessica thought she had never felt anything so wonderfully complete as the moment she felt him inside her.

They kissed, their tongues keeping pace with the frantic rhythm of their bodies.

They embraced, their bodies melding together so tightly that two heartbeats became one.

They whispered, their promises and demands and soft cries stirring the deep silence of night.

And they loved as if there were no tomorrows and no yesterdays, no past and no future, but only now and only them. Because nothing else mattered.

When it was all over, when the shudders of release had been spent, they fell back against the bed, still clinging to each other, still whispering to each other their promises and demands and soft words of love.

Pierce perched on the edge of Jessica's desk and watched her through the open door to the shop. She and a customer were talking animatedly about a silver spoon collection which had just arrived earlier in the week via Brandon Chambers.

At the thought of the buyer, Pierce scowled. He didn't care what Jessica thought of the man, he still didn't trust him, but so far he hadn't been able to justify his suspicions. Even Jay had said the man appeared to be on the up-and-up. But, of course, Jay Greene would be inclined to trust anyone that Pierce didn't.

Pierce moved back around the desk and sat down facing the computer monitor, but his mind wasn't on the figures he'd pulled up on the screen. He was thinking about the animosity he and his brother-in-law had always shared.

Pierce had never been quite sure why the two of them had taken such an instant dislike to one another, but from the moment Jessica had introduced them,

Pierce had known that Jay didn't trust him. He'd often wondered if Jessica's brother had somehow found out about his secret life, if Jay's animosity was indeed genuine concern for his sister.

Or was it something else? Something more personally motivated?

Pierce couldn't imagine what. The agency was top secret with very limited access, even among the highest echelon of the United States government. As a special naval attaché assigned to the office of the Joint Chiefs of Staff in the Pentagon, Jay enjoyed top-priority security clearance, but that still would not have privileged him with knowledge of the agency.

Unless he'd stumbled onto something by accident that he shouldn't have, Pierce thought, his frown deepening. Perhaps it was time he had another talk with his brother-in-law.

Pierce scanned the sales figures in the columns on the screen, and he whistled softly under his breath. Jessica had done an incredible job with the shop. Her accomplishments never ceased to impress him, but as he studied the entries more closely, a pattern emerged that began to bother him. Her largest sales, her highest percentages of profit came on the resale of items Brandon Chambers had sold to her.

Pierce backdated the journal entries, going back first a year, then two, three, four, until he reached the figures for the months following his disappearance. That's when the resale of items Jessica had bought from Chambers first began to appear in her records. The evidence seemed to place Chambers on the scene just shortly after Pierce had left it. At best, it was a worrisome coincidence, but Pierce didn't believe in coincidences.

Jessica finished with the customer in the showroom and then came into the office. Standing behind Pierce, she wrapped her arms around his neck and kissed him on the cheek, making it difficult to concentrate on Brandon Chambers, Jay Greene or anyone else besides her.

Pierce smiled. The past few days with Jesse had been incredible. They'd spent almost every waking moment together, but Max would be home tomorrow, and in spite of how much Pierce would miss the closeness he and Jessica had shared, he couldn't wait to see his son again.

"I miss Max," Jessica said, echoing his thoughts. They'd been doing that a lot lately, it seemed. It pleased Pierce to know that they were once again becoming attuned to each other's thoughts and moods.

"He'll be home tomorrow," Pierce said, turning his chair around to draw Jessica onto his lap. "So we'd better make the most of tonight."

She struggled a little, then gave up and settled against him. "What if a customer comes in?" she protested weakly.

Pierce kissed her soundly. "We'll hear them first."

"Maybe *you* will," she murmured, nuzzling his neck with eager lips. When she was with Pierce, she couldn't seem to concentrate on anything but him.

And now that he had her undivided attention, Jessica realized that something was wrong. She saw that distant look in his eyes that she remembered from the past. He'd had that look the day he'd disappeared. Panic welled inside her as she sat up on his lap and stared at him. "What's wrong?"

"What makes you think something is wrong?"

"Because I can tell by that look in your eyes.

Pierce, you aren't having second thoughts? About... us, I mean?''

His dark eyes seemed to melt as he met her gaze. ''No, sweetheart. How I feel about you and Max is the one thing I am certain of. I've been thinking about something Dr. Prescott said,'' he admitted. Gently he lifted her from his lap, then got up, walked over to the window and stared out. Jessica had the distinct impression that it wasn't the street outside that held his attention. It was the turmoil going on inside him.

Her heart began to pound even harder.

He turned and stared at her, his expression shuttered. Jessica had no idea what he was thinking. Until he spoke.

''I think you and Dr. Prescott were right, Jesse. I think it's time I see someone. A psychiatrist.''

Jessica's heart skipped a beat. ''Why? I mean... why now?''

''Because until we both deal with the past, I'll be worried about our future,'' Pierce said.

''But we *have* dealt with the past. We've put it to rest.''

Pierce let out a breath, shaking his head. ''No, we haven't. Not really. We've merely swept it aside. But it's still there, waiting to tear us apart. And until I can tell you the whole truth about myself, you'll never really be able to trust me, to trust how I feel about you. And how you feel about me.'' He turned back to the window. ''I've already made an appointment with Dr. Layton. He can see me within the hour.''

A sick feeling formed in the pit of Jessica's stomach. ''So soon?''

''The sooner the better,'' Pierce said. ''Isn't that what you said, Jesse? Isn't this what you want?''

No! Jessica thought. Not anymore. She'd come to terms with the past. She'd accepted the fact that she might never know what had happened to Pierce. In fact, she didn't think she even wanted to know anymore.

Maybe they were better off not knowing. What if Pierce found out he'd lived another life during those five years and that there was someone else he wanted...besides her? What if he remembered he didn't love her anymore, didn't need her? Could she handle that? Jessica asked herself desperately. Could she?

"I've made up my mind," Pierce said, coming to stand before her. He took her hand and held it tightly in his. "It's the right thing to do, Jesse. It's the only thing I can do."

"But I'm so afraid," she said, and stepped into his arms.

"I know," he whispered, his lips against her hair. "I am, too," he said.

He was being followed.

Pierce felt the familiar sensation the moment he walked out of the shop. Jessica's Audi was parked at the curb, and as he strode across the sidewalk toward it, he gazed around, trying to locate the invisible eyes.

He unlocked the door, climbed in and started the engine. As he eased the Audi into the light traffic on Washington, Pierce glanced in the rearview mirror. Half a block down, a dark green sedan pulled into the traffic behind him. Pierce smiled grimly, satisfied that his instincts had been correct. He was being followed—but by whom? Someone from the agency?

Or someone with a more dastardly agenda in mind?

Pierce decided there was only one way to find out. Swerving his car into the center lane, he tromped the accelerator, and the Audi careered past two cars. Up ahead, a traffic light turned yellow. Pierce didn't slow down. He sped through the intersection, then checked the mirror again.

Two cars behind him swished through on yellow. The sedan should have been caught by the red light, but instead, the driver ran the light, barely missing a blue Mazda turning left from the intersecting street. Pierce remembered that somewhere around here an alley cut through from Washington to Jefferson Avenue, the next street over. A restaurant located next to the alley had changed names, and Pierce almost missed it, but at the last second, he recognized it. Cutting the car sharply to the right, he headed down the alley, praying it wouldn't be blocked this time of day by delivery trucks.

The Audi bumped along the broken pavement and forced to slow his speed, Pierce cursed under his breath. A quick glance in the mirror told him the green sedan hadn't been able to follow him. At least, not yet.

The Audi emerged on Jefferson, and Pierce shot across the street toward a parking garage. He pulled into a space facing the alley and sat with the engine idling.

Several minutes passed and still no sedan. Had he lost it? Surely not. Not unless the driver was a rank amateur, in which case that would eliminate anyone from the agency. Evasive driving techniques, as well as surveillance, were all a part of the training.

Maybe the agency was slipping, Pierce decided, after several more minutes had gone by. Or maybe his imagination was simply getting the better of him. Whatever the case, the green sedan was nowhere in sight.

Pierce shifted into reverse and started to back out of the parking space just as a car squealed to a halt directly behind him. Instinctively he dived for the floorboard an instant before the sound of a gunshot blasted through the parking garage. The back window of the Audi shattered into a million jagged pieces.

Trapped, Pierce reached for the door handle, opened the door and crawled out. The parking garage was half-empty, with very little cover. He scanned the area, deciding the best course of action, but before he could make a move, he heard the unmistakable sound of a pistol being cocked not five feet from him.

"No sudden moves," a voice behind him ordered.

Slowly Pierce got to his feet and turned.

The sun shone through the open side of the garage, backlighting the man standing a few feet away and making him seem no more than a faceless shadow. A mirage. Pierce squinted, trying to put a face on the silhouette.

"Who are you?" he asked.

The man laughed softly, a familiar, eerie sound that set Pierce's heart to pounding. He knew him.

"Welcome home, Kincaid."

A memory flashed through Pierce's mind, but before he could explore it, a splitting pain crashed through the back of his skull. Pierce registered the blow as he fell to his knees. He heard the man say, "You hit him too hard, you idiot."

Pierce put up a hand and felt the blood. Then he pitched forward as his world suddenly faded to black.

Chapter 13

Jessica glanced at the clock on the kitchen stove. It was after six, and she hadn't heard from Pierce since he'd left the shop earlier that day. His appointment was at five, and if it ran an hour, he would have left Dr. Layton's office by now. Jessica wondered if he would call her before coming home, prepare her for what he had learned.

But as the minutes slipped past and the phone remained silent, she grew more and more anxious.

By seven o'clock, she had worked herself up into a real panic. She even phoned Dr. Layton's office, but only got a recording with a pleasant female voice chiming off the office hours and advising callers that Dr. Layton only saw referral clients. Jessica glanced at the clock again as she hung up the phone. Even allowing for traffic, Pierce should have been home by now.

It was foolish to worry, she knew. He was a grown

man, and he'd been gone for the past five years. She'd thought he was dead. Worrying because he was late for dinner seemed so ridiculous by comparison. But still, she couldn't imagine why he hadn't gotten home yet unless...

Don't say it, she scolded herself. Don't even think it.

But a sly little voice had already insinuated itself into the back of her mind. It whispered to her now like an icy wind in the dead of winter.

Pierce isn't here yet because he isn't coming back at all.

Jessica closed her eyes and leaned against the sink. Not a second time, she prayed. Please, not a second time.

Pierce woke up with a splitting headache. He gazed around the small cell-like room as a host of memories surged through him. He groaned, wanting to fade away the pain, but he knew if he did that, he'd never remember what happened to him all those years ago. He'd never be able to be back with Jessica completely.

He sat up on the cot and tentatively felt the lump on his head, then winced. Someone had really done a job on him. He remembered the gunshot, the man standing silhouetted in front of him, the pain, then nothing. Everything since then was a complete blank. How long had he been out, anyway? Jessica must be going out of her mind with worry—

His anxious thoughts broke off as the door opened and a man stepped through. They eyed each other warily, and Pierce thought the man looked somehow familiar. He was tall, perhaps six-two, and athletically built. His hair was brown and his appearance, apart from a thick brown mustache, was nondescript. Not ordinary precisely, but in no way memorable. He was exactly the kind of man the agency liked to recruit.

Pierce's gaze narrowed on him. "Who are you?" he demanded.

"My name's Walker."

"The man on the phone?"

Walker smiled and his mustache tilted at the corners. "One and the same. It's an honor to meet you, Kincaid. Your reputation precedes you."

"But you said we'd met in the Caribbean," Pierce said grimly. "And then at the café, the day I got back. I thought there was something suspicious-looking about you."

Walker inclined his head in acknowledgment. "I'd take that as an insult from anyone else." He took a few steps into the room, but his eyes never left Pierce. "Rumor has it, you used to be the best in the business. Until you turned, that is."

Pierce stared at him in shock as he fought a wave of nausea. His head hurt like a son of a bitch. "What the hell are you talking about?" he demanded.

"Five years ago you sold information to the leader of a two-bit Caribbean country that's hardly more than a blemish on the world map. We were looking to oust the generalissimo and install our own user-friendly dictator. You sold Valencio our game plan, and then he turned on you."

Pierce shook his head, unable to believe what he was hearing. "I worked on that case for over three years," he said. "We found out a double agent was on Valencio's payroll, someone selling him military information that could have jeopardized our whole peace plan in that region. It was my job to track down the traitor, to flush him out into the open.''

Walker's mustache flicked. ''A convenient assignment, considering you were the double agent. But, of course, you didn't count on your buddy, Valencio, double-crossing you, did you? He and his Cuban buddies got what they wanted, then threw you in prison for the better part of five years. We negotiated your release a few months ago.''

''A few months ago? I've only been back a few days. What happened? Where've I been?''

Walker shrugged. ''We don't know for sure. There was an explosion on board the boat bringing you in. You disappeared in the confusion, and we lost track of you until a few days ago when you showed up back here. We've been following you ever since you came through customs in Miami using a fake passport.''

Pierce shook his head, unable to grasp all that he was being told. He got up and walked over to the window. They were on the ground floor, but metal bars on the outside of the window nixed any thoughts of escape. He turned back to Walker.

''Where am I now?''

''Langley, Virginia. Your old stomping grounds.''

''Am I to assume I'm under arrest then?''

Walker's eyes were cold, hard, mercenary. The eyes of a trained professional. He said calmly, ''That's what usually happens to a traitor, isn't it?''

Pierce's voice was just as cold. Just as steady. And just as deadly. ''I'm not a traitor, you bastard.''

Walker smiled. ''Try telling that to the powers-that-be.''

''Give me the chance and I will.''

Walker shook his head. "Not yet. Not until we have a little more proof."

"Proof of what?"

Walker slanted him a look. "Of your innocence, Kincaid."

"My innocence? Are you saying you believe me?" At Walker's nod, Pierce's anger erupted. "Then what the hell was all that garbage about my being a traitor? Why am I here? What's going on?"

"I'm telling you what happened five years ago, before your disappearance," Walker said grimly. "That's what you wanted, isn't it? Why you were planning to see a shrink today?"

"How the he—the phone's tapped," Pierce said in disgust, shoving his hand through his hair. "I should have known."

"Don't be so hard on yourself. You've been out of circulation for years. No wonder you're a little rusty on the draw."

There was something troubling about Walker's voice, his attitude. Pierce watched him carefully.

"The double agent you were after got wise to you," Walker said. "He sold you out. He arranged an exchange of information with Valencio to make you look guilty. When the information turned out bogus, Valencio's henchmen, with the help of the Cubans, came looking for you. They nabbed you, took you back to their little island hideaway and worked you over good, trying to get the real information out of you. When that didn't work, they threw you in prison, hoping to use you as a bargaining tool at some later date."

"Wait a minute," Pierce said. "Are you saying that

the agency bought the double cross? They thought I'd turned?''

''The verdict's still out.''

Pierce muttered an oath he was surprised he still remembered. ''Is that why I'm here?''

Walker propped one foot on the cot and folded his arms over his leg. ''You aren't being detained by the agency, Kincaid. You're being detained by me.''

Pierce gingerly felt the bump on the back of his head. ''Detained? Is that what you call it these days?''

Walker ignored the sarcasm. ''I had you brought in because I didn't want you seeing a shrink. The agency went to a lot of time and expense, programming the fade-to-black trigger in you. A shrink could undo it without realizing it.''

''Fade to black,'' Pierce said slowly. ''A programmed response? I was trained to forget, wasn't I?''

''That's probably at least part of it,'' Walker agreed. ''The rest we can only guess, but we haven't much time for speculation. There are those in the agency who believe you're guilty of treason, Kincaid, but I'm not one of them. I know the real double agent is still out there somewhere, and you're the only man alive who can identify him.''

Pierce was across the room in two strides. He grabbed Walker by the lapels. ''You said there was no danger, damn you. You said Max and Jessica were safe from this.''

Walker looked Pierce right in the eye. ''They are, as long as he knows where to find you.''

Pierce shoved him aside and turned away in disgust. ''This whole thing makes me sick,'' he said. ''I can't believe I was ever a part of it.''

''You were the best,'' Walker said again. ''You

never hesitated to do what had to be done. Don't hesitate now, Kincaid. We have the perfect opportunity to catch him, to flush him out into the open. Sooner or later, he'll make a move on you, and when he does, we'll get him. After all this time, we'll finally nail that bastard.''

"And I'm just supposed to sit tight and let you use my family as bait?" Pierce retorted coldly. "No deal, Walker."

"Unfortunately you're not in any position to bargain. It's in your wife's and son's best interests for you to cooperate with us. As long as he knows where to find *you*, he has no reason to harm *them*. If you were to up and disappear again, he might try using them to get to you. Besides, you're the best protection they've got right now. The only thing you can do is exactly what you've been doing."

"Which is nothing, damn you."

"You know as well as I do that a good portion of an agent's life is spent watching and waiting." Walker drew a SIG-Sauer semiautomatic from his jacket pocket and laid it on the small wooden table beside the cot. He turned to Pierce and smiled, but there was no warmth in his eyes. Just an ice-cold resolve. Pierce wondered if he was seeing a reflection of himself five years ago. It was a thought that gave him no pleasure.

"Welcome back to the action, Kincaid. It's in our blood, you know. Men like you and me, we thrive on danger. We'd wither and die without it." Walker crossed the floor to the door and opened it, then glanced back. "By the way, the door was never locked. You were free to go at any time."

"You son of a bitch," Pierce muttered. Like five

years ago, he was left with no choice. He picked up the SIG-Sauer and followed Walker out the door.

The house was quiet except for the ticking of the grandfather clock in the foyer. Jessica noted almost every minute that went by. She stood glued to the living-room window, where she had a clear view of the street. Every few seconds, she would whip her head around to look at the phone, willing it to ring, then turn back to the window to stare out into the darkness.

A misty rain had started to fall, and the streetlights reflected in wavering beams across the pavement, reminding her of how she had always hated rainy nights. They made her think of all the cold, lonely nights she'd spent in the orphanage, and all the cold, lonely nights she'd spent during the past five years. They reminded her of the night Pierce hadn't come back to her....

She touched her reflection in the window with the tip of her finger as a wave of remembered loneliness washed over her. How would she stand it this time? How would she cope if Pierce had walked out on her a second time?

Shivering, she started to turn away from the window, but the sound of a car engine drew her gaze back to the street. A late model, dark-colored sedan drove slowly past the house. Under the streetlight, she could just make out the dark green color, but the windows were tinted and against the wet night, completely opaque. The car turned right at the next street, and fighting down a bitter swell of disappointment, Jessica watched the taillights disappear.

When the telephone finally rang at eight-thirty, she

nearly jumped out of her skin. She dashed to the phone and jerked it up. "Pierce?"

The only sound was static crackling across the line as if the call was coming from a car phone or a pay phone, perhaps. No one said anything, but just like the call a few nights ago, she knew someone was there. The back of her neck prickled with warning.

"Hello? Who is this?"

Still nothing. Jessica clung to the phone, listening intently. The caller remained silent for a moment, then the line clicked dead. Jessica cradled the receiver, her fingers trembling. It was just another hang-up call, she told herself. No need to worry.

But whether it was the fault of the rainy night or her worrying about Pierce, Jessica couldn't be sure, but suddenly she experienced an unprecedented sense of unease, an almost overwhelming premonition of danger. She imagined Pierce lying somewhere, hurt, bleeding, not knowing who or where he was. Not knowing how to get back home to her.

The house, quiet before, now seemed abnormally silent. Jessica didn't like the feeling of being frightened in her own home, but she couldn't shake the notion that something was wrong. She had the chilling sensation that the house was being watched. That *she* was being watched. But by whom? And why?

And where in God's name was Pierce?

She'd feel better if he were here. His presence had such a calming affect on her, a steadying influence—

Jessica stopped, realizing what she was thinking. Was she, like Max, already starting to rely too heavily on Pierce? It was a disconcerting thought. Jessica had long ago come to the conclusion that she could count on no one but herself, so why tonight, of all nights, did she feel she needed Pierce's protection?

Driven by a fear she didn't understand, Jessica dialed the number of the campsite that Sharon had left the first night when she and Max had called Jessica. Sharon had told her that in case of an emergency, the old couple who ran the park would be able to reach them. Jessica knew it was probably too late to be calling just because of a bad feeling she had, but she couldn't help it. She had to make sure her son was safe.

To her relief, the old woman who answered the phone was incredibly understanding. She knew just where the McReynoldses were camped, she assured Jessica. She'd get in her truck and go down there right now to make sure everything was okay. It was no bother at all. She had children and grandchildren of her own. It would take her a while to get there, though, so Jessica shouldn't worry if she didn't hear back right away.

Jessica hung up the phone and sat down in the chair beside it, waiting for it to ring again. Thirty minutes later, Sharon called her back. "Max is fine, Jessica," Sharon said for the third time. Jessica heard the exasperation in her friend's voice, but she couldn't help asking again.

"Are you sure?"

"Yes, yes, yes. He and Allie are already tucked in for the night. He was sleeping like a log when I checked him before I left."

Jessica let out a long breath. "I'm really sorry, Sharon. But I just had this feeling...I just knew Max was in some sort of trouble—"

"Look, it's okay. I'd probably be the same way if

I were away from Allie. But we'll be home tomorrow, okay? And then you can stop worrying.''

"Okay," Jessica agreed. "I'll see you tomorrow."

Satisfied that her imagination had been running away with her, Jessica turned to leave the room, then jumped violently when she saw a shadow in the doorway.

Her hand flew to her heart as she stifled the scream that erupted in her throat.

Chapter 14

He'd been so silent, Jessica hadn't heard a sound. It was terrifying to realize how vulnerable she was in her own home. The shadows in the hall made him look mysterious and dangerous, emphasizing rather than hiding the scar that twisted his brow.

Jessica put a hand to her heart. She could feel it pounding against her chest, so hard and so loud she wondered if Pierce could hear it, too.

"I didn't hear you come in," she said lamely. "You startled me."

"Sorry." The dark gaze held hers for the longest time. The uneasy feeling grew even stronger inside Jessica.

She said, "Do you know what time it is? I was so worried, Pierce."

He slanted her a dark glance as he stepped into the room. "Worried that I wasn't coming back? Maybe I shouldn't have," he said.

Jessica's heart skipped a beat. Had she heard him correctly? "What do you mean?" she asked fearfully. "Did you…did you learn something…disturbing?"

"You could say that." His tone was flat and seemingly devoid of emotion. Jessica wanted to scream at his calmness. He walked over to the window and stared out, much as she'd done earlier.

"Is that all you have to say?" she said angrily. "I was worried half out of my mind tonight. I thought for sure something had happened to you, Pierce. That you'd been in an accident or—or something. Don't you think I'm entitled to an explanation?"

At last he turned from the window and faced her. His dark gaze held hers until Jessica began to tremble with dread. He said, still in that toneless voice, "It's past time you had an explanation, Jessica. I'm going to tell you everything. I should have done it a long time ago."

"Then you…know?"

"I know more than I've told you. I've always known."

Jessica reached out blindly for a chair, felt it with her hand, then backed into it. She sat down, sensing somehow that what Pierce was about to say would change everything between them, everything they had worked so hard to rebuild.

Pierce turned back to the window, as if he could no longer face her. He said, "It all started when I was a senior at Georgetown. My parents had died the year before, and I'd inherited The Lost Attic from them. I wasn't much interested in running an antique shop until one day when a man approached me on campus. He had a proposition for me, a job offer of sorts. It seemed my reputation for recklessness, along with my prelaw and political science courses, had drawn some attention from a government agency that I'd never even heard of before.''

Jessica sat in stunned disbelief as she listened to Pierce's revelations about his secret life as an agent, how he'd used The Lost Attic to ferry information to and from foreign countries, and how his true identity became his deep cover.

When he'd finished, Jessica gazed at him for a moment, trying to absorb it all, then slowly she felt a red haze of anger taking hold of her. She got up and walked toward him, her back ramrod straight, her eyes dry.

"And what was I?" she asked coldly. "How did I fit into all this? Was I part of your cover? Did you think you needed a wife to complete the picture? Answer me, damn you!"

For the first time since he'd begun his story, Pierce let his gaze meet hers. Something flickered in his eyes. Something that looked almost like pity. Then he said, "Yes. You were part of the cover," and Jessica's world came crashing down.

"Oh, my God." Her hand flew to her mouth as she started to back away from him. It was a nightmare come true, hearing him confirm her deepest, darkest suspicions. "I knew it," she said. "Somehow I always knew it. I always wondered how someone like you could want someone like me. Oh, God." A wave of humiliation swept over her. Jessica turned, shoving her hands through her hair. "How could I not have seen it? How could I not have known?"

"It's not what you think, Jesse." Pierce reached for her, but Jessica flung his hand away.

"Don't touch me," she screamed. "Don't you dare

touch me again.'' She faced him, her anger blazing, but suddenly the tears started to flow down her face. She collapsed back into the chair, staring up at him. "How could you do this to me? How could you do it to your son? All these years—they've been nothing more than a lie. You never cared about us, did you?"

"I loved you more than anything," Pierce said. "I never stopped loving you. Please, Jesse, just hear me out."

"I've heard about all I can stomach," she said, wiping her face with the back of her hand. She stood and faced him. "I want you out of here. Now. Tonight. I never want to see you again."

"Don't say that. I love you—"

"What does a liar know about love?" she demanded. "You used me. You used your son. I don't even know you. I never did. And right now, I can't stand the sight of you."

"All right, that's enough," Pierce said, his tone hardening. He turned away rubbing his face, then spun back around to face her. "I can understand how you feel, and I won't force my presence on you any longer than I have to. But what you don't seem to understand, Jessica, is that right now neither of us has a choice in the matter. I can't leave you until this whole mess is cleaned up. Until the traitor is caught, I have to stay here and protect you and Max."

"*Protect* us?" Jessica asked sarcastically. "You're the one who put us in danger in the first place. If anything happens to Max because of you, so help me, Pierce, I'll never forgive you."

"Then that makes two of us," he said grimly.

Jessica wept until there were no more tears left to cry. Pierce hadn't married her because he loved her but because he needed a wife, someone to complete his cover. And poor unsuspecting Jessica had fitted the bill perfectly. He'd completely swept her off her feet. She'd adored him. She'd never done anything or asked any questions that might have jeopardized their relationship. She had blindly accepted everything he'd told her because she'd been so pathetically needy.

But she knew. Deep down she'd always known that someone like Pierce could never really love someone like her.

When the phone rang at one in the morning, Jessica had only been asleep for a few minutes. Exhausted from the endless tears and the self-recriminations, it took her a moment to get her bearings.

She eased up in bed and reached for the phone but barely had time to say hello before Sharon's frantic voice ripped her world apart again.

"I'm sorry, Jessica. Oh, God, I'm so sorry."

Jessica's heart slammed against her chest. She fought for breath and lost, making it impossible to speak. She clung to the phone, terrified. "Wh—"

"What happened?" Pierce demanded, his voice strong and clear and in control. Jessica realized dimly that he must have answered the phone the same time as she had.

Sharon's voice babbled across the line. "He woke up Allie in the middle of the night and told her that he and a friend had to help his dad. It was a secret mission, he said, and he couldn't tell anyone. He made Allie promise not to say anything to us, but after Max had left, she got scared and came and woke me up. I don't know what to do. Frank's out looking for him right now—"

"Have you called the authorities?" Pierce asked.

"I've got a call in to the sheriff's office at the nearest town, but no one answered and they don't have 911 service out here. What should I do, Jessica? Oh, God, this is all my fault," Sharon sobbed.

"It isn't your fault," Jessica managed to say. It was Pierce's fault.

Pierce said, "I'm coming up there right away. Just sit tight, Sharon. The local authorities won't be of any help in this matter, anyway. I'll take care of it."

"All right," Sharon said. "But please hurry. When I think of that poor little thing out in the woods wandering around in the dark…"

Dear God, Jessica thought. She'd been thinking the same thing. She'd had the same image since the moment she'd heard Sharon's voice. Her baby. Her poor baby.

Let him be safe, she prayed, as she hung up the phone and ran out of the room. She hurried down the hallway to the stairs. Pierce met her at the bottom. He didn't waste time with apologies. She had to give him that.

"I'll find him," he said. "Everything will be all right."

"You don't know that. Oh, God…." Jessica covered her face with her hands and wept.

Pierce grabbed her shoulders and shook her. "You have to be strong, Jessica. For Max. I'm leaving right now, but I want you to call the man I told you about—Walker. Have him meet me at the campsite."

Jessica shook her head, ignoring the tears streaming down her face. "I'm coming with you," she said.

"Jesse, it's too dangerous—"

"Don't," she warned. "Don't you try to talk me

out of it. I don't need you to protect me anymore, and I won't be left behind this time.''

Pierce took only a second to decide. "All right," he agreed. "Go get dressed and let's get started."

Within minutes, they were on the road heading for the campsite, which was a little less than an hour's drive from Edgewood. Pierce hoped to hell that the house was being watched as Walker had said and that Walker's men would follow him and Jessica. He had no idea what scenario they might be stepping into. All he knew was that he had to get his son back. He had to get to Max.

Jessica sat in the seat beside him, her face turned toward the window. She hadn't spoken two words to him since they'd left the house, but he knew from the drawn look on her face what she was thinking. This was all his fault.

Pierce concentrated on the road, his thoughts grim as the Audi ate up the remaining miles to the campsite. Thank God Walker had had the presence of mind to have the back glass repaired while Pierce had been out, he thought. Otherwise, precious minutes could have been lost procuring another vehicle. As it was, the seconds seemed to be ticking away too quickly, the miles passing too slowly.

Jessica felt numb. The same little prayer kept playing over and over in her mind.

Please let him be all right. Please let Max be all right.

It was like looking at the photo albums the other night. Bits and pieces of her son's life kept flashing through her mind. She saw his smile, his eyes, his mischievous grin, and her arms ached to hold him again.

Please let him be all right.

She felt Pierce's hand close over hers for a moment before returning to the wheel. Jessica looked at him, and their eyes met in the darkness.

"He'll be all right," Pierce said.

"How can you be so sure? That man has him, Pierce. He's using him to get you. What happens when he no longer needs Max?" What happens when he finds you? Jessica wanted to cry.

"I won't let anything happen to our son, Jesse. You have my word."

For what little that's worth.

Neither of them said it, but the unspoken words hung in the air between them.

Jessica turned again to the window and stared out at the flying darkness.

After a moment, Pierce said, "I'd like to tell you why I joined the agency, Jesse. I'd like you to know what my life was like."

Jessica looked at him in surprise. "You never wanted to talk about your past with me before."

Pierce shrugged. "Maybe I should have. Maybe I should have talked about a lot of things that I didn't. I know it won't change anything, but I'd like to make you understand at least why I did what I did."

When she didn't object, Pierce tapped his finger on the steering wheel a few times as if figuring out where to start. "My mother was forty-three when I was born, and my father was forty-nine. They were college professors who'd always dreamed of owning an antique shop. So one day they just up and left their teaching positions and opened The Lost Attic. It was a dream come true for them, and then I came along.''

Jessica saw his jaw harden, but his gaze never left the road.

''I was the old cliché, a middle-aged accident. They never wanted me, and they never pretended otherwise. If they ever noticed me at all, it was when I got in their way. They both loved to travel, and they didn't stop just because they had a child at home. I was left with housekeepers and baby-sitters and anyone else who would take me in. I was never wanted and I was never needed and I damn sure was never loved,'' he said.

''Maybe they just didn't know how to show it,'' Jessica said softly, moved in spite of herself. An image of a lonely little boy started to form in her mind, but it wasn't Max she saw. It was Pierce.

''By the time I was eleven, I was getting into trouble at school. Nothing serious, just some stupid pranks to get attention. My parents were…annoyed. They disciplined me and then forgot me again. By the time I was fifteen, I was working a full eight hours after school, first at a grocery store, then at a gas station, then at various other jobs that turned up. When I was sixteen, I bought my first car and paid cash for it. My parents didn't even ask me where I got the money. They didn't care, because by then they hardly ever saw me anymore. We all carried on with our separate lives, and everyone was happy.''

Everyone except you, Jessica thought, the ice around her heart starting to melt in spite of herself. She gazed at Pierce's profile, amazed at how little she knew about the man she had married. In so many ways he was still a stranger to her, but during the past few days, Jessica felt she'd gotten to know him better than she had in all the years they'd been married.

"Where did the agency fit into all this?" Jessica asked quietly.

"As I said, they approached me after my parents' deaths. You know what they said to me, Jessica? They said, 'We need someone like you, Pierce. You're exactly the kind of man we're looking for.'" He gave Jessica a wry smile. "Can you imagine? After all those years, someone was actually telling me that I was needed. That my life could mean something to someone. They didn't even have to ask me twice. I joined the agency, spent two years of grueling training and ended up right back at The Lost Attic."

"And then you met me."

"And then I met you." He slanted her a glance. "The agency had been telling me for several months that they thought my cover might be becoming suspect. They were the ones who suggested I think about getting married, starting a family."

The heaviness inside her was almost unbearable. Jessica wondered just how much more she could take. "So you agreed," she said, feeling the anger grow inside her again.

"No, I didn't," Pierce said. "Because by that time I'd already met and fallen in love with you, and I told them there was no way I would ever put your life in danger just for the sake of my cover. I told them I wanted out. I was through. I wanted to marry you and lead a normal life."

Jessica swallowed. Her hands were trembling, so she folded them in her lap. "Then what happened?" she whispered, almost afraid to hear any more.

"It wasn't as easy to quit as I'd hoped. About the

same time you started working at the shop, I got involved in this case. The players were already in place. The agency made me see that the whole plan would have been jeopardized if I'd tendered my resignation. They needed me, they said. No one else could manage the job. And so I stayed. And one year turned into two, then three, and then...well, you know the rest," he finished, lifting his hands from the wheel in a gesture of frustration.

"You put their needs before mine," Jessica said, stung by his revelations. Earlier tonight, she'd thought she couldn't be hurt anymore, but she'd been wrong.

"It wasn't like that," Pierce said quietly, helplessly. "It wasn't a conscious choice I made. I did what I thought was right. If I had to do it over again, well, it doesn't matter, does it? We can't turn back the clock, can we, Jesse?"

"No," she whispered. "We can never go back."

No matter how much one might wish it.

Chapter 15

Sharon was standing in front of the cabin, watching for them when they drove up. She came rushing out to meet them and threw her arms around Jessica as soon as she climbed out of the car.

"Did Frank find him?" Jessica asked quickly. "Is Max here?"

Sharon shook her head. "Frank got back just a little while ago. He couldn't find any sign of Max, but he's going out to look again, and Jessica, I...I called Jay. I hope you don't mind, but I just thought..." She trailed off as she glanced at Pierce. She didn't say anything else, but her message was loud and clear. She didn't trust Pierce to find Max. She didn't trust him period.

Jessica registered a faint prickle of resentment somewhere inside her. She said sharply, "Is he here yet?"

"No. At least, he hasn't come to the cabin. Shouldn't we call the state police or something?"

Pierce said, "I want to talk to Allie."

Sharon looked as if she was about to protest, but behind her, Frank's calm voice cut through the darkness. "Come on in, Pierce. I think that's a good idea."

As it turned out, Allie wasn't much help. She could vaguely recall the direction Max had gone off in, but not much more than that. When Jessica asked her about Max's friend, she pursed her little lips together and refused to say more.

"Allie," Sharon said, "please tell Jessica and Pierce everything you know."

The little girl looked doubtful, then nodded. "His friend came and got him."

Jessica's heart slammed against her chest, making her feel momentarily faint. She had to sit down on a nearby chair. Pierce said softly, "What friend, Allie?"

"Max's new friend. The one he played secret mission with."

A memory flashed through Jessica's mind. "You mean the little boy who moved in next door to Mrs. Taylor?"

Allie shook her head. "He wasn't little. He was like you," she said, pointing to Pierce.

"You mean he was an adult?" Pierce asked.

She nodded. "He said he was going to take Max up the mountains to a cabin. He said you were waiting for them up there. He said you needed Max to come get you. I watched them walk down the path until I couldn't see them no more. Then I went and got Mommy." Allie turned her big liquid eyes up to Sharon. "Am I in trouble?" she asked, her voice trembling.

Sharon hugged her daughter closely, making Jessica's arms seem even more empty. "No, darling," Sharon whispered, "you aren't in trouble."

Jessica put her hand to her mouth, stifling the sobs. "This is all my fault," she said. She turned her terrified eyes on Pierce. "He told me about this secret mission game days ago, but I didn't know...I didn't think... Oh, God. What are we going to do?"

"We're going to find him," Pierce said steadily. With his hands on her arms, he lifted Jessica until they were both standing face-to-face. He gazed deep into her eyes. "Listen to me," he said. "I'm going to go out there right now. I'm going to find that cabin and I'm going to find Max and bring him back to you. What I want you to do is stay here and wait for Jay. He'll know what to do."

"Please," she begged, "please don't leave me here."

"It's the only way," he said. He bent and brushed his lips across hers, and for just a second or two, Jessica clung to him. Then he turned, motioned for Frank to follow him, and the two men walked outside.

Jessica fought the urge to run after him, to make him take her with him. This time she knew he was right. This was his element. He knew what to do, and she'd only get in his way. She had to trust him to bring back her son.

She ran to the door and threw it open just as Frank was stepping back inside. Jessica brushed past him and ran outside. The first thing she saw was the gun in Pierce's hand. The metal glinted in the moonlight, as dark and deadly as Pierce's eyes.

They stared at one another for a moment, then Jessica whispered into the darkness, "Be careful. Please be careful."

And then he was gone, swallowed up by the deep shadows in the woods surrounding the cabin.

The moon had risen, and the path was easy to follow. There was a chance, of course, that they hadn't kept to the trail, but Pierce didn't think that likely. The whole point was to reel him in. He hadn't let on to Jessica, but she'd been right earlier. Once the traitor had Pierce, he had no reason to let Max go. He wouldn't. Not if the boy could identify him.

Pierce knew the game, knew how it was played, but he'd never had stakes this high before. It was harder to keep a cool head when he thought about his son, alone, frightened, needing him. But Pierce knew what he had to do. He'd promised Jessica he'd bring Max back to her, and he had every intention of keeping that promise.

He emerged from the woods onto the bank of a small lake. Moonlight silvered the water, making it look like a giant mirror in a darkened room. Keeping to the deep shadows of the woods, Pierce canned the area. He left the path and circled the lake, coming up behind a small cabin perched at the edge of the water.

It was a trap. Pierce knew that. There was only one way in and out of the cabin, but he also realized there was no other choice open to him. He watched the darkened cabin for several minutes, then crouching, he headed across the clearing, scaled the front porch railing, and kicked open the door.

Moonlight flooded inside what appeared to be an empty room. And then, just as he was about to leave, he heard a small voice whisper from the shadows, "Daddy? Is that you?"

Pierce resisted the temptation to run to his son. He flattened himself against the wall, his gaze roaming the cabin. His every sense screamed danger. He knew he and Max were being watched. He knew somewhere out in the darkness, a killer waited for him to make a move.

"I'm here, son," he said softly. "Where are you?"

"Over here. I can't move." He heard Max struggle and whimper. Pierce slid along the wall, following the sound.

Max was curled up in a corner, his arms and legs bound with rope. When Pierce knelt and touched the little boy's face, he felt the wetness of tears on his fingertips.

"It's okay, son," he whispered. "I'm here now. Everything's going to be okay." With his pocketknife he slit the ropes, and the second they were severed, he gathered Max into his arms and held him close.

"I knew you'd come," Max whispered over and over. "I knew you'd come."

Pierce held his son for only a moment longer, then he said, "We have to get out of here, Max."

Max gazed at him with wide dark eyes. "That man—he's not my friend, is he?"

"No."

"He just pretended to be. He brought me here so he could hurt you, didn't he?"

"He's going to try," Pierce said. He picked up his gun from the floor and saw Max's eyes widen even more. "We're not going to let him, though, are we, Max? You and I are going to get out of here, but I need you to do exactly as I say. Okay?"

Max nodded, his eyes still on the gun.

"Okay," Pierce said, standing, "I want you to stay behind me. There's a piece of railing broken on the side of the porch. It's hard to see in the dark, but you'll find it if you look. When I give you the word, I want you to crawl through that opening and run toward the woods. Run as fast as you can, Max. Do you remember where the path is? Do you think you can find it in the dark? Good. You find the path and you stay on it until you get all the way back to the campsite. Your mother will be waiting for you there."

"But what about you?" Max asked, his voice trembling in spite of his brave front.

"I'll be all right. I'm sending you on a real secret mission, son. Think you can handle it?"

Max nodded, lifting his chin. Right then, he looked the spitting image of Jessica. Pierce wanted nothing more than to haul his son into his arms again, hold him so tightly to protect him from the outside world. But he couldn't afford the time. He had to think with his head and not his heart. He had to be just as cunning and ruthless as the enemy who waited for them beyond the front door.

"Let's go," he said.

They edged toward the door. Caution was useless because Pierce knew they were being watched, their every move monitored. Keeping Max behind him, he moved out on the front porch.

He hesitated just a fraction of a second, his eyes scanning the immediate area around them. Then he said, "Now, Max!" and the moment the little boy took off for the side of the porch, Pierce dived toward the steps, hoping to draw the fire. A bullet splintered the wood beside him as he rolled to a crouch in the shadows of the steps. Another bullet whizzed overhead. Out of the corner of his eyes, he saw Max slip into the woods. Another shot rang out, and Max fell to the ground.

Pierce's heart stopped. Had he been hit? Dear God—

Suddenly a burning wave of rage swept over him. Oblivious to the danger, he stood and walked out of the shadows. "Let him go, you bastard," he yelled. "This is between you and me."

He heard a laugh, the same laugh that had tormented him for years, and then a voice he recognized said, "Throw down your weapon and we'll talk."

Pierce gazed at the woods where he'd seen Max fall. Was that a movement he detected? Was his son all right? Pierce knew that all he could do for Max now was to buy him some time. He tossed his gun to the dirt a few feet from him. After a moment or two, a figure materialized out of the shadowy woods. Pierce's enemy, his nemesis, the man who had sent him to hell five years ago, slowly walked out of the darkness toward him.

"You," Pierce said in disgust. "I should have known."

Chapter 16

The man who called himself Walker laughed again. "As I said earlier, you shouldn't be so hard on yourself, Kincaid. You've been out of circulation for too many years." Moonlight glinted off the gold eagle he wore at his throat, and suddenly Pierce remembered. A bird soaring against the sunlight. It had been Walker's medallion he'd seen that day.

"Why didn't you just kill me earlier?" Pierce asked, appraising his options.

Walker laughed again, the same laugh Pierce had heard in his prison years ago. "The agency's been following you for weeks. I couldn't take you out without bringing suspicion on me. I had to get you away from all those eyes, Kincaid. You know the game."

"Yes, I know," Pierce agreed grimly, inching forward.

There was a snapping sound from the woods as if someone had trod on a twig. Max! He was alive!

Pierce saw Walker's head turn just a fraction as if he was thinking the same thing. Pierce fought his own elation, knowing that he might not have another chance. He lunged toward Walker, and Walker fired. But he'd been thrown off guard, and the shot just missed. Then Pierce was on him. He rammed into Walker as hard as he could, and the momentum carried them both stumbling backward into the dirt. The gun went flying from Walker's hand, and both men saw it land in a bed of pine needles not three feet away.

Simultaneously they rushed for it, but a bullet kicked up the dirt mere inches from the weapon. It took Pierce a second to register the fact that someone else was on the scene. Someone else with a gun.

"Hold it," the disembodied voice ordered, as Walker whirled around. Brandon Chambers came out of the woods, his gun leveled first at Walker, then at Pierce. "Nobody make a move," he said.

"Chambers," Walker said in relief. He started toward the man, but Brandon lifted the gun, and Walker halted. He said in an excited undertone, "We've got him this time. He tried to kill me. He knew I was the one man who could put the finger on him."

Brandon's gaze swept over Pierce with icy disdain. "I've waited a long time for this night, Kincaid."

"Who the hell are you?" Pierce demanded.

"I'm with the agency, deep cover," he said. "I was assigned to your case the day you disappeared. I've been waiting for the day you returned."

"So you could kill me?" Pierce asked coldly. "I ought to kill *you* for using my wife the way you have."

"Using her?" Brandon shook his head. "You've

got it all wrong. We were helping her, making sure she and your son were provided for.''

"Somehow I don't think she'd be too grateful if she knew that,'' Pierce said.

"This is ridiculous,'' Walker said. "Let's take him in. Let me get my gun, Chambers.'' He reached for his gun, and another bullet hit the dirt. He glared up at Chambers. "What the hell are you doing?'' In one lightning move, he reached down, scooped up the weapon and spun, leveling it at Pierce. "You're going down this time.''

It happened so fast, Pierce had no time to react. He felt the pain rip through his shoulder before he heard the report of the gun. He stumbled backward as some-one—a woman—screamed. Then another shot rang out, and dimly he saw Walker pitch forward into the dirt. Pierce struggled to remain on his feet, but the pain was excruciating. Don't fade to black, he thought. Not yet. Not until he could find out everything he needed to know.

Chambers holstered his gun. "Dammit! I told you to let me handle this!''

Pierce looked around in amazement as Jessica came running out of the woods, followed more slowly by Jay, who carried the proverbial smoking gun.

"You were too slow to suit my taste,'' Jay said, tossing his own gun in the dirt at Chambers's feet. "I told you I don't like taking orders from a civilian, especially not some damn spook from Langley.''

Chambers muttered a curse. "You military stiffs are all the same.''

Jessica took one look at the blood flowing from Pierce's shoulder, and her face turned white. He thought for a moment she might faint, but Jessica was stronger than that. She'd had to be.

"Oh, my God," she said. "How badly are you hurt?"

"I'm all right," Pierce said. "Jessica—"

Jessica looked around frantically. "Where's Max? Pierce, where's Max?" she demanded.

"He ran into the woods," Pierce said. "Jessica, stay here while I go find him."

Her eyes widened as she realized what he was saying. She turned and started running blindly toward the woods. "Max! Baby, where are you? Please, Max. Answer me."

Pierce guided her in the right direction. He was at her side when they saw Max. He was lying still on the ground, his little face buried in his arms. He didn't make a sound, didn't move a muscle, and Pierce's heart stopped beating. Dear God, no, he prayed. Not Max. Not my boy.

Jessica screamed, "Max! Max!" Pierce tried to hold her back, but Jessica tore loose from his grasp. She ran to Max and flung herself on the ground beside him. "Max! Answer me, baby! Please be all right!"

"Mom? Is that you?"

Pierce thought for a moment he was hearing things. That his prayer was making him see things. Max lifted his head and peered up at Jessica, and then Pierce heard her laughing and crying at the same time as she pulled their son into her arms.

"Did I do it right, Dad?" Max asked, struggling out of Jessica's embrace. "I ran as fast as I could, but when I heard the gun, it scared me and I fell down. I pretended to be dead. That's what Superman told Lois Lane to do once. Was that okay?"

Pierce dropped to his knees beside them. His shoulder was throbbing, he felt sick to his stomach, and he was pretty sure he was going to pass out at any minute. But he had never felt so damned good in all his life.

"You did just fine, son," he said. "I'm proud of you."

Max beamed, then saw the blood on Pierce's arm. "Oh, wow," he said reverently. "Are you all right?" When Pierce nodded, Max said, "I bet you'll have another neat scar, huh, Dad?"

"I hope not, son," Pierce said, gazing at Jessica's tearstained face. "I think I've got a few too many as it is."

Max turned back to Jessica. She couldn't seem to keep her eyes off him. Her fingers fluttered up to touch his cheek as if she was reassuring herself he was really all right.

"Can we go home now?" Max asked.

Jessica nodded. "Yes. We'll go in a minute or two."

"Is Dad coming with us?"

Jessica's gaze met Pierce's for just a split second, then she looked away. Pierce felt a sinking sensation in the bottom of his stomach.

Jessica said, "Why don't you go tell Uncle Jay what an excellent job you did here tonight? I know he'll be impressed."

"Yeah," Max agreed, grinning proudly. He turned and shot past Jessica and Pierce, and when he had gone, the silence around them seemed deafening.

Pierce waited for Jessica to speak. She remained kneeling on the ground, her eyes lowered.

"Jesse?"

She still wouldn't look at him. She twisted her

hands together, giving away her nervousness. "Jay tried to keep me from coming up here with them, but I couldn't stay away. I had to be here...in case you needed me. But you didn't need me, did you, Pierce? You've never really needed me."

Pierce closed his eyes for a moment. The pain in his arm was nothing compared to the torment in his heart. "That's not true, Jesse. I do need you."

"As part of your cover," she said scornfully. "As part of your lie."

"No, sweetheart. As my wife. That part of my life is over. I couldn't go back if I wanted to. I don't even know the person I was back then."

A flicker of something that looked like hope passed through Jessica's eyes, then she lowered them. She shook her head. "I don't want you to come home with Max and me tonight, Pierce."

Pierce felt as if he'd taken another bullet, this one in the gut. "Why?" was all he said.

Jessica closed her eyes and took a deep breath. "You know why. Do you know what went through my mind when I saw Max lying on the ground just now? I thought he was dead. I thought our son was dead, and that you were responsible."

"I know," Pierce said softly. "I was thinking the same thing."

"But you're used to this sort of thing," Jessica said, reluctantly meeting his gaze. The look in her eyes tore Pierce up inside. She was closing him out of her life again, this time for good. "I can't live like this, Pierce. I can't. God knows when I'll even be able to sleep again, much less let Max out of my sight. It's too much happening too soon. I need some time to sort it all out. I need some space."

"How much time?"

Jessica shook her head, her expression resolute. "I don't know."

"You gave me a month," Pierce reminded her grimly. "You said thirty days."

"In that case, my timing is perfect," Jessica said with tears glistening in her eyes. "Because your thirty days ended today."

And so, just like that, it was over. Pierce had been debriefed in Langley, and slowly but surely all the pieces of the puzzle began coming together. Most of what Walker had told him was true, but what Walker hadn't known was that for some time Brandon Chambers had been on to him. He just couldn't prove his suspicions. It was Chambers who finally negotiated Pierce's release, but after the explosion aboard the boat—arranged by Walker, they suspected—Pierce had disappeared again.

When he'd turned up in Miami, Chambers had traced the passport he was using to a man—a doctor—living on a small island in the Caribbean. Evidently Pierce had washed up on shore after the explosion, near death, and when he'd finally regained consciousness, his memory was gone.

For months, as Pierce recovered physically, snatches of his memory began returning. He dreamed about Jessica and the life he'd had with her in Edgewood. As the anniversary of the day he'd disappeared approached, Pierce experienced an almost overwhelming sense of urgency. He knew there was somewhere he had to be, someone he had to protect.

Dr. Morales helped him forge a passport and gave him money to return to the States. From Miami, guided by his inner compulsion, Pierce managed to find his way back to Virginia, to Edgewood, and finally to the grocery store where he'd been headed five years ago. And then everything had clicked back into place for him. Everything except for the five years he'd been imprisoned.

Pierce remembered it all now. All the horrors, the despair, the intense longing for Jesse, for the son he had never seen. Everything Jessica had suffered for so many years, Pierce suffered now. He understood more than ever what she had gone through, and why she felt she had to protect herself from him. Pierce didn't blame her one damn bit. He'd put her through hell, and just because he'd suffered too, it didn't make what he'd done to her acceptable. But the facts didn't make her rejection any easier to take.

He was in Langley at CIA headquarters for three days, and at the end of that time, he walked out a free man. He'd tendered his resignation, the lies were over, and now it was time to start building a new life for himself. Pierce took a deep, cleansing breath.

But first there was something he had to do. Another part of his past he had to put to rest.

Jay Greene eyed Pierce's outstretched hand warily. He was wearing his uniform, and his attitude was very stiff and unyielding. Pierce wondered briefly if their antagonism toward one another had been the natural distrust that often sprang up between the military and civilians.

"You don't owe me anything," he said gruffly, but he accepted Pierce's handshake, anyway.

"You saved my life," Pierce said.

"You'd have done the same for me."

Their eyes met, and at that moment, Pierce realized that his brother-in-law was right. No matter how strong the animosity between them had always been, they were still family. Their love for Jessica bonded them together in spite of their feelings about each other.

"I always knew there was something suspicious about your activities," Jay admitted. "But I never could find out anything. That made me doubt you even more."

"You had good reason," Pierce said grimly.

"I only wanted what was best for my sister. I didn't want to see her hurt."

Pierce didn't blame Jay for the accusation in his tone. He said simply, "I've always loved her. That hasn't changed."

"Then what are you going to do about it?" Jay demanded.

"I don't know," Pierce said. "I don't know if there is anything I can do about it."

Jay scowled his disapproval. "That's what I've always disliked about you damned CIA spooks. You guys can't tell your butts from a hole in the ground. You couldn't make a decision—"

Pierce didn't wait to hear the rest. He just shook his head, grinned and walked off.

"When's Dad coming home?" Max asked again. Jessica had lost count of how many times she'd heard that question in the past week. She watched her son as he sat slumped in the lawn chair, idly dangling his legs. He scowled deeply. "It's boring around here without him."

Jessica had to agree. A week without Pierce and the

house had taken on the atmosphere of a tomb. She couldn't even muster up enough strength to work on the game room upstairs, and even the downstairs wore an uncharacteristic clutter. It was funny, but suddenly she'd lost the desire for a neat and orderly existence. She took a strange sort of comfort in leaving the dishes in the sink a little too long or letting the beds go unmade all day.

She hadn't even bothered to comb her hair since she'd gotten up this morning, Jessica realized, blowing away the bangs from her forehead. Much less put on lipstick. There was no one around to see her, anyway, except Max, and he seemed to be suffering from the same lethargy that gripped her. They both missed Pierce.

So call him, Jessica told herself. Call him and tell him you've changed your mind. Tell him how empty you feel without him. Tell him you like the excitement he brings to your life. Tell him that you need him. Desperately.

But instead, Jessica sat on the terrace and did nothing. What could she do? She didn't even know how to get in touch with Pierce. He'd only called once in the past week and then only to talk to Max. He hadn't even asked to speak to her.

It took Jessica a long time to admit just how much that had hurt her. She'd told him that night in the woods that she needed time to sort out her feelings, but it had only taken her one night without Pierce to know that she wanted him back in her life. More than anything.

But he was gone now. And for all Jessica knew, he wasn't coming back.

She took a deep breath and tried to quell the fresh batch of tears brought on by that thought.

"What's that noise?" Max asked, stilling his legs. He sat up and listened. "It sounds like a dog!" he cried excitedly. Before Jessica could say a word, he shot past her like a bullet, rounded the corner of the house, and headed toward the front yard.

Jessica jumped up and hurried after him. She didn't like the idea of a strange dog hanging around the neighborhood. "Max, wait!" But he had already disappeared through the back gate, heading for the street.

Jessica ran through the gate and hurried around the house. Then she stopped at the sight that greeted her in the front yard. A shiny red 'Vette was parked in the driveway, and Max was down on his knees in the grass, laughing wildly as a puppy, a little black-and-white mutt, avidly licked his face.

Jessica's gaze went from Max and the dog to the man standing near the front porch steps, watching them. Pierce immediately got a defensive look on his face. "Now, I know what you're going to say, Jessica."

No, you don't, she thought. You have no idea.

"But I found him on the side of the road. Someone had dumped him, and he had nowhere to go. I guess I sort of felt a kinship with him," Pierce said apologetically. "I couldn't just leave him there."

"No, you couldn't," Jessica agreed, smiling.

"I've already taken him to the vet's. He's had his shots and everything. I thought maybe I could keep him at my place, and Max could visit him there whenever he wanted."

Jessica's heart stopped. *His* place?

"You've...found a place to live?" she asked. Her

heart had started beating again at an awfully painful rate.

Pierce shrugged. "Not yet," he admitted. "But I'm sure I will."

"I know where there's a vacancy," Jessica said quickly, admiring her nerve.

Pierce gave her a strange glance. "Oh?" he asked noncommittally. "Is the rent reasonable?"

"Very. And there are lots of fringe benefits."

His jaw dropped, and Jessica almost laughed out loud. He took a step toward her. "Are you saying what I think you're saying?"

"Come home, Pierce," she whispered. "We need you so."

He closed the distance between them in no more than three strides. Jessica fell into his arms, and he held her close, kissing her eyelids and her nose and her mouth. Jessica's laughter mingled with her son's.

"I know I've made a lot of mistakes in the past," he said, his hand in her hair. "But, Jesse, I'll spend the rest of my life trying to make it up to you. I have my priorities straight now, sweetheart, and it feels good. It feels really good. My family is the most important thing in the world to me now."

"To me, too," she whispered. "Just don't ever leave me."

"Never again," he promised. "I'm here for as long as you'll have me."

She lifted her face for his kiss, and as their lips joined, sealing the vow, Jessica heard her son whooping with laughter.

"Hey, Mom," he yelled. "Krypto just went to the bathroom on my new shoe."

* * * * *

Three romantic comedies that will have you laughing out loud!

Favorite Harlequin Temptation® author

Stephanie Bond

brings you...

LoveStruck

Three full-length novels of romance... and the humorous missteps that often accompany it!

Get LOVESTRUCK in June 2003—wherever books are sold.

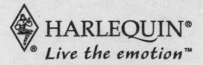

HARLEQUIN®
Live the emotion™

Visit us at www.eHarlequin.com

BR3L